HOSTILE TAKEOVER

EM LYNLEY

Dreamspinner Press

Published by
Dreamspinner Press
5032 Capital Circle SW
Ste 2, PMB# 279
Tallahassee, FL 32305-7886
USA
http://www.dreamspinnerpress.com/

Cover Art by Anne Cain
annecain.art@gmail.com

ISBN: 978-1-61372-728-7

Printed in the United States of America
First Edition
September 2012

eBook edition available
eBook ISBN: 978-1-61372-729-4

For all my wonderful beta readers:

You've given me support, inspiration, hugs, and commas! And you aren't afraid to tell me when it's just not working. Everything I write is better thanks to you!

AUTHOR'S NOTE

WHILE the Olympic Training Center in Colorado Springs is real, and fencers train there, there are no Olympic trials held to select the athletes for Team USA. That is completely fabricated for the purposes of this story.

In fact, the Olympic qualification system is quite complicated but ensures that only the best fencers in the world get a spot to compete. International fencing team rankings determine which countries can send teams and the individual athletes' points in competitions are used to select team members.

If the US team doesn't qualify for a spot, individual US fencers may still be allowed to compete based solely on point standings, similar to a wild-card slot in US Major League Baseball.

PART I

PROLOGUE

August 2012
Dallas, Texas

MATHIAS TOBLER fastened the strap on his fencing jacket and stepped onto the piste, feeling the weight of the once-familiar weapon in his hand. He slowly approached his opponent for one last bout, one final duel. The old thrill of the competition was absent today. Today he'd be fighting for everything important to him in the world, fighting against the man who once, years ago, had been everything in the world to him.

Once the closest of lovers, now they were the worst of enemies. How had he and Chase Richards ended up here, fighting each other, when they had such hopes and dreams for a future together? How had their love turned into… this?

CHAPTER ONE

July 2012
Dallas

"LEWIS, can you please come in here?" Mathias Tobler said into his phone as he glanced at the monitor on his desk. As CEO of the Tobler Group, he didn't usually pay much attention to the share price, but this morning, he'd noticed it had dropped at the New York open, and was still falling.

"Give me five minutes, Mathias." Lewis McDonald sounded rushed.

Mathias frowned. Since the previous day's close, the share price had dropped by 10 percent. He wondered why his Chief Financial Officer hadn't already alerted him. Mathias expected to be informed of huge price swings in the company value, rather than having to chase Lewis down and ask.

It was closer to ten minutes later when Lewis McDonald, CFO of the Tobler Group—the T-Group to insiders—hurried through Mathias's open door. Lewis was in shirtsleeves, his tie askew, dark hair mussed, and though it was barely past 9:00 a.m., he already looked crumpled and exhausted, in stark contrast to his usual neat-as-a-pin presentation.

"Lewis, what's going on with our share price?" Mathias kept his concern out of his voice, but Lewis's appearance told him this was serious.

"I was just on the phone with the exchange. That's what took so long." Lewis sat down in one of the chairs in front of Mathias's desk.

"Sounds serious. The market's been open less than an hour."

"It might be, especially if the price keeps dropping. The exchange could halt trading of our shares, which wouldn't be good for a lot of reasons." Lewis ran his fingers through his hair.

"Let's focus on what's going on now and why."

"Right. It seems someone's written a large number of put options—options to sell—on our shares, and that's driving the price of the cash market down. If whoever it is actually owns the shares, selling them would cause the price to plunge."

"It's already plunging. And why would someone do that? What's the strike price of the options?" Mathias asked, referring to the price at which the option allowed the holder to sell the shares.

"They're all over the place, but mostly lower than the current cash price."

"I don't get it." Mathias frowned. "Why fuck with the share price in the first place? And why us? Is this part of a broad market options strategy, or is it a focused attack on the T-Group?"

"I don't know. Yet." Lewis took a deep breath and shook his head. "I'll start with the things we already know. Maybe somebody's trying to drive the price down so they can make an arbitrage play— exploit slight price discrepancies," he explained. "Or it could be a prelude to a takeover bid."

"A takeover? But the price is falling—"

"Yeah. The put options depress the price, then they buy more shares as it falls, and before the market notices, they've got a head start. If it's a takeover bid, it's brilliant strategy." Mathias heard something approaching admiration in Lewis's voice.

"Who would want to acquire the T-Group?" He got up and started pacing the room. The concept was so ludicrous Mathias could barely wrap his brain around it. They made food items, for God's sake. The company owned machinery and buildings, but there was nothing sexy about the business. Not in a state full of oil and other energy and plenty of tech. Texas was full of sexy companies, and the T-Group was an old maid in a state full of beauty queens, at least as far as investments went.

"I've got my team working on that question right now, but all they've found is some holding companies no one's ever heard of."

"Holding companies?" Mathias searched for a link, a reason, an explanation, but he came up blank.

"Yeah, I wrote a few of the names down." Lewis handed a piece of paper to Mathias. "There are still a few trades we can't track down yet. And we haven't yet untangled ownership of these businesses."

The list contained half a dozen names consisting of initials or abbreviations—typical of holding companies or shell corporations trying to hide their true ownership. One near the bottom caught his eye.

It couldn't possibly be...

Mathias wasn't sure he wanted to share his theory, especially with McDonald. If he was wrong, it would be embarrassing. If he was right, the attack was personal.

"I might have an idea of who's behind this," he said tentatively. "RCC Industries—"

Lewis's cell phone rang. Mathias watched as he spoke for a few moments, nodded, raised his eyebrows, then shook his head slightly. He closed the phone and turned his attention back to Mathias.

"Looks like at least one of those holding companies can be tied to RichardsCorp." Lewis's voice wavered, high and tense.

"That's what I suspected." Mathias said, feeling his chest constricting. "RCC: it's Chase Richards's initials in reverse. Chase fucking Richards." Mathias banged his fist on the desk as he sat down in his chair.

Lewis didn't reply, he just sat back in his chair and raised a quizzical eyebrow at Mathias.

Fuck! Mathias could guess what was going through his mind. The fact that Mathias had made the connection—just from those initials—had triggered Lewis's curiosity. Mathias rarely got upset about *anything*, but just the mention of Chase Richards had gotten him pretty riled up.

Richards had a well-earned reputation for being unscrupulous in business, but Mathias admitted his reaction went beyond what Lewis would have expected, considering how little information they had to go on so far.

"How will this price drop affect our day-to-day business?" Mathias attempted to deflect attention away from his overreaction to Chase Richards's name.

"Banks might tighten up the line of credit if the value of the shares falls, since those assets are our collateral. It would put a strain on our cash flow. And if this *is* the beginning of a takeover, cash is exactly what we're going to need to try and fight it off."

Mathias wasn't completely surprised that Chase might be behind the share price manipulations and even a potential takeover. It was the way Chase Richards conducted business. Mathias also knew how Chase took care of personal issues—or at least the way he used to. They hadn't been in touch since business school nine years ago, except for the one meeting two weeks earlier when Chase had paid Mathias a surprise visit in this very office.

Unfortunately, Mathias knew all too well from personal experience what Chase Richards was really like.

Nine years earlier
Mid-May 2003
Venice, Italy

MATHIAS had been in Venice for a week. By himself. He'd been on the phone with Chase every single day, and Chase refused to say exactly when he'd be leaving Dallas to meet him. Mathias didn't want to go anywhere, see anything, or experience anything until Chase got there. That was the point, wasn't it? For them to be together, to wander around and discover Venice *together*? How romantic would it be for Mathias to traipse around on his own?

And it wasn't even that he had avoided all of the interesting places while he strolled around the city, or how much he missed Chase and wanted him to be here, wanted to be with him. Or that he wanted to ramble along the canals, holding hands, or kissing as they watched the sun set over the lagoon, or gliding under low bridges in a gondola. All those silly, clichéd things they'd promised each other they would do. Mathias didn't even mind missing out on any of that, or postponing it until Chase could join him.

What Mathias couldn't handle, didn't want to believe, was that Chase sounded as if he didn't *want* to spend the summer in Europe with Mathias.

They'd been planning the trip for the past year to celebrate receiving their MBAs—a last fun fling before they joined their respective family businesses. But Chase had sounded tired and frustrated and almost angry the last time Mathias had called from Venice. Half the time it didn't even sound like *his* Chase on the phone. Mathias was tired of asking "When are you coming?"

Chase's father had roped him into a project for a few days, but now it had been over a week. Mathias knew Chase was holding something back, and he had to find out what. Why couldn't Chase just explain why he hadn't come to Italy yet, why he'd kept Mathias hanging here, in the dark?

What's changed?

"Hello?"

"Chase?"

"Tee? I didn't expect you to call this early… it's not even seven o'clock."

"It's afternoon, here, Chase," Mathias said wearily. He was tired. Tired of waiting and wondering.

"I meant early for me." Chase laughed, but it didn't sound like he was very amused. "You woke me up."

"I wanted to catch you when you weren't too busy to talk." Mathias tried to keep the emotion from his voice. His heart was beating so loudly, he wondered if Chase could hear it over the phone.

"I'm sorry I've been so hard to get a hold of the past few days," Chase said. He sounded almost evasive. Mathias thought he'd noticed subtle shifts in Chase's behavior over the past month or so, even before he'd come to Italy. Now he was sure of it. Something had changed with Chase.

Chase had changed.

Mathias wanted to ask what Chase had been so busy doing in Dallas, but he stopped himself. *I'm not going to be the person who asks a million questions, trying to catch my partner in a lie....* And he wasn't going to paint himself the victim to make Chase feel guilty. No, he had more self-respect. He wouldn't force Chase into anything. He just wanted the truth.

"Chase, did you get your ticket yet? Are you coming to Venice this week?"

Chase's reply came a bit too late for Mathias's liking. "No," Chase said, then paused again. "I mean, not yet. I have something to do here that's not finished yet. Something important."

"I thought our trip was important to you." Mathias fought to keep his voice even. He balled his free hand into a fist. "We've been planning this since the fall."

"Oh, God, Tee, it is!" Mathias actually believed Chase. For a minute. Not quite a minute. Only until Chase opened his mouth again. "But this is important, too. It's my future, Tee."

"*Your* future? What about *our* future?" Mathias's heart ached, as if someone were squeezing all the love out of it. He wished he could see Chase's face right now, have some idea what he was thinking.

"I don't want to have to choose between you and...." He paused. "Don't make me choose."

"Chase? Choose between me and—"

"Look, I don't think I can meet you in Venice."

There it was. Chase had said it. He'd finally just come right out and said it. He hadn't even offered an explanation or suggested a compromise, and Mathias wasn't about to humiliate himself and ask for either. It had taken a week, but at least now Mathias knew where he stood. Alone, in the middle of St. Mark's Square, with Chase still in Dallas and not even preparing to join him.

Mathias wanted to smash his phone into a million pieces on the pavement, but he didn't. He wanted to scream and cry and give Chase Richards a piece of his mind, but he didn't. He wanted to ask whether the last three years had meant nothing, but he didn't.

"Does that mean what I think it means?" Mathias fought to keep his voice from shaking.

This time the pause was so long, Mathias didn't know whether Chase was still on the other end of the line.

"Yeah." Chase's voice was barely audible.

"Okay. Got it." Mathias was so calm he surprised himself. "Good-bye, Chase." He carefully closed his phone, slipped it into his pocket, and walked into St. Mark's Basilica by himself.

You're going to be doing everything by yourself from now on, so you'd better get used to it.

Present day
Dallas

MATHIAS sat alone in his office, watching his share price drop while he waited for more information from Lewis. He knew more than he wanted about Chase Richards and the way he operated. Chase was ruthless, and he didn't care who got hurt as long as he got what he wanted.

The Richards' style of hit-and-run business was well known. Chase had, after all, deposed his own father to take over as CEO of RichardsCorp. But this was the first time Mathias had been at odds with Chase over *business*, and he didn't like it any more than he had when their differences had been personal. This wouldn't end well. Chase never gave up until he got what he wanted, or he destroyed anything or anyone he saw as an obstacle. Everyone in Dallas knew that. Probably everyone in Texas.

The Tobler Group had begun as one tiny restaurant started by Mathias's great-grandparents with family recipes brought from Germany. The restaurant served large, affordable portions of delicious food and soon became a local favorite in Fredricksberg, south of Austin in an area that was home to many German and Eastern European immigrants at the time. Eventually, they'd opened more locations. Wary of banks, Mathias's great-grandfather, and grandfather as well, had kept their money in a safe at home, and when the Depression hit, while their business fell off, they were unaffected by bank runs and the resulting havoc in the financial system. As they recovered, the Toblers tried to help their friends and suppliers with loans. Unfortunately, not everyone weathered the downturn as well as the Toblers, and when their friends couldn't pay them back, the Toblers bought out the rest of their business—in many cases paying more than market value in order to help their friends out financially. Which is how they eventually acquired a food manufacturing plant, grocery stores, and a string of high-end department stores. Later their accidental acquisitions branched out to entirely unconnected industries.

Mathias's great-grandfather had built the company, and leadership had passed from father to son for three generations. Mathias's older brother Leo had been next in line, but he had gone to medical school and joined Doctors Without Borders. He didn't want anything to do with the business, but Mathias did.

Mathias had taken over the family business three years ago when his father had gotten too sick to work. Jerry Tobler had survived a rare form of cancer for years, but the treatments had taken their toll on his energy. Eventually, the cancer had gone into remission, but Jerry wasn't well enough to run the company on his own. For six months, Mathias worked closely with his father, getting up to speed on aspects of the T-Group until the Board of Directors named Mathias CEO.

Mathias loved the idea of a family business and tradition, and he liked building on what his family had made and making it better. He always wanted to improve things.

To Mathias, his company was all about people, the way his father and grandfather had taught him. When Mathias thought about the T-Group, he saw *people*, not things. He saw the faces of employees, of the people who bought their products. Every single employee called him Mathias, from the senior VPs down to the janitorial staff. He didn't want formality. He wanted people to like their jobs, so he respected their needs and listened to their problems and ideas, and didn't micromanage. He delegated authority to people he trusted. Employees felt a personal connection to Mathias and the T-

Group and wouldn't let him down. And he rewarded people for their good work.

Sometimes, Mathias even called up customers who wrote the company, whether the letter contained praise or a complaint. He was a hands-on CEO, involved in all aspects of the business, and inspiring people to do their best. The T-Group was his whole life.

To Chase, on the other hand, business was like a big chess game. Mathias knew that. Chase always saw things in black and white: the pieces he wanted or the pieces he already had and was done with and could discard—at a profit, of course. Everything was a means to an end, and he didn't stick with anything long enough to learn about it or make it better. Just bought and sold and piled up money. Most of the time, the companies he acquired and discarded were much worse off due to his interference. Chase's father taught him early to be ruthless, and Chase had been a star pupil from what Mathias could tell. The Richards family motto was probably "What would Machiavelli do?" Mathias though bitterly.

Chase and his father, however, had taken their cues from Enron. How to make money from buying and selling little more than the right to buy and sell. They acquired companies and didn't hesitate to carve them up into tiny pieces if it would net them a profit. It was a fortune built mainly on paper. Chase's keen financial aptitude had allowed him to come up with strategies that worked and were either completely legal, or not yet illegal. Few could be considered fair or ethical business practices, but that didn't matter, as long as they worked. He thrived on inside information that couldn't be traced to the source, and most people thought Chase had an army of people in his pocket, providing him information for payments, though he'd never been caught at it.

Outside of the oil companies, RichardsCorp was one of the largest businesses in Texas. And unlike the Tobler Group, which was a publicly traded company, RichardsCorp was still privately held. That meant that Chase was now one of the wealthiest men in Texas. Wealthiest and most ruthless—a dangerous combination. And he was setting his sights on Mathias.

Chase was fucking with his share price, pushing it down. And that meant only one thing. He was trying to take over the Tobler

Group. Once he got the price down far enough, he could place a tender offer and shareholders would jump at the opportunity to get their money back as quickly as possible. Mathias knew Chase had enough resources to swallow his company fairly painlessly. Painless for Chase, but Mathias expected that a takeover bid by Chase was going to hurt the T-Group severely.

I won't let him destroy everything my family's built. Not now. Not ever.

Mathias knew all too well what the fate of the business would be once Chase Richards got his hands on it. And Mathias wasn't going to let that happen without a fight.

CHAPTER TWO

Late May 2003
Dallas

EVEN though it hurt like hell, Mathias spent another week on his own in Italy before flying back home. He wouldn't let Chase Richards keep him from seeing what should have been the most romantic city on Earth. Not that he enjoyed any of it. Not the Byzantine beauty of St. Mark's Basilica, or the Bridge of Sighs, or even the grandeur and elegance of a trip along the Grand Canal. He looked at everything but saw nothing except his shattered dreams and an uncertain future.

When he arrived back at their Fort Worth home, his parents were surprised to see him more than a month earlier than planned. He hadn't felt like explaining, and although he knew his parents suspected something was wrong, they'd refrained from asking him directly about Chase.

His mom, Marta, tried to cheer him up by cooking his favorite foods.

"I'm not hungry."

"You haven't eaten a bite since dinner last night. And that was only a bite."

"I'm *not* hungry. I'll eat it later." He pushed the latest plate away with more force than intended, and it slid off the table and shattered on the kitchen floor.

His mother started crying. He put his arms around her and held her close. His heart stung even more when he realized how he'd taken his problems with Chase out on his family.

"I'm sorry, Mom." He wiped away his own tears before she could see. He wasn't ready to share this, not yet. Not until he sorted himself out first. But he loved her all the more for not pressing him to talk until he was ready.

He cleaned up the mess on the floor and made his mother a cup of tea before going back upstairs. He closed the door softly, though he really wanted to slam it so hard the whole house would collapse. He wasn't supposed to be living at home with his parents. He was supposed to be moving into a new apartment with Chase.

He lay on the bed staring up at the same ceiling he'd looked at since he was a kid. How many more nights would he stay here? His parents would do anything to make him happy, but nothing they did would ever fix what made his heart and body ache every minute of every day.

HE SLEPT late the next morning, the first night of good sleep he'd gotten since that conversation in Venice. He washed up and went downstairs. It was already lunchtime. And he was famished.

"Good morning," his mother said when he found her in the kitchen.

"Hey, Mom." He gave her a hug from behind as she stood at the counter chopping nuts. "You know, you make the best sandwiches in the world. Would you make me one?"

Without skipping a beat, she turned around. "Sure, roast beef or some turkey breast?"

"Roast beef, with Swiss cheese?"

"Give me a minute."

He sat at the table and watched her prepare the sandwich. There were tears in her eyes when she set it down and took the chair across from him.

The toasted bread smelled fantastic, with the tang of cheese and the sharpness of just the right amount of mustard. He devoured the sandwich in four bites and washed it down with a glass of water. Before he finished, his father, Jerry, came in and sat down at the table.

"You got a few minutes to talk?" Mathias asked.

"All day for you, Mattie." She pronounced it "Muh-tee," and the nickname always made him smile.

"Sure, son," his dad added.

"Chase didn't meet me in Venice like he was supposed to. I called every day until he finally admitted he wasn't coming because something his dad wanted him to do was more important," Mathias finally found the words—and the strength—to explain.

"Did he say what he needed to do first?" She put one hand over his, squeezing gently.

"No. He just said it had to do with his whole future and that if he was forced to decide between me and whatever, he was choosing whatever." He fought to keep the pain from seeping into his voice. "I guess that means we're over."

"Maybe he just felt like there was a lot of time pressure on him. You wanted him to meet you and his father needed him here. It sounds like it was just bad timing," Jerry suggested.

"Yeah. Maybe. I wasn't asking him to choose, though. I just wanted him to let me know what was happening." Mathias waved away a cup of steaming black coffee. "We could have rescheduled our trip, but he didn't suggest that. It all sounded so mysterious. He didn't seem to want to tell me what was going on. That's the part that upset and worried me."

"Why don't you go see him and just ask?" Marta was quick to take the practical, straightforward approach. "I don't think it's over just because he couldn't meet you in Italy."

"You don't think so? He said it was over."

"Honey, you've been together for three years. I doubt Chase could just throw that all away so easily. It must be something very important, and I'm sure he has a good explanation. He's never done anything like this before, has he?" Mathias shook his head. "So try and see it from his perspective." Marta continued. "I think you both just need to talk. You can't let it all end like this, without more information."

"I think your mom's right, Mattie." Jerry reached out to squeeze his elbow.

"Everything you've said makes sense. But I need a few days to calm down. I'm still pretty upset. And maybe he'll try and get in touch with me in the meantime." Mathias knew he was grasping at straws, hoping Chase would try and contact him.

"Well, just don't leave it too long," Marta said.

"Thanks." Mathias knew how lucky he was that his parents were so understanding and wanted to help him sort things out.

OVER the next two days, Mathias thought about what he'd say to Chase. He didn't want to apologize, because he thought Chase owed *him* an apology for leaving him alone in Italy. Had he pushed too much or had Chase never intended to meet him? If Chase had family commitments, why couldn't he just be honest about that? They'd never kept secrets from each other. At least not until lately.

Chase had never hidden his feelings—at least about Mathias. The only topic that they ever had any trouble discussing was Chase's family, and maybe that was why Chase had been so closemouthed about whatever was keeping him in Dallas.

I'll call Chase today and let him know I'd like to talk this over, Mathias thought as he paced around his bedroom.

"Mattie, honey," Marta's voice drifted up from downstairs. "You have a visitor."

A visitor? Chase? His heartbeat accelerated for a moment. *She would have said that.*

Mathias was completely surprised to see Alan Richards, Chase's father, sitting in the living room waiting for him.

"Good morning, Mathias." Alan stood and offered his hand.

"Hello, Alan." Mathias shook Alan's hand.

"I'm sure you're wondering why I'm here, Mathias. I wanted to talk with you, privately… about Chase."

They both sat down, Alan on the couch and Mathias in a chair facing him.

If Mathias hoped Alan was going to say how torn up Chase was after breaking up with him, he was very disappointed once Alan starting talking.

"I want to say I'm sorry that things ended the way they did between you and Chase. I was very surprised to find out when he told me. And I'd like to apologize, because I think I may have been responsible for part of what happened."

"Responsible, how?"

"Well, you know Chase came home to spend some time at RichardsCorp during spring break," Alan began. "He pitched a deal that I decided to finance, and the project was just winding down during the past few weeks. Chase insisted on being part of the team from beginning to end, to help to finalize everything. I hadn't realized that he'd put off your trip in favor of working on this deal. I'm very sorry for the timing. But it was Chase's decision, and it seems he ended up choosing work over...." Alan's tone softened and he looked away.

Mathias read the meaning loud and clear: Chase had chosen work over him.

"He stayed in Dallas to finalize a deal?" Mathias was stunned. "But why didn't he just tell me? He didn't explain any of this. I can certainly understand why he wanted to be here—be part of the team— for that. All he had to do was explain."

Alan's face was unreadable. "I think that he might not have wanted to tell you everything... because of the bonus."

"Bonus?"

"I offered him a pretty big incentive, and looks like he wanted to earn the bonus for completing the deal... north of a million dollars." Alan shrugged.

Mathias remained silent as he let that last bit of information sink in. Chase had kept the deal and the money a secret. He hadn't wanted to let Mathias know he brushed off their trip—their relationship—for a million dollar bonus. Was that how little he'd valued the past three years with Mathias? He wasn't as important as a deal and some money? Chase turned out to be a true Richards after all.

"I see," Mathias said, his mouth a tight, thin line. He got up out of the chair.

"I wish it hadn't come to Chase choosing between a job and his relationship with you. And I can't tell you how disappointed I am in the decision he's made. I'm sorry, Mathias." Alan stood and clapped a hand on Mathias's shoulder in a fatherly gesture.

"I appreciate your honesty," Mathias said as he showed Alan Richards to the door.

Stomach churning, Mathias watched Alan's black limousine glide down the driveway toward the street with a growing sense of uneasiness. He knew enough about Alan Richards to realize he couldn't possibly be as nice as he'd *appeared*. There was plenty below the surface to frighten anyone familiar with his ruthless ways. And over the years Mathias had never seen Alan this calm and agreeable.

Why on earth had Alan come today? To apologize on Chase's behalf? To make Mathias feel better? It seemed unlikely. Something else was going on here. But try as he might, Mathias was just too upset to figure it out.

Several days later, Mathias decided to take his place in the Tobler Group. It wasn't as if he was doing anything else, he reasoned. It was time to move on.

He had come to the unpleasant conclusion that Chase had sent his father to do his dirty work. So it was a shock when, a week later, Mathias's mother gave him the message that Chase had called.

He didn't return the call. Chase called every day for a week. They'd broken up over the phone, and Mathias never wanted to have another telephone conversation with Chase Richards for the rest of his life. If Chase had anything important to say, he could damn well get in the car and drive over.

That didn't happen. After another week, Chase stopped calling and Mathias tried to give up caring. He knew that would take a lot longer than a week. Mathias began to question himself. How had he fallen for Chase in the first place? Why hadn't he been good enough to keep Chase interested? Had he done something wrong? Maybe, he decided, he just had never known Chase as well as he'd thought.

It wasn't as though Mathias couldn't have seen this coming. He and Chase had both fenced in college and competed against each other in numerous intercollegiate tournaments. But when they'd finally exchanged more than a few words, Chase had acted like an overbearing jerk, practically from the minute Mathias had introduced himself. Maybe that's who Chase had been all along. Their lives had intersected only as long as it served some purpose to Chase, and then he'd tossed Mathias aside, like his father had dozens of other useless things. And Chase was, after all, a Richards.

But the memories of what they had—what Mathias thought they'd shared—lingered for a long time.

Which one was the *real* Chase Richards? Mathias wondered.

May 2000
US Olympic Training Center
Colorado Springs, Colorado

"I'M MATHIAS Tobler." Mathias introduced himself at the welcome party for fencing team hopefuls at the OTC. He said his name slowly, Mah-tee-us, so everyone would know how to pronounce it. He was tired of being called Mah-thigh-ass, which was how most people outside his family said it.

His heartbeat sped up at the excitement. He was one of three dozen of the top American fencers here, half men, half women, in competition for the few spots on the US Olympic team heading to Sydney in September.

"I know." Chase's tone was cocky the first time he spoke to Mathias. "But you already know who I am, too, don't you?"

"Yes, but my father always says it's polite to introduce yourself, and not to presume too much."

"My daddy says people should already know who you are if you're doing things right, so you shouldn't need an introduction," Chase replied. "But then again, I don't always do everything my daddy tells me. Do *you*?" Chase flashed Mathias a mischievous grin.

"No. No, I don't either."

Mathias had only exchanged a few words with Chase Richards after their fencing matches, but he knew who Chase was, of course. They'd kicked each other's asses in NCAA intercollegiate matches a few times over the years. Chase beat Mathias the few times he'd competed in saber, while Mathias had the edge in épée, his strongest weapon. If Mathias hadn't put his studies first, they'd probably have met in national or international competition long before this. It was only because the chance to be on an Olympic team was a once-in-a-lifetime opportunity that Mathias had decided to take the spring quarter off from Stanford University to come to Colorado Springs for the training and tryouts.

So here he was, along with a couple dozen other young men and women—including Chase Richards—who had won a spot at the prestigious training camp before the Olympic trials in July.

"You're from near Austin, right? That little German town...."

"Yes...." Mathias wasn't sure if Chase was insulting his heritage or stalking him. "How did you know?" Had Chase been researching him or something? That was just fucking creepy.

"I read your bio in the welcome packet," Chase replied and Mathias relaxed a little, though Chase's tone was still a bit too intense for Mathias's liking. "I'm from Dallas," Chase added.

That explained the overbearing attitude. Mathias knew there was a lot of new money in Dallas, and sometimes people went overboard trying to make sure everyone knew who they were, what they had, and how they'd acquired it. It was a different world from Fredricksberg.

Richards, Mathias thought as Chase droned on. He wondered why he hadn't put it all together sooner. Chase must be Alan Richards's son. Which made perfect sense. Alan Richards was a prick.

Like father, like son.

Anyone who did business in Texas knew Alan Richards's name—and reputation—and tried to stay as far away from him as possible.

"We have a house in Fort Worth, too," Mathias said, turning his attention back to Chase just to be polite. He'd try and get away from

Chase as soon as he possibly could. "My dad stays there a few days a week, since he moved his company headquarters to Dallas, but I haven't spent much time there myself. Mostly when my dad has company meetings in town. I'd rather stay at our ranch, though."

"You're missing out," Chase said, and went on to elaborate all the places and events that Mathias needed to visit or see in Dallas, as if Chase Richards himself had been the first person to discover all of them and make them famous and worth seeing. Mathias tried not to appear bored.

Somehow he let Chase talk him into going to a bar with a bunch of other people—mainly because there were other people going and Mathias wanted the chance to meet and talk with some of them in a casual setting before the training started. Mathias did his best not to guzzle his beer in an effort to blot out some of Chase's pretentious banter.

It was when Chase was into his third beer—Mathias his second—that Chase seemed to change. He laughed, his dark golden eyes sparkling in amusement, and he dropped the pompous act. He became funnier, more interesting, and much more *real*. Suddenly Mathias realized he didn't mind spending time with *this* Chase at all. He found himself laughing along as Chase told him a string of humorous stories.

Chase *was* attractive—almost *too* good-looking—with a collection of freckles on his nose and cheeks, which made him seem more down-to-earth than he probably was. Maybe it was because of the beer that Mathias found himself staring at Chase's freckles. He tried not to notice Chase's lips, which were full and perfectly shaped and exactly the kind of lips Mathias wouldn't mind kissing. Not that that was the *only* thing to cross Mathias's mind as he studied those lips.

Mathias ended up talking exclusively to Chase until the bar closed, and they headed back to the training center, knowing they had a very early start the next morning.

Present day
Dallas

MATHIAS struggled to bring his thoughts back to the here and now so he could focus on finding out exactly how and why Chase was fucking around with the T-Group. Still, he couldn't help the way those old memories kept racing through his brain. He wondered vaguely if he'd ever be completely over Chase. Even reminding himself of what Chase was really like didn't seem to help, because in the end, he still remembered *his* Chase: not the cocky kid with the overbearing personality, but the carefree, loving man with whom Mathias had eventually fallen in love.

But underneath that well-practiced façade of warmth and affection, Chase was first and foremost a Richards, still someone who used people up and spat them out when he got what he wanted. Chase's true nature had been clear when they'd met, but Mathias had let himself forget and believe in the illusion as their relationship grew.

Whichever Chase was the genuine one, Mathias wouldn't be dealing with either ever again, if he could help it. It had taken him too long to get over Chase Richards, and it had been a very long time before he'd let anyone else into his life, or his heart, again.

CHAPTER THREE

One month earlier
Dallas

IT WAS Saturday morning, and Chase Richards was reading the newspaper in bed.

Alone.

Just like every Saturday morning for the past nine years. Without the need to head into the office, Chase was pretty much at a loss about how to spend his weekends. There wasn't anywhere he really wanted to go, or anyone he wanted to spend time with. Not anymore.

He'd briefly considered heading to the Dallas Athletic Club and playing some tennis or golf, but the last time he'd done that it hadn't been much fun. He'd either run into people that disliked him over some business deal they'd lost out on involving RichardsCorp, or he'd have to avoid the people who wanted something from him and weren't afraid of making sure he knew it. They weren't afraid of him *yet*.

Chase flipped through the business section, but none of the headlines caught his eye. He had already heard rumors—or started them—and nothing in here was news to him. Work had been slow lately, and frankly, it bored him. He'd achieved everything he'd hoped for—businesswise. Lately, he'd been thinking about expanding his reach out of Texas and taking on bigger fish in a bigger pond.

Still mulling over that idea, he came across the society pages. He'd been about to toss the section aside when a photograph on the front page caught his attention. He read the headline and did a double take.

The photograph showed Mathias Tobler and a beautiful, petite brunette who looked somewhat familiar. Mathias flashed his usual million-watt smile, while the woman gazed at him as if he were Prince Charming.

"Local businessman to wed former Miss Texas," read the headline.

Now that *was* news. Mathias getting *married?*

After their breakup, Chase had seen Mathias around Dallas—they attended some of the same social functions, the occasional Fuqua alumni activities, and he had seen Mathias at clubs that in the light of day neither would admit to frequenting, though they'd had no actual contact since business school. Mathias always seemed to be heading in the other direction when they saw each other at social events; clearly he hadn't wanted to have anything to do with Chase. Why would he, after the way Chase had treated him?

The engagement announcement hit Chase with a pang he hadn't known he was capable of feeling, at least as far as Mathias was concerned.

Chase remembered that he *had* seen Mathias with Brooke Collier at the Athletic Club. At the time, he'd thought Mathias was simply overcompensating—a necessity in the homophobic business atmosphere of Dallas. But now, it looked like he was actually planning to marry the bimbo... *that's going too far now, isn't it? Well maybe she's good in the sack.*

For the first time in years, Chase realized just how long it had been. How many years he'd spent living without Mathias. Chase had moved on—in his own way—though he had never gotten Mathias out of his system, and suddenly the pain of it all came crashing down on him at the sight of one little photograph.

Mathias had clearly moved on and was beginning a brand new life. Did he still have feelings for Mathias? Chase laughed at the idea, it was so farfetched. Or was it? He might have broken up with Mathias, but he felt unexpected jealousy at the idea that someone else—a woman—would have him now.

Chase lay back in bed, thinking about Mathias marrying Brooke and making a commitment to living a straight life. Was Mathias really going to try and live that life? Chase didn't recall seeing him at even the most discreet gay bars in months, so maybe….

Did Mathias know what was in store for him? You didn't get to be a beauty queen in Texas without some claws, and Chase was pretty sure Mathias had no idea just how sharp they could be. Brooke couldn't possibly be as sweet as she appeared. But Mathias most definitely was. There wasn't a scheming or deceitful bone in Mathias Tobler's body, unless he'd changed completely from the way he used to be when he'd been with Chase.

Maybe this was just part of the stellar reputation Mathias had made for himself in the business community, leader of the T-Group and well-known local philanthropist. He would settle down and produce a brood of handsome little Toblers with the beauty queen. Chase laughed at the absurd picture in his mind.

And what do I have to show for myself?

Sure, Chase had worked hard since he'd gotten his MBA and grown RichardsCorp beyond what his father had ever dreamed of. But was that enough?

He had a lot of money and he'd bought a lot of things with it. The fastest cars, a few planes, this amazing house, considered one of the most impressive and opulent in Dallas and maybe all of Texas. He'd filled it with art and treasures from around the world. Well, *he* hadn't personally filled it. He'd hired someone to do all that since he'd been so busy with work.

The thought reminded him of a lazy Sunday morning with Mathias, back in Durham, reading the travel section of the paper together and planning a summer-long European trip, discussing the cities they'd visit and the things they wanted to bring home. But in the end, only Mathias had actually gone to Venice. It would have been nice if they'd managed to go to some of those places and bring beautiful things back—things they'd chosen together—for a house they'd intended to share when they returned. *Their* house….

With a rueful sigh, Chase rolled over onto his stomach, shoving the newspaper off the bed, watching it flutter and scatter on the expensive oriental carpet covering the smooth, polished wooden floors. The photo of Mathias landed facing up, and Chase could still see his face. He closed his eyes and tried to get comfortable, but all he could think of was Mathias, and it was getting him hard.

Chase slipped his pajama bottoms off and pressed his hips into the bed. The silk sheets felt cool and slippery against his cock, and he thought about how good it would feel to get fucked into these sheets, on this comfortable bed. He couldn't even remember the last time he'd bottomed, but it had been Mathias doing the fucking. Mathias had been the last person Chase had trusted enough for that. But not here. He'd never brought anyone into this house nor had anyone in this bed. Chase was the one doing the fucking now. That's all it was for Chase—just fucking—purely physical, bodies meeting briefly for one and only one purpose. There was no more making love for Chase. Mathias had been the last person Chase had cared enough about for that, too.

Memories came crashing back—of Chase face down with Mathias's hands pinning his wrists to the bed, Mathias's weight on him and Mathias's cock deep inside of him, filling him up. Chase could practically feel his hot breath panting against the back of his neck. God, how he missed the way Mathias used to move his hips slowly so his cock dragged across that wonderful place inside that made Chase see stars and come, shouting into the mattress until he couldn't remember his own name or anything but the way his body responded.

Now, the friction of the sheets against Chase's nipples was smooth but slightly painful, a sharp contrast to the way his cock slipped against the silk.

"Mathias," Chase whispered as he ground his hips hard into the bed. As he came, he shouted Mathias's name, hearing the sad echo around the empty house.

He felt like Kubla fucking Khan in his pleasure dome, full of treasures and no one to share them with. No one that mattered. *Fucking huge useless fucking house. Fucking pathetic life.*

Chase didn't even have anyone he called a friend. He hardly even had business acquaintances. He'd made a lot of enemies, burned a lot of bridges. His father had taught him to succeed, and Chase did as he was taught.

My father. Talk about pathetic.

He hardly ever thought of his father anymore. They'd been estranged since Chase had taken over RichardsCorp. Chase had wanted it that way.

When he was younger, he had adored his father. He had wanted to be just like him. Sometimes his father would bring him to work when he was just a kid. And Chase had followed his father around, repeating everything he said, acting as if he ran a big, important company.

Now Chase ran the company for real, and everyone listened to him. They did everything he said, never questioning any decision or order. And here he was enjoying the lifestyle that had gotten him. But at the moment it felt like nothing. He wanted more from his life. He wanted love and companionship, someone to share all of the things he'd acquired and give them some value—give *Chase* some value. Mathias had found that, so why couldn't Chase?

May 2000
US Olympic Training Center
Colorado Springs

CHASE knew he'd completely fucked up his first conversation with Mathias Tobler. From the day the names had been announced for the special training camp, Chase had been thinking about what he'd say to Mathias. And he'd still fucked it up. His university fencing team had competed against Mathias's for the past couple of years in NCAA matches. And even though he'd always been intrigued by Mathias's imposing physical presence and his engaging smile, Chase had been reluctant—admittedly too shy to speak to the object of his affections—to try and get to know him. Until one day six months earlier, when Chase had managed to beat Mathias at épée, Mathias's specialty. Chase hadn't just beaten him, he'd pretty much wiped the floor with him, even though Mathias was fencing well. Chase just happened to be having a particularly good day.

When they'd removed their masks after the bout and Mathias saluted Chase as was the custom, Chase fully expected to see a sour look or a fake smile. Instead, he was treated to the biggest, brightest smile he'd ever seen. A smile that went all the way to Mathias's eyes and had to be completely genuine. He looked pretty fucking hot in his fencing costume, the way it emphasized his muscular frame, tight in all the right places. Chase had forced himself to concentrate during the match, but afterward, his mind wandered across Mathias's broad chest and tight ass.

After that, Chase was smitten. He didn't dare speak to Mathias, but he couldn't stop thinking about him. What kind of person was Mathias, to smile like that after he'd been defeated so soundly? Chase was as intrigued by Mathias's personality as he had been by his body—a body Chase couldn't stop dreaming and fantasizing about. He wanted to peel back that fencing suit and slowly explore all six-feet-four-inches of Mathias Tobler hidden beneath. He wanted to do much more than explore. Some nights, he'd lie awake in bed, hand on his own cock, wondering what it would feel like to have Mathias's hand—or mouth—there instead.

After months of waiting and planning and fantasizing, Chase finally had his chance. Two months of training before the Olympic trials meant two months of opportunity to get to know Mathias and see what developed between them. It was unacceptable that he had nearly blown the chance to make a good first impression on Mathias. Chase had gone to the training camp hoping to impress Mathias, and he'd practically blown it at their very first conversation.

Chase knew his father would have planned a strategy and followed the plan, eventually achieving his goal, no matter how long it took. Alan Richards had been a fencer himself, and a chess player, and found a way to incorporate the strategies of both sports into his business. He'd drilled into Chase to prepare and wait for the right time to attack—timing was crucial—but Chase never seemed to get it right.

Meeting Mathias was just another one of Chase's failures—or near failures, at least. And yet somehow, Chase had managed to pull victory out of almost certain defeat that night in Colorado Springs, though he still didn't quite understand how.

He and Mathias had been talking for only a short while at the welcoming party, but Chase could see Mathias's attention was wandering. Just then, a girl with long, sleek blue-black hair came up to them. She was slim and tall—almost as tall as Chase—with dark crescent-shaped eyes indicating some Asian heritage in her family.

"Hi, I'm Arlene. Arlene Sinclair." She reached out to shake Mathias's hand.

"Oh, hey! Épée, St. John's right?" Mathias asked with recognition and a big smile. "I'm Mathias Tobler."

"You're at Stanford, aren't you? We were there in January," Arlene said.

"I'm Chase Richards," Chase interjected.

"Yeah, I remember that. Your team kicked our asses in épée," Mathias said to Arlene.

Chase felt like he was invisible.

"Not you, though, I think you ruined the men's perfect score that day!" Arlene turned a whiter-than-white smile at Mathias.

"Chase's great at épée, but saber's your main weapon, isn't it?" Mathias asked, and Chase silently thanked Mathias for remembering he was there.

"Richards?" Arlene rolled the name around on her tongue with a thoughtful look. "I can't remember, what school are you at?"

"Columbia," Chase replied.

"Oh, okay." Arlene paused for a moment, then said, "Too bad, they came to us this year. I would kill for a chance to visit New York! Anyway, group of us are heading out to a bar now. You guys wanna join in?" Arlene aimed another very inviting smile at Mathias. "This guy from Yale has a big SUV and won't be drinking. There's plenty of room!"

"Sounds good. Sure." Chase looked toward Mathias, hoping he'd want to go. If not, Chase was more than happy to stay at the training center's booze-free party.

"I'm only twenty." Mathias shook his head in obvious disappointment. "My birthday's not till July. I won't be able to even get in."

Chase could see Mathias really wanted to go. "I doubt a guy as big as you is gonna get carded," he joked, but Mathias didn't laugh.

"Go on without me. See you guys in the morning." Mathias started to turn away.

"Come on, Mathias, you have nothing to lose," Chase pushed.

"Yeah, I'm sure the driver would bring you back here if you can't get in, and we'll catch up with you later on," Arlene added.

"See?" Chase said.

Mathias finally caved, apparently unable to resist both of them. Chase hoped it wasn't because Mathias wanted to spend more time with Arlene. The three of them joined the group heading for the bar, and Arlene made the introductions before they all piled into the SUV. Everyone managed to get into the bar without being carded, so Mathias's concern proved unfounded.

The bar was noisy and crowded, and it was hard to make conversation with more than one or two other people at a time. Chase bought a round for everyone, but once people had their drinks, they drifted off in different directions. Chase found Mathias and Arlene chatting and went to join them. The three of them shouted at each other for a few minutes, until another carload of fencers turned up and Arlene ran off to greet the newcomers. Mathias glanced over in her direction, and Chase could see the indecision on his face. Mathias was too well brought up to run off and leave someone on their own, so he stayed and talked with Chase, who had been trying his best to impress Mathias, but seemed to be failing at every turn.

"Want another beer?" Chase asked Mathias, who was still sipping his first beer. Chase had finished his second ages ago and pretended to keep drinking from the now-empty bottle.

Good thing it's dark in here, Chase thought.

"Sure." Mathias sounded unenthusiastic.

Chase headed off to the bar and ordered two beers and a couple of tequila shots. He knocked both the shots back before heading to see if Mathias was where he'd left him. By the time Chase made his way back, the tequila was starting to give him a nice warm feeling. Mathias was still on his own near the back of the bar, and Chase fought off the urge to grab hold of him and start making out, because at that moment, that was the only thing Chase really wanted to do with Mathias. Obviously nothing he had *said* had made any impression on Mathias, but Chase was a damn good kisser. He restrained himself, remembering he was supposed to plan things out first, not just jump right in with both feet—or lips as the case may be.

Mathias gave Chase an odd look—apparently he must have had some idea what was going through Chase's mind—and Chase made a joke to deflect the attention. Soon Mathias was laughing, practically for the first time that evening. It was a beautiful sound, loud and deep and real, and Chase loved the way Mathias threw his head back when he laughed.

Maybe there's some hope for me yet. Chase crossed his fingers behind his back. A little superstition never hurt.

From that point on, their conversation flowed smoothly and naturally. Chase had no idea what they talked about, and he didn't even care. He just wanted to listen to Mathias for hours—to say or do anything to get him to shine that amazing, bright, beautiful smile down on Chase again.

It was 1:00 a.m. when the lights flickered in an attempt to get everyone to leave. Last call had been thirty minutes earlier, but most of the athletes were still milling about, chatting and laughing and making new friends of former foes. Neither Chase nor Mathias even realized how late it was.

"What time is the first training session tomorrow?" Chase asked, knowing he wasn't going to like the answer.

"Seven maybe? No, maybe that's when breakfast starts," Mathias said, pulling a folded up schedule from his back pocket. "Breakfast 6:30–7:30, then first training 7:45–9:00 a.m.," he read from the now-crumpled paper.

"Fuck, that's early!" Chase replied just as Arlene and two other women fencers came up to them. Arlene glared at Chase out of the corner of her eye, but apparently decided not to say anything, for which Chase was grateful.

"Let's get going." Arlene herded the fencers out of the bar. There was some general confusion as everyone piled back into the vehicles, and Chase ended up in the SUV while Mathias went back to the training center in someone else's car—the one with all the girls. Chase's driver got lost and had to contend with five half-drunk guys giving him conflicting directions, and it took half an hour to get back, by which time the group from the other car was probably already in bed. The only question on Chase's mind was "Whose bed would Mathias end up in?"

Mathias had seemed to respond to Arlene's initial flirtatiousness, but he had spent the rest of the time at that bar with Chase, hadn't he? If Mathias had been interested in any of those women, he would have found a way to talk to them well before the ride back in the car, Chase reasoned. It was just the first night; it didn't mean anything. *Did it?*

Not to worry, we're here for a couple of months, Chase thought, though he was disappointed. Impatience was his downfall in fencing as well as his personal life. Mathias wasn't going anywhere. Chase needed to slow down, relax, and plan. He vowed to take things more deliberately, more carefully, from now on.

Later that night, lying in bed, Chase went over that first conversation with Mathias in his head. Mathias hadn't responded to the confident persona that his father employed. It worked when his *dad* acted like that. People looked up to his father and respected him, didn't they? Alan Richards always got what he wanted in business, as well as in his personal life. So why hadn't it worked for Chase?

He couldn't think of anything he'd wanted more than for Mathias Tobler to notice him and want to talk to him, and he'd nearly blown it. He'd responded much more positively to Chase when he'd just been his normal, not-very-distinguished self and to the way he got slightly goofy after a couple of beers. Chase couldn't stop thinking about the way Mathias had smiled at him once he'd let down that almost disdainful wall and warmed up a bit. He would focus on that, and not how Mathias had left in a car full of female athletes, because that was just depressing.

The next morning, Chase got to breakfast as close to 6:30 as humanly possible. Only a handful of other people were already there, seated in a group at a large table and chatting quietly as they ate, obviously still half-asleep and conserving their energy. Chase smiled in greeting but headed to a smaller table on his own, hopeful that Mathias would notice him sitting by himself and join him.

No such luck. It was nearly 7:15 when Mathias finally showed up, tousled and looking as if he'd just rolled out of bed. Chase laughed, deciding Mathias must not be an early riser. He stopped laughing when he saw that Mathias had come in with someone else—a female someone, so definitely *not* his roommate. It was Arlene. Chase's mood descended another ten or twenty notches. They both looked guilty and slightly embarrassed and they were laughing as they made their way through the food line together.

Maybe Mathias hadn't just rolled out of bed; maybe he'd been rolling around *in* bed with Arlene. Chase cursed himself for assuming that Mathias was gay. The way Mathias had looked at him the previous night gave the impression he had a chance, but evidently Chase's gaydar was as fucked up as the rest of his social skills.

It was a huge disappointment, but Chase decided he was up to the challenge. Stranger things had happened, and Chase had managed to persuade more than one bi-curious guy to give it a shot, so maybe, just maybe...

Chase worked up the courage to approach Mathias during the first training session. "Mornin', sleepyhead," he said with a smile.

"Man, I feel like an idiot." Mathias ran a hand through his shiny near-black hair. Talk about bedhead! "I forgot to fix the time on my alarm clock and got up an hour late. My body's still on California time."

Chase's heart skipped a beat, especially at the images of Mathias's body forming in his brain. Maybe Mathias *hadn't* been with Arlene after all. Or maybe it just meant that Mathias *and* Arlene had overslept together because of Mathias's alarm clock.

Stop worrying. Eyes on the prize and stop second-guessing yourself.

But before he could dwell on things too deeply, practice began. Chase didn't just need to win Mathias, he needed to win a spot on the team. His father was counting on him.

The first practice session consisted of a number of drills, both with and without weapons. They practiced footwork, attacks, and defenses in every position, and they rotated partners after each drill, so that no two fencers would get too familiar with each other's moves.

This first day also allowed the coaches to size up the athletes and decide how to focus future training sessions.

Before they donned fencing suits for the weapons practice, Mathias wore only shorts and a T-shirt that left no doubt in Chase's mind that Mathias worked out, a lot. Chase didn't mind the view, either. The lunges and squats were especially nice to watch, and Chase marveled at Mathias's huge, powerful thighs, muscles straining beneath the skin.

After the weapons session, the men filed into the locker room to shower. Each man had been assigned a locker for his equipment, some of which the center provided, and most people had put personal items in their locker earlier that morning or the previous day. Chase had brought all of his shower items down the day before, taking a moment to note the location of Mathias's locker in relation to his own—thanks to the convenient nametags. It was located in the same bank, but opposite Chase's.

As Chase undressed, he fought the urge to turn around and check Mathias out, reminding himself that there was plenty of time, and he didn't want to act like a stalker.

"Fuck!" Chase heard Mathias exclaim behind him. "I forgot my gym bag. No shampoo!"

Chase turned, ready to offer Mathias his, but another guy was already handing him a bottle of shampoo, and they headed off together toward the shower. Chase tried not to pay too much attention to how Mathias interacted with the other guy, and chose a shower on the opposite end of the room so he wouldn't be tempted to spy on them.

Chase showered slowly, daydreaming, and by the time he got back to his locker, half the guys were already dressed and heading out. Mathias was still there, towel wrapped loosely around his waist, talking with someone else—a red-head with freckles in places Chase didn't know you *could* have freckles. Mathias nodded as Chase approached, and he returned the greeting, noticing how precariously that towel perched on Mathias's hips. Chase dressed, daydreaming some more about what was under the towel, listening to Mathias still chatting until the other guy finished dressing and rushed off to meet up with his roommate. When Chase sat to put on his shoes, he discovered Mathias still wasn't dressed. Apparently multitasking wasn't the guy's strong suit. But now they were the only two people in the locker bay.

"What'd you think of the first practice?" Chase watched Mathias's back as he pulled the towel off and applied it to his long, damp hair. Chase kept his own hair short and neat and usually disliked long hair on men. But on Mathias, it seemed a perfect complement to his personality, especially the way it spilled across his eyes like a dark curtain. Chase had noticed that the previous night when they'd been talking. Whenever Mathias got really animated, his hair seemed to join in the excitement. The thought of that made Chase laugh out loud.

"My thighs are still killing me. I guess they're going to work us pretty hard here." Mathias slid one hand along his thigh and Chase fought off his body's reaction to the sight. He tried to think of something unsexy to counteract Mathias's incredibly virile presence. "Maybe this is how they're going to weed us out, like Navy SEALs training or something." Mathias was still stroking his thigh, and Chase's brain had turned to mush, though his cock was anything but. "I'll bet the last three guys for each weapon who are still *alive* at the end of training automatically make the team," he added with that magical laugh that made Chase's heart speed up even more.

As Mathias spoke, Chase enjoyed the view of the powerful back and shoulder muscles rippling below his skin. And that ass! It was perfectly shaped and muscular and Chase imagined what it would be like to caress its beautiful curves or fondle it as he fucked Mathias, maybe bent over one of the benches in here. Thankfully, Mathias was the slowest dresser in the entire world, so there was plenty of time to look and definitely plenty of Mathias to ogle and daydream about.

Occasionally, Mathias turned his head in Chase's direction, and at one point, from the odd look on Mathias's face, Chase worried he had noticed the way Chase had been staring at him.

Fuck, Chase thought.

"What?" Mathias asked. "Something wrong?"

"I was just thinking about how much time you must spend in the weight room," Chase tried to explain, practically stuttering out the words.

Fuck! Could I have said anything lamer? That was the dumbest thing anyone had ever said, probably only exceeded by whatever he was about to say.

But Mathias didn't react the way Chase expected. To his complete surprise, Mathias turned around, still completely naked, and Chase finally saw exactly what Mathias had been hiding under that towel, and he was more than satisfied and definitely interested as he looked at Mathias's large and very beautiful cock. It more than lived up to Chase's late-night fantasies, and he just couldn't help staring.

"Take off your shirt," Mathias said.

"Huh?" Yup, that was now officially the dumbest thing Chase had ever said. Well, considering the fact that most of his attention was on Mathias's cock, maybe it wasn't entirely unexpected that he'd sound like an idiot.

"Your shirt," Mathias repeated, smiling, "take it off."

Chase smiled back and unbuttoned his shirt. This wasn't at all what he'd expected. Not that he was complaining. He just didn't think something like this would happen in the locker room; it was way too public. After he pulled off his shirt, Chase began to unbuckle his belt.

"Just the shirt, dude," Mathias laughed, and Chase felt like a complete fool again. It seemed that Mathias had something different in mind than Chase had hoped.

Mathias stared at Chase's upper body for a moment, letting his gaze linger here and there appreciatively. Or at least that's how it seemed to Chase. Chase knew he was in good—no, make that great—shape. He trained regularly, and he was here, for fuck's sake, trying out for the Olympic team. His chest and arms and back were hard, and he knew he looked damned good, if the stares he got on a regular basis from both men *and* women were anything to go by, but his muscles weren't as defined and chiseled as Mathias's.

"I could give you some workout tips, if you're interested." Mathias turned back around and pulled on a pair of skin-hugging boxer briefs, then loose, well-worn jeans. Chase couldn't understand why Mathias wanted to cover up such a great-looking ass under acres of denim.

"Yeah, okay, thanks." Chase hoped his disappointment wasn't obvious. But it was a start, and it meant Mathias would definitely be spending more time with him, without Chase having to initiate additional contact.

Mathias finished dressing and sat down on the bench, facing Chase, while he put his shoes on.

"You know, we could work out together if you want." Mathias offered Chase a smile that seemed to promise more than just working out, but Chase didn't want to get his hopes up again.

"That'd be great, thanks!" Chase said sincerely. At a minimum, he'd get to spend time with Mathias, and end up looking fantastic at the end of a couple of months.

And if Chase played his cards right, he might end up with a whole lot more.

The days soon blurred into a series of long morning runs, seemingly endless drills of footwork and sword work. Countless practice bouts were followed by daily strategy sessions, which bored nearly everyone, including one of the instructors, based on the way his eyes seemed to glaze over and lose focus, as if he were about to fall asleep.

But the highlight of each day, for Chase, was the time he and Mathias spent working out in the Center's well-equipped weight room. If Mathis ever realized the reason Chase needed him to demonstrate some of the moves several times, or required hands-on correction for form, he never let on. Chase grinned and found excuses for both, while Tee—he'd let Chase make up a nickname—smiled back and appeared to be enjoying the closeness and contact just as much. Soon they were spending nearly all of their free time together, earning more than a few curious glances from their fellow athletes and several disappointed glares from female athletes who realized they wouldn't have a chance with either one of the two hottest guys at the Training Center.

CHAPTER FOUR

Two weeks after publication
of the engagement announcement
June 2012
Dallas

"YOU'RE home so late, Matt." Brooke rushed into the living room before he'd even closed the door behind him. She wore a cream-colored dress with sparkly beads that made her look a little like a twenties flapper. Her hair, however, still looked like twenty-first century Texas: big and immaculately coifed.

He glanced at his watch and took a deep breath. No one called him "Matt." She thought he should like that she had a pet name for him. He'd always hated the nickname. "It's barely five-thirty. That's early."

"No, it's late. You need to hurry up and get ready."

A little muscle in his jaw twitched. What had he forgotten? "For…?"

"The fundraiser for Dallas Big Brothers Big Sisters. At the club. Tonight."

"Oh, right." That explained why she was so dressed up. He couldn't stomach a benefit tonight, but he wholly supported the cause. Not everyone had the benefit of a loving, supportive family, and he thought the program helped kids. The club was the Dallas Athletic Club, which meant at least some of his friends might be there.

She stood with her arms crossed, eyes narrowing and one foot tapping silently on the thick Persian carpet. "You're not hurrying."

"Brooke." He took her hand and led her to the couch. She sat, knees together facing toward him. "Honey, can we skip this one? You're not on the board, right?"

"No, but we are not skipping it. I got this dress." She stood and waved a hand along her body. She did a little shimmy so the beads danced and glittered. "We are not skipping this."

"I'm tired of being on display at these things. We hardly ever go out just the two of us. I miss that."

"Matt, we're engaged. You don't have to keep courting me." She looked at her own watch now and started the foot tapping again.

He reached for her hand and pulled her back down to the couch. "Promise me that next time it's just us. A date. We'll go to dinner and a concert. Or maybe a film at the Inwood." He loved the couches and the legroom there.

"Why?"

"I liked going places with you, and talking about the film or the concert. Now, all we seem to do is these charity things."

"Philanthropy is very important. It's how you make your reputation, you know that."

"I thought it was about doing good."

"Silly." She flashed a bright smile at him. "Now go get ready." She disentangled her arm from his grasp and glided into the other room.

He got up and went into his bedroom, where he found she'd laid out his tuxedo on the bed. He held it up and realized it wasn't his usual one. Instead, she'd gotten him one that complemented her dress. The tux, single-breasted, had wide notched lapels and a white waistcoat—like something out of *The Great Gatsby*. He sighed and slipped into the bathroom for a quick shower before dressing. He wouldn't think about how much the tux cost. He could afford it, but he'd rather give the money to the charity than the tailor.

After a brief shower, he toweled off and began dressing, wishing he didn't feel so resentful that Brooke scheduled him for so many society events. They hardly spent time together at those things.

Everything had changed in just a few short months. She'd swept into his world less than a year ago, and now he could barely remember his life before her.

They had first met at a charity event a year earlier. Brooke could have her pick of men, and not just in Texas, but anywhere in the US. She'd even been a Miss America runner-up a few years back, and she was every bit as beautiful now as she was then. But somehow, she had chosen him, and it had been more than a little flattering.

He'd been seated next to Brooke during dinner, and she'd paid a lot of attention to him. She'd even managed to convince him to dance, which was quite an accomplishment.

Despite her stunning looks, Brooke had seemed surprisingly down-to-earth, and Mathias had immediately loved her sense of humor. She was intelligent and made clever jokes. She mentioned some of her other interests—music, art, old films—and it made him realize how infrequently he went to a film or concert. He had divided his time between the T-Group and his family, especially after his father had gotten seriously ill. He realized he needed to expand his horizons and try to have a social life for a change.

A week after the hospital benefit, Brooke had called him at work to ask if he would escort her to another charity event the following week. He wondered why the idea had come as such a surprise to him. Yes, she'd paid him a lot of attention—spent most of the evening with him, in fact—but it hadn't really clicked at the time that she'd been interested in him. Or was she? Maybe it was just a friendly invitation and nothing more. Never mind what it was, he decided. He'd enjoyed her company and agreed to go with her to a fundraising dinner for the Dallas Symphony. That would be a good opportunity to enjoy a concert as well as get to know Brooke Collier a little bit better.

Soon, they were spending time together every week, going to concerts, the theatre, or one of the many fundraisers Brooke attended. She seemed to be on the board of a number of worthwhile charities, and Mathias was happy to support the causes she embraced

Brooke had inserted herself into his life the way Chase had years earlier. Chase had made the first move, and Mathias had followed, until suddenly one day, Mathias knew he couldn't live without Chase, without having Chase in his life in every way possible. So it had been with Brooke—one day, Mathias realized he'd fallen in love with her, and loved the way he felt whenever they were together. She'd made him happy and restored his self-confidence, so seriously damaged after Chase had unceremoniously dumped him. When Mathias was with Brooke, he felt as if he were the most important person in the world. She made a point of asking his opinion of the films they saw, or paintings in a museum, or what he experienced when he heard a piece of music she loved.

No matter that she'd been the pursuer at first, within a month he'd found he enjoyed her company so much, he was disappointed if occasionally one or the other of them was too busy to meet. And within another month, Mathias couldn't imagine not seeing Brooke as much as possible.

It had been a relief to find his affection for Brooke growing. After Chase, Mathias had given up hope of another meaningful relationship. He thought Chase had been his one true love and no one would ever replace him. He'd avoided entanglements, not willing to let anyone that deep into his life—or heart—again. Until Brooke broke through the cool, cynical wall he'd built.

"Matt, are you ready yet?" Brooke swung the door open as he finished his bowtie.

"Yes. How do I look?" He thought he looked pretty damn good. The tux was growing on him. He smiled and gave his reflection another glance.

"Your tie is crooked. Let me fix that." She was on him in two quick steps. She yanked the tie open and sighed deeply as she rolled her eyes. "We need to get going. I called for the car and the driver's waiting." She finished retying the knot and spun on her heel toward the door.

"I wanted to drive. We don't need the driver."

"I like being driven. We can make a nice entrance when we arrive. Besides, you're paying him, so we might as well make him work."

Mathias suppressed a response and followed her to the door.

THE Dallas Athletic Club had been transformed into a 1920s speakeasy. The ballroom was decked in gold and white, as was the small orchestra that played for two couples on the dance floor. Another room held a buffet spread, while a third had card tables, roulette wheels, and two bars—one at either end.

Mathias couldn't remember what time he'd eaten lunch. "Let's grab a bite first, then mingle."

"Go ahead. I'm not hungry." Brooke fluttered her fingers at some friends of hers seated at a table in the gambling room.

"You're not coming?" This is what he'd been afraid of. They'd gotten dressed up and he'd probably never see her the rest of the evening until she was ready to go home.

"I'll find you in a little bit. I want to see what Erica's wearing."

"Okay." He leaned down and gave her a peck on the cheek, then turned toward the buffet room.

"Oh, before you go, Matt, I need some money."

"Why? Isn't everything included?"

"To gamble, silly. A thousand will do."

"A thousand dollars?" He didn't normally carry even a hundred in cash.

"It's a benefit. You're supposed to gamble and the money goes to the charity."

"What about the tickets?"

"That's mainly for the food. It's not really your donation."

He slipped his wallet out of the breast pocket, and before he could even see what was in there, she pulled it out of his hand, took the cash, and handed it back. She gave him a smoldering look and disappeared into the crowd.

"Millie cleaned me out, too," a gruff voice tinged with humor boomed from behind his left shoulder.

"Hey, R.J., how ya doing?"

"Good. Good." R.J. Garrett, was one of Mathias's closest friends, and a fellow club member. "Let me get you a drink."

Mathias put a hand up. "Nope. I'm famished. Let's eat first."

"You want a drink."

Mathias was about to protest again but hesitated when he saw R.J.'s smile had melted away. "Sure. Knob Creek."

"Be back in a minute." True to his word, R.J. returned quickly. They had good staff here at the club. They should, given how much it cost to belong.

They sat at a table near the far wall, away from the bustle at the gaming tables.

"What's worrying you, R.J.?" Mathias took a sip of smooth amber bourbon, let it tingle on his tongue and waited.

"I didn't know whether or not to say anything, but Millie told me I should."

"I don't like the sound of that."

"We've been friends for a while, and I've never told you how to live your life."

Mathias took a gulp rather than a sip. He didn't like where this conversation was heading. He hoped it wasn't going in the direction of being outed. He hadn't been the most well-behaved half-in-the-closet bachelor in Dallas, but he'd been discreet. And he hadn't been with a man since he started dating Brooke seriously. What had R.J. heard or seen? "Unless you count a dozen or so blind dates over the years that nearly scarred me for life."

"Yeah, I admit to that. You're too good a guy to go through life alone. You need a good partner. That's why I was thrilled when you met Brooke…." R.J. shook his head and gulped his own drink.

Oh, fuck. Here it comes. "And?"

"And, buddy, I just don't know how to tell you this."

"Just come out with it." Mathias wished he'd chosen a different phrase.

"I thought it was just my imagination, but Millie saw it too."

"Saw what?" There was no way Millie Garrett had seen Mathias in a gay club. He relaxed. R.J. wasn't going to force that issue, at least not tonight. "You've got my curiosity piqued."

"Brooke. And the tennis pro, what's his name, Fences or Doors…."

"Gates. Ted Gates."

"She plays a lot of *tennis*, Mattie." R.J. said the nickname like his parents did: Mah-tee. Mathias liked that about him. "And I don't mean the kind with *yellow* balls."

"What're you saying?"

"She's been seen with this Gates guy outside the club. At a restaurant, and Millie swears she saw them together in the bar at the Palomar. If it wasn't Gates, it was some guy who looks like him. Another guy, Mattie."

Mathias swallowed the remaining bourbon and put the tumbler back on the table. The liquid blazed a warm trail down his throat and his head felt a little fuzzy. He didn't drink much and one drink had a powerful effect. That, plus R.J.'s news.

"It's probably not what you think." Mathias couldn't help looking around the room for Brooke. He spotted her throwing dice near the bar with her friend Erica. No sign of Ted Gates, at least at the moment. "There could be another explanation."

"Sure there could. You could ask."

"She'll think I'm checking up on her."

"You are checking up on her. It's Dallas, women want you to pay attention to them. So, pay a little attention—even a little too much—and see how she reacts." R.J. stood up. "Let me get us some refills, and I'll meet you over at the buffet."

"Yeah. I really need food now. More than bourbon." Mathias got up and watched Brooke for a few moments before heading into the dining room. He glanced at the spread but he'd lost his appetite. He didn't want to believe what R.J. had told him. It just didn't make any sense. He couldn't picture Brooke cheating on him. She didn't seem to be very experienced with sex, and the idea of her seeking it elsewhere was almost ludicrous.

He'd taken things very slowly with the physical side of their relationship, waiting months before getting intimate. Quite frankly, since Chase, he was out of practice with women who were anything more than a hookup. He was more used to picking guys up in bars or clubs, and there was very little finesse needed with those arrangements. With Brooke, however, Mathias hadn't wanted to make a mistake. Had she taken that for disinterest?

He'd found out fairly early in their physical relationship that she was quite particular about what she wanted. He'd start off slowly, but she rebuffed much beyond kissing, so he backed off. To his surprise, after their next date she'd practically pounced on him and they'd ended up in bed, with Brooke calling the shots.

For months he played it easy, letting her decide when and how they would make love. She rarely wanted to venture beyond the basics, even when he wanted to try new things just to please *her*. If she thought he was pushing, she'd freeze him out.

All other aspects of their relationship went smoothly, and they both had similar goals for the future, and Mathias could picture spending the rest of his life with her. After six months of dating exclusively, she suggested moving in and he'd been thrilled. But her Jekyll and Hyde routine seemed much more obvious now, and Mathias didn't know how to approach the issue.

Even when she was in control there were things she wouldn't even consider. He remembered how the first time his fingers had brushed her ass, she'd nearly freaked out and refused to let him touch her for a week. Now that they were living together, she'd retreat to her own room if he tried to take their lovemaking in a new direction, saying it was distasteful or possibly even aberrant. She was such a beautiful and sexy woman, but it seemed she either had minimal sex drive, or she simply didn't care for the way Mathias made love to her. He'd been shocked she still didn't feel comfortable letting go with him, especially after their engagement.

She couldn't possibly be cheating on him.

HE WAITED until the weekend to bring up the topic. He'd made blueberry pancakes, grilled thick-cut bacon, and even hand squeezed fresh orange and tangerine juice.

She picked at the food on her plate, but drank two cups of café au lait.

"Not hungry?" Mathias stabbed a piece of bacon and chewed, enjoying the smoky-salty taste. He didn't make bacon often, but he kept in good shape and figured he could splurge on fat and calories once in a while.

"You know I won't eat bacon."

"More for me." He grinned. Then he frowned. "Want to play a few sets at the club with me today? I booked a court for eleven."

"What?" She sipped more coffee. "No. I'm kind of tired."

He watched but her expression didn't change at the mention of the club or tennis. "I'll see if R.J.'s free. Come watch me play?"

"Sure."

So far, so good. She hadn't tried to get out of going to the club. "Why don't you see if Millie's free and we can all lunch together later."

"Okay, that sounds good."

"It does?" Mathias had expected her to say she didn't want to see Millie. "Hey, speaking of Millie, R.J. said she ran into you last week at the Palomar."

"I didn't see her."

She hadn't denied being at the Palomar. He wasn't sure if that was good or bad.

"You were there?"

"Yeah. I had a drink in the bar."

"She said she thought you were with a guy that looks like Ted Gates."

Brooke laughed, a trilling, musical sound. "It was Ted Gates."

Oh. He hoped Millie had been wrong.

"Why'd you meet him there?" He hadn't intended to ask so directly, but since she hadn't denied seeing Gates, Mathias took a chance.

"I didn't meet him there, silly." She slapped his wrist. "I was at the spa for a massage and had a drink after. He showed up and joined me."

Mathias forced out a weak laugh. "Oh, that's nice."

She grinned. "I think he might have been at the hotel for something naughty, you know. And he couldn't very well pretend I hadn't seen him." She took a sip of coffee.

Mathias nodded. "So, that's it? You saw him and he had to pretend it was just normal?" He speared another piece of bacon and bit off half. "I knew it wasn't anything. Millie overreacted."

"Overreacted? What do you mean?" She put her coffee cup down with a loud clank.

"She implied it wasn't an innocent coincidence." He shrugged, but as soon as the words were out, he wished he'd been more careful.

"You mean she thought I was goin' behind your back with Ted Gates at the Palomar?"

"Yeah, ridiculous, right?"

"You believed her?" Brooke stood up and glared. "You were checking up on me? Quizzing me to see if I'd say the wrong thing?" She started breathing hard and her hands balled up into fists. "Mathias Tobler, I can't believe you insulted me like that. And that underhanded way you asked. That's even more despicable." She smacked the pot of café au lait and it crashed to floor, shattering and spilling hot liquid across the kitchen tiles. She stomped out and slammed the door behind her.

"Glad I cleared that up," he said out loud as he bent down to clean up the mess.

She didn't speak to him for two days. She wouldn't let him touch her for another two after that. He took her on a shopping trip and promised her a dinner at the most expensive restaurant in town so she could show off the new dress and gold bracelet he'd bought for her. He made a reservation for the following week at the French Room—a jacket-required, near perfect on the Zagat scale and expensive enough to put a smile on Brooke Collier's absolutely perfect face.

CHAPTER FIVE

One week later
Dallas

MATHIAS was late meeting Brooke for their big dinner at the French Room and he knew she wasn't going to be happy about it. Brooke hated sitting alone at the table. Not because she hated being alone, but because she hated being *seen* alone, especially in the best restaurant in Dallas. Plus, this was supposed to be his apology for accusing her of fooling around with the tennis pro from the club.

It seemed he couldn't do anything right by her since they'd gotten engaged and she'd moved into his condo. Now Mathias felt like a screwup, even in his own house. He had no one to blame for being late but himself, and he'd brought a large bouquet of flowers, a collection of roses, lilies, and three things the florist told him didn't even grow in the Western Hemisphere. He hoped it would help make it up to her. She liked flowers, and these were impressive, so it couldn't hurt.

She was seated at a booth, drinking something alarmingly blue from a martini glass, when the maître d' escorted Mathias to the table. She looked gorgeous. Even sitting down, Mathias could see the midnight blue silk dress he'd bought her—also part of the apology—was stunning, with its low neckline that enhanced her beautiful cleavage. She was wearing the diamond earrings he'd given her as an engagement gift, and they sparkled brightly even in the dim light.

"Babe, you look amazing." He leaned down to kiss her.

She turned her head away, letting his lips brush against her cheek. She smelled as good as she looked. "Lipstick. Sorry," she said, with a light laugh that struck him tonight as not even remotely genuine.

He handed her the flowers, and she made some admiring noises as she glanced at them before putting them down on the table.

"I thought those flowers were beautiful, but they're nothing next to you, especially tonight." Mathias put an arm around her shoulders after he'd slid into the booth next to her. He knew he sounded incredibly corny, but Brooke just had that effect on him, and he really meant what he'd said. She never failed to astonish him with her beauty.

Mathias noticed that heads had turned when he'd sat down next to Brooke. That was no surprise. She'd been a pageant queen and was easily the most beautiful woman in the room. It wasn't why he'd asked her to marry him, though. She'd been so much more and until recently made him feel like the most important thing in the world.

Recently, however, Brooke's attention had been focused less on their relationship and more on the details of their wedding. And he was fine with that, until she had suddenly wanted to change so many things about him: their home, their lifestyle, his clothes, even the way he did things. He hadn't expected that.

"I'm Brad, and I'll be serving you tonight," the waiter said, startling Mathias back to the here and now. Brad handed them menus, and smiled. He was average height, with eyes the color of dark chocolate and short dark brown hair. Under his crisp white shirt, it was easy to see the man worked out, and he had a bright, engaging smile. There was something in the way he looked at Mathias, with a smile that seemed to offer so much more than just waiterly things. Mathias thought he was imagining it when Brad described the evening's specials as if he were listing the sexual favors he'd like to perform for Mathias. Until Brad came back to take their orders and kept his eyes on Mathias the entire time, not even once glancing in Brooke's direction. Mathias smiled back, acknowledging Brad's interest.

After they'd ordered, Brooke started up on one of her recent favorite topics, house hunting. "I've been talking with this terrific agent and she's found some fantastic places. Look." Brooke pulled some printouts from her purse and pushed them across the table at Mathias. "This one—" She tapped at it with a long pink fingernail. "—would be perfect. It's got a tennis court and stables."

"You don't ride."

She smiled coyly. "I might if we had our own stables."

Mathias took the sheet and glanced at the house, an enormous, stuffy-looking monstrosity that belonged on an English manor. The price nearly made him spill his Knob Creek. "It's so far out of town."

"It's like something from a magazine, Matt."

He held back a groan at the nickname.

"I like living right in Dallas. Close to the office and to the club. I know you love spending time there, with your friends. And all that tennis."

Brooke nodded, glancing around and looking a bit uneasy. "Tennis."

He wondered about her reaction; she'd assured him there was nothing going on with Ted Gates. "Didn't you play today? That's probably why you're glowing. All that fresh air and sunshine."

"Yes. I played a few sets with Erica."

"You two have been playing a lot, plus those lessons. When are you going to join the women's tour?" Mathias reached for Brooke's hand but she pulled it away.

"Oh, we don't play that well. Don't be so ridiculous." There was no humor in her tone or her eyes.

"Speak of the devil!"

"What?"

Mathias nodded toward the front of the restaurant. Brooke had to turn to see. "There's Erica. Why don't we have her and Tripp join us?"

"No!" She patted her hair. "No, I just spent all day with her. Let's just be the two of us tonight." She reached for Mathias's hand as Erica and her husband came up to their table.

"Why, Brooke Collier, wherever have you been hidin' your pretty self? Stood me up for tennis again and not returnin' my calls!"

Erica slapped Brooke's wrist playfully. "Hey, Mathias, you look handsome as ever tonight!"

"Erica. Tripp." Mathias gave them a polite nod and turned his gaze back to Brooke. She looked like she wanted to crawl into her martini glass. Bright spots colored her cheeks and she blinked a few times.

"Well, we'll catch up with you lovebirds later." Erica put an arm through her husband's and moved toward a table where their waiter stood ready to greet them.

Mathias wished they hadn't left because now he was alone with Brooke and he didn't know what the hell to say to her.

"Excuse me." She got up and headed for the powder room.

Mathias watched her go, trying to control his breathing. R.J. had said she'd been seen with the tennis pro on more than one occasion, but she'd explained it to his satisfaction. Nothing sinister in that. Though for what Mathias spent on her tennis lessons, the coach should be buying him a drink. Or something more. He grinned. That coach was a good-looking guy. He could imagine spending time with the man would be awfully pleasant.

But Brooke had lied outright to him tonight about being with Erica, and rushed off rather than stayed to hear Mathias's reaction. That was decidedly more sinister.

"Something more for you, sir?" Brad came up to the table, close enough that Mathias could feel the heat from his body. "Another drink, or—" He paused for a shade too long. "—something else?"

Mathias waved at his empty glass and avoided looked at Brad's face. "Yes, another. Thanks," he said in the general direction of Brad's waist, trying not to let his gaze move any lower.

Brad and the drink arrived before Brooke returned and against his better judgment, Mathias gulped it like a shot. Brad hadn't gotten more than two paces away before Mathias slammed the empty glass on the table, and the waiter turned almost immediately. "Another?"

"Yeah."

Mathias watched Brad walk away. Life had been so simple before Brooke. He still couldn't fathom her cheating. Her "alleged cheating," he reminded himself. She was almost… asexual was the only word he could find. She was sexy as hell, but she didn't like sex much—unless she started things. He couldn't imagine her screwing a tennis coach. He could barely imagine her screwing him—it happened so infrequently. She must have some real issues about sex she hadn't sorted out. Probably because she'd been putting her body on display practically since she could walk, thanks to an overzealous pageant mother.

Warmth from the bourbon spread through his body, reminding him it had been far too long since he'd been with Brooke. He liked sex, what was wrong with that? Brooke, for all her good qualities, seemed to like tennis and shopping more then she liked making love with Mathias.

Mathias knew he wasn't an unskilled or inconsiderate lover—quite the contrary, in fact—but they just didn't click in the bedroom. Mathias had been so frustrated he had considered going back to clubs to pick up guys. But he hadn't touched anyone else since she'd moved in with him. He hated the idea of cheating on Brooke, and promised himself he never would.

But it sure looked like she'd pulled one over on him. She was the only one having any sex now. Unless she was holding out until he bought her a three million dollar house.

He could just give in to her and do what she wanted, but he didn't want to start a precedent. It made him think back to how easy life had been with Chase. They'd wanted the same things, or didn't mind letting the other make a decision. They had shared so much more than Mathias suspected he and Brooke ever could. Then suddenly it all came crashing down, with no warning. It made Mathias wonder how long Brooke would be enough for *him*?

Brooke returned looking like she'd been powdered within an inch of her life. Maybe she'd been crying. Mathias couldn't tell. He did notice she didn't bring up the topic of tennis or Erica or that she'd been caught lying. Mathias opened his mouth to bring it up himself when Brad appeared at his side, holding aloft a platter with their first course.

"For the lady." Brad's hand faltered and a baby carrot rolled off the plate onto the pristine white table cloth. "Oh, pardon me." Brad smiled but Brooke glared at him so intently Mathias thought the waiter's hair would catch fire. "And for the gentleman. Today's special." Brad grinned and—did Mathias imagine a wink as well?—with a flourish he turned and strode away.

By mutual consent, while they ate, the conversation stayed on safe topics like their meal and whether Mathias wanted to go to the Symphony Benefit the following week. But he could tell something significant had shifted between them. Brooke avoided his gaze and whenever there was a lull in the conversation, she spoke to fill it, as if afraid he might bring up the lie.

As he ate, Mathias watched the waiter walk past as he served another table, and couldn't help noticing his very attractive ass, a deadly combination with the number of bourbons he'd inhaled on an empty stomach. The mood wasn't all that was shifting for Mathias tonight. What was at first a hazy idea quickly turned into a rock-hard plan. Brad had gone over to the waiters' station, and Mathias adjusted himself as he got out of the booth, grateful for the fact that he usually wore his trousers loose.

"I need to make a quick call, Brooke. I'm going to ask the waiter to hold our meal until I get back." She looked annoyed that he was leaving her sitting alone in the restaurant, but he ignored it. His attention was on Brad now.

Why should Brooke have all the fun? She hadn't even attempted to apologize for her lies, much less her behavior. Mathias headed over to the waiter's station.

CHASE RICHARDS also happened to be dining at the French Room that evening, and he'd been watching Mathias and Brooke. He particularly noticed how Brooke seemed annoyed at Mathias almost from the moment he'd sat down. It had been much more interesting than Chase's own dinner conversation with his companion. He'd be lucky if he even remembered her name the next day. She was one of a string of women he spent time with simply for appearances. Once in a while he even slept with them—also for appearances, because he never knew when they might talk with each other and he couldn't have any of them guess the truth.

Making small talk with Barbara—or was it Bonnie?—was hard work, and Chase was in a particularly lazy mood tonight. But when he noticed Mathias smiling as he spoke to the waiter, it more than piqued his interest. He decided to follow Mathias as he walked away from the waiters' station and didn't go back to his own table. Chase made some excuse to what's-her-name, then got up and, walking slowly, watched as Mathias went toward the telephones near the back of the restaurant, then just kept on going in the direction of the men's room and went inside, followed by the waiter at a very discreet interval.

Chase entered the men's room and walked to a urinal. *Well, what do you know*, he thought as he heard Mathias and the waiter together in a stall, the farthest one from the door.

Chase unzipped and moved closer so that it would look like he was actually pissing in case anyone came in. He had his cock in his hand, and as he heard the waiter's breath forced out of him with each of Mathias's thrusts, Chase found himself getting hard. He turned his head slightly in their direction and saw Mathias's huge hands high on the wall, pinning the waiter's wrists above his head. Chase kept listening, hearing Mathias's soft moans, remembering when *Chase* had been the one causing them, and now he was so hard he had to do something about it, so he quickly went into one of the other stalls. He could tell Mathias was close to coming by the way he sounded. Chase was still listening and remembering Mathias's body as he jerked himself off in the stall.

He heard the waiter grunting, coming—Mathias was so fucking *polite* he made sure the waiter came first, even against the wall of a bathroom stall. Mathias was still slamming himself into the man, until finally Chase heard that familiar intake of breath, followed by a soft groan as Mathias came, a sound Chase knew so well it tugged at his heart… and his cock, and he found himself coming, too, trying to stay silent as he spilled into his hand. As he cleaned himself up, he heard the men's room door open, presumably the waiter leaving, and then Mathias washing up at the sink, humming softly. Chase waited until Mathias had gone before he exited the stall, washed, and returned to his own table.

MATHIAS sat down in the booth with Brooke, and she gave him her usual slightly annoyed, pouty look at his return, then quickly recalculated and smiled, presumably to take his mind of the fact that he'd caught her in at least one lie already today.

"Hmmm, you smell so good," she said, sliding up unexpectedly and nestling against him. Apparently she decided the way to smooth her lies over was with her body. "Do you have a new cologne? I didn't notice it before."

Yeah, base notes of lust and sex, a hint of sweat, and a top note of waiter, he thought, but just shook his head in answer to her question. She snuggled closer and gave him a sexy look, a promise of something much more once they got home.

Given their argument, and her apparent intent to assure him she hadn't been sleeping with a tennis pro, he could easily avoid sleeping with her. He needed to think about what was going on in their relationship. She may have cheated with Ted Gates. He certainly had just enjoyed Brad's service. Maybe they were even now. God, how stupid it had been to vent his frustrations with Brooke by fucking a waiter.

They needed a long talk and he could put this behind them and think of the future, if she could. Not that he would mention the waiter. They had their incompatibilities, but he was prepared to make the effort to work through them, because she was kind and considerate and good company most of the time. Deep down Mathias loved her, and waves of guilt washed over him as she took his hand in hers and squeezed it, then planted a soft kiss on his knuckles.

Even though the dynamics of their relationship seemed to have changed, he desperately wanted Brooke in his life, and he'd figure out a way to make it work for both of them. He'd spoiled her by taking her wherever she wanted and buying expensive gifts. But he was certain they could come to some sort of compromise on everything else—where they lived, what kind of house, those things weren't going to make or break their relationship—but Brooke didn't even want to *discuss* their sex life. They'd have to now he had proof of her cheating. Either they'd work through the issues, or—he wasn't ready to call the wedding off just yet. He'd made a commitment and he'd try like hell to live up to it. He wasn't ready to give up on making things work with Brooke. The last thing he wanted was a sham marriage where they both found what they needed elsewhere.

He thought Brooke Collier was a woman he could make a future with. He hoped he hadn't been as wrong about her as he had been about Chase.

WHEN Chase got back to his table, his date was less than thrilled with the amount of time he'd been gone, but he only gave her half his attention as they finished their meal. He was watching Mathias and Brooke again. Brooke had seemed annoyed when Mathias first came back, but apparently he'd said something to placate her, and she'd cuddled up against him. Chase noticed how Mathias's face changed at that point. For some reason, he seemed more annoyed than pleased at the physical contact.

Very interesting, Chase thought, as he watched them interact for a few moments. They seemed to be on two different wavelengths while they ate their meal, speaking to each other but not really communicating. Even at a distance, it was easy to see how neither of them focused their full attention on the other. Which reminded Chase that he wasn't alone.

As soon as they'd finished their meal, Chase sent his own date home in a cab while he got into his limo. It had been more than a shock to discover that even though Mathias was getting *married*, he was fucking around with waiters in men's rooms. At the most expensive restaurant in Dallas to boot. That didn't sound like the Mathias he used to know. Well, the fucking in the restaurant sounded like Mathias—that had been a game between them, way back when— but the waiters, now that was something new. And it showed that while Mathias and Brooke *seemed* set for "happily ever after," there was something under the surface of their relationship that wasn't quite right, and now Chase was even more intrigued. He couldn't help the feeling of *schadenfreude* that crept on him that maybe Mathias hadn't found his fairytale ending after all.

But jerking off in the bathroom stall hadn't been enough for Chase, so he had his driver take him to a popular but discreet gay club where they parked the limo in the back.

Chase sent Sheppard, his driver, into the club, with instructions to find someone who met Mathias's description: tall, muscular, with dark, shoulder-length hair. It wasn't the first time Chase had asked for men of this description, and Sheppard knew the drill. He had a wad of cash, too, if that was what it took to get the right young man into his boss's limo.

After about fifteen minutes, the driver opened the rear door helped a tall young man wearing a blindfold into the back seat, and closed the door behind him. His appearance was close enough for Chase's tastes. But as Chase fucked him in the back of the limo, he discovered the young man didn't feel or sound enough like Mathias, and this was suddenly more important than ever. As soon as they were done, he opened the door and let the trick out of the car while he was still pulling on his clothing. After a few minutes, the driver got back behind the wheel.

"Sheppard, let's try another place." Chase raised the partition again and used a towel to tidy up the back seat.

"Yes, sir." He took Chase to another club where they repeated the entire process. This time Chase found the man more to his liking, and he kept the driver waiting outside the car for considerably longer than the first time. Afterward, Chase had his driver drop off the young man at home before driving back to Chase's house. He'd gotten the man's phone number, just in case, though he rarely took the risk of seeing someone again. He didn't want anyone to find out who he was, which is why he insisted on the blindfolds in the first place, and he didn't need the potential threat of blackmail. Chase hadn't come this far and given up so much for his success to risk losing it all for a good fuck. There were plenty of new tricks out there every time, and his driver was an expert at convincing attractive young men to take his offer.

CHAPTER SIX

OVER the next few days, Chase couldn't stop thinking about Mathias, couldn't get him out of his mind. He'd be in a meeting or on the phone and Mathias's face would pop unbidden into Chase's mind. For years he'd been looking for guys like Mathias at clubs, picking them up, fucking them, occasionally seeing one again, but all of that had just been about sex. About Chase wanting to fuck Mathias.

Now that he knew that Mathias wasn't completely satisfied with Brooke, it gave him ideas. *Definitely trouble in paradise.* Brooke wasn't enough for Mathias, that was more than obvious. Or she wasn't quite what he wanted....

Until he remembered the way Mathias had looked at Brooke. Whatever his rationale, Mathias really was in love with her, not just playing her for a beard. Mathias was attempting to have a straight relationship with Brooke. He'd looked at Brooke the same way he *used* to look at Chase.

Jealousy and loss bubbled up in Chase's stomach. No one had looked at him like that since Mathias. But was that love wasted on Brooke Collier? She'd probably reeled him in like a fish on a hook, but it seemed that now she had Mathias, she still wasn't happy. And Chase had seen her around the Dallas Athletic Club with other men, but only occasionally with Mathias. Was she up to something too?

There had to be a way to use this information—Chase's stock in trade.

Chase had never gotten over Mathias—never stopped loving him. But he had given up hope that Mathias would even speak with him after the way Chase had treated him—left him alone in Venice without even having the courage to explain why. But Chase had made

Mathias happy before, and maybe he could do it again. How could Brooke possibly know what Mathias needed or wanted?

Chase had spent three years with him, had known everything there was to know about him. He'd never seen Mathias as unhappy as he'd looked sitting at the best restaurant in Dallas with the most beautiful woman in the place, practically in the whole state. It was almost painful thinking about how disappointed Mathias had appeared that night from the moment he'd sat down next to Brooke.

What does Mathias want in his life?

After Chase found Mathias in the men's room with the waiter, it was clear he was still interested in something Brooke couldn't—or wouldn't—provide. He could stay with Brooke and see Chase on the side. Mathias might as well be fucking Chase instead of picking up waiters or tricks in clubs.

Or could Chase actually persuade Mathias to start up something more serious again? That was probably out of the question. Even if Mathias forgave him for the breakup, what kind of relationship could they have? Mathias hadn't liked having to hide their relationship in public before—at least in Dallas—but maybe if they managed to get back together, they wouldn't need to. Chase was willing to consider coming out—if it would win Mathias back. Did it really matter if people knew he was gay? He knew it probably *would* matter to the people he did business with, so it wasn't really in his best interest to come out. This was still Texas, and even if *Mathias*'s hometown had accepted him and Austin had a more tolerant attitude to gays, Dallas was a long way from accepting them, especially in the world of business. Alan Richards had been right on that count, at least.

Did Chase even need to impress anyone anymore? He was in charge and he could do what he liked with his business—buy or sell most of the others multiple times. But that wasn't who he really wanted to be anymore. Maybe he did need to play by Dallas rules for a while longer.

The one thing Chase was sure of—he had to see Mathias, couldn't go another day without it, wanted him back somehow. Chase wanted to prove to Mathias he wasn't the man he'd been nine years earlier when their relationship had ended. He couldn't understand why these feelings were back *now*. Feelings he hadn't had—or wanted to have—for years. It had *never* been about not wanting Mathias. It had been about Chase believing he wanted—needed, really—something else even more. Leaving Mathias hadn't been the only thing Chase had regretted in his life, but it was certainly the worst.

Chase felt a hope he hadn't had since he'd met Mathias. A feeling he could make a new start, right that wrong. Mathias brought up Chase's desire to be the man he'd been before he'd started working for his father's company, a different man than he was now—a vastly better man.

Chase couldn't just call Mathias up and invite him to lunch or a game of tennis. Even if he ran into Mathias at a public function, Mathias wouldn't give Chase the time of day, much less actually talk with him. They belonged to the same country club, the Dallas Athletic Club, but he knew Mathias rarely went there, except for tennis with Brooke or a charity event. Mathias wasn't the sort to hang out all afternoon playing golf and drinking at the bar afterward. No, Chase had to find another way to get to Mathias.

Then he came up with a germ of an idea. Mathias's two main interests seemed to be work and Brooke. Chase wasn't interested in Brooke—quite the opposite—so he'd have to reach Mathias through the T-Group. In nine years, Chase and Mathias hadn't crossed paths in business, so Chase was going to have to manufacture a believable excuse for suggesting a deal with Mathias now—a pitch he would actually consider. It would have to be a serious business proposal— the kind of business *Mathias* did. Chase was going to need some help.

He picked up the phone and dialed his CFO, Mike Killian.

"Mike, get me a workup on the Tobler Group."

"What have they got that you'd be even remotely interested in?" Mike asked, his tone skeptical, almost condescending.

"I'll know after I've seen the numbers," Chase said evasively. He honestly didn't know, but he didn't like that Mike had already figured out this was going to be something out of the ordinary for RichardsCorp. "Just do it. And I'd like it by tomorrow morning."

"What's the big rush, Chief? You don't even know what you're looking for!"

"Right now I'm about to start looking for a CFO who can follow one simple fucking instruction," Chase roared into the phone then smashed it back onto the cradle. He laughed when he thought of the look on Mike's face as he contemplated Chase's last remark. At least Chase knew he'd have the report on his desk when he got to work the next morning—even if Mike had to stay all night to work on it himself.

Two days later

THE intercom on Mathias Tobler's desk buzzed. "Yeah, Pam?"

"Chase Richards on line two for you," Pam's low, husky voice said cheerfully.

"What does he want?" Mathias kept his voice calm, but his heart was thudding in his chest. *Why is Chase calling?* Mathias hadn't heard from him since right after he'd gotten back from Venice, and they hadn't spoken face-to-face since.

He forced himself to calm down and breathe normally. How could Chase still have this effect on him after everything that had happened between them *nine years ago?* At this moment, he felt exactly like he had that day he stood in the middle of St. Mark's Square in Venice and listened to the worst news of his life.

"He didn't say," Pam replied.

"Tell him I'm in a meeting and find out why he's calling." Mathias wished he could take back the sharp tone he'd used.

"Sure thing, Boss," Pam said, in her usual bright tone, thankfully ignoring Mathias's mood.

A few minutes later, she came into Mathias's office and seated herself in one of the chairs facing his desk. She tucked a lock of hair behind an ear. Mathias battled the urge to ask about Chase. If Pam suspected how upset Chase got Mathias, she didn't say so, but he could tell she knew something unusual had happened.

"Chase Richards is interested in scheduling a meeting with you for a business proposal."

"What kind of business proposal?" He was confused. What business interests did he have in common with Chase Richards? Chase and his company were corporate raiders, and Mathias's company wasn't even a decent target for the kind of asset stripping Chase usually engaged in. The T-Group wasn't rolling in cash. Its balance sheets weren't in particularly good shape, and its earnings were modest. For once, Mathias was glad his company wasn't more successful.

"He didn't say. But he did suggest two possible times, and you were free for one of them, so I tentatively scheduled it for next Tuesday." Pam nodded, gazing a bit too intently at Mathias.

"What?" Mathias all but shouted. "You made an appointment for me? With *Chase Richards?*"

"That's my job, I'm the secretary." Pam's smile never wavered, but Mathias could tell his reaction had surprised her. "I always schedule appointments for you, and you show up for them. Division of labor and all that."

"B-but—" Mathias stuttered uncharacteristically. He turned toward one of the monitors on his desk pretending to read something there, hoping Pam hadn't noticed how the idea of meeting Chase had affected him. Too late. Pam knew him too well.

"But what? You've never turned down anyone who wanted to meet with you before. What's the deal with Chase Richards?"

What was *the deal with Chase Richards?* Mathias asked himself. He hadn't talked to Chase since that last phone call from Venice, and they hadn't spent any time together since the last night they'd spent making love before Chase had taken Mathias to the airport. Now Chase wanted to meet with him, and at the sheer thought of that, Mathias couldn't breathe because their past was coming back to him at blinding speed. He thought he was going to be sick.

"Mathias, are you okay?" Pam asked, a worried look on her face.

"Yeah, sorry, I just… I don't know," Mathias said slowly, trying to calm himself. Pam knew him too well to get anything past her, and he certainly didn't want to explain his past relationship with Chase. "Just put the appointment on my schedule. Thanks,'" he said absently, turning back toward his computer and effectively ending the conversation. He'd figure out an excuse later on to cancel or miss the appointment. No reason to bring any more attention to the situation right now.

As Pam walked out of his office, she glanced back at Mathias, and Mathias knew she was wondering why the thought of meeting with Chase Richards had scared the crap out of him. She might know they'd been at business school together as Chase's name appeared on alumni correspondence Pam handled. She could even figure out this appeared to be intensely personal, not just an old classmate trying to get in touch. He just hoped she wouldn't be too curious about the meeting. If she asked again, he'd just spin it that doing business with RichardsCorp was risky and had worried him—no need to bring anything personal into it. Mathias needed to get his emotions under control, and he hated the fact that Chase could still do this to him.

CHAPTER SEVEN

IT WAS late, and Mathias was exhausted. He'd had back-to-back meetings all afternoon after his conversation with Pam about Chase's appointment, and he'd spent the evening catching up on emails and skimming daily reports. Pam had ordered in dinner for him before he'd threatened to fire her if she didn't go home. That never worked anyway. Even when he fired her, she showed up the next morning as if nothing had happened. It had almost become a routine with them, he thought, laughing as she shared his dinner. Thankfully, the topic of Chase Richards hadn't come up again.

But Mathias was glad to finally be home. The condo was dark and silent when he walked in the front door. Brooke must already be asleep. It was apparently much later than he'd realized. He headed in the direction of the master bedroom and thought how nice it would be to snuggle into a warm bed against Brooke's comfortable curves. But to his surprise, he noticed Brooke's bedroom door was closed; she'd gone to bed alone and made it clear he wasn't welcome.

In the master bedroom—the one Brooke sometimes shared with him—he undressed, slipping out of his suit, carefully hanging it up in the closet. He stripped naked and pulled on a pair of thin cotton pajama bottoms before he washed up and settled into the soft bed under the thick, fluffy comforter. Brooke had bought new linens when she'd moved in, and Mathias enjoyed the luxurious feel of the sheets, though the king-size bed felt huge and empty without her.

He'd been so excited when she'd moved in, thinking how much fun it would be to spend more time together and start making a home—a life—together. Only since then, he hadn't been having much fun. He hadn't thought twice when she'd asked if she could have her own room. It seemed reasonable for her to have a space that was private, all her own. He hadn't counted on her wanting to sleep there half the time. He'd expected that once she moved in, they'd become even more intimate and adventurous, but neither the frequency nor the boundaries of their lovemaking changed.

There had been a short resurgence after the discovery at the French Room that she'd done something inappropriate with Ted Gates, but she'd cried and promised she'd be good and that he could trust her. They'd moved into a more comfortable intimacy, though still not as frequent or as thrilling as he'd like.

He sighed as he relaxed and let the tension of the day ease out of his body. A lot of things had changed since she'd moved in, some for the better. But he couldn't help the feeling of loneliness washing over him as he tried to fall asleep. He missed having someone there with him every night. Someone warm and welcoming and loving. And sometimes he just wanted someone to make love with before falling asleep in each other's arms.

As he tumbled into sleep, he thought about how long it had been since he'd felt really satisfied. Nine years? Had it really been that long since things had ended with Chase? Mathias couldn't help but remember how it had been with him, back when things had been good between them. More than good—fantastic. If only Brooke made Mathias as comfortable and content as those years with Chase....

Late May 2000
US Olympic Training Center
Colorado Springs

THEY had been dancing around each other physically for over a week, a slight brush here or a lingering touch when they were working out, as Mathias demonstrated moves and exercises for Chase in the weight room and helped him with the proper form when Chase repeated the moves. They'd had the weight room nearly to themselves since few other fencers trained much beyond the standard exercises and reps. But Mathias knew a lot of variations, especially with free weights, and Chase seemed eager to learn more new exercises.

At first Mathias hadn't thought anything about the way Chase's gaze lingered on his body at the gym—par for the course as Mathias demonstrated moves in the weight room. Then it hit him: Chase's interest went beyond working out. No one had ever looked at him quite that way before, and Mathias liked it—a lot.

Chase's attention flattered and attracted Mathias, and it didn't take long for him to realize his interest in Chase had gone beyond training and friendship. He found himself mirroring the look of near-hunger in Chase's eyes, enjoying lingering touches and the effect being near Chase had on his mind and his body. He craved Chase's company and found himself imagining them being together in so many ways—in private. Chase's jokes seemed funnier once he'd dropped that initial cocky, know-it-all act that made Mathias want to run. They soon became inseparable: daily training sessions, ate almost all of their meals together, and most nights they hung out in the common area long after everyone else had gone to bed.

One evening, Chase decided they needed to spend more time with the videos from the training sessions. He wanted Mathias's suggestions on some footwork he couldn't quite master and asked Mathias to come to his room to watch the videos. Chase's roommate was conspicuously absent, and Mathias suspected Chase's actual motive for asking him to come over had nothing to do with fencing. He wouldn't have gone if the feeling hadn't been mutual.

The more time they spent together, the easier it became for Mathias to decide he really *liked* Chase. Mathias had been attracted to men before, though he'd never actually done more than a little bit of fairly harmless fooling around once or twice. It seemed Chase Richards was destined to be the first for anything more serious.

They sat on the small couch in front of the television, their thighs nearly touching as they watched the DVD of épée practice. Chase paused the DVD for Mathias's opinion on his work with épée, Mathias's strongest weapon. Chase was more adept with the saber, and the two weapons had different strategies and moves.

Mathias was in the middle of making a suggestion, Chase's gaze on his face, taking in every word with rapt attention, when suddenly, Chase leaned in and kissed Mathias. A soft, slightly lingering kiss, but more than enough to get Chase's point across. Though it had taken

Mathias by surprise, he was aware of the light pressure of Chase's lush, full lips, the prickly feel of stubble, but mostly the way as soon as Chase broke contact Mathias wanted more and he wanted it immediately.

Mathias didn't even speak, just leaned in toward Chase, saying everything with his eyes, and when their mouths met again, Mathias's hand instinctively went toward Chase's head, pulling him in closer. Chase straddled Mathias's lap, one muscular thigh on each side of Mathias's, pressing against his legs, sending brand new signals up and down the length of his body. Their tongues met and tangled, exploring each other's mouths, gently at first, and then with increasing ardor. Mathias fought the urge to crush Chase against him. He'd never wanted to be this close to anyone before. Chase's arms held tight, the muscles gliding beneath the skin and only thin cotton separating their bodies.

They kissed for a long time, their hands seeking more contact, stroking each other's chests or shoulders, feeling the hard muscles beneath the thin fabric of their shirts. Chase broke the kiss briefly as he worked open the top button on Mathias's shirt. He glanced at Mathias to make sure it was okay—it was more than okay with Mathias—before his mouth fastened onto Mathias's once more, and he fumbled at the rest of the buttons.

Chase was wearing a pullover, and Mathias reluctantly pulled away so he could tug Chase's shirt off over his head, toss it away, and run his fingers, trembling with the excitement of discovery, along Chase's collarbones and shoulders, down his back, along arms corded with tight muscle. Chase moaned, the sound thrumming through his body, when Mathias's lips blazed a trail following the movement of his fingers, and he ground his hips against Mathias's.

Chase's weight in his lap felt so fucking good, and even better was the way Chase moved against him, tracing the outline of Mathias's muscles with strong, needy fingers, and licking hot, wet stripes along Mathias's chest and neck. Mathias's nipples ached and his cock got so hard it hurt. He couldn't wait to get his jeans off. Well, he wanted to get Chase's jeans off too. He wasn't exactly sure what he'd do after that, but he'd figure it out. Every single touch from Chase sent waves of pleasure through Mathias's entire body. He let his hands fall to Chase's hips, still moving against him, and he loved the way Chase's cock pressed against him through the denim.

Chase kissed and licked his way down Mathias's chest, stopping halfway to glance up at Mathias. He looked down into those caramel-colored eyes and thought he'd drown in their sweet, sticky depths. They pulled him in, sinking deep, unable to breathe or think or care about anything more than the pleasure those eyes seemed to promise.

When Chase's mouth closed on a nipple, sucking and nipping, Mathias lost any remaining shred of control he'd held on to. The way Chase writhed in his lap, the taste of him, the salty tang of his skin, the intoxicating scent of him—it was all too much. Shuddering and grunting, Mathias came, the pleasure almost eclipsed by his embarrassment at being unable to control himself and coming in his pants like some horny teenager.

He let his hands drop and his head fell back against the top of the couch.

"Oh, God. Oh, fuck, I'm so sorry…," he managed to mumble, turning his face away so as to avoid Chase's gaze. Mathias thought he might even be blushing with shame.

"Me, too," Chase whispered into Mathias's neck, then placed a series of kisses along his throat. "It's okay. I nearly did, too. Probably would have if we hadn't stopped just now," Chase added, making Mathias feel somewhat better.

"Really?"

"Really. Don't you know how hot you make me?"

If Mathias had any doubts, the need in Chase's wide-blown pupils and the low, gravelly purr in his voice dispelled them immediately.

"Let's find out." Mathias surprised himself with such boldness and began to unbuckle Chase's belt as Chase laughed.

Chase had on button-fly jeans, and Mathias popped the buttons open one at a time, slowly revealing Chase's cock, clearly outlined against the thin cotton of his shorts. Mathias ran his fingers along the rock-hard length of it and felt it twitch at his touch. He'd fooled around with another guy at a party once, but he'd been drunk. This time, Mathias was completely sober, and he wanted to be aware of each and every detail of the experience—every little thing about Chase Richards.

Chase's hands gripped Mathias's shoulders, and he watched as Mathias pulled Chase's boxer-briefs away. He stared at Chase's hard-on, the sight of it almost like a mirage—was he really doing this?—and took his cock into one hand, caressing it carefully, afraid to do the wrong thing. Chase moaned as Mathias touched him and Mathias grew more confident, applying more pressure and stroking up and down, twisting his wrist at the head, which was now slick and dripping precome. It took less than a minute before Chase came, covering Mathias's hand and his own chest with thick, creamy jets.

Sighing, Chase leaned down to kiss Mathias, then he grabbed his discarded shirt and cleaned away his come before sinking back against Mathias and kissing him long and hard.

"Do you want me to leave now?" Mathias asked tentatively, when the kiss ended.

"Of course not," Chase replied, clearly surprised by Mathias's question. "This isn't just supposed to be about getting off once. At least not for me."

"I didn't really know what you wanted." Mathias didn't know where to look. He was afraid what he might see in Chase's eyes.

"How about what *you* want?" Chase lifted Mathias's chin with a gentle touch.

"I like you, and I like spending time with you...."

"Is there a 'but' at the end of that sentence?" Chase gazed into Mathias's eyes.

"No." Mathias couldn't manage more than that, the way those eyes glittered and distracted him.

"In that case, I'd like it if you'd come to bed with me." Chase stood up and pulled his underwear up slightly. He didn't bother to do anything about his jeans, which hung precariously around his hips. He held out his hand to Mathias.

Present day
Dallas

STILL alone and half-asleep, in bed in his condo, Mathias remembered that very first time and how fantastic he'd felt—how *Chase* had made him feel. Mathias couldn't have asked for a more wonderful and special experience, and he was still glad it had been Chase. Even if they hadn't stayed lovers after that summer—though they'd become far more than that—Mathias would always remember and cherish those memories. No one had ever wanted him as much as Chase had—before or since, he realized with regret and disappointment— and it had made him feel amazing.

Even now, years later, Mathias's body responded to the same thoughts and emotions he'd had that night in Colorado. His rock-hard cock throbbed, aching with need and frustration. *Damn Brooke and her convenient prudery!* He wouldn't dream of forcing her into anything, but she never seemed to be completely willing and giving. Mathias had picked up guys in bars who had been more into him than Brooke seemed to be half the time. Could she ever be enough for him sexually? Mathias wondered. He'd been perfectly satisfied with women in the past, and he thought he'd satisfied her, but he realized he needed more than what she offered. Why did he find more satisfaction with strangers he picked up in a club than with his own fiancée?

And then there was Chase. As a lover, he was in a class by himself. Always giving, though he took as much as he wanted, and Mathias had been glad to give him everything and anything. They'd complemented each other, finding nearly every experience together exactly what'd they'd wanted—or needed—at the moment.

Chase had opened vast new sexual horizons for Mathias, but never once pushed him past his comfort zone. Chase made Mathias eager to try new things, with a level of trust between them that only enhanced their sex life. They had a balance that worked for them, and Mathias hoped he'd develop one with Brooke, too. But for now, they were as out of balance as they could possibly be.

Without his even realizing it, Mathias's hand moved to his cock, stroking and pulling and twisting, as he remembered curves and angles and valleys—not Brooke's, but Chase's. And when he came, shooting thick strands across his bare chest, he groaned out Chase's name. He fell asleep, temporarily sated and content with his memories.

Mathias didn't know how long he'd been asleep when a slight movement of the bed awakened him. Brooke had crawled in next to him.

"Mmmm, you're home, Matt." She leaned down and kissed him with uncharacteristic hunger. "I didn't even hear you come in, but then I woke up, and thought I heard your voice."

"I'm sorry, I lost track of time at work, and I know should have called…." His head was still fuzzy. He must have been deep asleep.

"No matter, you're here now, right?" She untied the front of her nightgown. Mathias could see her breasts in the pale moonlight. They were beautiful, full and heavy, nipples hard and peaked with arousal. He couldn't remember the last time she'd come to him like this. He grabbed her hips, settling her into his lap. She was wet and soaked through the thin cotton of his pajama bottoms, getting him instantly hard. He pulled her tightly against him, kissing her neck and throat.

"Mathias! You're… all… sticky!" She shoved Mathias away and pulled her nightgown back up over her body. "You've been jerking off again! You know how I feel about that!"

Fuck. Mathias let his head fall back against the pillow. He must have fallen asleep before he'd had a chance to clean up.

"When I got home you were already asleep…," he began, as if his frustration might actually get through to her.

"So, why can't you wait for me? You're just like some kind of… sex-crazed animal." Brooke got out of bed and strode toward the door before turning toward him. "Can't you ever get enough?" She stormed out of the room, and Mathias cursed out loud this time.

He went into the bathroom and cleaned up before getting back into bed. He slid under the comforter, feeling the chill of cold sheets go through his entire body. Rolling onto one side, Mathias closed his eyes and tried to sleep, but more memories and images of Chase filled his brain. Such a stark contrast to Brooke, Chase had always offered himself willingly and never made Mathias feel wrong for wanting him, or wanting anything of him—at any time. Chase would do or try anything, and Mathias had always felt the same. Tonight, though, Mathias would have to be satisfied with memories.

Alone in his bed in the Dallas condo, Mathias finally fell back asleep, wondering again whether his lack of connection with Brooke was simply physical or whether there was a much larger emotional disconnect. Maybe sex would interest her more if they had more of an emotional connection? Or had Mathias closed himself off from her, avoiding the intimacy that he thought he craved so much. Was it Brooke, or was it really Mathias who was the problem? Did he even know what the fuck he really wanted?

Yes, he told himself. He knew exactly what—or who—he wanted, and that was an impossibility. The man he'd loved was gone now. It wasn't just that Chase had moved on without Mathias, but that Mathias didn't believe that the kind, loving, open Chase he'd loved even existed anymore. His Chase would never have brushed him off so easily over the phone from thousands of miles away.

Mathias fell asleep wishing there were some way to find the old Chase again, and let him know how much he still cared, but Mathias knew that was something that would never happen.

Late May 2000
US Olympic Training Center
Colorado Springs

"… I'D LIKE it if you'd come to bed with me." Chase held out a hand to Mathias.

Almost shyly, Mathias took Chase's hand and stood up, letting Chase lead him into the bedroom. Chase sat at the edge of the bed and pulled Mathias to him by his belt. Slowly, he unbuckled the belt, then unzipped Mathias's jeans, which he let fall to pool around Mathias's ankles. Mathias carefully stepped out of them. Now he stood in front of Chase, the damp spot on his boxers embarrassingly obvious. Chase looked up at Mathias, smiled reassuringly, then pulled Mathias close to him, licking and sucking at his navel. It tickled and Mathias laughed, enjoying the way Chase's stubble scraped against the sensitive skin. He liked everything about the way Chase touched and aroused him and made him feel special.

Slipping Mathias's boxers down off his hips, Chase licked his way down to Mathias's cock, which was still damp and sticky, and gently began to lap at the come that clung to his skin. Chase's tongue on Mathias's cock—warm and gentle at first, then increasingly rough and hungry—soon got Mathias aroused again. Chase used his hands and mouth on Mathias, who was moaning almost continuously, until Mathias was nearly rock hard. In one quick motion, Chase slipped out of his jeans and shorts and lay back completely naked in the bed, waiting for Mathias to join him.

That was all the invitation Mathias needed, and in no time he was lying next to Chase, pulling him into his arms, and they began kissing as eagerly as they had on the couch, hands exploring each other's bodies, skin against skin, sharing each other's heat and passion. Every time their cocks brushed together, delicious electric shocks zoomed through Mathias's entire body.

"Mathias," Chase whispered. "Really want you… inside me."

"I, uh, never did this before… I mean not with a guy." Mathias's heart pounded at the thrill of Chase's invitation. As soon as he said it, he felt like an idiot.

"That's okay." Chase looked into Mathias's eyes and smiled reassuringly. They were lying side-by-side on the bed, and Chase's fingers traced their way along Mathias's shoulder. "We don't have to do any more unless you want to." He clearly didn't want to pressure Mathias into sleeping with him. That made Mathias want it even more.

"Oh, God, yeah, Chase. I want this. Want you." Mathias's words tumbled from his mouth, but he meant it. It was dim in the room, the only illumination now from the long-forgotten television screen. Mathias looked down at Chase's naked body—*God, he really is beautiful*—and realized he'd never wanted to be with anyone as much as this. And the way Chase looked at him and touched him, and spoke to him, Mathias had never felt as *desired,* despite his nervousness. Every single caress and stroke made him feel like they were the only two people in the world.

Chase gently took Mathias's hand—slightly shaky—and slicked the fingers with lube from a bottle he pulled from the nightstand. He grabbed a condom from the drawer and set it on the table.

"Can I?" Chase asked and Mathias nodded, not exactly sure what Chase was planning.

Chase lay back, spreading his legs wide, and took Mathias's hand, placing the index finger at his own entrance. Mathias watched, eyes wide, but thrilled by the sight of Chase laid open and waiting. Chase pushed the tip of Mathias's finger inside slowly. Tight and hot and—all Chase. Mathias's eyes went even wider. He pushed the finger in further, feeling the flutter of muscle clutching at him. His pulse raced again and his cock throbbed and leaked precome. Mathias wasn't sure how he'd handle any more excitement and he hadn't put more than a finger into Chase.

Chase showed him how to get him ready, letting him know when to add another finger. He explained how to feel for his prostate, and Mathias loved the way Chase's body shuddered as he probed at it with a finger. It didn't take Mathias long to figure out just what Chase liked.

"Are *you* ready?" Chase asked with a low moan when Mathias had three fingers inside up to the knuckles. "Because I definitely am."

"Yes," Mathias breathed. He was hard, and pushing his fingers into Chase had been so fucking fantastic that now his cock ached and throbbed, begging for attention.

"Put on the condom—or I can do it for you…."

Mathias slowly removed his fingers from Chase and reached for the condom, slick fingers fumbling with the foil. Finally he got it open, clumsily rolled it down over the length of his cock, then waited for the next instruction.

"Then insert tab A into slot B," Chase said, joining in with Mathias's chuckle. Mathias willed himself to relax.

Mathias took a deep breath, feeling the ache deep in his balls and a tingle through every other part of him, pressed the tip of his cock against Chase and very slowly began to slip inside, a whole new amazing feeling that he couldn't even describe. He'd only gotten the head of his cock in and Chase let out the most incredible sound Mathias had ever heard in his life: it wasn't a moan or a grunt or a groan, but some combination of all of them, and that *Chase* had made that sound because *Mathias* was inside him was even more thrilling. He felt like making some noise himself at the way Chase's body clenched hot and tight around his cock, but even more than that, Mathias wanted to hear Chase make more noises—wanted to pull those delicious sounds from Chase. He kept pushing in, surprised this wasn't hurting Chase, but knowing from the look on Chase's face and the sounds he continued to make that this was anything but painful. For Mathias, it was the most indescribably incredible sensation he'd ever experienced.

"Oh fuck, that's… sooo good," Chase half spoke, half moaned when Mathias was almost completely inside. "You can start moving."

Mathias did and thought he was going to come again on the spot. Thank God he'd already come once; hopefully he'd last longer this time, but he wasn't sure. Chase felt better than any woman Mathias had ever been with, and Mathias loved the way Chase made lots of noise so Mathias could tell what he liked. Chase's legs were wrapped around Mathias's waist, pulling him in deeper on every thrust, and soon Chase was writhing beneath Mathias, eyes closed and those beautiful lips parted only slightly as he groaned and purred.

Mathias tried different angles and depths, wanting to see what pleased Chase as well as himself, until he figured out how to make his cock rub against Chase's prostate.

Concentrating on what Chase liked helped Mathias stay in control. If he thought too much about how good Chase felt, the intense sensations from hands traveling along his chest and arms, how Chase pulled Mathias's head down into a passionate, breathless kiss, Mathias knew he'd come apart and it would all be over in a second. Every little thing Chase did or said brought Mathias closer to the edge, and he could barely think of anything else but Chase—the way he looked and sounded; the way he smelled and tasted. Mathias fought to keep his eyes open so he could watch Chase's face, thrilled at the pleasure he saw reflected here.

Chase clutched at Mathias, digging his strong fingers into Mathias's shoulders and arms, then suddenly gasped and grunted and to Mathias's complete surprise, Chase came in thick creamy spurts across his own chest and as high as his neck.

"Fuck, Mathias! What are you trying to do to me?" Chase asked, breathless.

"I'm sorry, I—"

"Don't apologize, for fuck's sake!" Chase laughed when he saw Mathias's stricken expression. "That was the most… amazing thing… I've ever felt!" Chase sputtered as he fought to catch his breath.

"Really?" Mathias let out a sigh of relief.

"Yeah, and you better promise to do that to me again… a lot!"

Mathias laughed and bent to kiss Chase, and he was already so close to the edge that the slight movement was enough to start Mathias's own orgasm. It surprised Mathias as much as the first time he'd come that evening, on the couch, but this time he didn't try to fight it, let it wash over his entire body.

Chase held onto him tightly as he came with eyes squeezed shut, a sharp intake of breath, and a long, soft moan. Mathias didn't remember anything else except the way his body experienced every little jolt of ecstasy, but everything blended together into one enormous explosion that left him breathless and shuddering and unable to think about anything but the pleasure and that he was with Chase. When it was over, he lay down on Chase and rolled them both over, so Chase lay on top, tightly wrapped in Mathias's arms.

"Well?" Chase asked eagerly when Mathias finally opened his eyes again. Chase watched him intensely, almost anxiously, with a huge grin. It was nearly too dark to see, but Mathias knew his eyes glittered the way they always did when Chase was thrilled or excited about something.

"Well what?" Mathias asked, unable to say much more than that. His mind and body were still blissfully incapacitated.

"Do you promise to do that to me again?" Chase asked.

"God, yeah," Mathias said huskily, then craned his head up to kiss Chase deeply. "But, only if you ask nicely," he added with a grin.

"Oh, I can be *very* nice when I want something," Chase said playfully. "And I want *you*, Mathias," he added in a more serious tone. Then he wrapped his arms around Mathias and kissed him again, in case Mathias might not yet be convinced. He was, but he certainly enjoyed the way Chase tried to make sure he got the message.

They snuggled together a while longer, falling into an easy intimacy, still trading kisses and gentle caresses. Eventually, Chase got up and padded into the bathroom, while Mathias disposed of the condom in the trash.

Chase climbed back into bed with a damp cloth. As Mathias let Chase gently wash him up, he didn't have a single doubt about what he'd just done. It wasn't just doing *something* he'd been thinking about—having sex with a guy. Instead, Mathias realized that with *Chase*, he'd found a person who made him feel so special and wanted—and worked so hard to let him know that—and it had nothing to do with being male or female. It was only about *Chase*.

They lay in each other's arms, not speaking for a very long time, just enjoying the sound of unfamiliar heartbeats and slow, deep, contented breathing.

CHAPTER EIGHT

Present day
Dallas
The following Tuesday

MATHIAS drove himself to the restaurant Chase had chosen for their appointment. Since the day Pam had told Mathias that Chase wanted to meet with him, Mathias hadn't been able to stop thinking and remembering details of their relationship. But he had to pull himself together now. He couldn't go into this meeting and let any of their past personal relationship influence him.

As much as he'd wanted to simply cancel this appointment, Mathias knew he had to go. Whether Chase's real reason for wanting to see him was business or personal, he had to face Chase and put his own feelings about the past behind them. It was the only way to keep Chase from having any further hold over his emotions. Mathias hoped this would leave him completely free of the past and able to concentrate on his future with Brooke.

Mathias just needed to keep everything professional and stick to business, no matter what Chase wanted to discuss with him. Chase had changed, and the man he had become was someone that Mathias wanted nothing at all to do with. The only way that Mathias could separate this Chase from the Chase he had known—and loved—was to remember how many companies and people Chase Richards had destroyed since he'd taken over RichardsCorp from his father. Mathias expected only the worst from this meeting, and as he walked into the restaurant, he braced himself for more than a little unpleasantness.

"WHAT are we doing here?" Mathias asked, sounding suspicious as he sat down at the table where Chase was already waiting for him.

God, Chase thought, Mathias looked great, better than ever, it seemed. He was wearing a beautifully tailored suit that fit him nicely—Italian, probably Brooke's influence. Mathias never went in for anything so expensive. Chase realized he didn't know what Mathias went in for lately. But he looked healthy, if a little pale. Mathias's raven hair was long, as usual, but it was cut well and looked good if not entirely professional, and Chase wanted to reach out and run his fingers through its soft length. He realized just how much he'd missed Mathias—missed everything about him—as Mathias seated himself across the table, and Chase wondered how he'd let so much time pass before he'd made any attempt to see Mathias.

It was a week after the night Chase had seen—heard, actually—Mathias fucking the waiter in the men's room at the French Room. Chase had considered choosing that same restaurant for their meeting, for a little private joke, but in the end, decided on one that was popular for business deals. That would make his offer seem more genuine, just business, and less personal, though his *true* intentions were entirely personal.

"Having lunch, or have you given up eating because you're too busy?" Chase asked amiably. "You do look a bit thin; you could probably use a good meal."

"I eat just fine, and I don't need your solicitude, thanks," Mathias said in a hostile tone. "Why are you suddenly so concerned about my health? I thought you had some sort of business proposal for me, though I don't know why I'd even consider doing business with you in the first place."

"Ouch," Chase said. "Didn't your daddy tell you to wait and listen before you jump to a conclusion, or something along those lines?" he asked, aiming for a light tone.

"Let's leave my father out of this," Mathias said, appearing to lose patience. "There's nothing personal—just business courtesy that I'm here at all. And I *am* giving you a chance… to get to the point."

Chase found Mathias's angry tone oddly satisfying. Mathias wouldn't be so upset unless he still had some feelings for Chase. If Mathias had really moved on, he'd be calm and neutral. *No, angry Mathias is good*, Chase decided.

A waiter came over to their table, offering menus, but Mathias waved his away without even glancing at the man. "I'm not having anything, thanks," he told the waiter, though his gaze remained on Chase.

Apparently Mathias had had his fill of waiters, Chase mused.

Chase ordered; then after the waiter had left, he pushed a piece of paper over to Mathias.

"I'm interested in buying a block of your companies. I had my finance team put together a valuation and offer," Chase said.

Mathias picked up the paper. Chase watched him scan the page and the slight reaction as he saw the final figure. Mathias was never any good at hiding what he was thinking, and Chase knew that openness would always be an obstacle for Mathias in business—just as it had been in his personal life before.

The offer was more than fair, Chase knew, and from a strictly business perspective, Mathias should be more than satisfied with the amount. It was a bit more than the block of companies was actually worth on paper.

"I'm not sure I even understand why you want these businesses," Mathias began, brow wrinkled in obvious confusion. "What do you want with three companies that produce machinery and supplies for the oil industry?"

"These companies don't really fit in with your core business, if you consider that retail and food would be your core business. Selling them off makes more sense than keeping them. I'm making you an offer that's more than fair."

"Right now with the price of oil where it is, those companies are doing very well. But I still can't see you making much of a profit after you strip them and sell off what little assets they have."

"That's true." Chase nodded. Mathias knew too much about his own companies and way too much about the way Chase did business. Had Mathias been keeping tabs on him, or was it so widely known how RichardsCorp operated? "The thing is, I'm not actually planning to sell them."

"What?" Mathias asked, his tone and expression skeptical.

"I thought I'd keep the group, and try running them, especially as now is a good time for the oil supply industry. Something new." Chase shrugged and let out a slightly self-conscious laugh.

"Something new?" Mathias echoed. "Instead of ruining companies on paper you want to try and do it for real now? Or are you just bored and think playing with people's livelihood might be fun for a change?"

"Touché." Chase said using a more-than-appropriate fencing metaphor as he mocked a pained expression, falling back on his usual over-confident persona in the face of Mathias's open hostility. "The truth is that I really do want to do things differently from now on. Maybe you can't believe this, but I really admire the way you—your family—does business, and I'd like to learn something from you." Chase hoped he sounded as sincere as he felt, but knew it would be a hard sell. It was difficult for him to be this open and honest with anyone, but Mathias had always made Chase feel safe. Only now everything between them had changed. "Look, I'm tired of doing business on paper, as you put it, and I want to try and take something and make it grow."

"Buy a plant," Mathias suggested in a sarcastic tone.

Chase could see Mathias wouldn't immediately believe he really wanted to change, but he'd at least thought he'd discuss the offer rather than dismiss it—and Chase's intentions—outright.

"I should have realized you wouldn't take me or my offer seriously. What can I do to convince you? How about add another 10 percent to the offer?"

"You can't fix everything with money, Chay…, Chase," Mathias added, clearly not wanting to fall back into their former familiar patterns by using the old nickname. "Didn't you learn your lesson nine years ago? Have you and your million dollars been happy together since then?"

How did Mathias find out about that million-dollar bonus check from my father? Chase wondered. That was weeks after they'd broken up, and they hadn't spoken to each other since that last conversation in Venice. Even though Chase had tried to contact him, Mathias had refused to return his calls.

"That was a huge mistake, a complete miscalculation and I'm sorry. My father—" Chase started.

"Your *father*? That's your excuse?" Mathias practically shouted; the contempt in his voice was more than obvious. "You can't blame your own actions on someone else!"

"No, not an excuse. Do you really want to hear what I have to say about that?" Chase's heart was racing. Would Mathias actually listen to him? Would it make any difference? Chase would gladly explain everything—even now—and maybe Mathias might actually understand *why* Chase had done what he'd done.

"No. That's ancient history. I've moved on." Mathias's tone of finality made Chase's heart sink. "Are you serious about this proposal, or is this just some ruse to get me to meet you?" Now Mathias sounded suspicious.

"I want to buy them," Chase said, though Mathias was right on the other point too. "Are you interested in selling… to me?"

"Not yet. Let me think about it for a while. When you said you want to change, you almost sounded like the Chase I used to… know, for about two seconds."

Had he been about to say "love"? Chase wondered.

"If you can find some way to show me you have changed, at least how you do business, then we can talk about it again. Right now, I have another appointment." Mathias stood abruptly, and walked away.

Chase watched him leave and kicked himself for the way he'd handled their meeting. He'd wanted Mathias to let his guard down, take him seriously, but Chase had miscalculated again. He'd assumed Mathias would behave a certain way, and been dead wrong. What he should have done was to prepare a formal proposal for running those companies, put a little work into it, to prove to Mathias he was serious. A piece of paper with a dollar amount at the bottom was the easy way, and Mathias knew that.

Chase had attempted to approach him as the *old* Chase would, not the hard-nosed businessman Mathias had undoubtedly expected to meet today. Mathias had always encouraged Chase to be himself, though when he'd tried today, Mathias had shot Chase down without a second thought. That wasn't how he used to work, but he'd come to their meeting suspicious and angry. Chase hadn't expected his proposal to be accepted, but he also hadn't anticipated meeting a completely new Mathias. It reminded Chase of a conversation and a promise—now broken—from a long time ago.

Late May 2000

US Olympic Training Center

Colorado Springs

CHASE and Mathias were lying together in bed, limbs tangled, after the first time they'd made love.

"Chase, can you tell me one thing?" Mathias's voice was low and gravelly. God, how Chase loved how he sounded right now, how he felt, how he made *Chase* feel, his voice vibrating through Chase's entire body and soul.

"What?" Chase he was almost afraid to hear what Mathias would say. Did he regret what they'd just done? Would he leave now and decide he'd rather sleep with women after all?

"Why did you act like such a jerk at first, when we first talked, that night at the welcome party? I didn't even want to talk to you for more than five minutes."

The question surprised Chase. And frightened him. He'd taken so many chances to get here with Mathias. What was one more? "Because I'm actually… shy," Chase practically whispered.

"Shy? You? I don't believe that!"

"I am, really. When something's important to me I get nervous, and shy. But if I pretend I'm someone else, someone who's not shy— someone much more confident—it's… easier for me."

Mathias rolled onto his side, facing Chase, looking into his eyes. He could probably tell from Chase's tone that this revelation was something important, and he gave Chase his full attention.

"I used to be worse." Chase paused, then continued when he realized Mathias wanted to hear this. "When I was much younger, I wouldn't talk to strangers or even my teachers. I hated school. My mom got this ingenious idea to sign me up for acting classes when I was about ten. I loved it. When I became someone else, I didn't have any trouble talking. I started trying that outside of the classes, and it helped me with my confidence. I got kind of used to doing that, and sometimes it backfires, like it almost did with you." Chase glanced away again. He wasn't ready to admit to Mathias that the person who Chase felt the least confident around was the one person he wanted to impress more than any other—his own father. Alan Richards had such high expectations of Chase that the only way Chase could even begin to feel confident enough to live up to them was to *pretend to be* confident and successful, just like Alan.

"Well, I'd like to just get to know the real Chase Richards, whoever he is in there. Not the cocky guy who thinks the world revolves around him, okay?" Mathias's voice was soft and sincere. "Because when you're being yourself, you're totally worth spending time with."

"You really think so?" Chase asked, needing the reassurance, and hating himself for it.

Mathias looked at Chase with some confusion, and Chase realized he shouldn't have any doubt about Mathias's interest in him. They'd just made love—and it had been Mathias's first time with a guy. That alone should have convinced Chase, but he still couldn't quite believe Mathias wanted to spend more time with Chase.

"Of course I mean it, Chase."

"Yeah, I can do that… and be myself, for you," he promised. It was a little bit frightening, but Chase knew Mathias Tobler would be worth it.

Early July 2000
Olympic Training Center
Colorado Springs

"TEE, tell me a secret," Chase said. They were in bed, Chase tangling his fingers in Mathias's black hair, soft as silk between his fingers.

"A secret? What kind of secret? Like something bad I did, or something embarrassing?"

"Anything. Just something you've never told anyone before. It could be good or bad."

"Why?"

"I have a secret to tell you, but I'm feeling kind of shy about sharing it," Chase told Mathias.

"Oh, so you want me to go first?" Mathias asked, his tone teasing.

"Yeah…," Chase replied, with a hint of embarrassment.

"Well…" Mathias started, thinking. He pulled Chase close so he could whisper. "I want to feel you inside of me, Chase. I want you to make love to *me*."

Chase gazed into Mathias's eyes, taken aback by what Mathias had said.

"Really?"

"Yeah, really," Mathias confirmed. "Soon, maybe after they announce the team and all the pressure's off here."

"We're probably both too exhausted to make it special now anyway."

"It'll be special. I'm sure of that, Chase."

Chase leaned over and began kissing Mathias. After a few minutes, Mathias broke the kiss, but they were both slightly out of breath.

"Hey, now it's your turn. Don't you have something you wanted to say?" Mathias reminded Chase.

"Yeah, but…." Chase looked down, he felt his cheeks heating up.

Mathias tried to give him a supportive look, but Chase could see he was really curious now.

"Tee…," Chase started, then hesitated. A look of resignation came over his face. "Mathias, I love you."

"Really?" Mathias asked, clearly pleased. "Because whatever happens with the team, I know I'm not ready to say good-bye to you when this is all over."

"No good-byes," Chase confirmed and they began kissing again. They really were both too tired to do much more than that lately.

For a while, they lay together, arms and legs tangled, and Chase heard Mathias's breathing change to a slow, deep rhythm and knew he'd fallen asleep. But Chase wasn't offended; in fact he was glad that Mathias had responded the way he had to Chase's revelation. Chase didn't want Mathias to feel obligated to return the sentiment, but it was clear Mathias had strong feelings for him too. And for now, that was good enough for Chase. Head on Mathias's chest, he listened to his breathing, feeling the now-familiar slow rise and fall, knowing there was nowhere else in the whole world he'd rather be.

CHAPTER NINE

Mid-July 2000
US Olympic Training Center
Colorado Springs

IT WAS Saturday morning, and the final Olympic roster was supposed to be posted outside the locker rooms by 8:00 a.m. Neither Chase nor Mathias were in any hurry to get up and rush down to find out whether they'd been chosen for the team. That wasn't strictly true, as they had woken up early and fully intended to take a quick shower then head downstairs, except somehow they ended up distracting each other in the shower, trading blow jobs in the cramped space, but thankful for the luxury of their own bathroom.

They'd actually been exceedingly lucky in that regard. About a week after the first night they'd spent together, Chase's roommate had gotten tired of either being asked to "disappear" for a while, or walking in on something he'd rather not see again, and the guy had decided to avoid a repeat by trading rooms with Mathias, leaving Chase and Mathias as roommates. There weren't any rules at the training camp about a situation like theirs, and no one made any move to prevent it, so Chase and Mathias simply enjoyed the opportunity. They weren't the only couple to hook up so far during the training: two straight couples had gotten together, though in one case it hadn't even lasted a week, and a couple of girls had followed Mathias's example and effected a similar roommate switch.

The end result was that Chase and Mathias had a room to themselves with its own bathroom and all the privacy they could want.

"What if one of us makes the team and the other one doesn't?" Chase asked as they embraced under now-lukewarm water.

"If you make it, you can bet I'm going to Sydney to watch you compete!" Mathias enthused.

"But what about the rest of the summer?"

"I can get an apartment in town and stay right here while you're training. Or would I be too much of a distraction for you?" Mathias asked with a devious grin.

"Yes, you would be a terrible distraction, but I wouldn't want it any other way," Chase told him. "And if you make it, I'll stick around."

"Even though you missed most of spring semester? Don't you need to do summer school to catch up?"

"Fuck summer school," Chase said, laughing against Mathias's neck. He pulled Mathias's head down into a kiss that was very convincing.

"Well, let's just wait and see what happens. Maybe we'll both be going to Sydney in September."

Everyone else had already learned their fate and headed in to breakfast by the time Mathias and Chase, both with hair still wet, made their way toward the locker rooms. A few people shouted mild congratulatory remarks at them, causing them to quicken their pace. Had they both made the team? That would be amazing luck, and an experience of a lifetime.

"I can't tell if she was upset that she didn't make it or what," Chase remarked as they received another halfhearted thumbs up.

"Well, here we are. The moment of truth," Mathias said as they neared the bulletin board. "You go look."

"No, we look together," Chase said, tugging at Mathias's elbow.

They walked up to the bulletin board, their fingers loosely interlaced, and skimmed the names of the men's teams. Neither of their names was on the list. Instead, they were on the list of alternates, Chase on the Men's Saber team and Mathias on Men's Épée.

"Fuck," Chase said, and Mathias nodded.

"Yeah, 'fuck' is right. Now we have to keep training our asses off, *and* we won't even know until the last minute if we'll even end up competing," Mathias said.

"We can just quit now—" Chase leaned in to whisper into Mathias's ear. "—and go back to bed and fuck till autumn term starts."

"That does sound tempting." Mathias grinned suggestively. "But I'm not quitting," he added decisively as they turned away from the board and headed for the cafeteria. "Just think; we get to spend the rest of the summer here—together—then a free trip to Sydney."

"Good point." Chase handed Mathias a tray as they got in the line for breakfast. "Sydney's got an awesome gay district. We could have a lot of fun there, *especially* if we're not competing."

They were just starting to eat when Chase's cell phone rang. He pulled it out of his pocket and glanced at the display—HOME.

"Hi." Chase started off in a cheerful tone because he had a pretty good idea how the rest of the conversation would go, and he hoped to head that off for a few minutes at least.

"Chase, we've been waiting hours for your call!" Alan's voice boomed out of the phone, and Chase could tell that even Mathias heard not only the words but the tone. Chase's father was angry. "Didn't they post the team roster this morning?"

"Yeah, Dad," Chase paused. "I'm an alternate for saber!" That was actually better than Chase had expected, he had to be honest with himself. His rivals for the team were all in excellent form during the trials, at least as good as anyone he'd faced recently at an international meet.

"*Alternate?*" the voice roared. Chase thought even people on the other side of the cafeteria might be able to hear, it was so loud, so he excused himself silently from the table and went into the hallway to finish the conversation. If it could be considered a conversation when all Alan did was express his displeasure at Chase's *failure* very vociferously.

"The coaches said they'd have a hard time choosing," Chase said, trying to placate his father. "Everyone was in top form after the training camp, and we were all really evenly matched. Mathias's an alternate, too," Chase added, trying to recreate some semblance of a conversation.

"Mathias? Mathias!" Alan roared again.

"Yeah, I mentioned him—"

"So tell me who *made* the team?" Alan cut in, his tone demanding as he refused to drop the subject, and Chase went back down the hall to read the names off the list for his father. "Chase, you beat every single one of those men before and have had winning records against two of them overall for the past three years. How the holy fuck did you not make the team when *they* did?"

"Like I said, we're all training with the same coaches, so we all ended up—"

"Chase, you just don't get it, do you?" Alan's condescending tone sliced right through Chase's heart. "I didn't send you to the training camp for you to learn how to *fence*. You've been training with a top coach for years—I've got the bills to prove it. I sent you there to learn how to *compete*, how to beat the rest of the competition."

He took a deep breath and blinked away the pain of his father's reactions. "What's the difference?" Chase never quite understood why hard work and skill weren't enough to win, at least according to Alan.

"You spent weeks watching your opponents every single day. You're supposed to pay attention to their weaknesses, use that against them. That old adage 'know your enemies' is entirely true—maybe I should have tattooed that on your ass so you wouldn't forget!" Alan barked and berated Chase. "You get to know them, find out how to trip them up. *That's* how you win. It's not just a matter of skill—you've got more than enough of that! It's about *tactics*! That's why you still don't win all the time, when you *could*! Should!" Alan paused for a second. "Chase, those men didn't win—*you lost*!" Chase's heart dropped at his father's harsh, biting words and cruel tone. "It's time for you to understand the difference. Fencing is good training for life—for your future in business as well as every other challenge you'll face. Don't forget that." Each word was like another jab, another blow, sending Chase's emotions reeling, knocking him off balance.

"I won't, Dad." Chase's reply was cut off by the beeps indicating Alan had already disconnected. He closed the phone. *I did my best,* he whispered to himself, wondering when that had ever been good enough.

His dad had been there since Chase had first started fencing when he was just a kid, and had encouraged him, practiced with him, and hired the best coaches for years, and now Chase had come so close to fulfilling the dream of competing in the Olympics—and the chance to win an Olympic gold medal. Suddenly Chase's world championship medals faded into insignificance. He'd worked his ass off for more than ten years, and he'd failed. He had only just realized how important making the team really was—to his father. It wasn't *Chase's* dream, he acknowledged as he fought to calm the pounding in his chest and start to breathe again. He closed his eyes and tried to relax.

Familiar feelings of failure and shortcoming came rushing back, and he felt lightheaded and slightly sick to his stomach. He leaned against the wall for support and found himself sliding toward the floor, suddenly unable to stand. He hadn't felt such paralyzing fear for a long time, and he hadn't realized his father could still have this effect on him. He'd let his father down—again.

Firm hands and strong arms tried to lift Chase off the floor, surprising him, and he opened his eyes to find Mathias bending over him with a worried look on his face.

"Chase, are you okay? What happened?" Frantic words tumbled from Mathias's mouth as he peered down, searching Chase's face.

"I'm okay, yeah, Tee. It's all right," Chase said, for his own benefit as much as Mathias's. "Just… I don't know… I got kind of dizzy." Chase didn't elaborate on Alan's displeasure. He didn't want to get into *that* with Mathias—not yet. He still wanted Mathias to think he was strong and confident and normal and not an enormous failure.

"Your dad didn't sound too happy," Mathias said, but he must have realized that this wasn't a topic Chase wanted to discuss, so he quickly changed it. "His call reminded me to phone my parents and let them know I'm heading to Sydney, even if I might not end up competing." He sat down on the floor next to Chase, their shoulders touching.

"What did they say?" Chase was glad to turn the attention to Mathias's family. He honestly didn't know whether everyone's parents were like his father or not.

"They were really excited, and they're already booking plane tickets and a hotel. No one in my family's ever made it to the Olympics before."

"Weren't they disappointed that you didn't make the team?"

"I did make the team, sort of." Mathias laughed. "But as long as I'm happy and feel like I did my best—and above all, had fun—that's all they care about."

"Wow." Chase didn't manage to hide his surprise. He could tell from Mathias's expression that might have been the wrong thing to say, but he stopped caring. Mathias's good mood brightened Chase's as well.

"Maybe you'll feel better if you finish your breakfast?" Mathias suggested and Chase just nodded.

Mathias hopped up and pulled Chase to his feet, and they headed back to the cafeteria. A few people turned to stare at Chase. They must have heard his father, Chase thought gloomily as he sat back down at the table he'd vacated only ten minutes earlier. Chase could only manage to take a few bites of his now-cold breakfast, and he pushed the remnants of food around his plate, battling to keep what he'd eaten down.

"You want me to get you something else?" Mathias offered, his steely blue eyes dark and his brow furrowed.

"I'm not hungry." Chase sighed and gave up the idea of eating. "Can we just go back to the room?"

"Yeah, sure."

They got up, took their trays to the rack on one side of the cafeteria, and went back to their room, Mathias's fingers skimming along the back of Chase's arm, offering silent comfort from just a simple touch.

Chase lay down on his bed and stared at the ceiling in silence for a few minutes.

"Do you want to talk ab—"

"No, I don't!" Chase's tone came out much harsher than he'd intended, and he could see how surprised and hurt Mathias was. "I'm sorry, I didn't mean... it's just really... complicated," he added, in a much softer voice.

"I can leave you alone if you want. Maybe I'll go work out or run or something." The pain in Mathias's eyes belied his neutral tone. He got up and headed for the dresser. "I'll be around later if you want."

"Don't go... I really want you here, and I *do* want to talk to you, I just feel so...." Chase knew he sounded too needy, so he shut up, hoping he hadn't frightened Mathias away. Why would Mathias want to be with him if he was such a loser?

But to his surprise, Mathias sat down on Chase's bed and started to stroke his arm, gently and soothingly. It still surprised Chase that a big guy like Mathias could be that tender and loving, and Chase knew how lucky he was that he and Mathias were together. The last thing Chase wanted to do was to fuck *that* up, too, and the possibility frightened him even more than his father's anger and disappointment.

"Scoot over and make some room for me?" Mathias asked, and Chase complied.

Mathias lay down on his side next to Chase, still stroking Chase's arm, not speaking, just waiting, obviously not wanting to pressure Chase into talking until he was ready.

"I really let my father down," Chase said after a while, his voice heavy with disappointment. "I wanted him to be proud of me, and I fucked it all up."

"You mean because you're not on the team yet?"

Chase just nodded, not trusting his voice. He hoped he wouldn't cry in front of Mathias.

"Chase, is this about *you* or about him?" Mathias asked. "Is the issue that you wanted to be on the team that badly, or because you think he's upset that you're an alternate?"

"I wanted to be on the team." As soon as the words were out, Chase could tell Mathias knew he was lying. Chase didn't want to admit that his father might love him less if he weren't a success. That's what Chase feared, at least. Maybe Mathias wouldn't care for him any more if he knew Chase was so inadequate that his own father thought he was useless.

"I guess I didn't realize it meant that much to you," Mathias said, wrapping his long, strong arms around Chase and holding him tight, offering simple comfort and acceptance and not asking anything in return. Chase wasn't used to being treated that way by anyone, and he marveled at how easily Mathias had made him feel special and worthwhile. It was like Mathias had some extraordinary power that a laugh or a smile or simple hug could turn Chase's despair around so easily. Almost as easily as Alan's harsh words had brought it on.

They lay together for a long time, neither speaking, and eventually Chase felt normal again. He leaned into Mathias more closely, and Mathias opened his eyes. Chase gazed into them long and deep, emotion welling up inside that he was suddenly unable to express. He traced a finger along Mathias's wonderful, distinctive sideburns then touched his lips to Mathias's, hoping he could convey how much he appreciated and loved Mathias for just being there and accepting him as he was.

Present day
Dallas

IF ONLY Chase had trusted in Mathias—in himself really—Chase thought back ruefully to that long-ago conversation. With Mathias's love, Chase felt comfortable being himself for a *long* time. During their senior year of university—Mathias back at Stanford and Chase at Columbia—they'd spent occasional weekends together in one place or the other. And their relationship continued smoothly for most of the two years they'd been together in business school. Chase was fine when it was just the two of them. He felt secure being himself around

Mathias, because Mathias never expected too much from Chase, and loved Chase simply for himself, his *real* self.

But eventually, Chase reverted back to safety, pretending he was someone else, and this time the new persona worked so well, he started believing that's who he really was. It had started during the spring break of their second year at Fuqua. Chase had returned to Dallas, at his father's insistence, to attend several RichardsCorp meetings in preparation for joining the company once he completed his MBA later that spring.

At B-school, Chase was a great student. Always prepared, participated in class, turned in assignments done well and pretty much on time—unless he'd gotten distracted by Mathias—but back in Dallas at his father's company, in front of his father and the other executives, once again he felt terrified, out of his element—inadequate—and his first defense against the onslaught of panic and pressure was his old standby—acting like the person he *thought* he should be. All those years of following his father around and mimicking him as a child kicked in, and before Chase knew it, he was doing it again. He had practically *become* his father, at least outwardly. He used his father's mannerisms and style of speech, and much to his surprise, people were listening to him. They asked him questions in meetings, showed him pages of figures and asked for his advice or opinion, and Chase responded. He was quick to catch on, had good ideas, and he worked on one deal with a small team for three days straight before they presented it to his father. Alan was thrilled with the proposal and decided to do the deal.

Later that week, the day before Chase returned to Durham, Alan took him to the country club for a special lunch. It was tradition for Alan to bring Chase here for a special occasion or achievement, to commemorate or celebrate. It happened so rarely, Chase could count the number on one hand. This time, Alan said how proud he was of his son and the way Chase had jumped right in; he'd even called him a natural.

Chase would never forget that conversation, though it had taken some time before he truly understood what it had meant.

Mid-April 2003
Dallas Athletic Club

"CHASE, I want to tell you how impressed I've been with you this past couple of weeks," Alan began, and Chase smiled. His father's praise was hard-won and rare, and in Chase's experience, Alan had rarely been this free with his approval of anything Chase had done. Alan expected the best, and Chase had always worked as hard as possible to succeed and live up to his father's high expectations. In his entire life, Chase had only failed once, and the resulting loss of his father's affection stuck with him. He'd do anything to avoid repeating the devastation he'd felt.

"You've definitely lived up to my expectations for you, and I'm glad you're going to be joining the business. That deal you put together is already on track, and we'll make a huge profit when it's finalized," Alan said. "I'm going to give you a bonus of 10 percent of the profit, once it's on the books."

"Ten percent? That's over a million dollars!" Chase was shocked. He'd spent his life around huge sums of money—on paper—and putting this multi-million dollar deal together was so far just an exercise in math. But his dad paying him a million dollars for an idea that only took him half an hour to come up with? That was a new and electrifying experience.

"It could be much more than that. I think your estimates were too conservative. I expect we'll net at least 50 percent more than your forecast," Alan raised a glass of ancient Cognac in salute. "You won't get that big a bonus on every deal, but I want to reward you for showing me how you've matured in the last couple of years. And I want to drive home to you what business is all about. It's hard work, then once you've finished the job, you can sit back and rest and enjoy what you've earned."

"Yes, sir, I understand."

"I hope so," Alan said, in a tone that Chase couldn't recognize. "What I need from you is to follow through on this deal, and close it out as soon as you move back from Durham. It's your deal, and you should participate fully in the execution."

"Move back?" Chase asked, beginning to worry about how quickly this was all happening. He thought he'd have at least the summer off before taking up his role in the company full time.

"Sure, take a week or so to move back, settle in, and relax after graduation; then I expect you to take your place on the executive team by mid-May."

"Mid-May?" Chase repeated, a sinking feeling growing in the pit of his stomach that his well-laid summer plans were about to be demolished.

"Chase, I'm sensing some hesitation here. Are you or are you not in on this deal? No deal, no bonus." Alan put his glass down with a loud *thunk*.

"I was planning to go to Europe with Mathias for a couple of months—we've been planning the trip since last year—*then* come back and get immersed in the business, at the end of the summer."

Alan picked his glass up again and looked into the amber liquid for a few moments. He nodded. "Sure. Just think what a nice trip you'd have after you earned that million dollars." Alan turned his gaze directly on Chase.

That would be something, Chase thought. He'd love to take Mathias on a really luxurious trip—stay in the best hotels, eat at the best restaurants, buy him something beautiful. They'd be able to see and do anything they wanted. He just needed to figure out a way to come back, finish the deal, and then travel with Mathias. It would make a wonderful surprise, since Mathias had been expecting backpacking and hostels or guest houses, not the Ritz or the Riviera. They both had wealthy families, but neither liked to abuse the privilege.

So after finals and graduation, both Chase and Mathias moved back to Texas from Durham. Chase moved back into his parents' house, while Mathias had his things sent to his family's place in Fort Worth. They hadn't decided where they'd live yet, but Chase wanted them to get their own apartment—live *together*. They hadn't shared a place in Durham, but they'd spent every night together, in one apartment or the other. During the trip they'd have plenty of time to decide the details. The only real problem was that Alan didn't want

Chase to be out in Dallas because of how it might reflect on him and RichardsCorp. The Toblers didn't care one way or the other; they just wanted Mathias to be happy, and would support him in whatever decision he made.

Mathias and Chase didn't need to make a decision right away. They'd been planning that trip to Europe, and they could wait until they came back to figure out how to work everything out between themselves and Chase's family.

But Chase hadn't closed the deal yet. He'd made the commitment to the company, and more importantly to his *father*, and he wouldn't let his father down, not again. Chase's past failure still ate away at him, though his father acted as if it no longer mattered. But it mattered to Chase. He would not disappoint his father like that again, not when it was something within his power to avoid.

Chase also wanted to surprise Mathias with the bonus, so he hadn't told him any of the details of his plan. They'd already bought plane tickets, but Chase said he needed to stay a few more days in Dallas, so Mathias should go, and Chase would fly out later. Mathias didn't mind postponing departure until Chase was finished, but Chase insisted he start on the trip. It would be much more enjoyable for Mathias than waiting around while Chase had to go into the office.

So, on schedule, Chase took Mathias to the airport, and waited with him at the gate until his flight left. Since Chase had a ticket for the same flight, he'd been able to get through the security checkpoint, and he'd simply canceled his seat on this flight once they'd gotten to the gate. He figured he could just change the date on the unused ticket after he'd closed the deal.

A few days dragged out into a week, and Chase had to decide whether to leave the deal to meet up with Mathias, or stay, earn the bonus, and make his father happy, then hope the fantastic trip would help him make it up to Mathias. While Mathias waited in Venice, growing increasingly impatient and suspicious, Chase waited for his father to give the signal that they should close his deal.

That deal. The big surprise of the bonus.

How could he have been so naïve?

CHAPTER TEN

The day following Chase's offer
to buy the oil-supply companies
July 2012
Dallas

MATHIAS considered Chase's point about those oil supply companies not fitting into his core business. The T-Group needed to be streamlined, and they owned several companies that didn't make business sense.

Mathias hadn't wanted to make too many changes when he took over, hadn't known how his father would take it, considering his illness. Mathias wanted to avoid upsetting him, but that had also kept him from doing what was best for the company over all. He really should sell those oil supply companies. It was a good time, while high oil prices meant he could get top dollar for them and put the profits back into the T-Group, making it stronger too.

But he'd be damned if he was going to sell to Chase Richards. Mathias didn't believe a word of his bullshit story that he'd changed—or wanted to change because he admired Mathias so much. If he'd thought so much of Mathias, why had it taken this long for Chase to contact him? Why had Chase even dumped him in the first place?

Mathias picked up the phone and dialed Lewis McDonald. Ten minutes later, he came in without knocking and sat down.

"Lewis, I think now's a good time to sell those oil supply companies. What do you think?"

"I don't think there's a better time to offload them."

Mathias handed Lewis Chase's offer. There was no letterhead on the page to indicate the source of the figures.

Lewis looked over the numbers for several minutes. "I'd say this valuation is probably spot on. I'd have to check a few figures, but this is public data, so I don't see that my calculation could be far off."

"Can you put someone on that today? I'd like to formulate an appropriate asking price and put word out on the market as soon as possible."

"Did you put this together?" Lewis asked and Mathias shook his head. "If this is a genuine offer, why not go with this figure?"

"No," Mathias replied firmly. "I'd like you to work up a list of potential buyers, and begin approaching them. Let the usual suspects know—quietly—that these companies are up for sale."

"Will do. I'll bring the figures by in a day or two, along with a list of potential suitors."

"Sounds great, Lewis, thanks." Mathias stood and clapped his hand on Lewis's back.

When Lewis had left, Mathias sat back down and thought about whether Chase really had changed.

THE day after his unsatisfying and unexpectedly short meeting with Mathias about the oil supply companies, Chase settled down at his desk with a thick stack of reports: the research for a proposal he intended to put together for Mathias—proof that Chase had a legitimate plan for purchasing and running the block of companies as a going concern, and not merely to be stripped and sold off piecemeal the way RichardsCorp normally did business.

Once Chase got into the project, he found himself enjoying the work more than he'd expected. Originally, he'd only made the offer in order to appeal to Mathias by playing by his rules. But the oil industry and its particular challenges and opportunities intrigued him. He felt intellectually stimulated in a way he hadn't since he'd first begun working for his father, when putting together deals was still new and exciting.

Within a day, Chase had a good grasp of the industry and pages of notes for changes he thought could improve the performance and profitability of the companies. He would work up some estimates, crunch some numbers, and write up a proper report. That ought to be enough for Mathias to realize Chase was serious.

The research reminded him of the innumerable case studies they'd worked on in B-school. Unlike most of his classmates, Chase enjoyed those exercises and found each one challenging and fun. It was like solving a puzzle with more pieces than necessary, and the first task was to figure out which pieces to use and *then* how they fit together. Chase was so absorbed by this new possibility of buying and running these companies that he nearly lost sight of the ultimate goal—Mathias.

Mathias. Chase couldn't even express quite how much he wanted and *needed* Mathias back in his life. He'd simply been existing since he'd broken up with Mathias, deluding himself that he wanted what he had, because he knew he'd given up his chance to have what—who—he really wanted. Chase's feelings hadn't disappeared; he'd only been ignoring them, ignoring the emptiness in his life, and wearing a mask to cover the truth, even from himself. But now, Chase wouldn't let Mathias slip away from him again. He was willing to do whatever it took to win Mathias back.

ONCE Lewis McDonald put the oil supply companies up for sale, it didn't take long for one of the larger oil companies to put in an acceptable—even generous—bid, which McDonald advised Mathias to accept. Letters of intent to sell were signed and a few days later, the oil company put out a press release to announce their plans to acquire the companies from the Tobler Group.

IT ALSO didn't take long for Chase to discover that Mathias had sold those companies right out from under him. It hadn't been two full weeks since they'd discussed his offer, and Mathias had said he'd consider it if Chase could show he'd changed. During the intervening time, Chase hadn't begun any new acquisition deals, and he'd been researching the oil supply industry, even coming up with some medium- and long-term plans for growing the businesses. His proposal was done—just fine-tuning to make it perfect—proof to Mathias that Chase could make big changes.

Why couldn't Mathias have given him a chance? Chase had gone into this with good faith, but Mathias hadn't. He'd lied. That wasn't the way he did things, and it surprised Chase that Mathias had outmaneuvered him in business.

He picked up the telephone, realized he didn't even have Mathias's direct line. Chase decided not to call. Instead, he buzzed Alicia, his secretary, and asked her to have his car waiting for him downstairs.

He'd take care of this in person. He wanted to see Mathias again, and face-to-face, he could be more convincing about how he'd changed. Let Mathias see the difference.

Sheppard was already waiting when Chase got downstairs. On the way, Chase went over what he would say to Mathias. He reminded himself it's a long-term plan here—plan being the key word. He had to stay calm and take it slowly, one step at a time, and make a more positive impression than the last time they'd met.

The corporate headquarters of the Tobler Group was in a large building, more functional than fashionable and not especially aesthetically pleasing, even inside. The reception area was large and bright, with unremarkable but comfortable-looking furniture. Portraits of Toblers past and photographs of their properties hung on the walls. There was nothing impressive or eye-catching about the place, just a utilitarian space, in stark contrast to the well-appointed lobby of his own headquarters. First impressions were key, and Mathias hadn't made much use of that, unless he wanted people to think they were visiting a boring, old-fashioned company. *Whatever*.

No one stopped Chase as he got into the elevator, which deposited him on the top floor, just outside Mathias's office. Mathias's secretary smiled as Chase introduced himself, and he was surprised that she waved him toward an open door.

"Go right in there, Mr. Richards. Mathias's not too busy to see anyone." She'd even called him "Mathias" and not "Mr. Tobler," he noticed. *How interesting.* Not too busy? Maybe it was easier managing the Tobler Group than he'd thought. He'd expected running all those restaurants and stores would take a lot more effort.

Chase walked into Mathias's office. Mathias was at his desk, head bent as he read a printout on his desk. His sleek hair spilled into his eyes as he concentrated on the report. He looked up with surprise at Chase's approach and brushed stray strands out of the way.

"Chase, I didn't expect to see you."

"Obviously not." Chase glanced around the office. It had a view to rival his own, but that was where the similarity ended. Where Chase's office was light and spacious and elegant, Mathias's office was almost the polar opposite. It gave Chase the feeling of stepping back in time about a hundred years. The walls were wood paneled, and exquisite Oriental rugs covered the floor. The mahogany desk was large—probably hand carved—and very clearly an antique. Chase suspected it had been his grandfather's desk. It really was rather magnificent and a definite work of art. It served as the focal point of the room, and the other furniture paled in comparison.

On top of the desk were a pair of lamps with slag glass shades that gave off more of a glow than strict illumination, but they were lovely. Nowadays, people called things like that "vintage," and they'd become trendy, but Chase suspected every item had been here since it was made, because that's what the Toblers were like: they bought quality and kept it; they didn't go for fashion and fad—or anything modern. This room probably hadn't been redecorated since Mathias's grandfather's time. It was more like a museum than an office.

In front of the desk were three large leather-covered armchairs for guests and a couch, low table, and another set of four chairs on the opposite side of the room. Floor-to-ceiling bookcases held a collection of old books—probably also antique—and gave the room more the feel of a den or library than an office where someone conducted business. It was actually sort of cozy, Chase decided. Maybe Mathias would offer him a glass of port while they sat around and discussed their business.

"So, what brings you here?" Mathias's tone was neutral. He didn't get up to shake Chase's hand.

"It's about those oil supply companies we discussed a couple of weeks ago."

"Ahh, right." Mathias straightened up and sat back in his chair, motioning Chase to take a seat.

"I saw the announcement that another firm has closed the deal to acquire them." Chase kept his voice even as he settled himself in the chair. *Very comfortable. Surprisingly comfortable.* "I thought you were going to consider my offer. It was for quite a bit more than you settled on."

"I didn't realize you were serious about that offer, Chase."

"I went through the trouble of putting together a fair valuation and offer. What about that didn't seem serious?"

"I guess I'm just used to your reputation for fucking with things rather than taking a long-term approach to business. You have to admit, this certainly doesn't fit with your usual *modus operandi*. I couldn't in good conscience even consider an offer from you—even a substantially larger one. I would feel personally responsible for all the employees once they'd lost their jobs."

"Does this look like I was fucking around?"

Mathias looked up and seemed to notice for the first time that Chase was carrying a folder. Chase pulled out a thick sheaf of papers and tossed them onto the desk. Mathias picked up the report and skimmed the first page.

"That's the plan I put together for running those companies. I also have some suggestions for streamlining their operations. Ideas that I think would make them more profitable—as a going concern and not as a pool of assets to sell off piece by piece." Chase found it increasingly difficult to keep his temper under control.

"You're serious?" Mathias cocked his head, clearly thrown for a loop by Chase's enthusiasm about getting into the oil supply business. "You can't blame me for not taking you seriously, Chase. Not after everything I've seen you and your family do over the years. In fact, I once thought your father was the champion, but you've gone and surpassed even him."

"I'm trying to change how I do business, but it's not going to happen overnight. I thought this could be a good start," Chase knew his tone betrayed his disappointment. "I guess I shouldn't have expected that you'd even give me half a chance." Chase was losing control over his emotions, and hoped his words hadn't come out as hostile.

"Look, throwing together a few facts and figures and some ideas doesn't make a leopard change its spots, Chase. You're a leopard, and you always will be. You're just like your father—worse, since you seem to be so much more devious." Mathias didn't disguise his malicious tone. "I'm sure you have an ulterior motive for wanting to buy those companies, and it had nothing to do with this." Mathias picked up the report from his desk and let it fall back down, making a loud *slap* on the surface of the desk that startled Chase. "I won't get burned again by a Richards. You and your father both made a fool out of me—it won't happen again. So, take your new leaf and leave me alone!"

Chase stood up, surprised by Mathias's vehemence and anger. Now his own mood matched Mathias's—he was furious. Not only had Mathias thought Chase was bluffing, but he'd insulted Chase as well. He'd never be anything like his father! Alan Richards was in a class by himself when it came to scheming and trickery, and Chase had only reached that level once: when he'd taken RichardsCorp away from his father.

Now that Chase really *did* want to change, to become a better person, a more responsible businessman—thanks to Mathias really— all he got were insults and abuse. Mathias had been cruel and judgmental. He'd been right all along. Mathias had changed. He wasn't the same man Chase had fallen in love with.

But this wasn't over, not by a long shot.

"I won't forget this," Chase knotted his hands into fists, but he kept his voice calm and steady as he stood up, turned on his heel, and stormed out of Mathias's office.

MATHIAS watched Chase walk out of his office and marveled at the transformation he'd witnessed. Sometimes, he looked and sounded just like the Chase that Mathias had fallen in love with all those years ago—the Chase he admitted he still dreamed about. The way his eyes sparkled when he got excited about something. That's how he'd sounded when he was talking about making a new start and working with those companies, rather than selling them off in bits and pieces.

Mathias picked up the report and glanced at it. Chase had paper-clipped a personal card to the top page, with his direct office number, home, and cell phone numbers. Mathias was about to dump the whole thing in the trash when he stopped himself and decided to take a quick glance through it. Fifteen minutes later, Mathias had come to the surprising conclusion that Chase had put together a fairly impressive and comprehensive proposal and business plan.

But Mathias knew better than to believe a word Chase said—or any report. Not anymore. This was one of Chase's games, and Mathias vowed not to get caught again. It was impossible to know where the scheming, unethical businessman left off and this new "softer side" of Chase began. That was probably just an act anyway, and Mathias wanted no part of it.

Chase even looked better than ever, Mathias thought, recalling the light in his eyes and the charming way he turned up one corner of his mouth, and the little bounce in his step when he'd arrived. Still devastatingly gorgeous, like some living version of *The Picture of Dorian Gray*. With disgust, Mathias wondered what Chase saw when he looked in the mirror.

ON THE way back to RichardsCorp, Chase called Mike Killian from his car.

"Mikey, I'm on my way back. Have your ass in my office when I get there."

"Sure thing, Chief," Mike replied, sounding intrigued. "Wha—?" Chase jammed the phone shut on Mike's question and closed his eyes.

My father? Mathias thinks I'm just like my father! Chase stewed in the back of the limo as his driver darted through traffic. If only Mathias knew how dead wrong he was. Or was he? Alan *had* turned Chase into a copy of himself, only Chase hadn't discovered just how little he wanted to be like his own father until it was far too late.

As a child, Chase dreamed of being just like Alan, working with him, making him proud to call Chase his son. And for nearly twenty-five years, Chase had done everything his father had ever asked of him—done anything, given up anything—to make his father happy, because that had made Chase happy too. Until his father had asked too much, and Chase saw the kind of man Alan Richards really was. Cold, selfish, manipulative. Chase hadn't wanted to be that kind of man at all, but despite his best intentions, that's what he'd turned into. And now, Mathias would see exactly who Chase had become and what he was capable of.

Mathias was going to be sorry he hadn't given Chase a chance. He'd only asked for a *chance* to show, to prove, he'd changed—or was trying to change. But Mathias had kicked him to the curb on those oil supply companies, not even giving him the courtesy of letting him know they were officially up for sale or politely turning down his offer. And Mathias's only excuse was that Chase was a Richards and there could be no way he could be trusted. No way Chase would really stick with those companies for the long run. There wasn't anything worse Mathias could have said, striking directly at exactly the part of Chase's life and behavior he desperately wanted to change.

Still a leopard? Chase mused. He'd show Mathias, make him sorry for brushing him off so cavalierly and rejecting Chase's own idea of who he really wanted to be. Well, he'd take something from Mathias, too, and Chase knew precisely what in the world was most important to Mathias Tobler.

WITH light traffic, it didn't take Chase long to get back to his office. He found Mike waiting for him, sprawled out on the couch at one end of the spacious and expensively furnished office. Floor-to-ceiling windows on two sides of the room provided a fantastic view—such that it was—over downtown Dallas.

"So, what's your sudden interest in my ass this afternoon?" Mike asked, with a rather suggestive tone. He wasn't wearing his suit jacket, and his tie was more than slightly loosened, making Chase wonder what Mike had been up to while he had been over at T-Group headquarters.

"In your dreams, buddy." Chase shook his head, though he couldn't help laughing. The truth was, Chase suspected Mike would be more than willing to sleep with him, and not just because he thought it might help his career. But Chase kept things strictly business with Mike, most of the time, anyway. He'd never sleep with any of his employees; there were too many things that could go wrong, and Chase was careful to avoid all of them.

"I can wait," Mike replied, and he sounded like he meant it.

Mike was the closest thing Chase had to a friend. Mainly, it was because they both knew too many of each other's secrets to let the other one get too far out of sight. Mike was one of a very few people at RichardsCorp who knew Chase was gay. Chase's secretary, Alicia, was another—out of necessity—since Chase had brought men to his office on more than one occasion. But Mike pulled his weight at RichardsCorp, and his financial prowess had made them plenty of money during the years since Chase had taken control, so the secrets weren't the only reason Chase kept him around.

"This is *business*." Chase's tone left no room for doubt.

"Nothing wrong with mixing business and pleasure." Mike flashed a wide grin.

"Just concentrate on the business for now, okay?" Chase shot a warning look at Mike—the fun was over for the time being.

"Sure. What is it?"

"Do you still have that analysis we worked up on the Tobler Group?" Chase asked.

"Yeah, but—"

"I'd like to put together another plan."

"I thought those oil supply companies had been sold. What else do you want from them?" Mike sounded intrigued with Chase's sudden interest in the Tobler Group. "You're not thinking about buying up something else just to *keep* are you?" It was clear from his tone that he thought Chase had been insane for even considering the purchase of the original three companies.

"No, not this time. This time, it's business as usual."

"Oh good, I was afraid we'd gone over to the light side or something." Mike attempted an evil villain voice, but Chase wasn't in the mood to appreciate it.

"I'm going to take over the Tobler Group," he announced in a self-satisfied voice, leaning back in his chair as if he'd already succeeded.

"Why the fuck—?"

"Because I can."

CHAPTER ELEVEN

Late July 2012
Dallas

Two weeks to the day after Chase stormed out of Mathias's office, the T-Group share price started to plunge, giving Mathias the first indication that something was up.

Following Mathias's initial meeting with Lewis regarding the stock price drop, Lewis developed a set of strategies to counteract Chase's put options. The plan required cash, more money than they had available, and Mathias knew the company would have to borrow—heavily—to fight Chase off. They needed to buy back shares to prop up the price, and to retain as much voting power as possible. The Tobler family owned only 35% of the outstanding shares, which meant they would need to get hold of an additional 16% to retain control. They could appeal to shareholders to let Mathias vote their shares for them, but Mathias was afraid that calling a shareholders' meeting would backfire. All Chase had to do was to offer them more than the current price for their shares, and they'd fall all over themselves to sell, and Chase would easily be able to buy up enough shares to counter the Toblers' personal voting power in the company.

The first order of business was to find a bank willing to extend the necessary credit, and that meant Mathias would have to personally speak with bankers, explaining how he was going to fend off Chase Richards' takeover bid.

Mathias had made a quick trip to his parents' house to talk with his father about the takeover threat and the strategies that he and Lewis had to choose from. As usual, Jerry was well up on what was going on, both from newspapers and from the several telephone conversations they'd already had. Jerry knew a number of local bankers and several more around Texas, men he'd known from business school or simply friends he'd made from years in business. Jerry might not be healthy enough to run the T-Group, but he was more than capable of paving the way for Mathias and Lewis. He had set up a half dozen appointments with banks he thought would back their takeover defense.

Mathias then spent a week going from bank to bank in Dallas, but no one—not their regular banks, or Jerry's contacts—would agree to a loan. Dallas bankers were either afraid Mathias would lose and the debt wouldn't be repaid, or they were simply afraid of Chase Richards. More likely the latter, Mathias thought, feeling as if they were already defeated.

The following week, he and Lewis approached another set of lenders in Houston, with the same result. Mathias realized he had to go to New York, to escape Chase's sphere of influence, before he'd be able to find a bank willing to help.

"MATT, baby, why do you have to go away again *now*?" Brooke snuggled up to him on the couch in his condo as he broke the news to her. "You were in Houston for two days, and now New York? There's a benefit for the Zoo and the Dallas Community Service awards we're supposed to attend this week. Can't you postpone the trip? I hate going to those things by myself." Suddenly her face brightened. "Or take me along with you! I love New York, and we could see a couple of shows, and eat at the best restaurants—I've just been dying to go back to Boulud and Jean-Georges! And the shopping! I could look for a wedding dress and—"

"No, Brooke, I'm really sorry, but it just can't wait. It's business—" Mathias tried to soothe her, but she cut him off.

"All you think about lately is business! You come home late every night, and then you're on the phone with Lewis McDonald even when you *are* home." Her smile faded as if it had melted right off her face. "I don't want to hear about *business* all the time!"

"Oh, honey, I'm sorry." Mathias pulled her to him. She let him wrap his arms around her, but her body was rigid, and she didn't lean against him or snuggle against his chest. "I know you don't like me to bring work home, but right now we're in a really tough position. Someone is trying to take over the company, and it's taking all my time to prevent that from happening."

"If someone wants to buy it, why not just sell it? As long as they pay what it's worth." She shrugged. "Isn't that how business is done? Mergers and acquisitions...."

Mathias squinted a little as he looked at her. She'd never liked speaking of business, though she listened when he occasionally brought it up. Apparently more had sunk in than he'd realized. "It's not that easy. See, the person who's trying to buy it isn't going to run it the way we do. They're going to sell off pieces and close the stores and restaurants, so people are going to lose their jobs. I can't let that happen to people who have been loyal employees to the company and to my family. And the offer isn't close to what the company's really worth, so the current shareholders won't get a fair price."

"I don't really know much about business. I studied history." She shrugged one shoulder and smiled. "But I'm starting to understand this is more than just numbers to you. What happens if they win?"

Mathias wondered whether she was worried that he wouldn't be as wealthy as he was now, if the takeover succeeded. He chided himself for thinking that she had such base motives for being with him. Of course, she would be concerned if they couldn't retain the same standard of living they had, but he hoped it wouldn't matter that much to her. They loved each other, and that should be enough to overcome some temporary financial difficulties, shouldn't it?

"If you mean me, personally...?" he asked and she nodded, a serious expression on her face. "Well, I wouldn't exactly be poor or anything, but I wouldn't have as much, or as many assets as I have right now. And I wouldn't have a job. But that's not why I want to save the company. My great-grandparents started this business, from one tiny restaurant all those years ago, and my great-grandfather ran it, then my grandfather, then *my* dad, and now me. My family's built something out of so little. That means more to me than just money in the bank or a nice house or fancy car. You can understand, can't you?" he asked, almost imploring her to see the situation from his own perspective.

"I didn't realize you felt that way about the business." Brooke turned toward him, putting her arms around him and squeezing. "It's nice hearing you so passionate about something."

"I'm very passionate about this company, but I know you don't like me to talk much about work, so we've never really discussed these issues." How could Brooke *not* know how he felt about the business? Had she been tuning him out all these months? It served him right, since he was certainly guilty of that himself—more than ever recently.

And it wasn't just the takeover. Being back in contact with Chase brought old feelings and memories to the surface. Emotions Mathias thought he'd buried years ago when he'd discovered just where Chase's priorities lay—with his family and his desire for money and power. But Mathias discovered that those feelings for Chase—the Chase he used to know—were anything but history, and it made the current situation even harder to deal with.

"Who's trying to take over the T-Group?" Brooke sounded as if she were genuinely interested—and concerned.

"It probably won't mean much to you, but it's Chase Richards, of RichardsCorp." Mathias fought to keep his voice level as he said Chase's name, not wanting to betray his history with Chase, business or otherwise.

"Chase?" Brooke sounded surprised, but not as surprised as Mathias to discover that not only did Brooke recognize the name, but she appeared to be on a first-name basis with Chase. "I know him," she said, confirming Mathias's fears. "But why would Chase want your company?"

"You *know* Chase Richards?"

"Yeah, he belongs to the Dallas Athletic Club, and I see him there once in a while," Brooke said innocently. "I never met him until recently, but I recognized him—I mean, who wouldn't? He's very attractive…. And then I played tennis with him about a week or two ago. Well not *with* him, *against* him. Mixed doubles. He was Erica's partner. He's really good, and they kicked our asses." Brooke's laughter filled the room, back to the bubbly good mood Mathias missed, and so badly needed, while everything else around him was stressful.

Mathias wondered how Chase had time for tennis, when it was all Mathias could do to get home before Brooke got bored and went to bed on her own, especially lately. Since Chase's company didn't actually *do* anything, he probably didn't have much to do at work besides plot against Mathias. He certainly didn't have to worry about keeping factories running or making deliveries to customers or supporting thousands of employees, the way Mathias did. But Mathias loved his job, and he loved his company, and he'd do whatever it took to keep them, and to keep them safe from corporate raiders like Chase.

"You're not even listening to me are you?" Brooke's voice rose and turned strident. She punched Mathias in the shoulder a bit harder than a simple playful gesture, and he realized he must have completely tuned out whatever she'd been saying.

"I'm sorry, honey. I know I've been distracted. But once this is all over, I promise I'll make it up to you. We'll go together to New York, and no business—just shopping and restaurants and museums, and spending time with each other." Mathias hoped that when it was all over, he'd still have the Tobler Group, in good shape and not suffocating under a mountain of corporate debt. "Now what were you telling me?"

"About our tennis match."

"Right. Who was your partner?" Mathias feigned interest. Figures and strategies were still spinning around in his mind. Some time with Brooke would be relaxing so he could concentrate on work later on. He tried to focus his attention on her.

"Mike something. Has a shaved head. Normally, I think it looks vulgar, but on him it's very attractive. Do you know him, too?" she asked.

Now she had Mathias's entire attention. The only Club member with a shaved head he could recall was Mike Killian. Chase's CFO. *What the fuck was he doing playing tennis with Brooke?*

"Yes, I know him, too," Mathias said, his mouth a tight line.

"How do you know all these people when you're hardly ever at the Club anymore?"

"I know them from work. They're not at the Club all the time, you know. They have jobs, too," Mathias reminded her.

"So how do they manage to work and have time for tennis when you don't?" Her tone grew petulant.

That's a good question. Aside from the looming takeover, the T-Group wasn't difficult to keep running smoothly. He had good, honest people working for him, people he didn't have to spend every waking minute managing. Why did he prefer to be at work, rather than at home? Yes, he loved his job and the company and even though he felt obligated to his family, customers, and employees to do the best job, it never felt like a burden. Maybe he should be asking himself why he didn't want to spend more time with Brooke?

What was missing in their relationship that he could only find at work? At the T-Group, Mathias knew what he was doing. It wasn't so much that he was in charge, but more that he knew what he needed to do and he did it. He was respected and appreciated. But with Brooke, Mathias felt out of his element. He never quite knew what she expected, as loved and appreciated by Brooke as he used to feel, or as he had hoped to feel again.

Would anything change after they got married?

August 2012
Dallas

MATHIAS and Lewis spent a week in New York, visiting bank after bank. They didn't have many contacts there, and the ones they had were unwilling to help them, considering the T-Group a bad risk, or perhaps too concerned about having Chase Richards know they'd been helping to keep him from his goal. *Has Chase's influence spread this far?* Mathias wondered.

They found themselves repeating the same details of their company, the situation, and their plan over and over. Finally, they found a small bank that helped them come up with the required amount of capital at a fairly reasonable rate. Mason, the head of the bank, told them he needed a few days to get everything approved by his board before he could disburse the funds, and they all shook on the deal, which was good enough for Mathias; that's how they did business in Texas.

The next afternoon, Mathias let himself into his condo back in Dallas, following a crowded and tiring flight home. He was exhausted, but cautiously optimistic. Once they had the money, they could start to fight back against Chase. It wasn't a foolproof plan, but it was the best they could come up with, given their resources. He left his suitcase in the hallway and sprawled out on the couch, intending to take a quick nap, then head into the office, but he was afraid he might not wake up if he let himself fall asleep.

"You're back?" Brooke came into the living room from the direction of her bedroom. "How was your trip?" She sounded as if she'd missed him and finding him at home was a pleasant surprise.

"Long." He pulled her down onto the couch next to him and kissed her. He'd missed her more than he'd thought he would. She smelled warm and familiar, and he liked having her greet him when he returned, even if it hadn't been planned. "But successful."

"Successful how?" she asked.

Mathias was even more pleased that she was taking more interest in his business than she'd shown before. He took that as a sign that this crisis was bringing them closer.

"Lewis and I managed to secure financial backing for our plan to fight Chase's takeover bid." He planted a kiss on her neck. "But you don't want to hear about all of that, do you? I was just going to take a quick shower, but I can take a long one if you want to join me," he suggested in a low, inviting tone. He needed a long-overdue physical release. "I promise you'll enjoy it." Mathias smiled and ran his fingers slowly down one of her bare arms.

"Honey, I just did my hair, and I'm supposed to meet Erica at Hibiscus for dinner in an hour…. I'm sorry! We can save that for later, okay?" She gave him a quick, apologetic peck on the cheek. "But tell me about this plan you and Lewis have cooked up. I don't get how all that works."

"You're really interested?" Mathias was surprised but thrilled with her growing attention to business.

"Of course! If it's important to you, it's important to me." Brooke slipped behind Mathias and began massaging his neck and shoulders, earning a low, pleasured moan.

Mathias spent the next ten minutes outlining the strategy, and Brooke even asked a few thoughtful questions.

"So Mason was the only bank that was willing to lend you the money? That seems odd."

"New York bankers don't know us the way Texas bankers do. So it's much harder to convince them we're a good risk, considering the situation we're in right now. We're more than just figures on paper, and that's when knowing the bankers can make all the difference."

"Well, all this financial stuff is certainly more interesting than I ever expected. But I've kept you from your work—and your shower—too long. I have to meet Erica at Abacus."

"I thought you said Hibiscus?" Mathias asked.

"Oh, I always get those two places mixed up." Brooke shook her head, giggling. "Silly me!"

"Let me jump in the shower real quick, don't leave before I get done, okay?" Mathias got up and strode toward the master bedroom.

"Of course not," Brooke said. "I'm not ready anyway." She went back to her room, where the closet already overflowed with her clothes. She was working on filling up the closet in the master bedroom as well, but she preferred to dress in private, and Mathias didn't mind. He always enjoyed the thrill of seeing her all ready to go out, though he missed the intimacy of watching her dress and fix her hair. Or of getting to help her—or get in her way. He and Chase used to distract each other and show up late a lot. Why did he suddenly remember that? The memories that flooded back meant he did more than wash up during his brief shower. Brooke was dressed and ready to go when Mathias emerged from the bedroom in clean clothes but with his hair still damp.

"I'm leaving now,"

"Have fun at dinner, honey." He kissed her neck before she headed out the front door. "You may get home before I do."

"I will. We'll probably stay out late, so don't feel bad if you end up working till late, okay?"

Mathias was pleasantly surprised at her understanding. He'd been distant the last few weeks, focusing on work—and on Chase—and had more than a few late nights. Finally, Brooke seemed to realize how important the fight for the T-Group was and had been more supportive and understanding than ever.

Twenty minutes later, as he headed down to the garage, he felt energized, thinking that surely his luck had changed.

CHAPTER TWELVE

October 2001
Durham, North Carolina

CHASE and Mathias had been in Durham for six weeks, and in classes at Duke University's Fuqua School of Business for about a month. It had been a hectic, busy month, and the first exam period was just over a week away. Chase had been at a study group meeting for the past three hours, and he was ready to explode. They'd planned to meet in Chase's apartment for a nice, quick, stress-relieving fuck, then go out to dinner. Then they both had assignments to finish for the following day.

Chase unlocked his front door, dropped his bag on the floor, and started unbuttoning his shirt before the door was even shut behind him. "God, Tee, that study group went on forever," he shouted from the hallway as he kicked his shoes off. "I hope you're ready and waiting, and I don't have to waste time with your clothes, too." He was half-hard just thinking about Mathias waiting for him— preferably completely undressed.

Chase walked into the living room with his shirt unbuttoned, hand on his unbuckled belt, to see Mathias sitting on the couch, still fully clothed. And he wasn't alone.

"Dad!" Chase said, surprised and more than a little embarrassed. At least his mother wasn't here, too. *Thank God for small mercies.* He did his belt up, took a deep, calming breath, and then sat down on a chair near the couch.

"I didn't know you were in town," Chase said as calmly as he could manage. Any trace of a hard-on had disappeared as soon as he'd seen his father.

"I distinctly recall mentioning I would be here for a conference in early October." Alan Richards' voice was even colder than his gaze. He held a half-full glass of scotch, and took a large swallow as he stared at Chase. "Button up your shirt, Chase," he added as if Chase were five years old.

"You know, Chase, I'll just wait in my apartment. Call me later." Mathias got up from the couch. "Nice to see you again, Mr. Richards." He nodded and flashed a smile.

"Alan. Why do I need to keep reminding you?" Alan asked in a tone that Chase could tell wasn't meant as jokingly is it might have sounded, but Mathias was still smiling, apparently unfazed.

"Alan," Mathias repeated.

Chase grabbed his hand as he walked by and pulled Mathias down for a kiss that he hoped hinted that their plans weren't canceled, simply postponed, not caring that his father was watching.

After Mathias left, Alan turned his attention to Chase.

"A group of my buddies from Wharton are also in town for this conference. They've invited you along to dinner tonight. Go put on a good suit and be ready to leave in fifteen minutes. There'll be a lot of people you should meet." Alan's tone left no doubt that this wasn't merely a suggestion.

"But, Dad, Mathias and I have plans, and I need to get an assignment done for tomorrow."

"Forget the assignment."

"What?" Chase was surprised at his father's lax attitude. "You've always wanted me to get top grades. What's with the sudden change?"

"Up until now, your grades *were* important—getting into an Ivy League university and then a top B-school. But do you honestly think you're at business school to learn something? You have a job waiting at RichardsCorp. You don't need to worry about every single assignment the way most of the other people here do," Alan said. "The most valuable thing you'll need in business is *contacts*, and this is the place to start making them. That's how you get information, and how you get ahead of your competition."

"And Mathias...."

"Chase, you won't get ahead by staying home and fucking your boyfriend, unless you happen to be dating Warren Buffet. Forget about him for one night, and do something that's going to be crucial for your *future*. Am I making myself clear?" Alan's voice was sharp, and Chase knew he wasn't going to take "no" for an answer.

"Yes, sir." Chase resigned himself to his fate. He got up and headed into the master bath, washed his face and fixed his hair before going into the bedroom and choosing a blue pin-striped Prada suit and a pale blue hand-tailored shirt, tossing the clothes he'd worn that day onto the bed, and changing. He picked out a tie Mathias liked, one with large red flowers on a tan background. He knew his dad wouldn't approve of it, but Chase didn't care. Alan could allow him this one concession, since he'd shown up and started making plans for Chase without any warning. His future? To Chase, Mathias *was* his future, but his dad talked like Mathias didn't matter at all.

He pulled his cell phone from his discarded pants and speed-dialed Mathias, who answered almost immediately.

"I guess you're not on your way down, huh?" There was no anger in his voice, more an amused resignation. They both knew how commandeering Alan could be, and how focused he was on preparing Chase for his future at RichardsCorp.

"Sorry, Tee, I'm being dragged to some Wharton reunion bash tonight completely against my will. Call the SWAT team if I'm not down there by midnight, okay?" Chase whispered into the phone, one eye on the bedroom door. "I'll more than make up for the delay," he added in a low, promising tone and blew a kiss.

"I'll hold you to that. Go and have fun—" His tone was ironic. "—I'll be here whenever you get home. Though I might call the SWAT team anyway when I finish this assignment; they're usually pretty hot. They can keep me company till you escape." Mathias's laughter bubbled over the line and made Chase miss him already. They hadn't seen each other all day except for the two uncomfortable minutes when Chase got home to find his father waiting.

"Well, that sure as hell is incentive for me to get out of this thing as soon as humanly possible. If not sooner."

"*Catch* you later, Chase." It was a familiar joke between them.

"Love you, Tee." Chase blew another kiss, but Mathias had already hung up.

Chase smiled as he adjusted his tie in the mirror, but his good mood quickly faded as he contemplated the dinner ahead. Chase definitely felt like a five–year-old and not a man who was about to meet some very important business contacts. Why did Alan always treat him like a child, but still expect him to act like a confident businessman? The only way he would make it through the evening was to put on that cocky Chase persona that had helped him through so many similar situations in the past—through just about everything—until he'd met Mathias.

When Chase was ready he went back into the living room and waited while his father gave him the once over.

"Do you have to wear that faggy tie?" Alan spoke condescendingly as he looked over every detail of Chase's appearance.

"There's nothing wrong with this tie. It's Kenzo." Chase showed his father the designer's label, and Alan just shrugged dismissively.

"Fine." Alan sighed loudly, letting Chase know he didn't care to argue the point anymore. "Let's get going. My driver is waiting downstairs, and I don't want to be too late." Alan shuttled Chase out the door.

FOUR hours later, a slightly tipsy Chase let himself into Mathias's apartment. Mathias was lying on the couch, knees bent, reading, and he looked up eagerly when he heard Chase shut the front door.

"Hey," Chase said with a grin. He settled next to Mathias and leaned down for a very long-overdue hello kiss.

"Oh, I must be dreaming," Mathias said when Chase finally let him up for air. He reached for Chase's tie and gave it a little tug.

"What're you talking about?" Chase was just thankful Mathias wasn't angry that he got back so late from the dinner.

"You know, it's one of my fantasies to be bent over a desk and fucked by a hot guy in a four thousand dollar suit." Mathias sat up and tugged Chase's face close to his.

"Is that so? Tell me more about this fantasy." Chase laughed and hoped he didn't sound too drunk, because he really wasn't, just pleasantly buzzed. And horny. Way too fucking horny, but this sounded fun. Mathias didn't randomly start talking about his fantasies very often, and Chase wanted to make the most of it. And do whatever he could to turn that fantasy into reality.

"I'm sitting in front of the guy's desk, like it's a job interview…." Mathias started tentatively, and a look of slight embarrassment flashed across his face. He put his notes down on the coffee table, obviously playing for time. "And, well, he asks some very inappropriate questions…." A smile began to bloom as Mathias looked directly at Chase, no longer self-conscious. "And then does some even more inappropriate things to me."

"So, Mr. Tobler, tell me why I should hire you?" Chase decided to turn the fantasy into a game. He went over to the dining room table and sat down. "Have a seat right here. I have a few questions for you." He indicated the chair to his left, and Mathias laughed, then went and sat down.

"You're serious?" Mathias asked, before turning the chair so he was facing Chase.

"So, are you a virgin, Mr. Tobler?" Chase ignored the question and stayed in character.

"No," Mathias laughed. "You can call me Mathias. Mr. Tobler's my dad or my grandfather."

"Lovely thought." Chase tried desperately not to laugh and ruin the mood. "So, Mathias, do you like cock? Because this position involves a lot of cock. *My* cock." He unbuckled his belt and unbuttoned his pants.

"I love cock," Mathias flashed a bright grin and his eyes sparkled like sapphires. Chase could see he was really getting into their role-play.

"What do you love about it?" Chase aimed for a businesslike tone—totally out of sync with the topic of conversation—making it all the more fun. Acting—playing almost any role—came so naturally to him, but now with Mathias, he had an outlet for the role-play that was fun, rather than using it as means for survival as before. The way he had at that unbearable dinner with his father's buddies.

"Sucking it, for a start. I give great head." Mathias's mouth curved into a wicked grin.

Chase could barely wait to let Mathias put his money where his mouth was. "Now would be a good time for a demonstration of your skills." He spread his legs.

Mathias got out of his chair tentatively and knelt between Chase's knees, looking up almost shyly from under shaggy bangs. He reached up to palm Chase's cock through the fabric of his pants with a look of determination that made Chase want him even more. Chase was hard before Mathias touched him, a few strokes from Mathias's skillful hand had him moaning and nearly writhing. It wouldn't do to let the job applicant see him so easily aroused, but he was ready to explode.

Mathias unzipped Chase's pants and pushed his boxers down to free his cock. "You have a really beautiful cock, Mr. Richards." Mathias grinned and admired it for a moment before he bent down to lick up and down the length.

"You have a very… talented tongue." Chase moaned and trembled as Mathias's lips and tongue caressed his cock. "I'm sure they'll get along very well."

Mathias's huge hands went around Chase's waist, pulling him in closer. Mathias's mouth closed around the head of Chase's cock, and he began to suck eagerly. Chase tangled his hands in Mathias's hair while he relaxed back into the chair—not the most comfortable location for this, but he barely noticed—enjoying Mathias's skills almost *too* much. He remembered that he needed to get Mathias onto the desk—this was supposed to be *Mathias's* fantasy, not Chase's.

With a gentle tug of Mathias's hair, Chase attempted to get Mathias's attention, but Mathias was too absorbed in his demonstration to notice. Chase tugged a bit more forcefully, and Mathias looked up, mischief dancing in his eyes, mouth still at work.

"This is a little unfair, don't you think?" Chase asked. "Let's see what you've got under the hood."

Mathias used one hand to start unbuttoning his shirt.

"Not like that," Chase remonstrated. "Get up and give me a good view."

"Oh, yeah, okay," Mathias said as he finally let Chase's cock slip from his mouth, lips shiny-wet.

Mathias straightened then stood up, stepping back a few paces. Chase could see the outline of Mathias's hard-on, and it made him happy to see how much Mathias was enjoying this.

Slowly, Mathias began to unbutton his shirt, gazing at Chase with a mixture of shyness and playfulness that Chase found as arousing as the way Mathias had sucked his cock. Mathias still worked out religiously, and his body was proof enough of that. Every time Chase looked at Mathias or touched him, he realized how lucky he was to be with someone as gorgeous on the outside as well as the inside. But right now, Chase was more grateful that not only did Mathias have an incredibly hot body, but that he liked showing it off for Chase.

Mathias slipped his shirt off one shoulder, and Chase just watched, enjoying the view as Mathias peeled the garment off completely and tossed it to one side.

"Beautiful," Chase said, eyes taking in the well-muscled chest and torso, thinking about running his hands over that body, licking and sucking at the brown nipples. "Lose the pants now," he added in an authoritative tone.

Mathias bent his head as his hands went to his belt, but he looked up at Chase with that sly smile. His fingers fumbled with the belt, taking their time while Chase squirmed involuntarily in the chair, waiting and wanting more of the game, more of Mathias.

When Mathias had unbuckled his belt, he pulled it slowly out of the belt loops, tossing it in the direction of the discarded shirt. Chase noticed how the heavily muscled chest made Mathias's waist look even slimmer, and how without the belt, his jeans slipped low onto his hips. God, Chase wanted to run his fingers along those hipbones and blaze a trail with his lips down the faint trail of hair that disappeared into the waistband of his jeans. He was pretty sure Mathias knew *exactly* what he was doing to Chase at this point.

Mathias unbuttoned his jeans, and as he began on the zipper, Chase realized Mathias wasn't wearing any underwear. It made him wonder who had started the game after all, but as soon as Mathias's jeans slipped down his hips, pooling at his ankles, Chase didn't care. Mathias was hard, his cock long and thick and dark. With one hand Mathias stroked himself, his other hand moving lower to cup his balls. Completely unaware, Chase mirrored the motion with his own hand.

God, he couldn't stand it anymore. Chase's entire body was on fire. He hadn't realized that now he was still fully clothed while Mathias wasn't just naked, but on display for him, teasing him.

"Just how badly do you want this job?" Chase nearly groaned, trying to get his mind back on the roles they were playing.

"Pretty. *Fucking*. Bad," Mathias said, drawing the words out so they sounded incredibly obscene. Chase thought he could come just from listening to Mathias's voice, and his hand tightened slightly around his cock.

"You think you can work for me, follow my directions?" Chase asked suggestively.

"Yeah, I can… take orders from you."

"Then come here," Chase said sharply, and Mathias complied, stepping carefully out of his jeans and walking slowly and gracefully to stand in front of Chase, his cock practically in Chase's face.

Chase pushed Mathias back a few inches and stood up. His pants and underwear slipped down his hips. As they did so, his cock poked out between the shirttails. Chase ran his hands along the soft smooth skin of Mathias's chest, enjoying the contrast with the hard muscle it concealed, letting a thumb brush against one nipple and relishing the way it made Mathias's body shudder as a tiny groan escaped Mathias's mouth. Chase let his hands wander lower, taking a firm grasp on Mathias's cock, loving the moan that Mathias couldn't contain. He stroked once, roughly.

"Well, Mathias, you have a pretty impressive cock, too, don't you?" Chase asked.

Mathias seemed to be speechless as he looked down at Chase's hand wrapped around him, and he just nodded.

"I'll bet with a cock like that, you're the one doing the fucking," Chase commented, and again Mathias nodded. "So, let's see if you can follow instructions. Turn around," Chase said, and as he let go of Mathias's cock, he took hold of one shoulder, and in one smooth move, he had Mathias bent across the dining room table.

Chase ran his hands along Mathias's back and ass, fondling more than caressing him, appraising his anatomy like he was at a livestock auction. Beneath him, Chase could feel Mathias shudder and groan at the slightly rough treatment, and he smiled as he thought about what he was going to do next.

"Yes, you've got a sweet ass, too, don't you? I'll bet my cock's gonna like that as much as it likes your mouth," Chase said in a mildly threatening tone.

"You mean you're gonna *fuck* me?" Mathias asked, in mock concern, or so Chase thought.

"Are you going to tell me you won't follow instructions?" Chase asked, just to be sure.

"Are you gonna fuck me into this desk, hard and rough and so deep I won't forget it?" Mathias asked hopefully.

"Yeah, that's what I was planning," Chase said, thrilled with the way Mathias had told him exactly what he wanted.

"Oh," Mathias said, sounding as if the thought both excited and worried him, and Chase knew he was just getting more into the game.

Chase pulled a tube of lube from his inner breast pocket and set it down on the table near Mathias's hip. He spread Mathias's legs farther apart, squeezing and fondling his ass roughly, treating his balls much more delicately, but still not quite lovingly. Mathias wanted to get fucked, and Chase was more than happy to oblige. He slicked up the fingers of one hand with lube and began to prep Mathias, gently at first, then more roughly as Mathias grew louder and more aroused and desperate.

Chase was really looking forward to this. Mathias usually topped, and that was more than fine with Chase, because as he'd said, Mathias's cock was not only a thing of beauty, but he sure as fuck knew how to use it. But tonight Chase was excited about the chance to fuck Mathias without a condom. They'd decided over the summer that they were ready for that step, taken all the tests twice, and there was no doubt that they were exclusive. Just the thought of pushing into Mathias with no barrier between them got Chase even harder—if that were actually possible.

"I thought you were going to fuck me," Mathias said almost petulantly, as Chase slicked more lube on his aching cock. He leaned forward and grabbed a handful of Mathias's hair, pulling Mathias's head around slightly so their eyes met.

"I'm the one making the decisions around here, don't forget that!" Chase told Mathias, hand tightening as he pushed himself unceremoniously into Mathias, enjoying Mathias's gasp of surprise and delight as much as the pleasure that shot through his entire body just from entering Mathias's tight heat and feeling it squeezing around his cock in a whole new way.

Mathias was groaning and pushing back against Chase as Chase fucked him roughly into the smooth, cool surface of the highly polished table. They'd purposely bought a table that could withstand something like this, not some delicate piece of wood that would shatter under the sort of sexual antics they'd both planned. This just happened to be the first of what would undoubtedly be many similar encounters.

Chase was still wearing his suit jacket and hadn't even loosed his tie, and he was burning up. The buttons were probably digging into Mathias's back and the fabric was probably scratchy against his naked skin. It was an odd sensation, being mostly dressed and not feeling Mathias's skin directly against his own, while his bare cock was pushing hard and deep inside of Mathias. Chase just concentrated on those sensations as he listened to the remarkable sounds he was drawing out of Mathias.

"Can you come when I tell you?" Chase grunted between thrusts when he knew he couldn't hold out much longer.

"Yeah, now, soon, please?" Mathias groaned in reply, his hand reaching beneath his body to wrap around his cock.

"Right… now," Chase gasped as his orgasm overtook him, and he grabbed onto Mathias tightly. Under him, Chase could hear Mathias coming and felt the spasms around his own already overstimulated cock squeezing even more ecstasy from him as he shot hot and hard deep inside of Mathias.

Still lying on top of Mathias, Chase wished he hadn't come at the same time as Mathias after all. He wanted Mathias to experience the amazing sensation of feeling Chase's come shooting inside him, the way Chase finally had as Mathias came. This time Mathias was probably too preoccupied with his own orgasm to notice the wondrous feeling, but next time Chase topped, he'd remember to do it that way.

They were both breathing hard, Chase gasping for air, chin digging into Mathias's back.

"Well?" Mathias asked, craning his head around to try and catch Chase's eye.

"Well what?" Chase asked, in parody of their conversation after the very first time they'd made love, when the roles—and the words—were reversed.

"Did I pass the interview?" Mathias asked, reminding Chase of their game.

"Oh, yeah. You're hired," Chase said, completely exhausted. He stood up and flopped back into the nearest chair, nearly tripping on the pants and boxers that were still tangled around his ankles.

Mathias straightened up, turned, leaned down again between Chase's knees and lovingly untied and removed his shoes, then his pants and shorts. Next, he helped Chase out of his jacket, tie, and shirt. Neither of them spoke a word, just enjoyed the quiet intimacy as Mathias carefully undressed Chase.

"You wanna come to bed now… Boss?" Mathias asked softly, adding that last little reminder of their game.

"In a minute," Chase said. "I was just wondering how long you've had that fantasy, since you never mentioned anything about it before," he inquired.

"Oh, from about the time I saw you walk in the door wearing a four thousand dollar suit a little while ago," Mathias said with his million-watt smile. Then he leaned in and kissed Chase, and Chase decided he was the luckiest man in the world, and he'd never, ever let Mathias Tobler get away.

CHAPTER THIRTEEN

Present day
Dallas

NEARLY a week had passed since Lewis and Mathias had returned from New York, and Mathias was in his office scanning the financial screens again, unable to believe what he was seeing. The T-Group share price was still descending. There was no time to waste, and he desperately needed that funding from Mason immediately.

Chase's puts were worth even more now, and he'd be able to exercise the calls and use the proceeds to acquire even more of the T-Group at the lower price. *What in hell is going on here?* Mathias punched numbers into his phone, trying to get in touch with Mason in New York. His secretary said he wasn't available but would call back as soon as possible. Mathias slammed the phone down on his desk again and tried to slow his racing pulse. Mason had been incommunicado for two days. This was very, very bad.

An hour later Mason returned the call. "Mathias, sorry for the delay. We've had some developments over here, and we aren't going to be able to finance you at this time," Mason said, not even attempting to sound apologetic.

"What? What happened? And why am I just hearing about it now? I needed the money last week. A few more days, and it'll be too late." Mathias willed himself to stay calm and professional, but alarms were going off in his head. Everything could be over before it even started if this funding fell through.

"Yeah, we had a change of ownership here, and the Board put several decisions, including your financing, on hold until everything was finalized. I thought you had gotten the notice."

"Change of ownership? I didn't hear a thing." Mathias had a bad feeling about this. "Isn't there supposed to be some notification to your clients?"

"We didn't have anything signed, so it must have slipped through the cracks of our legal department," Mason sounded evasive. "It was a buyout by another private firm and—"

"How could this have happened so quickly?"

"Well… RichardsCorp—"

"RichardsCorp? *Richards*?" Mathias shouted down the line, then slammed the phone down on the desk, shattering it into a million tiny pieces of plastic and metal. He didn't have time to find new financing now. It had taken long enough to get Mason to work with them in the first place. Fucking Chase had acquired an entire New York investment bank just to keep Mathias from fighting off his takeover? How on earth could Mathias compete against that?

Another question flashed in his brain. How had Chase known which bank he'd been working with? Mason had given him the impression that his business was confidential at their first meeting, despite the lack of paperwork.

Enough of this! Mathias got in his car and drove to RichardsCorp headquarters. He needed to find out what the fuck Chase was trying to prove. This couldn't be because Mathias sold the oil-supply companies Chase wanted to buy; clearly it was much bigger. Mathias fought to keep his mind on the road and for the first time, cursed his habit of always driving himself. Most men in his position had a car and driver, and for once he saw the advantage of a few minutes to concentrate and prepare before having to deal with a situation like this.

Mathias parked in a visitor's spot at the RichardsCorp building and calmed himself as he walked into the lobby. It wouldn't do to storm in there. He wouldn't let Chase's tactics twist his normally calm demeanor and pleasant personality. He greeted the receptionist cheerfully, calling her by name after looking at the nameplate, and said Chase was expecting him. It wasn't entirely a lie: it certainly shouldn't surprise Chase that Mathias had shown up after hearing Mason's news. The receptionist smiled and told him to go on up.

Arriving at the top floor, Mathias greeted Chase's secretary in exactly the same friendly fashion, and she didn't even try to stop him as he burst into Chase's office. Mathias suspected that Chase had been expecting him when he saw Brooke there. Her back was to the door, and she didn't see him come in, but Mathias saw everything in one horrible flash of understanding. Chase sat on his couch, Brooke on the couch next to him one hand on his thigh. Chase wasn't even looking at her; he was concentrating on Mathias's face. Brooke's head whipped around as she heard the door open and let out a startled gasp; then she laughed when she saw it was Mathias. She gave him an unapologetic smile as she removed her hand and slowly buttoned up her blouse. Her face was slightly tilted down but Mathias could see the trace of a smile on her lips.

"Oh, Mathias, I wish I had a camera right now. The look on your face is just priceless!" Chase said, his voice dripping with arrogance.

"Fuck you, Chase," Mathias spat the words out forcefully. He'd never meant them more than he did at this moment.

"Well, we were just getting to that, weren't we, Brooke?" Chase said with a derisive laugh. Brooke sat on the couch, not quite meeting Mathias's eyes. "Mathias, I guess you'll have to come to the conclusion by now that everything you had is going to be mine sooner or later."

"You bought the whole fucking bank! At least now I know how you found out about that," Mathias said, looking at Brooke, unsure which made him angrier: Chase's tactics or Brooke's betrayal. Now all of her questions about how he'd save his company, and the sudden interest in his difficulties obtaining financing, made sense. Not to mention her "late dinners" with the ever-changing companions. And Mathias hadn't even suspected anything. Had he trusted Brooke too much, or had he simply been oblivious to what was happening under his nose because he'd stopped paying enough attention to her? Probably both, Mathias conceded, and he'd pay dearly for that lapse.

"Brooke, I'm not even going to ask you for an explanation. I'm just really disappointed in you. I don't think this is going to work out the way you thought it would; just remember that later on. I'm sorry you'll end up being destroyed in this whole thing, too."

"Destroyed? What are you talking about? Chase's going to take better care of me than you can, definitely better than you will be able to once he gets your company. I'm sorry for you, but he's just hard to refuse, you know," Brooke said with a giggle, leaning against Chase on the couch, the way she used to lean against Mathias.

"Do you think Chase's going to *marry* you, and you two will have a nice big magazine house with a stable and a few kids and live happily ever after?" Mathias asked.

He could see from her expression that Brooke hadn't really thought that far ahead. She glanced over at Chase, whose face was typically blank, then back at Mathias, and he saw a tiny flash of doubt in her eyes.

Mathias knew Chase didn't want Brooke unless she had some value to him, and at this moment her worth was about zero. She'd revealed Mathias's business strategies, and now that he knew about her betrayal and collusion with Chase, she offered no further use, not even to embarrass Mathias by rubbing his nose in the fact that she'd chosen Chase over him. Chase might play straight for appearances the way Mathias did, but Brooke would never be in his league, if he were to decide to marry anyone, and she'd figure that out soon.

Mathias was disgusted with himself that he couldn't even summon up more than a token amount of pity for her. The knowledge of what Brooke had done erased any pain or sadness he might have felt for the loss of her love and companionship, such that it was. Their relationship hadn't been perfect recently, but this went far beyond the scope of any of their differences. This was no longer a personal issue between himself and Brooke. Now it involved his entire company, their employees, and their customers, not to mention Mathias's family.

"Brooke, I just don't understand *how* you could do something like this? And why?" Mathias said. "I didn't treat you badly. I don't deserve this kind of betrayal."

"Well, I understand. I understand everything now that Chase's explained it." Her voice got low as if she was concentrating on controlling her words. She took a deep breath. "I should have known you were some sort of pervert, the way you wanted me to do things to you or let you do things to me—in bed." As she continued, the pitch of her voice rose. She seemed to be losing the battle with her emotions.

"What are you talking about?" Mathias asked, truly perplexed. "Understand what?"

"That you're gay!" she shouted, giving up any pretense at self-control. Her chest heaved and she paused for a moment, sitting up straight on the couch. "I didn't believe him at first. Maybe just because I didn't want to. You don't *look* gay or anything. But the more I thought about it, the more it made sense."

This threw Mathias for a loop, and he glared at Chase, who had a look of absolute innocence on his face—and made it seem completely believable.

"He told me how you had a *boyfriend* in business school, and how even now you pick up men—" She shuddered and her voice wavered. "—men in *gay* bars and have *dirty* sex with them." She punctuated her comments so that her shock and disgust were obvious. "He even said he'd seen you in the *bathroom* at the French Room with *our waiter*!" She practically whispered the last part, as if just saying it made her feel dirty.

Mathias was utterly shocked Chase could stoop this low, that he could tell Brooke about Mathias's B-school lover, knowing full well that *he* had been that boyfriend. That drove home to Mathias just how little Chase must have thought of their relationship. And Chase had seen him with the waiter? Mathias would need to be a lot more careful from now on. Unfortunately, everything Brooke had said was true, so Mathias couldn't even accuse Chase of lying.

"You aren't even going to try and deny any of it?" Brooke asked, her voice a cruel blade twisting through his body. "At least now I know where you were all those nights you said you were 'working late'." She pressed her lips into a thin line, but Mathias saw they trembled as much as her voice. Tears rolled down her cheeks. Any semblance of smugness or anger had been replaced by pain.

Mathias couldn't deny any of that—except he had been working late—but at the moment he didn't even care to defend himself to Brooke. She didn't deserve a response—or apology—not after what she'd done, not just to him but to his entire company: employees, shareholders, customers. It was hard to balance that against any grievance she might have had against him.

"Brooke, could you let me speak with Chase alone?" Mathias asked, his voice even and his eyes on Chase the whole time.

She threw a questioning glance at Chase and he nodded. She sniffed loudly, wiping tears from her face, and got up and went through a door in the back of Chase's office. She didn't meet Mathias's gaze. *Probably got a bed in there or worse*, he thought.

He didn't know if he was angrier with Chase for telling Brooke the truth about his past sexual relationships, or for the way she'd believed everything Chase told her without even asking Mathias if it was true. What would he have said to her if she had asked? She never would have understood the truth, or forgiven him for lying to her, he knew that much at least.

"Mathias, you have no idea how easy it was to steal Brooke. You really should be embarrassed," Chase said in a cocky tone as soon as Brooke had closed the door behind herself. "All it took was paying some attention to her and listening to her."

Mathias didn't reply.

"And you know what? This is the best part." Chase laughed again. "The fact that I didn't want to sleep with her was a plus. She thought I was a real gentleman because I said I'd wait until *she* wanted to do anything."

"You sonofabitch. Why couldn't you just keep this between us? Keep it to business. This doesn't have to be personal. You didn't need to ruin everything between Brooke and me."

"Mathias, you still haven't figured out that this is entirely personal? It has nothing to do with business. You told me that I was just like my father, so that's what you're getting: my father. And for the record? I didn't ruin things between you and Brooke. You did that all by yourself. I just used your lies and incompatibilities to my advantage. Besides, you know and I know that she's not what you really want, is she?"

Again, Mathias was silent. He hated that Chase still knew him so well.

"Someday, you'll thank me for saving you. It's perfectly obvious Brooke isn't capable of keeping you happy; don't even try to deny that. You'd never be truly happy again with a woman. That's not who you really are. Just admit it to yourself."

Chase paused, watching Mathias, as if hoping for a reaction, but Mathias refused to give him one.

"Mathias, I have a proposal for you," Chase said, snapping Mathias out of his thoughts. "Let's get this over with. One final battle for the whole thing. Company, Brooke, everything. How about a duel?"

Cute touch, mentioning Brooke. He must still have some use for her, Mathias mused. "A duel? What are you talking about?"

"A fencing match... how's that? Appropriate, don't you think? Look, we both know this takeover battle is hammering your share price and ruining your company, and if it keeps up you'll have nothing left whether I take over the T-Group or not. Let's call it a duel for *your* honor." Chase laughed at the irony of that. "If I win, I get your company. You win, and I leave the Tobler Group alone, *and* you get Brooke back. I do hope you'll invite me to the wedding, though."

What wedding? Brooke didn't want to have anything to do with Mathias now, given her reaction to Chase's revelations about Mathias's sexual activities. Quite frankly, Mathias didn't want her back after her betrayal. Mathias almost admired Chase's style in offering to fence for their final showdown, considering the fact that they'd first met—and fallen in love—while training for the Olympic Fencing Team. Chase's attack on Mathias couldn't be more personal, more than stealing Mathias's family business, or his fiancée. Chase had focused on their past relationship, a relationship *Chase* himself had brushed off like sand from the beach: fun while it lasted, until it became a dirty nuisance.

"Fine. Let's just do it and get it over with. When and where?" Mathias wasn't sure why he'd agreed. He was just so fucking tired and upset he couldn't think straight.

"Next Saturday, at the Club. Noon work for you?"

Ten days from now, Mathias thought.

"Which weapon?" Mathias asked. He expected Chase to choose the saber; it had been his forte.

"Why don't we draw to determine that? Just before the match. Then neither of has any advantage," Chase suggested. "Does that seem fair?"

"Yes, it *seems* fair," Mathias replied through tight lips. Chase would find a way to rig that, too, he suspected. He'd probably pay off the referee as well. Chase never played fair anymore, not since they'd fenced against each other in college. In business—and love—Chase definitely didn't seem to follow any rules but his own.

"Okay, so that's all settled." Chase's tone indicated Mathias could leave.

"Fine." Mathias was anything but fine at this moment. His hands clenched into fists as he tried to slow his pulse. Nothing at all was settled, at least not for him. "And, in the meantime? What about my share price?" Mathias was still standing in front of Chase, and he drew himself up to his full height to remind Chase that he wasn't backing down.

"I won't make another move in the markets. I promise. You'll take my word on that, won't you?" Chase's tone was smug, as if daring Mathias to call him a liar.

"Against my better judgment, yes." There wasn't anything else for Mathias to do, and Chase probably knew that. At least he had the satisfaction of knowing he'd played fairly during the entire takeover attempt, though that didn't count for much at the moment.

"Good. Glad to see you haven't changed a bit. Some people might say that you're just slow. Not me. I'm impressed with the way you stick to your principles, despite the fact that it hasn't really been working all that well for you." Chase's tone was cold and cruel.

"Ten days, and it's all over," Mathias replied just as coldly, turning to walk out of the office.

"Now, where were we, Brooke?" Chase said calling to Brooke in the back room as Mathias opened the door to leave. He could hear Brooke's voice as he closed the door behind himself.

For one brief moment Mathias had to suppress the urge to laugh. When he'd walked in on them, Brooke looked like she was about to give Chase a blow job. She'd never been that eager when she'd been with Mathias. Well, at least he knew he could give better head than Brooke, and by now Chase had already come to that conclusion himself. In bed, Brooke could be more trouble than she was worth, and Chase was demanding. He liked to fuck, and he could go all night—and not always the nice, tender lovemaking Brooke liked. The kind of things Chase liked to do in bed—or have done to him—would shock her. Was she more willing to do them with Chase than she had been with Mathias? He honestly didn't give a flying fuck at this point.

There couldn't be a worse match than the two of them. Mathias smiled slightly to himself. The thought of his two traitorous ex-lovers—together—was the only thing that kept him from being sick to his stomach at everything he'd just discovered. Between Chase's animosity toward him and Brooke's duplicity, they belonged together. Mathias didn't want anything to do with either one of them. The two people he'd once believed had loved him had not only both betrayed him, but they had somehow ended up together trying to take away the thing that was most important to him: his family's business.

Mathias wondered what that said about his ability to choose a partner. He felt like a failure at everything he'd tried to do with his life.

CHAPTER FOURTEEN

CHASE watched Mathias's retreating back knowing he'd almost defeated him already. This was even easier than he'd thought it would be. Mathias was so easy to read—so easy to play. He could easily out-fence him and win the company. Or he could crush it in the market if he happened to lose the match. It almost didn't matter anymore. Whether he won the T-Group or not, he'd taught Mathias a lesson. That already felt good.

He barely noticed when Brooke seated herself on the couch again, waiting for him.

"So, what did he say?" Her tone betrayed her malicious curiosity. She pulled Chase back down onto the couch and snuggled up against him, apparently willing to pick up where they left off. She reached toward his cock, and he stopped her. He certainly didn't want what she was offering now, and he wondered whether he still needed her for his plan to pay back Mathias. She tried to climb into his lap, and he tried to stand up but she pulled him back.

"Brooke, I have work I need to take care of now."

"Can't you go back to work after we have some fun?" she asked, giving him a teasing, sexy look. She'd clearly recovered from her earlier tears. Had that only been a performance? He wondered if she'd done it for Mathias's sake—or for his. Chase looked at her and any charm and beauty she might have had evaporated. He'd never been interested in her physically, but suddenly he was shocked by how easily she'd not only betrayed Mathias, but by how much she seemed to be enjoying it, had enjoyed twisting the knife into Mathias when he'd walked into Chase's office.

"Now's a bad time," Chase told her, his voice even and unapologetic.

"I can't exactly go back to Mathias's place now, can I? Now that he knows about *us*." She lowered her voice to an intimate tone that suddenly made Chase's skin crawl. He cursed himself for failing to realize that now he was responsible for her, and he'd have to offer her a place to stay—temporarily.

"You're right," he said resignedly. "There's plenty of room at my house. I'll have a car take you to Mathias's to pick up some of your things and bring them to my house—I'll let my housekeeper know to expect you. Then you can have the driver for the rest of the evening. Take yourself and a friend out to dinner or shopping or something. Don't wait up for me," he said, disentangling himself from her and standing up.

She clutched at him to sit back down on the couch, but she wasn't strong enough to have any effect on him. He pulled out his wallet and peeled off a few hundred dollars, then handed the crisp new bills to her. He already knew her well enough to be certain this would appease her. She loved shopping and fine dining.

"Thanks, Chase, I'll see you later." She stood up to take the money and kissed him, but he turned his head and her mouth brushed his jaw. Her expression told him the money had placated her for the time being, but she wanted more than that from him. "You're letting me have the limo tonight?"

"No, I need the limo later for... business." He noticed disappointment flash across her face. At least she didn't seem curious about precisely why he needed it. "You can have one of the Mercedes. If you wait in the outer office, Alicia will arrange it all for you."

"Okay." Brooke nodded, but he knew she took it as a personal slight to be downgraded. He gave her enough of a hug and kiss to coax a small smile—she could be dangerous if she was unhappy, that much he already knew. Chase didn't need Brooke to turn on him. He'd make sure she didn't have any ammunition to use against him in the future.

Brooke walked toward the door and turned to flash Chase a coy smile before she sashayed out of the office, but he could see her giving Alicia an unpleasant sneer as she sat down near the secretary's desk.

Chase shut his door behind Brooke, then went to his phone and asked Alicia to arrange the car. He hung up and went back to the couch to think about what had just happened.

The image of Mathias's face when he discovered Brooke here had been a thrilling little victory, and it had gone to Chase's head. But what lingered in his brain was the defeated look when Mathias had left. Chase had chewed him up and spat him out and it showed on Mathias's face, in every inch of his posture, in the way he walked out the door like he was going to the gallows.

That wasn't how this was supposed to go. Chase hadn't started out to destroy Mathias. He'd been trying to win him back, only when that hadn't gone as expected, Chase had acted like his father would and reverted to the tried-and-true Richards way: knock down everything in his path. Now Chase had more chance of winning the Nobel Peace Prize than he had of getting Mathias to love him again. He'd never speak to Chase again, even if he won the damned duel.

That wasn't the plan. That wasn't what Chase wanted. He wanted Mathias back. He'd fucked that up, for damn sure.

I never believed it, but I really have turned into my father. And I have just as much to show for it as he did: everything in the world and no one to share it all with. No one to care if I live or die. I'll never get another chance to show Mathias I'm not like my father, because I am.

He wanted to pick up a chair and hurl it through the window, but he thought he might end up going right after it. Down twenty stories. That couldn't possibly be as painful as the memory of Mathias's face this afternoon. Chase's heart stung.

Business had been easy for Chase because most of the time he didn't fucking care whether he got what he wanted or not. This time, all he wanted had been Mathias. The fear of losing him forever—to Brooke or anyone else—had driven him to a desperation he barely understood, and it clouded his judgment. In his quest for revenge, he'd threatened two of the things Mathias loved most: his family business and his fiancée.

All Chase knew was he'd never stop loving Mathias and the pain of losing him again would be too much to bear. There had to be a way to put the shattered pieces of their love back together.

MATHIAS went back to his office after he left RichardsCorp head-quarters. He walked past Pam's empty desk and went into his office, slamming the door behind him. His open-door policy was over for the foreseeable future. He needed privacy and a quiet place to think.

At least Pam had already gone for the day. Mathias couldn't face her, or explain his state of mind; she was far too sharp for his mood to go unnoticed. As he approached his desk, he noticed that someone—most likely Pam—had cleaned up the pieces of the broken telephone and replaced it with a new one. Yes, she definitely knew something far beyond ordinary had happened.

Sitting down at his desk, Mathias glanced at the monitor that for the past several weeks had been dedicated to T-Group share price data. The market had closed with their stock down *again*. If the price fell another ten percent, shareholders would be lining up to accept Chase's latest tender offer for the company. Chase promised not to continue interfering in the market, but Mathias still had no reason to believe him. Even if he stopped playing with options, unfavorable market sentiment could continue to push the price down into the danger zone that would make Chase's offer look attractive, or leave the T-Group open to a bid from another company. They weren't safe yet.

Mathias squeezed his eyes shut, head in his hands, and tried to clear his mind and think. It was impossible. He'd fucked things up royally, and he was just waiting for shareholders or his family to begin demanding answers as to how this had happened. How could he possibly explain that Chase had done this just to take revenge on Mathias, or that Mathias had told confidential information to his fiancée and she'd leaked it to Chase? Even if he managed to keep the company out of Chase's hands, Mathias was probably through as CEO. It might be a family business to *him*, but to Wall Street and the shareholders it was only about business, and Mathias had failed as spectacularly as possible. He'd let his family down and hundreds, even thousands, of people would pay the price.

The harsh sound of his cell phone pulled him out of his despair, at least temporarily. He glanced at the caller ID—his mother. She'd always been there when Mathias needed support or advice, and he desperately needed it now, but he wasn't quite ready to discuss what had happened that day. He hoped a conversation with her would pull him out of his current troubles, even if only temporarily.

"Hi, Mom." Mathias tried to keep his tone positive.

"Honey, I'm sorry to disturb you, since I know you have a lot on your plate right now." Marta Tobler's voice sounded as weary as Mathias felt. It could only be bad news—something about his father—but Mathias hoped he was wrong.

"I always have time for you, Mom. You know that. How are you, and how's Dad?"

"Mattie, hon, that's why I'm calling. Your dad's not doing very well, and—"

"I'm leaving now, I can be there in a few hours," Mathias said, interrupting her.

"No, don't come… yet. He's going for some tests tomorrow. We'll know more when we get the results. You should wait and visit then, okay?"

"Are you sure it can wait?"

"Positive," Marta said. "And I have a message for you. Your dad thinks you're doing a great job right now. He knows you're doing everything you can, and he's proud of you, no matter what happens."

"Thanks, Mom," Mathias said quietly. Tears began pouring silently down his cheeks. His father was sick—possibly dying—and he wanted to make sure Mathias knew he was still proud of his son. It killed Mathias to know that right now his father was worrying about him and not focusing on his own health. There was no way Mathias could let them know that the financing had fallen through. His only chance now was to beat Chase in the duel the following week, or it wouldn't only be the company that would be hurt by Chase's actions; Jerry Tobler's health might also be at risk.

"I'll call you as soon as we have any news."

"Okay, Mom. Love you and love to Dad." Mathias closed the phone and laid his head on his arms, realizing how close he was to losing every single thing that he loved. Chase hadn't just gone after the company and Brooke. Now Mathias's dad was going to end up being another casualty.

How on earth had Mathias ever cared about Chase? Chase had said he often acted like other people as a way to overcome his shyness. Could he have been *acting* for the three years they'd been together? Chase couldn't be that good an actor; no one could, Mathias decided. The Chase he'd talked to today, the one who had stolen his fiancée and was still trying to steal his family business, was nothing like the man that Mathias had loved years ago. Mathias knew he still loved *that* Chase. But he hated the one that was trying to ruin his life now—and getting damn close to succeeding. Mathias doubted that their past relationship could have meant anywhere near as much to Chase as it had to Mathias. Or else how could Chase just have thrown it all away like that... for money? And now, Chase was proving to Mathias just how little he'd meant to Chase.

For the next several hours, Mathias sat in his office, staring out the large picture window, watching the sky get progressively darker and darker as his thoughts followed suit. He tried to concentrate on work, but his mind kept turning over the day's events, bringing him closer and closer to absolute despair. He knew he should head home and get a decent night's sleep, but he couldn't bear the thought of walking into the condo and seeing so many reminders of Brooke— and her now-obvious treachery.

He'd wondered lately whether he belonged with her, but she'd answered that question loud and clear. How could he have made the same mistake again? He'd avoided anything approaching a real relationship after the pain of breaking up with Chase. He survived on casual sex and poured his heart and soul into the T-Group. When Brooke had come into his life, he'd been caught off guard. She'd brought a light and warmth back to him he'd thought he'd never feel again. Had she just been putting on an act to lure him in? Today the mask had come off completely, just as he'd found out years before that he meant less to Chase than a job.

Now his two ex-lovers were together, both having gotten revenge on Mathias. They deserved each other—for however long *that* would last. And Mathias was alone again. He'd never trust anyone again. His heart was shattered, and he couldn't bear the thought of enduring more agony. He looked around the office, at the reminders of everything his family had built. He'd lost that too. He'd loved too much and it only heightened the anguish of loss.

Finally, he took the elevator down to the garage, got into his white Lexus GS Hybrid, and began to head for home. Against his better judgment, he found himself taking a detour which brought him past a club where he'd go when he was looking for a quick, no-strings fuck. That sounded pretty damn good right now, and he pulled into the parking lot. He wasn't really dressed for a club, but he hadn't come to impress anyone. He knew what he wanted and how to get it. Once inside, he headed for the bar, ordering two shots of Lapiz Platinum tequila and downing them in quick succession. He fought off the impulse to order a whole bottle. Well, maybe afterward, he thought. No one could blame him, could they?

He turned around on his barstool with his back to the bar, facing the room so he could scope out who was here tonight—and who might be what he was looking for. Instinctively, he found himself noticing well-built men with dark blonde hair who bore any sort of resemblance to Chase. *Fuck Chase Richards*, Mathias thought. He couldn't even get Chase out of his thoughts despite everything he'd done. Either he wanted to kill Chase for fucking with his company and making him jump through hoops to save it, or he found himself daydreaming about the way things used to be between them. The way they'd loved each other, and the relationship they'd had. It had been good—nearly perfect—right until the very end when Chase had finally shown his true colors, when Chase chose work—and a million dollars—over Mathias.

He needed to get the images of Chase out of his brain. He'd pick someone here who was the complete opposite of Chase, maybe that would work. Mathias prayed it would work. He turned toward the bar again and ordered two more shots.

"Hey." Mathias heard a voice behind him as he put down the glass after he'd knocked back the second one. When he turned to look he saw a short, slight man in his midthirties, wearing a limo driver's uniform. Not exactly Mathias's type, but certainly dead opposite from Chase. He must be pretty drunk already if he was even remotely considering going in the back with this guy.

"How tall are you?" the man asked Mathias.

"What?" This was an odd approach, but he was intrigued. Yeah, he was on the way to getting completely fucked up if he was actually talking to a limo driver. No doubt about that now.

"How tall are you? Six-three, six-four?"

"About six-four," Mathias confirmed. "Why?"

"You work out?" The guy asked as if he were reading from a questionnaire.

"Okay, what the fuck is this?" Mathias started to get annoyed with the third degree.

"My boss, he has a certain *type*, you know," Limo Driver explained.

"Your boss?"

"Yeah, you're his type and he'd like to spend some time with you, outside." The man craned his head in the direction of the parking lot.

"Oh, really?" Mathias was just messed up enough—and desperate enough—that he was actually considering the possibility. "Doing what?"

"He's got a limo out back. He'll fuck you, then I have $1000 for you afterwards. More if he really likes you," Limo Driver said nonchalantly, as if he were ordering a cheeseburger at McDonald's. "He'll use a condom and lube, and he won't hurt you or force you to do anything that you don't want to. You just have to wear a blindfold."

"What the *fuck*? Why on earth would I want to do that?" Mathias shook his head and motioned for another shot. "How do I know I'm not getting in a car with an axe murderer or something?"

"It's safe, you can trust them." The bartender poured another drink for Mathias. "His boss comes around here few times a month, and no one's ever complained. Trust me, I woulda heard about it if the guy was hurtin' people," he added. "People won't put up with that, even for a thousand bucks. No one's that desperate in this place."

Limo Driver nodded convincingly. Mathias couldn't believe he was seriously considering this offer and listening to a bartender's assurances, but he was in a dangerous mood tonight. The idea of doing something as risky as what this driver proposed seemed like just the right thing. Just let someone else be in charge for a while. No one had fucked him for a very long time, and now he was going to let some complete stranger do it? Maybe afterward Mathias would come to his senses and realize he had to stop going to places like this. He had to make a decision: either be straight and marry a nice, deserving woman and be a real husband to her, or admit he really wanted to be with a man. Unfortunately, he couldn't be with the one man who had made him truly happy—and truly unhappy—but if he came out, he could try to have a genuine relationship with someone, and get Chase Richards out of his system.

"Okay. Deal," Mathias said in a businesslike tone. "Lead the way." He'd probably regret this, but at the moment, for some unfathomable reason, he was actually looking forward to it.

They went out the back door, where a sleek black stretch limo was parked. When they got to the rear door, the driver carefully tied a black silk blindfold on Mathias. He felt disoriented, but strangely not worried or frightened at all. He knew he should be, and that was what really scared him. The fact that climbing into a limo and getting fucked by a complete stranger was suddenly a turn-on. He was actually getting hard just from wondering about what was going to happen to him. He was so fucking tired of making decisions that he liked the idea of ceding control to someone else and not having to think for even a little while.

He heard the driver open the limo door and felt the man gently guide him inside. He could tell it was dimly lit, but he couldn't actually see a thing. He knew someone else was inside with him because he'd heard the man's sharp intake of breath when Mathias had bent down to climb inside. But the man hadn't spoken yet.

CHASE couldn't believe his eyes when Sheppard came back with the trick and it wasn't simply a Mathias look-alike—it *was* Mathias. The real Mathias Tobler—*his* Mathias—was here, in his limo, having agreed to let Chase do whatever he wanted. At one level, Chase was thrilled with the chance to be with Mathias again. God, how he'd missed his body, the way he looked and felt and tasted, and the way that body made Chase feel when Mathias touched him.

But under the surface of the thrill at having Mathias here was the horrible knowledge he had sunk so low as to let strangers pick him up and fuck him. Had he been that unhappy with Brooke—so sexually unfulfilled—that this was how he found his substitute? It scared Chase to think of the danger Mathias put himself in tonight, and he wondered how many times he had done this. Not all the guys who did what Chase did were as careful as he was. Plenty of them would hurt the tricks or refuse to use a condom.

Then a horrible notion flashed through his mind. Had *Chase* driven him to this? Pushed him into a corner financially and threatened everything that Mathias cared about—personally and professionally? Could it be Brooke's betrayal with Chase, causing Mathias to lose his financial backing, sealing the fate of the Tobler Group? Chase had once considered using Brooke a real stroke of genius, but conceded he'd gone too far.

While Chase wondered what had brought Mathias here, his eyes took in everything. As soon as Mathias climbed into the limo Chase noticed the hard-on tenting his trousers. It both pleased and frightened Chase. Mathias had gotten aroused simply by the idea of stepping into the unknown. At least Chase would take good care of Mathias, but hoped like hell he never did anything like this again.

But for tonight, Mathias belonged to him again, and Chase intended to make the most of the opportunity.

Chase wanted more than anything to pull Mathias close and kiss him for a very long time, but he knew that he couldn't do that. Kissing didn't much happen in these situations; *fucking* was what happened. Yes, he wanted to fuck Mathias, but he also wanted to shout how much he still loved him and wanted him back, and Chase bit his tongue so he wouldn't. He wouldn't just use Mathias like another trick—like some toy he'd bought and paid for, even if that were essentially true. Instead, he was going to make sure that the time they spent together tonight would be as good for Mathias as it was for him.

He moved close to Mathias, taking in his still-familiar scent. They hadn't been this close in nine years, but the way Chase's body reacted to Mathias made it seem as if hardly a day had passed. He still felt everything as intensely as the last time they'd made love. He reached out and ran the back of his finger along Mathias's jaw, enjoying the end-of-the-day stubble. Mathias flinched slightly with surprise at the touch, but relaxed under Chase's gentle touch. This close, Chase could smell tequila and wondered how drunk Mathias was, whether that had influenced his behavior tonight. Again, Chase was thankful that Mathias had ended up here and not with someone else who might take advantage of him.

With one fingertip, Chase traced the outline of Mathias's lips—the closest he could get to kissing them, before letting his hand travel down his throat to his collarbone. He began to unbutton Mathias's shirt, slowly revealing the beautifully muscled chest. Mathias still took excellent care of his body. A shame it had been wasted on the undeserving Brooke. Well, not anymore, thanks to Chase. At least tonight Chase would properly appreciate every single gorgeous inch of Mathias's body.

"Mmmm, nice." Chase whispered as he ran his fingertips across Mathias's chest, caressing him, lingering to rub and pinch the nipples into hard, tight buds, enjoying the sharp intake of breath from Mathias. Chase leaned down, first licking, then fastening his mouth on one nipple, making Mathias groan and shudder as Chase sucked at the hard nub, carefully scraping his teeth over it as he pinched at the other nipple.

Instinctively Chase's body remembered just how and where to touch Mathias, and he responded as he always had, arching into Chase's touch. Mathias's breath was getting shorter and shallower, and he leaned against the seat, head thrown back, offering himself up for Chase to touch him as he pleased, clearly trusting him.

Chase had been hard from the moment he first touched Mathias, and by the time he'd gotten Mathias's shirt off, his cock throbbed and his balls ached. He unzipped his own pants to get more comfortable, then went back to Mathias. He slowly unbuckled Mathias's belt, brushing his fingers across Mathias's hard-on through his pants, feeling it twitch and hearing his moans.

As Chase pushed Mathias's pants down his hips, he could see the damp spot on his shorts, and wanted Mathias's cock in his mouth.

He'd always loved sucking Mathias's cock. From that very first time, when he licked him clean, Chase was mesmerized by it.

"Lift your hips." Chase realized Mathias might recognize his voice and tried to exaggerate his accent to disguise his voice. Mathias complied, helping Chase slip his pants and shorts down, kicking off his own shoes as Chase pulled his clothing away.

Chase couldn't help but just stare at Mathias's hard, beautiful cock, and he remembered the very first time he'd seen it—that day so long ago in the locker room in Colorado Springs, when Mathias had practically teased Chase, showing off his body to see how Chase would react. This time Chase's reaction was so much stronger—with memory and longing and almost wonder at his own luck to have Mathias here with him again tonight—despite the animosity that had grown between them and come to a peak earlier that day in Chase's office.

He knew he'd only made a deal to fuck Mathias, but Chase couldn't help the way his mouth watered at the sight of Mathias's cock, and Chase didn't even bother to stop himself, so he leaned down to take as much of Mathias into his mouth as he could. Mathias groaned a mixture of surprise and pleasure as Chase's mouth went to work.

Oh God, how wonderful and familiar he tasted, Chase thought as his tongue slid up the length, flicking across the slit and around the head before taking it back into his mouth and sucking some more. It was so fucking good having Mathias's cock in his mouth again, and Chase thought he might actually come just from sucking Mathias off. That wasn't quite what he'd planned, so after a few delicious moments, he reluctantly let go, giving a few last licks to the head as he turned his attention to the rest of Mathias. He let his hands and mouth travel along the chiseled muscles of Mathias's chest and six-pack. Chase finished undressing himself as he did, then got Mathias on his hands and knees on the long seat that ran the length of the back of the limo.

Mathias's ass was just as perfectly shaped as the rest of his body and Chase rubbed his cock along the crease while his hands fondled the familiar curves, moaning at how good it felt to be with Mathias again. He fought off the urge to moan out Mathias's name, but it was difficult. So many ingrained memories of so many times they'd made love that Chase had to consciously fight. He tugged and played with Mathias's balls briefly, knowing how much he liked that. Chase wanted to make this as good for Mathias as it was for him. The danger in that was that it might encourage Mathias to do this again, but for now, Chase had to take that risk. He certainly didn't want to hurt Mathias, just to teach him a lesson.

"You're gonna put on a condom, right?" Mathias asked, sounding slightly unsure.

"Yeah, don't worry," Chase said in his fake, thick Texas accent, hoping he sounded reassuring.

"Can you put it on now, so I'm sure… before you do anything?" Mathias insisted, and Chase was actually glad. At least he was being careful.

"Sure," Chase said. He opened up a condom and rolled it down onto his cock. He had been kneeling behind Mathias, but he moved to Mathias's side, then he guided Mathias's hand and placed on his cock, so he could feel that Chase had put the condom on. At the touch of Mathias's fingers on his cock for the first time in nine years, Chase couldn't control the groan that escaped his lips, as his body reacted to the familiar touch that had always given him such pleasure in the past.

"Thanks." Mathias visibly relaxed, completely unaware of the effect he had on Chase, who was even more grateful he'd insisted on the blindfold.

Chase grabbed the lube and slicked up the fingers of one hand and moved to kneel behind Mathias. With his index finger, Chase traced a circle around Mathias's hole, gently applying pressure, wanting to get Mathias worked up for this. Chase wondered how many times Mathias had let some stranger fuck him like this. If he did this blindfolded with strangers, he must be letting anyone fuck him nowadays. When they'd been together, Chase had bottomed most of the time, and topped only now and then. The thought that god-knows-who had been fucking Mathias cut through Chase's gut, and he fought back jealousy. He had no right to feel any of that, but it didn't lessen the pain.

He pushed his finger into Mathias a bit more forcefully than he'd meant to and Mathias stiffened at the rough intrusion. Chase wriggled the finger around, pulling slightly to the side, opening Mathias up. He tried a second finger, but Mathias wasn't loose enough yet.

"Damn, you're tight," Chase said with some surprise, but also even more excited by the knowledge of how good it was going to be once he was inside.

"Been a pretty long time since I've done this," Mathias said casually. "Years."

"Really?" Chase asked before he could stop himself. Well, at least no one had been in here for a while, he thought with an unexpectedly enormous sense of relief. He tried not to go as far as to hope that he'd been the last one, but he couldn't stop himself. "I'll be careful," Chase added in order to put Mathias at ease.

He slipped a second finger in, and worked them around. This was going awfully slowly, Chase thought, not that he was in a huge hurry. He did want to get his cock in there, but he also didn't want to hurt Mathias, and he planned to take his time and enjoy playing with him and making it enjoyable for both of them. He pulled both fingers out and heard Mathias's surprised gasp. That was nothing compared to the sound Mathias made as Chase leaned down and licked around Mathias's tight, pink pucker. A few more swirls, then Chase eased just the tip of his tongue inside, causing Mathias to moan and push his hips back.

Chase had never done this with anyone he'd had in the limo before, but with Mathias it just seemed right. Mathias's body was safe, familiar territory for Chase, and he also knew how much Mathias loved being rimmed—as much as Chase loved doing it.

"Oh, yeah." Mathias groaned as Chase thrust his tongue in deeper, licking and prodding and twisting it inside. He kept fucking Mathias with his tongue, feeling his own cock get harder and heavier with each thrust and every groan from Mathias. He worked a few fingers in there, too, so he could brush against Mathias's prostate and enjoy the way Mathias's body shuddered and squeezed around his fingers as he groaned uncontrollably. A few more minutes, and Mathias was pretty close to ready. But still, Chase licked and sucked and slurped at Mathias's ass. Finally, he pulled away.

"Ready for my cock now?" Chase's own hunger and impatience crept into his voice.

Mathias nodded and groaned and shoved his hips back roughly. He definitely needed to be fucked now, that much was obvious from the way he was acting. Chase was so hot and hard at this point, he wasn't sure how much longer he could wait. He needed to fuck Mathias even more than Mathias needed it.

"I didn't hear what you said," Chase said roughly.

"Yeah. God, yeah. Fuck me!" Mathias growled. "Fucking fuck me already, you fucking tease!"

That did it. Chase jammed himself deep into Mathias with one rough stroke, and Mathias groaned again wantonly, as if he'd have died if he hadn't gotten a cock into him that instant. The intensity of Mathias's response surprised Chase, but it got him even hotter and he fucked into Mathias like a jackhammer. *Oh God*, Chase thought, *this is even better than I remember.*

"So hot… and tight… and so fucking… amazing." Chase was unable to stop himself from blurting the words. He'd come if he kept up his pace, so he slowed himself down. He leaned back slightly so he could watch his cock gliding in and out of Mathias, taking his time now and savoring the sight as well as the sensations. Mathias kept grunting and thrusting back at him, wanting it harder and deeper. In all the times they'd been together, Chase had never seen Mathias like this, like he'd given up every inhibition and just needed someone to teach him a very rough lesson, begging Chase to go faster and harder. Chase didn't want to treat Mathias like a whore; he wished he could make love to him and treat him gently and lovingly, but that wasn't an option. God, he had to admit he liked this Mathias and wanted to fuck his brains out right now, and then again later on and again after that. He wondered whether he could get Mathias to stay in the limo with him for another session later on. How long could he keep Mathias here before he got suspicious or tried to take off the blindfold?

Not long enough, Chase knew—only *forever* would really be long enough—so he concentrated on fucking Mathias here and now, slightly speeding up his movements again. The way Mathias moved and the noises he made nearly sent Chase over the edge several times and he had to concentrate to hold back his orgasm. Every groan vibrated through him and amplified the sensations zinging all the way to his toes. It was all going to be over way too fast for Chase, and he had to slow things down again, draw out the experience—and the pleasure—for both of them. He could tell from Mathias's grunts and half sobs that he was very close as well. Chase thought maybe he wouldn't let Mathias come yet, maybe he could get Mathias to fuck him instead, but realized that was asking too much in the current situation. When Mathias's hand moved onto his own cock, Chase pushed it away roughly.

"Don't worry… I'll take care of you," Chase said.

"Wanna… feel… your cock in me… when I come," Mathias grunted out between Chase's thrusts.

Chase wrapped his hand loosely around Mathias's cock, feeling how hard and heavy it was, and loving the way Mathias groaned as he increased the pressure of his grip. He stroked a few times.

"Harder!" Mathias begged, his body beginning to shudder and he thrust his hips up against Chase, head nearly down on the seat on front of him, giving him plenty of leverage to push back.

Chase reached out with his other hand and grabbed a handful of Mathias's hair, partly to balance himself and partly because he'd wanted to touch it since Mathias had entered the limo. He knew Mathias liked having it pulled as much as Chase used to like pulling it. As Chase yanked roughly, Mathias's head snapped back and he let out a shout that would have frightened Chase except he could feel Mathias coming as his body spasmed around Chase's cock and Mathias let go, splashing his own chest and the leather seat below him with thick creamy strands. Chase didn't care, because he was coming, too, shouting and gasping for breath as wave after wave of pleasure crashed through his body and he held onto Mathias for dear life.

This might not have been the best orgasm Chase had ever had—though it was probably close—but it was certainly one of the sweetest. *Bittersweet.* Because he knew that this was undoubtedly the last time he'd ever be with Mathias. Chase had fucked things up beyond repair with him, and Mathias was never going to forgive him—even if Chase lost the duel, and Mathias kept the T-Group. Chase had to imprint every last detail of tonight in his memory, and that would have to sustain him through a future of unsatisfying anonymous sexual encounters.

Chase didn't know how much time had passed when he finally opened his eyes. He was sprawled on top of Mathias who lay face down on the seat, slick and sticky from his own orgasm. Chase caught his breath and knew he couldn't keep Mathias here much longer without risking Mathias discovering his identity. The blindfold was slightly askew, and Chase leaned down to straighten it. He let his lips brush against Mathias's back, trailing soft kisses here and there along the base of his spine, knowing how much more he wanted to give—and to take—right now.

"I'm sorry." Chase mouthed the words silently, lips pressed against the small of Mathias's back. "I love you," he added in the quietest of whispers, half wanting Mathias to hear it.

Slowly, reluctantly, Chase pulled out of Mathias and disposed of the condom before helping Mathias put on his underwear and pants. He handed Mathias a damp washcloth and watched as Mathias blindly dabbed at his chest, not knowing where to clean. Chase took the cloth and carefully wiped him clean. He'd never helped anyone before. He'd never even offered the cloth before, he realized, suddenly ashamed of how he'd treated the men who'd been in here before Mathias.

"Thanks," Mathias said as Chase cleaned him up.

No one had ever thanked Chase before either. Jesus, what a complete asshole he'd been. Mathias had been right to compare him to his father… and right then Chase's own self-righteousness burned bitter in his stomach. He'd learned a lot of lessons today, and each and every one had been agonizing as he discovered how much he'd become exactly the thing he'd despised. He wanted more than anything to change—to go back to being the kind of man that Mathias might care about again, whether or not he got him back. Chase couldn't live with himself, with the depths of his ruthlessness and just how little thought he'd given to the consequences his actions had on others.

He helped Mathias finish dressing, taking his time and allowing his fingers to linger here and there, knowing he'd never have the chance—or the right—to touch Mathias again like this. Chase pulled his own underwear and pants on then donned his shirt, leaving it unbuttoned. After caressing Mathias's face one last time, Chase reluctantly opened the limo door and guided Mathias out, steadying him so he wouldn't fall, while remaining in the limo. He'd never helped anyone out before either.

Once Mathias was on his feet, Chase pulled the door shut, finished dressing himself and poured a large whiskey from a heavy crystal decanter in the limo's bar. He gulped half of it down then sat back heavily in his seat and waited for his driver to take him home. He was shattered and exhausted and he could still smell Mathias on himself, in the car, and he couldn't stop thinking about how Mathias had felt with him earlier—and how good it had felt to be with him again. Chase sighed deeply, startled as he heard his driver open the front door and get back inside the limo.

"MR. RICHARDS?" Sheppard asked over the intercom after he'd started the engine.

"Yes?" Chase opened the window between the front and the back of the limo. The driver turned around and held up a wad of cash.

"He wouldn't take it?" Chase asked.

"Yeah, he did. But then he pulled off one bill and said 'Here's a tip,' then he handed all but that one bill to me."

"Well, in that case, keep it." Chase received a startled look in response. "It was his to do with as he wanted, and if he wanted *you* to have it, then so be it." That sounded exactly like something Mathias would do. It wasn't like he needed the money.

"Oh, and one more thing… he kept the blindfold."

"Don't worry about it," Chase told him, then closed the partition.

He sat back in his seat and smiled. He wouldn't be needing that blindfold ever again. Tonight would be the last time he picked anyone up in the limo. He also knew the driver was probably more surprised at Chase's attitude than the fact that Mathias had given him a $980 tip. Well, Chase would surprise a lot of people from now on, or at least he hoped so.

CHAPTER FIFTEEN

MATHIAS got into his car and sat behind the wheel for a long time, thinking, trying to clear his head. No, he didn't want to think clearly after all, he decided. What he really wanted was about twenty more shots of tequila, but he knew that wasn't a good idea. Maybe he'd do that when he got home, but he was careful about drinking and driving. He could just get a taxi home, but he didn't really want to hang out in the bar now either. Not after that bartender knew he'd just been in the limo with the mystery man.

Mystery man, Mathias thought. He'd gone along with the whole ridiculous scenario just trying to get the idea of Chase Richards out of his head and his body. Chase had been the only man who'd ever fucked Mathias—until tonight. Mathias had hoped letting some complete stranger do it would obliterate any last trace memory of Chase's body from Mathias's mind, but he'd been wrong. Worse even. For some reason, everything about that man tonight had made Mathias think about Chase. The way he touched Mathias, stroking him, kissing his body, even the way he sucked Mathias's cock made Mathias think about Chase.

What the fuck is wrong with me? There wasn't anyone on the planet that he despised more than Chase, yet he still wanted to be with him, still remembered the way it felt to make love with Chase, and now, after everything that Chase had done to him, Mathias couldn't get him out of his mind. He felt that he was seeing, hearing, *feeling* Chase every fucking place and it was making Mathias crazy.

But why did Chase Richards still have such a hold on him? How could it be that even after all these years, Mathias couldn't erase the feeling of Chase's fingers caressing him, or the way Chase had made love to him that very first time back in Colorado? And why was that all Mathias could think about when he'd been in the back of some stranger's limo parked behind a club where he'd let him fuck him for money? Mathias put his head in his hands and wondered whether or not he was going mad. The shocking truth was that Chase was still part of Mathias, down to his essence, whether Mathias wanted him to be or not.

Mid-July 2000
Rocky Mountain National Park, Colorado

THEY had a week break between the trials and the start of official Olympic training. Even though they were alternates, they were expected to attend all the training sessions and stay in peak condition. The fencers who hadn't made the team had a few days to pack and leave, before everyone else began the most rigorous training of their lives.

The break coincided with Mathias's birthday, and Chase and Mathias decided to camp for a few days in the Rocky Mountain National Park, a few hours' drive from the training center. Chase rented an SUV and bought a new tent and sleeping bags and everything they'd need. He'd even shopped for food and made reservations for camping permits. Mathias could see how much Chase enjoyed planning their little excursion, and all he had to do was go along for the ride.

"Chase, we're only going for a few days, why did you buy all of this stuff? You could just have rented," Mathias said as they drove to the park.

"Much easier than renting, plus this is the best gear out there. You'll be glad we got the good stuff, trust me. And when we're done, I'll donate it to some kids' camp around here. There's gotta be a dozen of them nearby. It won't go to waste, trust me," Chase had said.

The drive to the park took about three hours, with a detour loop around downtown Denver and its associated traffic. Even miles away from the Eastern entrance to the park, the Rockies—still snowcapped in mid-summer—rose majestically, and Mathias and Chase were both excited about the break from training.

For the first day's hike, they chose a moderately difficult trail to a field where bighorn sheep grazed all summer. They saw a small herd and sat quietly watching the sheep, far enough away to avoid disturbing the animals. Chase leaned back against a tree and Mathias sat between his legs, leaning back while Chase twisted his fingers in Mathias's long hair. Mathias smiled, loving the feel of Chase's body supporting him and the way even the smallest touch of Chase's fingers—in his hair, on his arm—made his heart race. Their vantage point was visible to anyone coming along the trail, so they decided—reluctantly—to wait until they got to their campsite before fooling around.

They hiked back to the car then drove to the trailhead for their campsite, another two-mile trek from the road. The gear weighed a ton, but hiking with packs made good conditioning for fencers, excellent for building lower-body strength, and they made good time. The tent took fifteen minutes to assemble, and there was still plenty of light as Chase went about preparing dinner, which entailed heating up canned soup and toasting bread over the small fire they'd built in the fire ring. They ate hungrily, and after dinner Chase surprised Mathias with a small chocolate birthday cake on which he'd placed a single candle.

"But my birthday isn't until tomorrow," Mathias protested, though he was thrilled that Chase had thought to get a cake for him.

"It's tomorrow somewhere by now, so hurry up and make a wish before we start a forest fire!" Chase joked, and Mathias quickly blew out the candle. Chase planted a large sloppy kiss on him before producing the second surprise: a bottle of champagne.

"It's not as cold as it should be, but I'm sure it will do the trick." Chase expertly opened the bottle, not spilling any of the contents and pouring champagne into plastic cups. "Now you're legal—for everything." Chase gave Mathias a wicked grin.

They knocked their cups together, splashing some liquid and laughing, before drinking.

"Thanks, Chase! This is amazing, spending this birthday with you, here."

"So, Tee, what did you wish for?" Chase cocked one eyebrow and traced his hand slowly up Mathias's leg, from the knee toward his thigh.

Mathias playfully knocked the hand away, though the touch had already gotten his dick stirring.

"I certainly didn't waste my wish on sex," Mathias said. "I don't need to wish to get that, do I?"

"No, you don't." Chase shook his head then kissed Mathias in a very promising way. "What did you wish for?"

"I can't tell you or I won't get my wish, now will I?"

"Ve haff vays of makink you talk," Chase said in a fake Eastern European accent. He stood up and pulled Mathias to his feet, then tugged him in the direction of the tent.

Even in the height of summer, at the elevation of the park it was freezing once the sun had gone down. Inside the tent, though, it was warm and cozy, and Chase and Mathias snuggled together under top-of-the-line sleeping bags, zipped together into one large pocket that fit both of them.

"Now I'll bet you're not complaining that I bought brand new gear, are you?" Chase teased.

"No, you were right," Mathias conceded.

"I like how that sounds. Can you say it a few more times?"

"Once is plenty, and I'll probably never need to say it again." Mathias landed a playful punch on Chase's shoulder.

"There are better things to do than argue, aren't there?" Chase pulled Mathias close and kissed him deeply, definitely getting the point across.

It didn't take long for them to get out of their clothes as they explored each other's bodies hungrily with mouths and hands.

"Chase, tonight, I want you to make love to me... so I can feel you inside me," Mathias whispered before he resumed kissing Chase's neck and throat.

"You're sure?"

"Yes. Positive." As certain as Mathias thought he was about this, he admitted to himself he was a little frightened. But he truly did want to be close to Chase, and this was the closest they could get, so Mathias wanted it.

Chase unzipped the sleeping bags partway, to make more room for them to move comfortably, and reached toward his backpack for lube and condoms, which he set down on the tent floor next to them, then turned his attention back to Mathias.

Mathias lay on his back, Chase hovering over him. The sleeping bag was still too constricting and Chase just unzipped it all the way open.

"Not too cold for you?"

"No, just fine," Mathias answered. "You always get me hot, you know that."

Chase kissed his way down Mathias's body, lingering at his nipples, and Mathias remembered the first time they'd been together. His nipples were so sensitive, and Chase was almost cruel to pay too much attention to them, but Mathias knew how much Chase loved the way Mathias reacted to his fingers or mouth, loved to drive Mathias crazy like this. Chase kept kissing and licking a burning, wet trail down and around Mathias's navel before encountering Mathias's cock, hot and hard and begging for attention. Chase happily went to work with his mouth as he squeezed some lube into his hand.

With one gentle finger, Chase slowly circled Mathias's entrance, applying only light pressure around the outside. He'd had a finger inside of Mathias before, but until now that had been it. Tonight Mathias knew Chase would take his time and be gentle. Mathias moaned and spread his legs wider as Chase worked his finger around. Mathias closed his eyes, letting Chase know he was enjoying this so far. When Chase tried to push in a second finger, Mathias tensed. Realizing Mathias wasn't ready, Chase kept on with the first one, brushing up against Mathias's prostate, and Mathias couldn't contain the sounds that exploded out of him as the finger brushed the sensitive spot. They'd done this before, too, but somehow tonight it felt even more mind-blowing. When Chase tried again to slip another finger inside, Mathias once again tensed up.

"Tee, let's try this. Get on your hands and knees for me?" Chase patted his knee and Mathias changed position.

"I wanted to see your face when you make love to me." He wanted it to be like it had been the first time he'd been with Chase. This position didn't seem right for his first time—not intimate enough.

"Don't worry, you will. I'm still getting you ready. Then you can lie down on your back again, okay?"

"Okay." Mathias couldn't see what Chase was going to do.

He found out soon enough as Chase spread Mathias's cheeks apart and then something warm and wet swirled around his hole—Chase's tongue! Chase definitely hadn't done *that* before, and Mathias couldn't decide whether he liked it or not. Yes, it felt so good, but it was also so… wrong. But damn if it didn't make his ass all warm and tingly, so he couldn't help squirming back against Chase for more. Then something even more exquisite happened when just a tiny tip of tongue pressed him open and darted inside. It was shocking and wonderful and strange and the most amazing thing Mathias had ever experienced. The unexpected touch on his sensitive skin sent shivers and heat radiating through him, concentrating at his entrance, but heat and ache pooled in his balls too. Oh, dear God, he might shoot his load right this second. Chase kept licking and thrusting inside of him, occasionally sucking and gently biting at the skin around his entrance, and Mathias's nipples tingled and his cock thickened and throbbed, so hot and hard, and he fucked himself back onto Chase's amazing tongue and let loose a string of words that surprised even him.

Chase gently pushed a finger in along with his tongue, and soon another finger, and before Mathias had realized, Chase had three fingers inside, all working and twisting and stretching him open as Chase licked and sucked. Occasionally, Chase stroked Mathias's cock or tongued and fondled his balls shooting lightning bolts of pleasure, and Mathias knew he was ready, couldn't be any more ready, and wanted Chase inside him.

"Chase, yeah, now! Gonna fuck me now?" Mathias begged, barely recognizing his own voice.

"No, Tee, no fucking."

"Why not? Want you so bad." He turned his head and his eyes stung. He needed it.

"Me, too," Chase said, "but I'm gonna make love to you, like you wanted."

"Now," Mathias growled, thrusting his hips back in a way he hadn't known he could. His body had taken control from his brain, and he couldn't think straight, just wanted more of Chase inside of him as hard and as deep as possible to fill that aching, pulsing void inside him that took his breath and thought processes away. "Chase...."

Chase eased Mathias down and onto his back, then slipped a condom onto his own cock, before he lay on top of Mathias, kissing him and caressing him, whispering.

"Hurry, Chase!" Mathias had never wanted anything as much as this before, and he was amazed at the way Chase's hands and mouth could drive him so fucking crazy.

"I'm here, Tee," Chase said in a low, soothing voice.

He pressed his cock against Mathias's hole and slid the head inside slowly past the first ring of muscle.

Too slow! Mathias grabbed at his hips to pull him in deeper. Needed him deeper.

It *hurt*. Hurt more than Mathias had expected. Even with all the lube and the spit and the slow, careful prep and the warmth and the needing. Mathias hadn't expected or prepared for any pain, and he gasped and opened his eyes wide.

"Shhh, Tee, just relax." Chase stopped and waited for Mathias to let him know it was okay to continue. "Do you want me to pull out?"

"No," Mathias gasped out. He knew it would feel good again, and that Chase was going slowly and gently. "No! Please keep going."

Chase stroked Mathias's hair and cheek until his breathing calmed, then Chase moved in more slowly. Eventually, Chase was completely inside.

Mathias panted with every emotion he'd ever experienced and then some. Chase Richards was inside him! The sensation was nothing like he'd expected, and he was a little disappointed and worried. Maybe he was doing this wrong.

"How're you doing? Ready for me to start moving?" Chase's voice was full of concern, but soft and soothing.

"Yeah, but slow?" Mathias blinked to get his mind off the lingering pain.

"Of course," Chase said, his gaze locked on Mathias's.

And very slowly, Chase moved, and Mathias relaxed enough so that he began to enjoy it, though not as much as he'd expected, and nowhere near as much as he'd liked the fingers and Chase's tongue. But soon, the sting was a distant memory, as Chase thrust in and out of Mathias, hands and mouth whispering across his body, murmuring words of love and encouragement. Chase's cock swept against that sweet spot inside of Mathias and he lost track of everything around him but Chase's body and how it made him feel.

Mathias could hear himself groaning and panting and begging for more from Chase until finally, it was all too much, and Mathias's body surrendered, his cock twitching and splashing hot sticky jets all over himself and Chase. And all the while, Mathias was laughing and shouting and crying, and the world was made of white light and shooting stars. In all of his excitement, Mathias very nearly missed the fact that Chase was holding onto him just as tightly, grabbing at Mathias's hair and saying his name over and over as he shuddered with his own orgasm.

It might have been minutes or hours or days that they lay together, the hot, wet stickiness like adhesive binding them together, while their labored breathing returned to normal, and they held each other close, not wanting the moment to end.

"That was really… amazing," Mathias finally said, his voice hoarse. He couldn't think of any other way to describe everything he'd just experienced and felt, and more importantly, how Chase had treated him so lovingly and carefully.

"I'm sorry if I hurt you at first." Chase's lips whispered an apology against Mathias's throat. "I thought you were ready."

"You made up for it later on, that's for sure." Mathias tightened his grip around Chase. "I don't think I'd mind if you did that to me again, you know."

"Well, I will if you beg me like that again." Chase rolled away from Mathias and reached for his discarded shirt, which he used to clean them up as much as possible.

"Beg you again?" Mathias was confused.

"You were begging me for all sorts of things while I had my tongue inside of you," Chase teased, tossing the shirt across the tent and snuggling back into Mathias's embrace.

"Oh." Mathias felt heat creeping into his cheeks, glad it was too dark for Chase to see.

"You were very vocal," Chase added, and Mathias felt even more mortified. "But I loved knowing how much you enjoyed what I was doing. That you enjoyed it as much as I did."

To shut Chase up, Mathias leaned up and kissed him deeply. Chase's mouth tasted of lube and something that Mathias couldn't identify and then he realized he was tasting himself. He nearly pulled back, but decided if Chase wanted to taste him, then there was nothing wrong with it.

"Chase?"

"Hmm?"

"Thank you."

"For making love to you?" Chase asked.

"For making love to me like *that*." Mathias smiled. "Letting me know that you love me."

"I do love you." Chase looked into Mathias's eyes, stroking his cheek and sideburns.

"I love you, too, Chase." Mathias's heart was pounding like a bass drum. He'd wanted to tell Chase for a while, but he'd been too afraid. But tonight, Mathias had never felt closer to Chase—to anyone—and it made him feel safe enough to reveal the depth of his emotions to Chase.

"Didn't anyone tell you that you're supposed to *accept* gifts when it's your birthday, not give them?" Chase asked softly.

"To me that was a gift, Chase. Making my first time so special," Mathias whispered. "Again."

"It was special for me, too." Chase planted gentle kisses on Mathias's face. "And now, telling me you love me, too, I feel like those are the most amazing gifts I've ever gotten. Thank you."

They kissed in silence for a few moments, then Mathias pulled Chase in even more tightly, and they lay in each other's arms again.

Mathias looked up at the sky through the small clear window in their tent and watched the stars twinkle above them as he listened to Chase fall into a deep sleep on his chest. The stars had been shining down on earth the same way for millions of years, Mathias thought, but for him, the world would never be the same, not since he'd met Chase Richards.

Present day
Dallas

AS MATHIAS drove home from the club, he thought back to that night in the tent with Chase. He remembered the wish he'd made, when he blew out the candle on his cake: that Chase Richards would always be part of his life. He'd gotten what he'd wished for, all right, and at this point it was the last thing Mathias wanted. All he wanted was for Chase to disappear and to be able to forget that Chase Richards ever existed.

But his main memory of that night in the Rockies was of how careful and loving Chase had been toward Mathias. He had opened himself up that night—heart and body—but Chase had made him feel safe and loved. His body had responded to Chase's careful and loving touch, but tonight, as some stranger blindfolded him and fucked him in the back of a limo, Mathias's body had felt exactly the same way; the man's touch had even made him think of Chase's hands and mouth on him all those years ago. All Mathias could think about was how his body had betrayed him as it found comfort and pleasure in that stranger's touch.

When he arrived back home, his initial thought was to jump in the shower and scrub the last memories of the man in the limo away, but for some reason he couldn't comprehend, he didn't. Instead, he picked up the black silk blindfold, enjoying the smooth texture as he caressed it and thinking about the man who had possessed his body that night. Mathias undressed himself completely and lay down naked in the bed in the extra bedroom, not the room he'd sometimes shared with Brooke, or Brooke's own room, but one that held no memories at all, and fell asleep, the silk blindfold still tangled in his fingers.

CHAPTER SIXTEEN

AS THE limo headed toward Chase's house, he thought about what had happened that day. It had all started so long ago, been put in motion years before, and now it had come down to this showdown he'd forced Mathias into.

The truth of the matter was that Chase didn't even *want* the fucking T-Group. He hadn't even wanted those oil supply companies either, at first, but once he'd spent some time looking into the industry, he'd gotten a rush he hadn't felt for years—how to take those companies and actually improve them rather than stripping them down. After Mathias had sold them to someone else, when he hadn't given Chase a chance, Chase had only wanted to teach Mathias a lesson. Now he was positive Mathias would never forget any of this. He'd never forget—and certainly never *forgive*—what Chase had done to him, personally and professionally.

What the fuck had Chase been thinking? He'd started the recent chain of events simply because he'd wanted to see Mathias again, because he'd never gotten over Mathias, despite having been the one to end their relationship. Chase used to make excuses to himself for his behavior, saying he was just acting and that none of it was the *real* Chase. Whether he liked it or not, he'd *become* that Chase, and the only time he could remember who he used to be was when he remembered the way he'd been with Mathias. Chase had been happy then. Happy to be himself; happy to make Mathias happy. He'd do anything in his power to erase what he'd done to Mathias now—to erase all the pain he'd caused.

The kernel of plan began to form. He couldn't just back down from the duel now. Mathias would probably just think that was another trick. They'd have to go forward, but Chase could make sure Mathias would win. Chase was an expert fencer—even if he was out of practice, and he could throw the match without anyone even noticing. That's what he'd do! He'd make it look good but let Mathias win. At least Mathias would keep the Tobler Group. He had absolutely no chance of getting Mathias to trust or care about him again; that was obvious. Mathias probably wouldn't even speak to him again, but Chase deserved no better. And this time, he couldn't even blame any of it on his father.

When he got home all he wanted to do was crawl into bed and forget about the duel, forget about the Tobler Group, and forget how he'd crushed Mathias's spirit that afternoon in his office. He wanted to think about the way Mathias's body had felt in the back of the limo that night, and the pleasure—and pain—he felt at being with Mathias again after so many lonely years.

But as Chase walked into his bedroom, with no tie, shirt half-buttoned and untucked, with the delicious smell of Mathias still on his body, he got a shock. Brooke was in his bed. She was asleep, but apparently was expecting him because she was nude, the crumpled sheets revealing as much as they concealed. She really was beautiful—former beauty-queen gorgeous—and Mathias must have appreciated that, but Chase had absolutely no interest in joining her. Especially tonight.

Silently, he backed out of his bedroom and went down the hall to the room that held his home theater system. He went over to the cabinet and slipped a hand-labeled DVD into the player, grabbed a bottle of bourbon from another cabinet, then made himself comfortable on the couch with one of the blankets that his housekeeper, Claudia, kept there for herself. She liked old movies and sometimes stayed after she finished work to watch, curled up on the couch. Chase didn't mind—at least someone was using all this expensive equipment.

Kicking his shoes off, he lay back and clicked on the plasma television. He sipped from the bottle as he watched the DVD—one he had watched many times over the years. It was partly old training sessions, from the summer he and Mathias had been in Colorado Springs, but there were a few other clips on there, of the happy days they'd spent in Rocky Mountain National Park, some of their adventures in Sydney at the Olympics, and of a scuba-diving trip they'd taken to the Caribbean later that year, during winter break. Chase smiled at how young he, and especially Mathias, looked in the videos. But seeing how happy they had been brought tears to his eyes, especially when he thought about the European trip they'd had so much fun planning and had never gotten to take.

Late Autumn 2002
Durham, North Carolina

"SO, IN Florence, of course there's Michelangelo's *David*. We can't miss that," Mathias said. "They're going to do a cleaning and restoration for its 500th anniversary."

They were lying in bed in Mathias's apartment one Sunday morning in late fall of their second year at Fuqua School of Business. They'd been sipping coffee out of large mugs and reading the Sunday papers, not bothering to get dressed. Most Sundays they never even felt the need unless they had to meet classmates for group projects. But at Mathias's, it was perfectly normal to spend the better part of the day naked—much of it in bed. Mathias had been flipping through the Travel section of the *New York Times*, and it got them talking about the trip to Europe they'd planned for the following summer.

"Really?" Chase asked. "Imagine being the guy that got to clean David's cock."

"Your mind moves in mysterious ways, doesn't it?" Mathias's mouth quirked and he let out an exasperated sigh.

"What's so mysterious about that? I mean the guy's naked for God's sake; his cock is the first thing people notice. You can't tell me you haven't looked at it yourself."

"I'd rather look at yours, 'cause I can touch it, too." Mathias leaned over to stroke Chase's cock gently—just enough to appreciate it, but not enough to get him hard—and gave him a mischievous grin.

"Excellent point, Tee," Chase agreed with a sigh. "I wonder how big it is—David's cock I mean. Certainly not very big in proportion to the rest of his body... unlike you." Chase smiled. "Hey, maybe we can hide out in the museum overnight and fuck right in front of David. Are you up for that?"

"Hmm, interesting idea," Mathias said. "But it's Italy; I can't imagine that's very outrageous. How about if we do it in front of Buckingham Palace, and see if those guards notice that!"

"Oh, you're getting creative. I like that." Chase ran his fingers along the muscles of Mathias's chest.

"Your turn."

"Let me think…. How about at the Vatican?"

"In the museum?"

"No, how about right in St. Peter's Cathedral? Loud enough for the Pope to hear us," Chase suggested. "Right under the cupola so the sound will echo through the whole place."

"Oh, you are definitely one naughty boy, coming up with that one." Mathias shook his head.

"I can be naughtier if it'll help."

"Help with what?"

"Help you figure out what to do with me?" Chase cocked an eyebrow.

"Oh, I have a few ideas," Mathias said in a low voice as he took Chase's coffee mug away and set it on the bedside table.

Present day
Dallas

WATCHING the DVD through tear-filled eyes, Chase eventually fell into a fitful sleep, until his housekeeper found him there the next morning and gently shook him awake.

"Mr. Chase, your guest is having breakfast in bed, sir. Do you want me to make up a tray for you, too?" Claudia asked. Nothing surprised her anymore, he was pretty sure of that, but this morning he could see confusion in her eyes as to why he was sleeping here while a *woman* was in his bed. Usually his "overnight guests" were male and stayed in the pool house. Chase never let anyone into the main house except Mike, a few friends, or his mother on the rare occasions she visited.

"No, thanks, Claudia." He rubbed his eyes. "I'm not hungry."

"You probably want to eat something." She disapprovingly at the half-empty bottle on the table next to the couch. He really hadn't drunk much the night before, but he knew his eyes probably looked red and swollen—from crying—and Claudia assumed he was hung over.

"You're right." He gave in to her gentle mothering as he always did. She was the one person in Texas who got away with telling him what to do, and he appreciated her more than she'd ever know. "Can you please make something for me and bring it into my study in about a half an hour?"

"Yes, sir." She nodded, one corner of her mouth turning up, as if she understood that he wasn't interested in the female guest, but didn't want to make any mention of that.

"Thanks, Claudia," he said sincerely, with the closest he could come to a smile this morning.

When she turned to leave, Chase pulled himself together— mentally and physically. He buttoned his shirt and made a decision about what to do with Brooke. Then he headed down the hall to talk with her.

"Chase!" Brooke said happily when he came through the doorway of the huge master bedroom. "You never came to bed last night!"

"I had to… work late, and I didn't get home till this morning." He stood at a safe distance near the foot of the bed.

"So, come join me now." She moved the breakfast tray to the night table and pulled the sheet slowly down her still-naked torso. She patted the bed next to her.

"I can't." Chase stepped back a pace, out of her reach.

"You *can't?*" she joked, sounding as if this were some sort of game.

"Well, I need to change and get to the office. I have a—"

"Don't tell me you work all hours of the day and night like Mathias does," Brooke huffed. He could see anger brewing as a result of her failed seduction.

"I don't, not normally, but until this takeover thing is settled, there're a lot of things that need my attention just now." Mustering his resolve he sat next to Brooke on the bed. He didn't know why he didn't just throw her out. Damn her for making herself at home in *his* bed and then expecting his housekeeper to wait on her with breakfast in bed.

"And I need to do some practice training for our bout next week. Need to save up my energy for that, you know." What he really needed to do was to clear his mind and think of some way to get out of the duel—out of the entire takeover bid if at all possible. The last thing he needed was Brooke around, distracting him and demanding his attention. He didn't know how long he could avoid her physical advances.

"Oh, right. I didn't even think of that." Brooke smiled and nodded as if impressed at Chase's dedication to fucking over Mathias. "You're saying I'd take up too much of that energy and maybe you wouldn't beat Mathias if you spend any time in bed with me?" She glanced at him coyly. "I'd tire you out, you mean?"

"Yes, that's exactly what I'm worried about." Chase gave her a nervous smile.

"You are just too sweet and gentlemanly, you know that, Chase Richards." Brooke leaned over and planted a kiss on his mouth.

"Yeah, that's me," Chase said self-consciously and laughed. "So, how about if you stay in a fancy hotel for the week, while I'm doing business and fencing training? I promise we'll have a big celebration after I kick Mathias's ass at the Club." Not that there was going to be a celebration—or ass-kicking for that matter—Chase was going to make sure Mathias won. He just couldn't have Brooke around right now, and he thought he knew her well enough to entice her away from the house—and him.

"If that'll help you win, sure, honey. Which hotel?" She asked in a tone that made it clear she had a preference.

"Whichever one you choose. You take your time with breakfast, then Claudia will arrange for the driver to take you to whichever hotel you like. I'll call you later on to see how you're settling, in, okay?" Chase leaned down to kiss her, knowing she'd be more likely to leave if it didn't seem as if he were throwing her out. So far, he'd managed this more smoothly than he'd expected. But he had been right about what he'd said to Mathias the day before. Just pay enough attention to Brooke, treat her like a princess, and she was easy to handle. He felt some guilt about manipulating her, but it was tempered by the knowledge she'd been manipulating *him* all along as well—she'd made herself at home in his bed, hadn't she?

"Okay, honey," she said to his back as he headed into the bathroom and locked the door behind him.

Back against the door, Chase held off what was nearly a panic attack coming on. Seeing Brooke naked in his bed, waiting for him, *wanting* him, brought back the harsh reality of what he'd done. Much of what had happened since that fateful conversation in his office with Mathias was a blur now—except for having Mathias in the limo. That memory was still crystal clear in Chase's mind.

MATHIAS woke up in the early morning in his guest bedroom, his brain full of hazy memories of the previous night. He was still clutching the blindfold, and everything came rushing back to him in an instant: the confrontation in Chase's office; his despair at finding out how Brooke had betrayed him; and finally, what he'd done in the limousine.

Mathias was disgusted with himself for enjoying it, and confused about the feelings that surfaced when that man had touched him, caressed him, almost reverently. Yes, the man had also fucked him—hard and rough and very satisfying for both of them—but it had been a very *caring* sort of fuck. Mathias wished it had been painful and brutal. Why had that stranger brought back memories of Chase? Mathias hated Chase more than anyone he'd ever met. Yet he couldn't stop thinking about how wonderful things had *been*—or had seemed—with Chase.

How the hell, after all these years and all the ways Chase Richards had ripped his world—and his heart—apart, did Mathias still think of him, still want him so badly? He must be insane to hold any fondness for the man. Just recalling that scene in Chase's office yesterday had Mathias shaking and his chest constricting. But something deeper, in his core, felt a loss more devastating than losing Brooke or even the T-Group. Had he somehow thought there might still remain a shred of affection between himself and Chase, even now?

Pulling himself out of this useless reverie, he threw the sheet off and sat up in bed, running his hands through his hair, clearing his mind for the important tasks ahead of him. He needed a shower. He got up, still holding onto the blindfold. He tossed it into the drawer of the bedside table and strode out of the guest room, heading for the master bedroom.

After a long, very hot shower, finished off with a refreshing blast of ice-cold water, Mathias got dressed and tried to focus. How was he going to approach this upcoming duel? Chase was probably already preparing for their showdown. But Mathias wasn't sure whether he should be training this week, honing his old skills and reflexes, or just wing it. *Has Chase been fencing recently?* It didn't matter what *Chase* did… Mathias had to do something—everything in his power—to prepare. It wasn't only his future resting on the outcome of the duel.

He could really use some advice from his dad, but Jerry Tobler would be at the hospital for tests all day. The last thing he wanted to do was to spring something like this preposterous *duel* on his dad right now. But he knew where to get the fencing advice he needed.

Resigned, he got up and called his old coach, Sergei Gorsky, who had trained him during junior high and high school. After a few minutes catching up, Mathias steeled himself for the inevitable explanation of why he was calling.

"Maestro." Mathias still honored him with the standard form of address for a fencing master. "I've gotten myself into a situation. I could use your help," Mathias didn't quite know how to explain.

"What sort of a situation, Mathias?" Sergei asked. For years, Mathias had spent more time training with Sergei than he'd spent at home, or so it had seemed. They'd formed a close personal bond as well, even though they hadn't met in years. Sergei had been almost a second father to him, and Mathias could be honest about what was happening.

"I've been challenged to a duel, and—"

"A duel?" Sergei let out a deep knowing chuckle. "Not over a woman!"

"No, Sergei." The response didn't surprise him. "For my company, actually."

"Oh." Sergei stopped laughing. "That is not at all amusing. Explain this."

"Someone's trying to take over my family's business, and somehow it's come down to a fencing match to settle, rather than a more traditional takeover bid." Mathias hoped Sergei wouldn't ask for more details.

"Well, you were Olympic class, why do you think you need my help to win this?" Sergei asked.

"My opponent is also an experienced fencer. That's why he thought this would be a fitting resolution."

"Who is opponent?"

"Chase Richards," Mathias answered as calmly as he could manage.

"Chase? You are fighting Chase? But I thought you two were friends!" Sergei paused. "More than friends… no?"

"What?" Mathias was taken aback to hear that his old coach knew the nature of his relationship with Chase. *Former* relationship, he corrected himself.

"Fencers talk. Of course there are not so many secrets," Sergei said, and Mathias could picture him pressing his lips together and nodding. There was no hint of judgment or disapproval, only a sort of acceptance Mathias appreciated.

"It wasn't really any secret, I suppose." Mathias tried to keep the unhappiness from his voice, not wanting to discuss the topic of his personal relationship with Chase any further. "But that's all been over for years."

"Ah, I see," Sergei said. "Well, as for this current situation, I don't think I can help you prepare properly," Sergei said. "I cannot help you to win."

"Why not?" Mathias asked, more than a little disappointed.

"You need Chase's coach. Only he can teach you Chase's secrets, and that is what you need. For that, I am useless."

"What? Why would Yuri Petrov help me?" Mathias assumed he'd be busy coaching Chase.

"Yuri is living now in Dallas, and also a friend of mine," Sergei continued enthusiastically. "You want this? I can call him and arrange it."

Mathias paused for a moment. It would be taking a page from Chase's own playbook—literally—to train with *Chase's* old coach. It sounded exactly like something Chase would do. He had to fight fire with fire, though it went against his personal moral code. It felt like cheating, *especially* in a sport that was all about honor and sportsmanship. Mathias reconciled himself to do whatever he could to beat Chase's dirty tactics. And while, historically, a duel was an issue of honor, it was still a violent and ugly way to settle a dispute. There was no other choice.

"Yes, Sergei!" Mathias responded, fighting mixed feelings. "That would be fantastic. I'd like *both* of you to work with me, though...."

"I arrange it and call you back, Mathias. Don't worry!" Sergei hung up.

Less than an hour later, Sergei called and instructed him to appear at Yuri's fencing school the following afternoon. They would discuss a training plan and schedule after they watched him fence again.

The next afternoon, Mathias arrived at Yuri's fencing studio on the outskirts of Dallas and was greeted warmly by Sergei, who made introductions. He learned that the two older men had been good friends, and rivals, back in Russia—the old Soviet Union at the time. They had even been on two Olympic teams together in their youth.

Yuri watched Mathias spar with Sergei, then Sergei watched Mathias fence against Yuri. The two coaches chattered noisily in Russian for several minutes while Mathias looked on blankly, wishing he'd studied the language.

"Okay, Mathias. You must come here for practice at least three hours a day," Yuri began. "We will get you ready to compete, and I will help you win."

"Did Chase call you to help him train?" Mathias asked Yuri, though he felt he shouldn't be prying. But he knew that if the roles were reversed, Chase would be gathering information about him.

"No. He didn't call to ask for my help," Yuri replied. "If he asks, I will tell him I am not available. You requested my services first, and I cannot coach both of you."

"Don't worry, Mathias," Sergei added, sensing that Mathias wasn't sure whether or not to believe Yuri. "Fencing is all about honor. Yuri tells truth to you. He is going to help you, and you can trust him, same as you trust me."

"Thank you, Yuri, Sergei." Mathias shook both men's hands, but he wondered why Yuri didn't have more loyalty to Chase.

"Okay, time for first training session. Now!" Yuri barked and Mathias simply followed instructions.

During the next week, Mathias spent the mornings at T-Group headquarters and afternoons and a few evenings at Yuri's. He quickly got back into the rhythm of fencing, training with all three weapons but spending the most time with saber and watching Chase's old matches on video. Yuri pointed out Chase's habits and weaknesses and taught Mathias techniques to defend against them and to exploit them in order to score.

"You're still hesitating on the attack, Mathias!" Yuri had told him every day. "Break!"

Mathias nodded to his sparring partner and stepped off the piste to talk with Yuri. He pulled his helmet off and wiped away the layer of sweat with a towel Yuri handed him. "I know. I'm just used to waiting for the opening, like in épée. Waiting for my opponent to make a mistake."

"Saber isn't chess. Stop thinking and let your body take over. Focus on the attack and you do not have to worry about defense."

"I'm hung up on right of way." In saber the fencer who starts the attack has priority and can score a hit, but Mathias was used to a different set of rules and strategies.

"You must get over that or you will lose. Break time is over!" Yuri grabbed the towel away from Mathias and motioned to the other fencer to get back on the piste. "En garde!"

Driving home from that practice session, Mathias recalled a conversation he'd had with Chase back at the Olympic Training Center one night after they'd trained all day and used what little energy they had left to make love.

They lay in bed, arms and legs entwined, on the edge of sleep.

"Tee, why didn't you stay with saber?"

"I've always been épée. Just covered in a few matches when one of our sabrists was injured so Stanford could have the chance at the points."

Chase nodded. "I kept hoping I'd compete against you again, after that first time. But I never really had a chance to talk to you again. Never a good way to get to you without being completely obvious." A shy grin spread across his face.

Mathias smiled. So Chase had been watching him for that long? Two years?

"You weren't bad. You could have done well if you stuck with it."

Mathias shook his head. "Well, saber was never really my weapon. It's not how I think. I'm a planner, not so much of an action man. Plus, I was always getting hung up on right of way. I'd hesitate and get scored on. My coach was always yelling at me."

"My take on right of way? Who cares? I go in for the attack and don't worry about it. If you attack enough and get enough hits, you'll outscore your opponent just by the numbers, even if some of the time you don't have right of way." His eyes glittered as he thrust forward with an imaginary saber.

"That's the secret to saber?"

"That's the secret to everything." This time he leaned forward with a rough kiss.

Mathias should have remembered that about Chase. It described his strategy on life, love, and business to a T.

At least Brooke was no longer a distraction to Mathias. The day after the confrontation in Chase's office he'd discovered that she'd come and removed many of her belongings from the condo while he'd been out. He'd taken her belongings from the master bedroom and dumped them in her room. He didn't care when or how she took them; he just hoped she wouldn't come to retrieve them while he was home, and so far she hadn't. She'd come back a few more times that week; he could tell because the mountain of clothing seemed to be getting smaller. He didn't know whether or not she was with Chase, and he didn't want to. Let Chase take care of her because Mathias was finished with worrying about what happened to Brooke.

The day before the match, both Sergei and Yuri felt confident that they had done as much as they reasonably could in the time available, and Mathias was prepared to take Chase on and had the strategies to beat him. He only hoped that Chase hadn't practiced as much, but mental preparation was as important as physical training, and he forced himself to concentrate and to remember how much was riding on this one bout. He just hoped to hell he was ready.

CHAPTER SEVENTEEN

Late August 2012
Dallas

WHAT the fucking *fuck* was he doing, Mathias asked himself on Saturday morning as he put on his fencing suit in the changing room at the Dallas Athletic Club. How had he let Chase talk him into this? Why did he think this could actually be a solution? One thing he did know, if the takeover fight didn't get resolved soon, there wouldn't be much left of the Tobler Group. Chase could live without Mathias's business, but Mathias couldn't. It was all he had and so many people depended on him. He wasn't sure which was worse, losing the company to Chase or letting Chase's stock market shenanigans damage the company and therefore the people that relied on Mathias for their jobs. Well, it would all be over soon, and why not this way? Physically, Mathias felt evenly matched with Chase, whereas he wasn't ruthless enough to beat Chase in any other kind of battle.

He walked out of the changing room door to the fencing room, where he saw Chase was already waiting for him, mask in his hand and a serious expression. Mathias was shocked not to be greeted with Chase's trademark cocky smirk on his face, a face so beautiful it was almost hard to remember the ugliness it covered. As soon as Chase spoke, however, Mathias expected to be reminded.

"Well, here we are, Mathias," Chase said, almost pleasantly, surprising Mathias yet again. He'd been expecting smug, überconfident Chase and the associated egotistical banter Mathias had been subjected to in Chase's office the week before. Most likely, Chase was simply trying to psych Mathias out with this uncharacteristically polite and sportsmanlike greeting.

"I'm here, on schedule," Mathias said, barely squeezing the words from his mouth. He concentrated on breathing and trying to *relax. Don't let Chase's fuckery distract you*, he reminded himself.

"Looks like we'll have an audience," Chase added with some surprise, indicating the gallery above the fencing strip. Mathias looked up and saw Brooke standing right at the railing. She looked away when their eyes met. Just like Chase to put Mathias's potential humiliation on public display. So far, the whole fiasco had been conducted in public—not including Brooke's role. The dispute might be between Mathias and Chase, but hundreds, possibly even thousands of people would end up being touched by it: people who had lost money on their investment or could possibly even lose their jobs, thanks to Chase's dirty tactics.

"And, here's our referee, Jake Roberts," Chase said. "I don't know whether or not you've fenced here before?"

"No," Mathias replied as the Club's fencing instructor arrived and introduced himself to both men.

It turned out that Chase had never fenced at the Club, either, and hadn't met the man before. Mathias felt a bit more confident that Roberts would be neutral and he wasn't walking into an ambush.

"Wow, it's quite an honor to meet two former Olympic team members," Roberts said after shaking their hands.

Roberts went over the basic rules, although it was hardly necessary. Match to fifteen points or touches, Olympic rules.

"And the weapon?" Mathias asked.

"I told you we'd draw for it," Chase reminded him. "Let's have our referee handle that."

"Write the names of the weapons on a piece of paper," Roberts told Mathias, as he handed a pen and paper over. "Then Chase will pull the name out of a mask."

Mathias did as requested and Roberts ripped the paper into three pieces, folded them, and put the pieces into Mathias's mask. He held it out for Chase to choose one.

"Saber," Chase announced, unfolding the piece he'd chosen and showing it to both Mathias and Roberts.

Of course Chase would be thrilled with that result, though Mathias couldn't deny the result had been fair. He'd written the slips himself. The saber was the most tactically aggressive and the hardest to defend. That was Chase's favorite weapon—the one he'd been an Olympic alternate for—while Mathias's weapon had been épée. Historically, the épée was considered the traditional weapon for a duel, back in the days when duels were actually fought, but the saber—based on the cavalry sword—required another level of skill and aggression to win.

Mathias and Chase entered the fencing piste and saluted each other as was the custom. Fencers choose distinctive salutes, especially those who compete extensively, and Mathias was caught off-guard when Chase used Mathias's own salute. *Just another mind-fuck*, Mathias decided, hoping his expression hadn't given away his surprise, as they saluted the referee and the handful of spectators who had gathered in the gallery—also customary.

They donned their masks and went *en garde*, sabers up.

The referee shouted, "En garde. Prêt. Allez!" Ready, set, go.

Chase started out aggressively, with a double advance lunge and aimed for Mathias's waist and arms, which along with the head were the only legal touches for saber. Mathias countered and then took the offensive, moving toward Chase and trying to score. Only the fencer on the offensive, or right of way, could score, even if the defender touched his opponent first. Mathias cursed himself for not checking the referee's impartiality beforehand, since scoring on saber relied heavily on the referee's interpretation of body language and footwork.

The first touch went to Chase, followed by two points to Mathias, who scored with a move that Yuri had taught him. Chase evened the score to 4-4.

"You've been practicing," Chase shouted, his voice muffled by the mask.

"Yes," Mathias acknowledged. "Haven't you?"

"No." Chase's tone was hard to fathom through the protective gear.

Mathias thought as he parried against Chase's attack and clashing steel echoed in the room. Chase assumed he was still good enough to beat Mathias without even training? Why had he expected anything less from the arrogant sonofabitch?

After the first few points, Mathias came to the conclusion that the referee was indeed impartial, agreeing with all of the calls. At least so far. Mathias knew he'd made a couple of mistakes, mainly from being out of practice. He certainly wasn't anywhere near his former skill level, but neither was Chase. And that made Mathias wonder, as they repositioned for the next point. Chase *said* he hadn't practiced, or was he simply trying to lull Mathias into a false sense of security by making simple errors during the first part of the bout, hoping that Mathias would underestimate his true skill?

After each point Chase scored, Brooke leaned over the railing of the gallery and waved at Chase, who raised his saber toward her in a halfhearted salute. Mathias knew Chase's behavior was all for show, all for Mathias's benefit—or his discomfort—but he didn't let it faze him. He'd expected to see Chase gloating more at each point he scored, and he didn't seem to be playing to Brooke the way Mathias had expected he would. But Mathias couldn't afford to let his concentration break at all, and he willed himself to ignore the interaction between Brooke and Chase. Everything Mathias had or wanted rode on this bout, and he needed to focus on winning.

Mathias expected Chase to hit him harder on the points… but Chase was taking everything completely by the book—nothing about Chase's behavior today was what Mathias expected. But why? Was Chase just trying to psych him out, or… could it be that Mathias had misjudged the situation, misjudged Chase? *Not fucking possible*, Mathias thought as he remembered how he'd discovered Brooke with Chase. No fucking way Mathias had misinterpreted *that*!

Brooke no longer mattered. Even if Mathias managed to win, he didn't want her back. At least when Chase had betrayed Mathias, he had chosen his family business over Mathias. While it hurt, somehow it was easier to understand than what Brooke had done, though there was still that million dollars. Mathias needed someone he could trust in his life, not someone whose loyalty would always be in doubt. He wanted a *partner*, someone who loved him for himself and not what he provided, and he needed someone who would stand by him, no matter what—or who—came between them. Neither Chase nor Brooke even remotely fit those requirements.

Chase had so far been taking his time, backing Mathias into a position where he couldn't score, but when he hesitated for a shade too long, Mathias took advantage and moved in to score another point, his blade whirring through the air to land on Chase's shoulder.

CHASE had been amazed at how well Mathias was fencing, specifically how he'd exploited Chase's own mistakes and weaknesses. He really had practiced, Chase thought, noticing that Mathias had brought his old coach Sergei Gorsky along today. During a pause in the action while the referee determined the touch, Chase spotted his own former fencing instructor Yuri Petrov arriving and seating himself next to Sergei, then nodding a greeting toward Mathias. *Has Mathias been working with Yuri, too?* Chase wondered. *Perfect!* He hoped Mathias would beat him. He'd given up any interest in winning long ago.

But Chase had also noticed that on the first few touches, Mathias had hit him hard—much harder than customary in a bout—and he fully expected to have a few bruises from the force of Mathias's hits. But then again, this wasn't a regular bout, was it? Mathias was fighting for his company; it wasn't unexpected that he'd be striking out against Chase like that.

But Mathias wasn't at his top form, and Chase scored on a few mistakes. By the time he'd reached five points he'd gotten into the rhythm of it. It brought back so many memories! How they'd met, how they'd spent an entire summer at the training center, and even though they'd rotated opponents, Chase and Mathias spent time after official practices sparring. It had been such a big part of their courtship, and the sheer physical exertion and competition had heightened the sexual tension for both of them in a public way. And afterward, they'd go back to their room and make love just as passionately until they were exhausted and fell into deep contented sleep.

AT EIGHT points, the referee called an official break and they each retired to their end of the piste to catch their breaths and have some water. Mathias noticed Brooke sitting with Chase, stroking his sweat-dampened hair, but Chase kept brushing her hand away. Despite his curiosity about Chase's annoyance with Brooke, he willed himself to focus on the match. He sat with Sergei and Yuri, but he caught the look of surprise on Chase's face when he realized Mathias had been working with Chase's former coach. He gave Mathias a nod of approval, and what looked like a genuine smile, which was even more surprising.

Why isn't Chase angry? Mathias wondered briefly, but turned his attention back to his coaches.

During the break, Yuri and Sergei offered additional strategy and warnings, but he already knew most of it. He still knew how Chase moved and thought better than anyone, and once Mathias had picked up his rhythm, he'd been able to even the score easily.

Back for the second half of the bout, they were so evenly matched that Mathias was able to successfully parry almost every one of Chase's attacks, and he got into the rhythm of saber. Chase's words from long ago came back to him: "attack whether you've got right of way or not." He'd been waiting to discover an opening where he could attack and score successfully, which is why Chase had evened the score practically without breaking a sweat during the first half of the bout. Now, Mathias attacked consistently, as did Chase, and neither scored for several exhausting minutes.

Slowly, they matched each other point for point, pausing only when the referee halted the action to award the touch. By the time the score was 12-12, they were both breathing hard again. For Mathias, it was so much more than mere physical exertion.

As they fought, Mathias couldn't help remembering other times they were together, this close. Scenes flashed into his mind of kisses and making love and holding each other. Of their first encounters and getting to know each other physically and emotionally that summer in Colorado where they ate, drank, and slept fencing—and each other.

So physically close to Chase now, Mathias's memories flashed into his mind unbidden. He just hoped his body wouldn't betray him as he remembered the feelings.

CHASE also had to fight off his own memories and discovered he was enjoying this bout more than he'd ever expected. Then, almost too late, he remembered the stakes here, especially for Mathias, and concentrated on how he could lose gracefully. But he'd gotten so caught up in the pleasure of fencing that it was already tied at 13, and he scored the next touch almost too easily.

It has to be now, Chase realized. They were tied at 14-14, and this was the last point. He'd started off too quickly and soon had Mathias backed into the corner. All Chase could do now was to guess how Mathias would feint to mislead him. They'd been in this position before, and Mathias almost always used the same move. But this time, Chase anticipated Mathias's tactics, knew just how he could set up the action so he could allow Mathias to take the final touch.

THEY were so evenly matched, especially with Yuri's insight, and the bout dragged on, neither scoring, until they were both hot and soaking, sweat dripping under their suits. Finally, Chase fell for a chest feint and Mathis scored with a cut to the head. Now they arrived at the crucial moment, the score 14-14. This was the final point and everything would be decided on what happened next. The winner could be decided in the next few seconds.

Chase had Mathias pinned near his end of the piste and Mathias had only one move to make to get away from him—taking advantage of his superior reach, he needed to feint in just the right way to get Chase to make the wrong move, leaving himself vulnerable for a strike. Yuri had drilled this move into Mathias over the past week.

But now, he wondered what this entire struggle had been worth. How much damage had it caused the company? His relationship with Brooke? His father's health? Suddenly, Mathias didn't even know why he kept fighting this long when he'd just been making things worse. Mathias felt he'd failed everyone: the company, the shareholders, his father, and himself. Could he repair any of that even if he won and retained control of the T-Group?

He had only a split-second to extricate himself from the corner. He moved, correctly anticipating Chase's feint, but his foot came down unsteadily, and instead of moving forward to steady himself, Mathias consciously moved backward.

CHASE responded to Mathias's attack, and realized with relief that Mathias had anticipated exactly that move and was about to score the final touch. But suddenly, Mathias stumbled slightly and Chase's forward momentum carried him right into Mathias—Chase had the right of way and scored, though it had been the last thing Chase had intended. He didn't know how Mathias could have possibly misstepped.

On second thought, Chase knew exactly how. He realized Mathias had lost on purpose. A cold anguish washed over Chase, sinking deep into his bones. Mathias had given up. Chase had more than defeated Mathias, he'd taken away his very will to keep fighting. Chase was suddenly thankful for the mask that hid his expression of shock and disgust at what he'd just done.

MATHIAS raised his saber toward Chase—the final salute to his opponent, the referee, and the spectators. Then he shook hands with Chase, as custom demanded, before turning away without saying a single word.

Chase had won. Because Mathias had let him. He'd had enough of this entire war. Best to end it now and pick up whatever pieces he could and try to move forward, although Mathias wasn't quite sure what *forward* meant for him anymore. He didn't know how to even begin to repair the damage. All he could do was to leave the T-Group with his reputation and integrity intact. And hope that Chase wouldn't ruin his family business and harm his employees. Mathias could go home and start fresh and figure out a way to start a new company and try and hire them back.

Mathias ignored the cheers from the viewing gallery and the cries of people coming down onto the strip to congratulate Chase. Instead, Mathias shook hands silently with his coaches, thanked them with just a nod, and walked slowly into the locker room, alone.

CHAPTER EIGHTEEN

CHASE didn't have time to think about anything more because people were shouting and streaming down to clap him on the back, congratulating him. He stayed at one end of the strip for a while, making uncomfortable small talk with the dozen or so people who had watched the bout. At least none of the spectators knew the stakes that had ridden on the match. Brooke was hanging off one arm and Chase hated her touch, couldn't wait to get away from her, but he couldn't escape to the locker room just yet. He wanted to give Mathias time to leave in peace. There was no point in trying to talk with him now, Chase knew that much. Mathias would assume Chase had gone in there to gloat, and an apology now would mean nothing to Mathias.

As for Brooke, Chase would make sure she went back to her hotel tonight because he couldn't bear to be around her or listen to her. She hadn't been the reason Chase had treated Mathias so badly the past couple of months, but he was ashamed at how he'd let her give him more ways to twist the knife in Mathias's heart, when that was the last thing that Chase had intended. He'd fucked things up even worse by using Brooke, not only because it had hurt Mathias so much, but because it had just reminded Chase of how much like his father he'd really become: using people and discarding them when they'd outlived their usefulness.

After Chase was sure Mathias had left the changing room, he went in and showered quickly and changed, then collected Brooke, only because he really didn't have any choice this time; he knew there was a chance she'd make a public scene if he didn't. He'd take her back to the hotel so he could be alone. Chase needed to figure out what he was going to do now about Mathias and the T-Group. Maybe he could just talk to Mathias and call off the takeover bid and—

"I had my driver go back to the hotel to get my things and bring them over to your house during the match, Chase," Brooke said, surprising Chase out of his thoughts as they walked out of the Club to Chase's waiting car and driver. "I thought that would be convenient and save us the trouble of doing it."

"What!" He was so shocked by her audacity that he barely suppressed the anger that bubbled up within him.

"You mentioned we were going to have a celebration after you beat Mathias, right?" Brooke reminded him, her tone cheerful and eager. "So, I had him check me out of the hotel, and move those things into your house. I still have tons of clothes at Mathias's. You can help me figure out how to get them, can't you?" she added in that helpless Southern belle way that most men couldn't refuse. Brooke was so focused on herself that she hadn't even noticed Chase's look of surprise or the resentment in his voice.

Chase didn't even know what to say or how to respond. She'd completely blindsided him. The way she'd moved herself into his bedroom the week before, despite his having Claudia make up a guest room for her; the way she'd treated his personal staff as if they were her own; and worst of all, that she had simply assumed she could move right out of Mathias's bed and life into Chase's. Yes, he'd used her to get confidential information on Mathias's business plans, but he'd never offered her the slightest hint that he was interested in anything more from her than at the most some casual sex. Perhaps he'd wooed her a bit more strongly than he'd thought, or she simply had to have someone in her life and now she wanted Chase, the way she'd wanted Mathias until a few days earlier.

Of course, Chase felt more than a stab of guilt over having used Brooke as harshly as he had, but what he'd discovered about her since the confrontation—most disturbing was the way she flaunted her physical interest in Chase—in the office made him wonder what Mathias had seen in her in the first place. Though to be honest, while she might have overstepped her authority with his staff, she seemed genuinely excited and affectionate toward him. None of that was an act; it was simply unfounded and more than unwanted. But at the moment, he was in no mood for a confrontation. He'd have to take her home with him after all and find some excuse to send her packing—again.

In the back of the chauffeured Mercedes sedan on the way home, Brooke chattered about how much she'd enjoyed watching Chase beat Mathias, and how nice Chase had looked in his fencing suit and how exciting the match had been—like something from an old movie. She whispered things in his ear about what she wanted to do when they got home and seemed ready to get started in the car, trying to kiss Chase while looking shyly in the direction of the driver because the privacy partition was down. Chase wasn't about to raise it and give her any opportunity to get physical with him. He could see that she was disappointed at his lack of response, but she said she expected he was tired after all that fencing, so she was happy to wait until they got home.

When they arrived back at Chase's house, he sat her down in the living room and calmly asked her to collect her things and leave. Brooke appeared completely taken aback by this turn of events, expecting the celebration he'd promised and not a dismissal, and when she realized Chase was finished with her, she began to scream and cry and knocked over a vase that cost a small fortune, smashing the beautiful pottery into tiny particles of dull powder.

He really didn't care much about the vase, though it was a terrible waste of something so lovely, but her complete lack of respect for his home and belongings turned his anger—so far directed at himself for actually beating Mathias—toward Brooke. He fought to keep it in check, though she had strained his limits of self-control.

"Brooke, trust me. You really just want to leave right now," Chase told her, a warning in his voice that she didn't pick up on.

"Why? You won, fair and square. You get the company, and me, and Mathias can't say or do anything to protest any of it, can he? So I don't understand why you don't want me anymore. I gave you information and helped you take over his company, just like you wanted." She looked and sounded genuinely surprised and disappointed. It seemed that she really thought Chase was interested in her for more than just information. She'd clearly imagined much more from him than he'd even hinted at.

"You don't want to stay, not with me, Brooke," Chase said coolly.

"Yes, I do. I don't want to go back to *Mathias*. Now that I know what he is."

"I wasn't entirely truthful when I told you about him."

"What do you mean? That he's gay? He didn't even try and deny any of it. Not the boyfriend, not the *waiter*. What *else* could there be?" There was a tone of dread in her voice as if what she already knew about Mathias couldn't possibly get any worse than it was.

"The thing is, Brooke, that Mathias isn't gay. He's *bi*." Brooke gave Chase a confused look. "That means he actually does like women, likes sleeping with women. He liked sleeping with you, he just happens to like men too. But he didn't lie when he told you how he felt about you."

"I don't understand."

"Mathias really loved you, Brooke. Couldn't you figure that out? Even I could see that. He loved you and wanted to marry you and have a bunch of beautiful kids with you."

"He lied to me. He couldn't really care about me if he did those things."

"No, Brooke. Mathias doesn't lie. Not to other people. All of that was true, or he wouldn't have proposed to you." Chase couldn't believe that Brooke still didn't understand the depth of Mathias's feelings for her, or how crushed he'd been when he'd found her in Chase's office, despite the fact that even Chase could see that Mathias wasn't still blissfully happy with Brooke. But Chase's tactics had destroyed any chance of Mathias and Brooke working through whatever problems they'd had.

"What do you mean 'to other people'?" She blinked and a new stream of tears slid down her cheeks.

"Since I've known him—a dozen years or so—he's still scrupulously honest. He may lie to himself, like whether your marriage would work, because I know he wanted it to, and he would have done anything in his power to make it work."

"Like having sex with waiters?"

Chase couldn't let her get away with that. "You weren't completely faithful to him, were you?"

Brooke avoided his gaze for a moment, then turned back, eyes narrowed. "That tennis pro was just a harmless little fling. I tired of him quickly. And Mathias was so much—" She glanced in the direction of her shoes. "—*better* at everything."

Chase suppressed the urge to mention that irony. "Cheating aside, knowing you'd told me his business plans really cut him. That was worse than betraying him because it hurt everyone involved in the Tobler Group. Doesn't that mean anything to you?"

"Well, what does that matter? Now *we're* together," Brooke insisted, trying to pull Chase toward her.

"You really shouldn't have tried to trade the prize you already had for what was behind Door #1." He shook his head in disgust as he pushed her hands away.

"Why not?"

"Life's not a game show, and it's not all about *you* either. Everything we do, every choice we make, affects someone else. We both figured that out too late, but you don't seem to care, so you'll keep making the same mistake over again," Chase said, his voice somber. He looked at Brooke but she had a blank expression on her face.

"Why should I care so much about Mathias? He lied to me—about what he really was!" was her only response.

"Didn't you wonder how I knew all of that about Mathias? How I knew exactly how to get to him, how to hurt him?"

Brooke remained silent, watching him. He looked at her for a moment before he continued. He was taking a risk with Brooke, but he couldn't even begin to put anything back together with Mathias as long as he continued to lie.

It was time to be honest.

He took a deep, resigned sigh. "Brooke, the truth is that Mathias's not gay, but I am. *I'm* the boyfriend he had in business school."

"What?" she shouted, and her eyes widened in surprise. "Okay, now you really are playing some sort of game with me. Aren't you?" she asked, hopefully.

"No. And I have absolutely no interest in women, *especially* you." Chase's tone was icy, but his words were finally sinking in. Brooke was starting to understand that maybe she shouldn't have been so quick to turn against Mathias, or take such delight in his pain and downfall. None of today—or his plans—had turned out the way Chase had intended, but both he and Mathias were better off without Brooke, and someday soon Mathias would come to the same realization. Chase wished he hadn't been the one to open Mathias's eyes to her true nature.

"But we kissed and in your office... you got excited, and you *wanted* me... I don't believe you!" she cried as if repeating it might change the truth.

"Kissing's the same with a guy or a girl, but I don't want anything else from you. Fact is that Mathias's cock's been inside me more times than it's been in your pussy, I can bet you that." Chase could tell by the look of absolute horror on Brooke's face that she believed him now. "Still want to stay here with me now?"

She stared at him for a moment, as if searching his eyes for the truth, and then a change came over her face, a sudden realization.

"You're still in love with him, aren't you?" she asked in amazement.

"Yes, I am," he admitted, suddenly feeling more vulnerable and afraid than he could remember, but he glared back at her in defiance.

Had history repeated itself?

There'd been only one time in his life he'd felt like this. He'd made the wrong decision then. Not a day went by that he didn't wish he'd had the guts to stand up for what he loved—who he loved. For Mathias.

May 2003
Dallas

THEY had graduated from Fuqua with shiny new MBAs and Chase was home working for his father. He just needed to close out that deal he'd worked on during spring break and then he and Mathias would be off for their European summer blast. It was hard to focus on the spreadsheets and briefings after the stress of exams and moving home. All Chase wanted to do was relax and catch his breath—or get hot and sweaty and out of breath with Mathias.

The thought got the blood pumping and Chase felt his cock swelling. He shifted in his seat and reminded himself in a few days or a week they'd be twirling pasta or kissing as a gondolier steered them along the Grand Canal. Ahhh, Venice.

Alan quickly spotted Chase's distraction and called him in for a discussion. Alan explained that he knew Chase wouldn't disappoint him *this time*; he had faith in Chase to make the right decision. Alan reminded his son that the only time Chase had ever disappointed him before was when he didn't get on the Olympic team. Alan explained that he'd spoken with the coaches after the team was selected, and learned that they didn't think Chase put enough of his energy into training. He'd been distracted, and he'd formed too close of a friendship with Mathias, and they couldn't train effectively together. The coaches had felt they would have both made the team if they'd been more focused on fencing and less on each other. The team wasn't just chosen based on skill, but on teamwork and attitude, and while they were among the most skilled, their deficiencies in the other areas had been enough to keep them off the final team. They'd been made alternates because they really were much more skilled than anyone else who hadn't made the team.

So Alan told Chase that he needed to make some decisions here, and whatever he decided, Alan would accept. Did Chase want to be successful and keep moving forward, or did he want to have something holding him back, keeping him from being his best? Chase had the whole world open to him, if he worked hard and smart and focused.

Chase had loved working with his dad, and he'd enjoyed using what he'd learned in the MBA program, putting it to work, seeing things connect. It was a great feeling when the theory became reality, and you could feel like you were really doing something. There were long hours, and the adrenaline was pumping, and after Chase got to work on his first deal and follow it to the end to see the final numbers—and yes, he'd get a check for well over a million dollars—it was turning into one of the most exciting experiences ever. But it had been nothing compared to the way Alan had praised Chase and made him feel as if *finally* he'd lived up to his father's expectations.

Mathias had been in Venice nearly a week and called Chase every day and it was getting more and more difficult to keep putting him off without explaining about the deal and the bonus that Chase wanted to be a surprise. And each day Chase asked his father if they could finalize the deal. Finally, Alan called Chase into his office for a closed-door conversation.

Today must be the day, Chase thought with excitement as he walked across the wide expanse from the door to his father's desk.

He sat down facing his father, who was leaning back in his chair behind the desk, then glanced around the enormous office, beautifully decorated and looking like something a Wall Street executive might have. There were smaller bowling alleys, Chase thought with a laugh. But as soon as his father started talking, his tone immediately serious and businesslike, Chase's brief good humor evaporated.

"Chase, I'm a little concerned about your priorities right now," Alan began, and immediately Chase tensed. This was not at all the conversation he expected to be having right now. "I need for you to decide if you want to keep doing this. Whether or not you're capable of doing this job. You can stay, and be on my team, and make a commitment to this company. It's not a commitment to me; there are more people involved now. Or you can take the money you earned, have your vacation, then figure out what you want to do with your life."

"Can't I just have a vacation and come back to my job here?" Chase asked, feeling panic welling up inside. "Mathias's already in Venice, Dad, and he's expecting me to join him."

"No, I'm sorry, but that's not an option right now. I can't treat you differently than the other team members, just because you're my son. You can't leave in the middle of the project that *you're* running. You begged me to be part of a real deal when you were here before, and I let you. And I need you to focus, or all the money we've invested might be wasted if this thing goes south. I put you in charge because I thought you could handle the responsibility. Are you telling me I made a mistake about your abilities?"

"No, Dad, I can do it," Chase said, feeling like he was a child again. He took a breath and resigned himself to showing his father he could do what was expected of him. He felt that feeling of confidence slowly start to come over him, as he let that other persona take over. "It's just that based on my forecast, we've already locked in profits double what I had anticipated. I think we can close it any time now."

"That's not how we do things around here. We don't just take our piece and run home when there's still more profit we can squeeze out of it. I'm using this as a training exercise for you, so you can learn from it," Alan explained and Chase just nodded. He loved working with his father, having his father teach him things, and he definitely wanted to learn. "But I'm getting mixed signals from you. I need to know if you are committed to seeing this project through, no matter how long it takes."

"Yes, Dad, but what about M—"

"Chase, there comes a time when you have to decide what's most important to *you*. What you want for your future. I see you as eventually taking over from me here at RichardsCorp, running the company, carrying on our name. Someday, all of this could be yours." Alan swept his arm up, taking in the expanse of the office, and Chase's heart began to race. He'd always wanted to be the one sitting at that desk, since he was a little boy. And his father had been telling him since then that Chase could have it. "But I don't know whether you're committed to putting in the hard work and dedication that it's going to require."

"Yes, Dad, I want that, you know I do!" Chase insisted. Was his father now saying that he didn't think Chase could do the job? Of course he couldn't do it yet; he was just starting his career. He had so much to learn from Alan, and he was looking forward to it. They'd only worked on that one deal so far, but it had been the most amazing thing. Chase couldn't wait to show his father some of the other projects he'd come up with.

Alan paused for a moment, looking into Chase's eyes, then smiling reassuringly before continuing.

"Good, I'm glad to hear that. But you know you have to earn that, right? It's not going to come to you just because your name is Richards. I'm going to choose the man who's shown he most *deserves* the job. The man who knows what his priorities should be, and won't let anything—or anyone—hold him back. Do you understand what I'm saying?" Alan asked.

"I think so," Chase almost stammered. Suddenly he wasn't sure what Alan was talking about, and he dreaded not living up to his father's expectations.

"It's for the best, son, and you'll be safer, too, in lots of ways. We can't have people finding out you're gay, or it could do serious harm to your career—to the company even," Alan added, as if he were trying to assuage Chase's indecision.

It took a few moments for Chase to realize exactly what—or who—Alan saw as the obstacle to Chase's success: Mathias. His father was telling him he had to make a choice between them because Mathias was just going to hold him back, keep him from putting all of his energy into the business, and possibly even inadvertently outing Chase.

"Are you saying you want me to give up *Mathias*?" Chase's heart pounded like timpani in his chest. He could already feel the dizziness settling in, signaling another panic attack. He'd thought he was past the point where his father could still do this to him. Thought he'd earned his father's approval.

"I'm not saying that at all. But right now I need you to be a man and make the right decision for your future, not your past. I wouldn't want to see misplaced loyalties hold you back."

"But *Mathias is* my future, Dad. I love him and he loves me. We want a future together and we support each other in everything. He'd never hold me back here." Chase had to make Alan see that he needed Mathias in his life and could be successful with him—there was no need to choose.

"I indulged you while you were in school, but I never really approved of Mathias. In the real world of business—in *Texas*—a relationship like that is going to be a handicap to you. And I can see right away I'm always going to question where your priorities lie—with RichardsCorp or with Mathias."

"I don't understand why I can't have both."

"Chase, I need to know I can trust you—trust your priorities and your judgment. That you'll be able to carry out any orders you get from me—for the good of the business. I don't want to be disappointed with the faith I've put into you, bringing you into the company. People who work for you or do business with you also need to have faith in your judgment. Otherwise they won't do business with you."

"You can trust me." Chase's head was spinning and his gut churned. He didn't want to disappoint his father. He couldn't do that to him again, not like he had about Sydney. Letting Alan down in business—the family business—would be a million times worse than not making the Olympic team. And Chase couldn't bear to hear disappointment in his father's voice again.

"Good, because I only want what's best for you. And I only want you to have the best of everything. You know how much I love you and I want you to make the right decision, even if it's difficult. I'm here supporting you. And I know you'll do the right thing. I have faith in you, Chase." Alan said and sat back in his chair.

Chase thought he was going to faint, and he could never do that in front of his father. Of course his father loved him and wanted what was best for him. And Alan knew what was best—he always had. But what about Mathias? Chase loved Mathias more than anything… didn't he? But did he honestly love Mathias more than his father? Chase knew he needed Alan to keep loving him and to keep trusting him; he was absolutely certain of that. If the only way to ensure that he got and kept his father's approval was to stop seeing Mathias, then Chase would have to break things off. He needed to be a man and make the right decision, do what was best for his father, for their family. It made his decision so much easier....

Chase fell back on acting like the person he thought he wanted to be, a successful businessman. And he had enjoyed how he'd been accepted so easily into the business. But it wasn't the *real* Chase that people liked and worked with. It was the made-up, confident, even manipulative Chase. But now there was no room in his life for his other personality. His father had taught him to be assertive—even ruthless—to succeed. That's what the job needed, that's what everyone expected from him, and he hated disappointing people—*especially* his father.

He wasn't really choosing between Mathias and his father; he was doing the right thing for the family name and honor, and in the end he chose the business.

CHAPTER NINETEEN

Present day
Dallas

"WELL, you're never going to get Mathias back now, are you?" Brooke practically snarled the words, capping them off with a derisive laugh that chilled Chase to the bone before she headed to the bedroom to pack her belongings.

Chase watched her go with a mixture of relief and dread, then turned and went into his study and shut the door quietly. He poured himself a large whiskey and sat down on the large leather-covered couch at the far end of the room. He could hear Brooke's high heels tapping on the marble floor of the front hallway as she made several trips, obviously taking her belongings back out to the car that Chase had asked to wait outside for her.

Nothing about this day had gone as he'd hoped, and he felt more miserable than ever. First, he'd inadvertently beaten Mathias, and now, he'd had to be so cruel to Brooke to get rid of her. She'd lashed back, though, and now not only did she know Chase was gay, but she had also figured out how he still felt about Mathias. He just hoped she wouldn't use that knowledge to take her own revenge on Chase, but he knew it was a distinct possibility. Maybe he even deserved it after the way he'd treated her.

Mathias had been right: Chase had also ruined Brooke in his power play, using then discarding her when she held no more value. True, Brooke's easy betrayal of Mathias also disgusted Chase, but that didn't justify his behavior. He really was no better than his father, and she wasn't the only person Chase had treated like that. But he vowed that she would be the last.

Remorse over the way he'd treated Brooke paled in comparison to his anguish and misery over how he'd destroyed Mathias. He'd taken everything away from him, when Chase never wanted any of it. The irony of all of this was that the only thing Chase wanted—*needed*—was Mathias, the one thing he had absolutely no chance for at this moment.

Chase had never felt more despondent in his entire life. But he also knew he didn't deserve to feel any other way right now. Everything had been his fault, and it was only fitting he should be as miserable as anyone else at this moment.

There was no way Mathias would want him now, not even want to speak to him, Chase knew that. Not the man who had destroyed Mathias's life. Chase was not going to be that man anymore, that clone of Alan Richards who treated people like pawns in a life-size game of chess.

Chase had to stop being that man; he had to peel back the façade he'd created and worn as a disguise for so long that he hadn't even realized he'd turned into someone else. It had been too easy to ruin Mathias—financially and emotionally—and Chase had never hated himself more.

He gulped down the last swallow of whiskey and grabbed for the bottle on the low table in front of the couch. It was empty. He hadn't realized he'd finished it. He put the glass down on the table with a crash and lay down on the couch.

Chase needed to find the man he used to be and start over with Mathias, go back to being the man Mathias used to love. It was the only way to dig himself out of this mess—the only thing that Mathias would respond to.

If only I'd started out that way, Chase thought as he stared up at the ceiling.

THE day after the duel, Mathias scheduled an emergency shareholders' meeting for one week hence, where he said Chase Richards would present a new bid for the company, and that the details of the offer would be made public before the meeting. Shareholders would vote on whether or not to accept the RichardsCorp bid at the meeting.

A week later, at the meeting, Mathias had no choice but to stand up in front of his shareholders and announce his support for Chase's latest bid and recommend the shareholders accept it. He did his best to answer questions as to why he'd stopped fighting the takeover by explaining how the T-Group would be stronger if RichardsCorp ran it, rather than depleting their cash reserves and threatening solvency by continuing to prop up the share price or repurchasing their own shares on the open market.

Mathias let Chase field the questions about what he planned to do with the company once he had control. Most of the shareholders didn't seem to care once they got their money back, much to Mathias's surprise. He wondered why he'd expected anything different. Chase claimed he would continue to run the company the way it had always been run, and he wasn't planning on making any major changes—especially no personnel changes, and he went so far as to encourage Mathias to continue as CEO—though there would be a thorough review of the business which might suggest substantial changes.

Mathias left as soon as decently possible after the meeting—where Chase's bid was overwhelmingly approved—and avoided speaking with Chase the entire time. He had nothing to say to Chase, and he didn't want to hear anything Chase had to say to him. There was no way he'd stay on and work for Chase! Mathias had made his decision on that last point during their bout, and he'd kept to his bargain by convincing the shareholders to accept Chase's bid.

Afterward, Mathias went home. He had a lot of thinking to do about his future. He hadn't decided whether or not his family should sell their stake in the company. They didn't hold any significant voting power anymore, but if they kept their shares, at least they could cash in when Chase made his move and started dismantling nearly a century's worth of hard work. He was slightly disgusted at the idea of making a profit on seeing his family business destroyed, but he liked the idea that it was almost as good as taking money out of Chase's own pocket.

Mathias woke up in the middle of the night and glanced at the clock. It was 3:00 a.m. and he'd barely slept an hour. The events of the day were still milling around his head. The shareholders' meeting, seeing Chase again, leaving the meeting knowing Chase now controlled his companies, even though the ownership transfer hadn't yet gone through. Mathias had no place with the T-Group anymore. His employees and his family business were now in Chase's hands, which frightened Mathias more than realizing he suddenly had no direction in his life.

He rolled onto his back and stared at the ceiling. He'd been sleeping in the guest room since the night he'd found out Brooke had betrayed him—since he'd been in the limo with the stranger. He hadn't wanted to sleep in the bed he'd shared with Brooke ever again, but why should that mean he had to stay in the guest room?

Before he knew it, he was out of bed, heading into his own bedroom. A sudden burst of energy took control over his body. He hadn't slept in here since before he'd walked in on Brooke in Chase's office. Memories flooded back of the way she'd felt and smelled and the way she'd kissed him. Had that all been a joke to her? Playing with him, when she'd really been on Chase's side. And for how long? How many days and nights had he spent with Brooke when she had merely been a spy, or found the whole situation so humorous that she would toy with Mathias?

In a rage, he pulled the pillows and linens off the California king-size bed, heaping them in a corner. Then he dragged the mattress out into the living room, followed by the box spring. It was heavy, but he was strong and needed to do this now. He had to get rid of any remaining trace of Brooke, at least in his bedroom. By the time he cleared the bed, he was panting with anger and frustration as well as exertion, but he didn't stop.

Next, he moved the guest room bed—not as large or as heavy, but just as comfortable—into his room, then haphazardly dragged the larger bed into the guestroom to replace it. He looked around the room for a moment and was about to slam the door shut on the whole sorry memory when he realized he'd left one thing in there he still wanted. He walked to the night table and opened the drawer slowly, reassured when he saw the black silk blindfold lying in the shadows at the bottom of the drawer. Mathias picked it up, fingers gliding over the smooth surface and he turned and walked out, this time slamming the door with satisfaction.

There would be time enough later on for erasing any further traces of Brooke and the life Mathias had thought they would share here in this apartment. He was looking forward to making the place his own again, though deep down he knew he desperately wanted to find someone to share his home and his heart.

Early August 2001
Durham

THERE was nearly a month before classes began at Duke's Fuqua School of Business, but Chase and Mathias had already moved to town, temporarily taking a suite at the Washington Duke Inn & Golf Club, courtesy of Alan Richards, while they looked for apartments. Make that *one apartment*. Alan had leased a spacious penthouse apartment in the best building in Durham for Chase, and a decorator—hired *and* directed by Alan—was already hard at work well in advance of the start of term at the beginning of September. Chase could move in within the week.

They only needed to find an apartment for Mathias because they'd decided that it was best to have two places: one apartment they could use for study groups and entertaining, and the penthouse would be perfect, while the other would be smaller and homier, a private place they could keep just for themselves. They didn't expect to keep their relationship a complete secret, or pretend to be straight, but they hadn't intended to come out to the world at large either. They'd decide with whom and when they would share more about themselves and their relationship.

Alan had warned Chase not to come out to his classmates for fear that it would hurt him professionally in the future, and Chase was inclined to agree with his father. They would, for all intents and purposes, let people think they were best friends who had separate apartments, but who spent a lot of time together. If anyone figured out their true relationship, so be it.

In the end, it was easiest for Mathias to take a smaller two-bedroom apartment in the same building as Chase's penthouse than to spend a lot of time running around Durham trying to compete for apartments with the rest of the crop of new students. They talked about the possibility the following year of renting a nice house far enough off campus that none of their classmates would want to come by and pry into their private lives. But for the first year of their MBA program, they'd mainly live in Mathias's apartment, which was ready to move into immediately, and Mathias received the keys as soon as he'd signed the lease.

"You're going to need furniture," Chase said while they ate room-service breakfast in their suite the following morning. "At the bare minimum, a bed."

They were sitting at the table near the window of the spacious living room, looking out onto the beautifully manicured golf course that was the main draw at this hotel, which was actually located right on the Duke campus.

"*That's* the bare minimum?" Mathias asked with a laugh.

Chase reached out with his fork to spear one of Mathias's pancakes and dropped it onto his own plate, smiling mischievously.

"Hey!" Mathias cried and reached to retrieve it, but Chase deflected his fork with a knife as if they were fencing, laughing as he did so.

"Tee, you are so out of practice, it's not even funny," Chase teased. "Maybe we could practice some later on."

"Dude! If you want pancakes, *order* pancakes!" Mathias huffed.

"I don't want *any* pancakes." Chase's grey-gold eyes flashed a flirtatious gleam. "Just *your* pancakes." He reached out and stroked Mathias's hand.

"Fine." Mathias refused to be placated.

"Fine." Chase cocked his head. "Have some of my omelet...."

"I guess that'll work... for a start." Mathias let his voice go low and provocative.

Chase slid a portion of his omelet onto Mathias's plate.

Mathias smiled and met Chase's glance, and they gazed at each other for a moment, both imagining what Mathias might want from Chase besides omelet.

"So, back to the subject of furniture," Mathias said, before they completely went off-topic and he never got Chase to focus.

"Right!" Chase replied. "All you really need is the bed."

"No desks or chairs or tables?" Mathias asked skeptically.

"No, we can just sit on the floor when we're not in the bed," Chase joked. "Though I can't really see why we wouldn't just be in bed all the time."

"Good point," Mathias agreed. "Then I guess we should go bed shopping today."

"I can't wait!" Chase said. "It's the first time I've ever gotten to choose my own furniture."

"You mean my furniture, don't you?"

"*Our* furniture." Chase put his hand back on Mathias's and squeezed.

"I like how that sounds." Mathias leaned over to kiss Chase, distracting both of them from thinking about furniture—or pancakes—for approximately an hour.

When they were ready to concentrate again, they made a list of furniture stores and drove to the nearest one in Chase's brand new Jaguar XK8 Convertible, one of the gifts his parents had bestowed after he graduated from Columbia University in the spring.

They spent the next half an hour testing out nearly every mattress in the store. This one was too hard, that one too soft; this one was tall, that one was too noisy. The ones Mathias liked didn't appeal to Chase. It turned into a game as they tried to find the most ridiculous reason to reject each one until they'd tried them all, bantering and bickering like an old married couple. Finally, they agreed on which one to buy. They moved on to the furniture department—much less fun than testing the beds—and found a bedroom set they both liked. Mathias paid for the furniture and arranged delivery for the following morning.

"I'm exhausted," Chase joked. "I might need a nap after bouncing around on beds with you all afternoon." He tugged at Mathias's arm, pulling him in the direction of the exit.

"And that nap would mean getting in bed in our hotel room?" Mathias asked. "Would it entail any more bouncing around, by any chance?"

"It might," Chase admitted with a sly grin.

"Do you think you could stay 'awake' for a little longer while we buy some sheets and towels and stuff like that?" Mathias asked in a slightly sarcastic tone.

"Wow, you are so organized. I wouldn't even have thought about sheets and towels!" Chase said. "I guess my decorator is supposed to make sure that I have all that stuff when I move in."

"My mom gave me a list of stuff I need, and I'm just working my way down the list," Mathias admitted. "I think I'll need a break once we start working on the kitchen. There's a lot of things on the list for the kitchen. Good thing we have a few weeks before classes start."

"On the other hand, there are plenty of restaurants in Durham, aren't there?" Chase reminded Mathias. "Who says we actually have to cook anything ourselves?"

"I *like* to cook. It'll be fun."

"Fun for who?" Chase asked. "I wouldn't say you were exactly Julia Child in your place in Palo Alto."

"Whom," Mathias corrected, though his expression quickly turned pouty as he realized Chase had insulted his culinary skills. "You always ate everything I cooked. What are you complaining about?"

"It was love. That's the only explanation." Chase shrugged, but one corner of his mouth turned up.

"And you don't love me anymore so you won't eat my cooking?" Mathias pushed his chin out just enough to let Chase know he was still offended.

"Oh, I'll eat it, but I won't necessarily *enjoy* it anymore," Chase teased.

"Fine," Mathias said in a huff, folding his arms. "I'll remember this conversation the next time you expect me to suck your cock."

"Shhh," Chase warned quietly, noticing a few customers turning to look at them after Mathias's last remark. "This is still the South. It's probably not a good idea to mention that sort of thing so loudly...." Even though Chase was whispering, the tone of his comments was sharp, and Mathias felt like he'd been jabbed with one of Chase's well-aimed fencing attacks.

"Oh, you're right. I wasn't thinking," Mathias said as he looked around apprehensively. It was late on a weekday morning, and most of the other customers were women or people who appeared to be students. He was suddenly aware of how close he was to Chase and backed away half a pace, though it wasn't necessary. They hadn't been touching or had more than slight physical contact with each other in the store, even in the mattress department.

"I guess I need to be more careful," Mathias added. But he'd lost the joking mood for the time being. Durham might be a fairly progressive town, but they were still in a state where most of the residents wouldn't approve of their relationship and they might be in actual physical danger if the wrong person overheard them.

"C'mon, let's go get some coffee or something, then start working on the list again. How does that sound?" Chase suggested, obviously trying to lighten the mood.

"Yeah, okay," Mathias agreed without much enthusiasm. They left the furniture store and walked down the block—Mathias still consciously monitoring his physical proximity to Chase—until they came across a diner that was uncharacteristically busy for the time of day.

Chase opened the door and immediately they were greeted by a medley of appetizing aromas that made them both smile. They went inside and settled themselves in one of the two available booths. The place was buzzing with activity, and it was clear they'd stumbled on a local hot spot. Soon, a waitress came by to take their orders.

"Can we get menus, please?" Chase asked.

"Oh, you must be new in town, then," the waitress said in a friendly tone. "Regulars don't need menus, and I forget to bring them.

I'm sorry! We usually don't start getting new faces for a couple more weeks. You know, just before term starts," she explained over her shoulder as she grabbed a couple of menus from under the cash register and returned a moment later. "I'll give you some time to look over them, but I can start you off with some peach tea if you'd like," she suggested. "It's our specialty."

"That sounds good," Chase said, and Mathias just nodded, and the waitress headed toward the kitchen. A few minutes later, she returned with two glasses and a pitcher of iced tea with slices of fresh white peaches floating among the ice cubes. She put the pitcher down and smiled.

"I'll let you finish looking over the menu. Enjoy!" she enthused before rushing off to wait on another table.

Chase poured them each a glass of tea, which was lightly sweetened and very refreshing now that the temperature was rising. It might not be as hot as Texas, but it was much more humid and that was even worse.

"Wow, this tea is great." Mathias poured himself a second glass after quickly gulping down the first. "Let's remember this place."

"The menu looks pretty good, too, but I'm not hungry again yet, are you?" Chase asked, and Mathias shook his head in reply. Chase flipped the menu shut. "Magnolia Grill," he read the cover. "Definitely need to come back here with an appetite next time."

"I agree. I'm happy with just tea," Mathias said, but his mood was still subdued. "I'm not feeling up to eating anything," he added. He felt slightly sick to his stomach, partly about his sudden realization that he'd been acting too "out" in this potentially dangerous southern town, and partly at the way Chase had scolded him. In the year they'd been together, Chase had never spoken to him like that, and it still hurt. He knew Chase hadn't intended to sound that harsh, but it had still taken the joy out of the day for Mathias.

"So, let's take a look at that list again," Chase said. "How about we find the kitchen store next?"

"Maybe tomorrow," Mathias said listlessly. He'd lost his enthusiasm for shopping—and cooking—after their sobering conversation in the furniture store, and even the unique tea and the delicious-sounding items on the menu couldn't raise his flagging mood.

Chase picked up on Mathias's tone and looked at him for a moment, concern in his eyes.

"Hey, if it's the thing in the store…," Chase started.

"I wasn't thinking, I know," Mathias said, mentally beating himself up. "I'll be more careful, I promise. I'm just not used to having to think about what not to do or say."

"We've been really lucky so far, most of our time has been spent in New York or around San Francisco where it's easy to get too comfortable," Chase tried to explain in a soothing tone. He looked like he was about to reach toward Mathias's arm, but he must have thought better of it and put his hand back on the table. He glanced around at the other patrons for a moment before leaning forward slightly and continuing, "Maybe once we spend more time around here we'll figure out what's acceptable, but until then, I think we should—"

"Act like we do in Dallas?" Mathias said, a touch of resentment creeping into his voice, even though he tried—not very hard—to hide it. The fact that Alan told them to tone things down whenever they visited still rankled Mathias, and it remained one of the few areas of friction between him and Chase. Not so much that Alan had said it. What bothered Mathias was that Chase just accepted his father's dictates and didn't stand up for himself—or Mathias.

"Yeah, that's what I mean," Chase agreed, sounding relieved. "That's a good plan."

"Fine," Mathias said a bit more curtly than he'd intended, but if Chase noticed he didn't react.

"So, let's finish the tea, then I'd really like to go to the kitchen store and get you everything you need to outfit that kitchen properly," Chase said eagerly, sounding as if shopping for pots and pans might possibly be more fun than oral sex.

"I thought there were enough restaurants in town that we didn't need all that stuff," Mathias said glumly. "Did you change your mind or something?"

"Absolutely," Chase told him. "I'm looking forward to a home-cooked meal tomorrow night… then we can break in the new bed," he added in a whisper. "Deal?"

"Deal, I guess," Mathias said, one corner of his mouth turning up in a reluctant smile. Chase was trying to cheer him up, and even though sex was involved, Mathias could tell that Chase felt bad, not only about his harsh reaction in the store, but also about the way he'd criticized Mathias's cooking. "If you're sure you want to eat something I've cooked," he said, only half joking, the pout back in full force.

"I'd eat anything you cooked *for me*, okay? Look, I'm sorry I teased you before," Chase said, and Mathias could tell he was sincere. Under the table, Chase's knee was pressing up against Mathias's, further emphasizing his words. "I love you," Chase mouthed the words and looked into Mathias's eyes in a way that left no doubt.

"You, know, I'm thinking I might need a nap after all of this tea," Mathias said with a slight wink.

"Can we get our bill, please?" Chase said loudly in the direction of the waitress, without taking his eyes off Mathias.

Present day
Dallas

AS MATHIAS went back to the master bedroom he knew he'd just slammed the door shut on a chapter of his life—he was ready to put Brooke and everything she'd done out of his heart and his mind. It was time to move forward and stop looking back. As unpleasant as it had been to discover that Brooke had cheated on him and revealed his plans to Chase, Mathias had no doubt that he was much better off without her.

He'd been a fool to think that Brooke—or any woman—was going to make him happy in the long term, and he needed to be honest with himself about what he really wanted from any future relationship. Not that he was ready to consider looking for anyone new at this point. There were too many more important things he needed to take care of, not the least of which were finalizing the change of ownership of the T-Group and handing things over to Chase, and his father's health.

Mathias knew his next relationship—if there ever was another—was going to be with someone who appreciated him for himself and didn't want to make him hide who he was or what he really wanted, either in public or in private. Mathias was tired of pretending he was someone else, and he deserved more than what either Chase or Brooke had offered him. He just hoped he could find that person; otherwise, he'd be back to a series of unfulfilling sexual encounters that satisfied his body only temporarily, while the empty hole in his heart grew deeper.

CHAPTER TWENTY

September 2012
Dallas

MATHIAS next saw Chase two weeks later, at his lawyers' office, to oversee the transfer of ownership of the Tobler Group. The Toblers had been required to sell their stake in the company as part of the process after all. They'd be receiving healthy checks for their shares, but it was a hollow replacement for losing the company they'd built up over a century.

The ownership change would be finalized within thirty days or as soon as all the other shareholders completed their own transfer paperwork—a small mountain of forms even for small stakeholders, but a necessary part of the legal and financial process.

Chase and his lawyers sat across the table from Mathias and the necessary officers of the T-Group, as well as their legal counsel. Chase was uncharacteristically subdued and let his lawyers speak for him most of the time. Mathias studiously tried to avoid meeting Chase's eyes during the entire uncomfortable meeting. He succeeded, except for once near the end, when for a moment, their gazes met, and Mathias couldn't describe what he saw there. He'd expected a haughty expression of victory, but the reality showed the much darker, hollow look of a man who seemed haunted by something. He gave Mathias an apologetic, almost embarrassed, look, and Mathias wondered whether this was just another act. But Chase's whole tone and demeanor were nothing like the last time they'd actually spoken, that day back in Chase's office.

Mathias was looking at an entirely different man.

Signing the papers—personal and corporate—took hours, and afterward, Mathias went home—utterly exhausted both physically and emotionally—to his empty townhouse to think about what had happened, and how he'd ended up here.

Pam had packed up his personal belongings from the office, including family photos and mementos, and had them delivered to Mathias's condo. Mathias really wanted his grandfather's beautiful desk, but that was company property, not his own, and he wasn't up to dealing with Chase to get it. In fact, he was reluctant to mention how much it meant to him for fear of giving Chase even more reason to deny Mathias.

He'd spent a week with his parents in Fredricksberg after the shareholders meeting, and even though they tried to convince him that they didn't blame him or hold him responsible, Mathias knew it was his fault. He'd lost the bout. Not just lost it, but *thrown* it. He'd finally admitted to his parents that they'd dueled for the company—the height of nonprofessional behavior—but not that he'd given up at the last moment. He barely admitted to himself how worthless he'd felt. Not just because of what Chase had done to him—because it *was* Chase. The takeover, Brooke, the duel were all completely personal between them, and Mathias just couldn't fight Chase any longer. He'd lost the will to win.

He'd also lost everything his family had achieved. He knew his father must be devastated, though Jerry denied it vehemently, but Mathias didn't believe a word of that. His father's health had deteriorated, and the recent test results showed the course of treatment wasn't working. Jerry's doctors insisted he check into the hospital, where he would have top-notch, round-the-clock care. The private nurses weren't enough anymore, and reluctantly, Jerry had finally complied with medical advice and was back in the hospital. Mathias suspected the timing of his father's relapse was in no way coincidental and blamed himself for that.

After discussing the loss of the T-Group, explaining to his family what had happened with Brooke was adding insult to injury, and Mathias simply gave them the barest of details. Eventually, he'd explain how Brooke's betrayal helped Chase engineer the takeover, but for now, he just let everyone think it was simply incompatibility.

He knew his mother had never really taken to Brooke, but still, she'd been devastated at news of the breakup, especially given the timing. If she suspected a connection, she didn't mention it, and focused on trying to cheer Mathias up.

Now, back in Dallas for the time being, Mathias was at a loss for what to do. In his huge, top-of-the-line kitchen, he heated some leftover takeout for dinner, but ended up pushing the food around his plate because he couldn't eat a thing. He heard a loud, jarring noise, and it took a few moments before he realized it was the telephone. He snapped out of his funk and picked up the receiver, mumbling an incomprehensible greeting.

"Mathias, how are you?" It was Brooke. How stupid did she think he was? She didn't care how he was, and how the hell *should* he be right now? She was calling because she wanted something, though he couldn't make himself care what.

"This really isn't a good time, Brooke." That was an understatement. "Should I send the rest of your things to Chase's house?"

"My things? Chase's…? No…." She paused, and he could tell she was crying. So Chase had already discarded her. "I was hoping…," she started again, but faltered.

Mathias suspected she couldn't bring herself to admit he'd been right about the extent of Chase's interest in her. She hated to lose. He didn't have the energy to care about her right now

"Matt, could we maybe…."

"Could we *what*?" Mathias asked, raising his voice. "You made it clear how you felt about me in Chase's office." He thought he would still be angry, but hearing her voice just left him cold. Cold and empty. Not even a twinge of pain at the core where his heart had once been.

"I was wrong about a lot of things, and you're one of them," she said. "I don't mind if you used to like men, too. I should have talked to you about it, instead of just believing Chase."

"Brooke, everything he said about me is true. All of it, even the part about the waiter. I should have told you the truth, but I thought I could be happy with you. I was wrong."

"We were happy! I was. I know I made mistakes—before Chase—and I'm so sorry for not realizing how I treated you—" Mathias hadn't expected to hear that from her, but even her apology left him untouched. "—maybe we could try it again! I know you loved me before, for real, and I'm the one who made the mistakes…."

"That day in Chase's office he and I made a deal. When I lost the bout, I lost my family's business, and I lost you, too. I know that, and I'm resigned to it." Mathias wondered why he avoided saying no to her. Did she deserve better? "Brooke, things are over between us. No matter what happened between you and Chase or anyone else, and whether or not you care that I'm gay and I cheated on you with men. But I can't get over how you betrayed me to Chase and the effect on my family and my business. I have a lot of things to sort out right now, and I just don't have the energy to try and fix your problems, too. You let me know when you decide where I should send your things."

"Mathias, I didn't realize what would happen. It seemed like a game at first. I had no idea how it would end up."

"Why would you even play a game like that?"

"I'm better at playing games than dealing with reality." Her voice broke and he heard her start crying. She'd summed herself up pretty well and Mathias wondered when she'd become so aware of her problems. "My whole life has been putting on one show after another. Pageants are just a game and I learned how to get what I wanted. I treated you like another prize, but it took Chase to make me realize how big a mess I made of everything."

Brooke and Chase had plenty in common, besides having fucked Mathias over. Maybe they would have been happy together. Mathias didn't need Brooke's baggage; he had more than enough of his own.

"I'm sorry how things ended, Brooke. I really am, but there's nothing left of whatever we had."

"Nothing at all? Not even a little bit of love that we could start with?" She sniffed a few times.

"Maybe I only ever loved you as much as Chase did."

He should feel worse about how things had turned out for her, but he was better off with Brooke out of his life. It never would have been fair to her if they had gotten married, unless she knew the truth. He wished he'd had the courage to end things himself before Chase had gotten involved and used Brooke against him. Mathias had to stop trusting; it had never turned out well for him.

He heard her crying again and he was about to hang up when she spoke. "There's something you don't know. About Chase."

"There's nothing more I want to know about Chase, Brooke." Now little prickles crawled up his spine.

"You should know this. He still loves you, Mathias. I don't think he ever stopped loving you."

He disconnected without saying a word. What could he say to that?

PART II

CHAPTER TWENTY-ONE

Three weeks after Tobler Group ownership change
September 2012
Tobler Ranch
Near Austin, Texas

MATHIAS had, for all intents and purposes, moved out of Dallas and onto his family's ranch in the hills outside Austin. He was outside playing with his dogs, Oskar and Trinka, throwing sticks and watching them run and retrieve, when he saw a dusty pickup turn off the main road onto the winding track that led toward the ranch house. He didn't recognize the car or the man until he got out. It was Chase.

During the past nine years, he'd never seen Chase in anything but impeccably tailored suits and fashionable clothes. Now he was wearing an old shirt and faded, worn jeans that fit him like a second skin. *Damn how good he looks in those jeans,* Mathias couldn't help but think, and he cursed himself at how quickly he'd let himself forget everything that had happened since the last time Chase had been here.

He dusted off his hands and sat down on the front porch, steeling himself for what promised to be an uncomfortable encounter.

AS CHASE pulled off the main road, he was instantly reminded of happier times he'd spent here. He and Mathias had spent part of two summers at the ranch, and Chase had been warmly welcomed by Mathias's family and the ranch staff, and had quickly grown to love the place more than he'd ever expected. Mathias had taught him how to ride Western—he'd only ever ridden English style, and never across the wide-open spaces in the rolling hills that made up the local terrain. For a city-bred boy like Chase, it was a completely different world than the one he'd been exposed to, and he'd enjoyed every minute of it.

Chase hesitated for a moment before he got out of the truck as he looked at the man sitting on a bench on the wide front porch of the ranch house. He almost didn't recognize Mathias. If it wasn't for the extra height, he'd barely know the man. Mathias obviously hadn't shaved for at least a week, his hair was long and unkempt, and his clothes hung on his frame as if he'd lost weight. He hadn't been taking care of himself for a while, that much was more than patently clear. Chase glanced at the dogs and saw their coats were thick and shiny. The horses in the paddock between the main road and the house were fat and had adequate food and water from what Chase could see. Of course, Mathias would never neglect his animals; he only forgot to take care of himself.

It gave Chase a feeling of revulsion knowing he'd done this to Mathias. He realized that he'd broken Mathias's spirit completely. Not only had Mathias lost the bout on purpose, but even now, he seemed to have given up living. Finally, Chase opened the door and stepped down from the truck. As he walked up to Mathias, the dogs barked, baring their teeth menacingly. *Of course they don't remember me after this long.* Chase noticed Mathias didn't try to calm them down.

"Why'd you come by, Chase? Just to gloat? Or maybe you want to take my family's ranch this time?" Mathias shouted bitterly as Chase approached him. "How about my dogs? Need some cattle? There's not much here that would interest a man like you." Mathias remained seated on the bench, making Chase go up to him.

Good. At least he's still fighting back, hasn't completely given up after all. It didn't even matter that Mathias was angry at him, as long as he still felt something. Chase knew once you gave up and stopped caring, you'd fall into the darkest place you could be. He'd been there before, and ironically, it had been Mathias who had provided the incentive for Chase to pull himself back, though Mathias didn't know and Chase wasn't about to tell him.

"That's not why I'm here." Chase walked to the foot of the steps and stood in front of Mathias, but didn't go up onto the porch. "But really, I haven't taken anything I didn't offer to pay for. You'll have a big pile of money, Mathias. I paid you fair value for your business. More, actually, since I know I fucked with the share price, and the final offer included compensation for that. Neither you nor your shareholders got cheated out of a dime." Chase stopped himself.

That wasn't what he'd intended to say to Mathias today. Why did Mathias constantly put him on the defensive? He felt himself slipping into the old patterns, behavior he'd been trying so hard to put behind him.

"You couldn't possibly calculate the value of the hard work, dedication, and love three generations of my family before me put into our business." Mathias folded his arms across his chest and glared.

Chase knew Mathias compared his family's experience to the relative ease with which the Richards had acquired their fortune—taking advantage of people, rather than *earning* it. He had nothing to counter the truth.

"So, tell me how much is left? By now you must have figured out how to sell it all off to line your already-overflowing pockets."

"Haven't touched it. Everything's running just like it was when you sold it to me. Haven't even fired anyone," Chase replied in an ironic tone. He tried to laugh.

"Money's not everything, Chase, but you probably wouldn't understand. That's not how your father brought you up to think. Or maybe I should say how he *told* you to think, because I'm not sure you ever had an original thought when it came to ethics or honor, at least not during the past nine years," Mathias practically spat the words at Chase. "And definitely not when it came to dealing with me."

Mathias had hit the nail on the head about everything, but this wasn't the time to go into the subject of honor or Alan Richards and exactly how he'd groomed Chase to follow in his footsteps.

But mention of Alan reminded Chase about Mathias's own father's illness. Jerry Tobler had always welcomed Chase warmly and kindly and treated him like a son. Jerry had supported their relationship, wanting Mathias to be happy with whomever he chose. If people truly got what they deserved in this world, Alan would be the one in the hospital right now.

"How's your father? I hear he's not doing so well," Chase said, his voice soft and sincere as he felt a pang of sadness for what Mathias must be going through right now. First the business, then Brooke, and now his father's illness. None of it was Mathias's fault; Chase had engineered all of it—the first two, at least—but he knew Mathias probably blamed himself for Jerry's relapse.

"Wow, small talk. Not getting straight to what you want this time? Must be something big or you wouldn't waste time beating around the bush." Mathias paused. "If you really care, my father's back in the hospital. The doctors don't think he'll be coming home this time. It's pretty close to the end for him, and I wouldn't be surprised if my losing our family business didn't have something to do with it. Thanks for asking." Mathias's voice was neutral and unwavering. It was clear he'd resigned himself to what sounded like his father's imminent death, and something about that touched Chase. He hadn't known that Jerry was quite that ill. If the situation were different, Chase would have liked to visit Jerry, but of course that would likely do more harm than good, given what Mathias had said.

He climbed the steps slowly and seated himself at the far end of the bench Mathias was sitting on. Oskar raised his head and growled symbolically, but stopped as soon as Mathias began to stroke him gently. Mathias looked down at the dogs curled up at his feet, avoiding Chase's eyes, probably not wanting Chase to see the pain and vulnerability he undoubtedly felt.

"I'M SORRY," Chase said, sincerely, his voice quiet and soft, a sound Mathias hadn't heard for nine years. "I'm really sorry."

"It almost sounds like you mean it." Mathias glanced at Chase's face, trying to figure him out.

"I do. I know you don't believe that now. I'm sorry for everything that's happened lately. I never wanted it to turn out like this. I never wanted Brooke or the T-Group. I didn't even want to win that fucking duel. When I saw you with Yuri Petrov I was thrilled! You should have won, but I know you gave up," Chase said, surprise and sorrow both evident in his voice.

Mathias looked down at his boots again. Had it been *that* obvious? Of course it would have been to someone of Chase's caliber. Well, no matter, there was no going back now.

"Well, it was just a matter of time. You aren't known for backing down, and I was just so fucking tired of fighting you off. You were right, my personal principles did work against me. I hated the fact that to compete with you I had to be more like you. I couldn't do it. I'd rather lose the company than turn into you, Chase."

"You can stop fighting now. I'm actually here to make you an offer."

"What kind of offer?" he asked, before he realized he shouldn't care, shouldn't want anything else to do with Chase Richards, the man that had ruined his life in so many ways over the years.

"How'd you like to run your company again?"

Mathias sat up straight and stared at Chase, not believing what he'd just heard.

"Oh, and how much would that cost me?" he asked, skeptically. "You know I'd probably pay whatever you asked, you son of a bitch." Mathias raised his voice, the heat and anger flaring up again. He felt his hands balling into fists and forced himself to relax, stroking Trinka's head in order to calm himself.

"Nothing. In fact, I'll pay *you*," Chase said evenly, not responding at all to Mathias's tone. "I want you to run that part of my business for me, just like you'd run it if it were still yours. I'll pay you half share in the business; you'd be my partner."

"I don't like how you do business, and I don't trust you. I'd never be your partner in anything." Mathias said through gritted teeth, though in truth he was surprised by Chase's offer. There had to be some catch. Chase wouldn't destroy Mathias the way he had in order to get the T-Group and then suddenly decide to give it back. There was something else Chase wanted. Mathias just had to figure out what, and he wasn't about to ask.

"You used to be my partner," Chase said, his voice softening, reminding Mathias yet again of their long-ago time as lovers, this time clearly on purpose. Chase must know he still had some hold over

Mathias, and it was clear that none of this was strictly about business. It had nothing to do with business.

"Forget what 'used to be'." Mathias's reply sliced the silence. *Is that what Chase wants now: me?* That would never happen, not after everything they'd just been through. "I guess my biggest question is why?"

Chase shook his head, gazing off in the distance. "I have everything I want—or *thought* I wanted. To tell the truth, I have too much. I don't want more businesses or money or *things*. I'd give it all up and trade it in for something else." He shifted his gaze to meet Mathias's. "I'd really rather have something to build on, something to grow for the future. And I need someone to help me with that. I need you."

Mathias looked up at him through narrowed eyes. Chase was still trying to manipulate him. He'd been using a voice Mathias hadn't heard since B-school. That let's-run-away-together-happily-ever-after voice. The voice he'd used when they'd planned their European summer. The sound of lies. It sent slivers of memory like knives through Mathias's soul. Chase had taken nearly everything out of Mathias that meant anything to him. And now he wanted *Mathias*.

"I used a lot of people and made a lot of mistakes, trying to get what I thought I wanted. What I thought would make me happy. But none of it made me happy. I've lied to so many people even I can't trust anyone anymore. Not a single person who works for me, or anyone I do business with. I don't have anyone I'd really call a friend, just a string of old lovers who'd stab me in the back if they had a chance." Chase paused for a moment. "But I only need one thing, but I fucked up and let it go a long time ago. I don't know why it took me this long to try and get it back. Something I never stopped loving or thinking about. Some*one*. You."

Mathias couldn't tear his gaze away from those caramel-brown eyes. They pulled him yet again into their sweet, deceptive depths. He wanted to dive in and lose himself, let himself be lost, carried away with the emotion Chase's voice and words and those goddamned seductive eyes stirred up.

Trinka growled at something and the sound gave Mathias a chance to breathe. He pulled himself out of the mesmerizing gaze and brushed off his pants as if brushing off the past.

"You have a really good speech writer. Have you considered going into politics? You'd be perfect." Mathias hoped his tone didn't betray the emotions surging through his brain and body.

"It wasn't a speech, Tee."

Mathias stared, chest again tight and painful. Chase hadn't called him "Tee" since they'd been lovers. Just more of his manipulative fuckery. "Even if I were interested in working with you again—which I'm not—how could you expect me to trust anything you say? You said yourself you're a liar."

"Would you believe this?" Chase pulled some papers out of his back pocket. Mathias recognized the share-transfer documents. "How about if I just burned these? The deal isn't final, and the checks haven't been cut. Nothing's legally changed ownership. I can make sure everything goes back to you, your family, and the other shareholders, just like none of this ever happened. We craft a public explanation for the deal not going through. I'll have my lawyers find something in the contract to dispute and—"

"Somehow I don't think destroying the contracts is going to fix everything," Mathias observed wryly. "Those aren't the only copies."

"Fine, we can burn down my office, and my lawyer's office to make sure and get them all, if it'll make you feel better. If you don't want to be my partner—be with me—I'll give you everything back, just undo everything. I've unwound the options and the share price is nearly back to the original level. You decide how you want it. Just tell me how I can fix things. I know I can't erase what's happened or how I've treated you. But maybe someday you'll trust me again, and we could even try…." Chase kicked some dirt with the toe of a boot and Oskar started to lunge forward.

Mathias snapped his fingers and the dog settled back down near his feet.

"What makes you think I'd go for any of that? Or want anything to do with you ever again? How pathetic do you think I am? Just because you dumped me all those years ago, and then you seduced my fiancée into telling you my business plans? You're nothing like the man I lo—" He bit his lip. "—*used* to love." *Fuck fuck fuck fuck fuck.* Mathias cursed his stupid mouth. His heart pounded a mile a minute. He didn't want Chase to know there were any of those old feelings left, and now he'd just spilled. Maybe he hadn't caught the slip.

If Chase heard the slip, he didn't acknowledge it.

"Tee, I hate the man I became after we split… after I broke up with you," Chase admitted in a tiny voice. "You know I wasn't always like this. You can help me be a better person again. I want to be like you. But I need you to help me figure out what my priorities should be. Not what my father drummed into my head."

Mathias saw Chase's chest rise and fall, like he couldn't take in enough air. A familiar sensation. Chase blinked a few times and he took a slow, deep breath. Mathias tried to ignore the way Chase's shirt hugged his body, still-hard lines of muscle, powerful shoulders and arms. Mathias had trouble breathing himself, and his mouth was like the inside of an old shoe.

"Tee, it might not mean much now, but he was the one who made me think I had to break things off with you." He glanced away, humiliation and shame playing across his brow and moist eyes, the bowed head. Then Chase pulled himself together and looked Mathias in the eye. "I can't believe I listened to him. You wouldn't have held me back. You would have made me a better person. You did, while we were together. He taught me to look at what use I could make of people, not to appreciate anyone for who they actually are. But no matter what happened to you—in business, in life, in love—*you* never changed inside, Tee. You're still the same man I loved—still love. I admire you more than you could possibly know."

Mathias didn't reply. He *had* changed. He'd given up. He'd let Chase defeat him. But he also wasn't about to go running back to Chase just because he'd apologized and offered him the chance to run the T-Group again. How the fuck could Chase even begin to think Mathias could forgive or trust him again? Just words. Manipulative, well-chosen words. *Aren't they?*

"You're insane if you think anything you've said today is going to make me want to have anything to do with you—ever again." Mathias stood up to make it clear the conversation was over. He couldn't process any of this yet. Not with Chase standing there, strong and handsome as ever, professing his love. He started to turn back toward the front door.

"I understand. I know I've lost every shred of credibility I might ever have had. I've gone about everything completely the wrong way, which only served to prove to you that I'm as bad as you thought. But I need your help." Chase's tone shifted yet again and Mathias could hear a tremor of fear just below the surface. He'd heard it before, and he also suspected Chase didn't even recognize it for what it was. But Mathias had figured it out: the very first time he'd heard Chase panic—when he'd let his father down by failing to make the Olympic team.

The sincerity in Chase's voice made Mathias sit back down to let him finish.

"I need your help, Mathias," Chase repeated. "I told you I want to keep the T-Group and try and run it… not sell it off for parts. I've done some research and talked to staff and tried to take in the big picture—on the ground, not on paper," Chase began tentatively. "It's going to be a lot more difficult than I'd ever expected. Not only don't I know enough about the industry, but obviously no one trusts me, from the executive team down to the guy who waters the plants. I'm not sure that I'm going to be able to do a very good job at it."

"Bit off more than you can chew?" Mathias asked smugly. God he *was* turning into Chase, he realized, and wiped the smile off his face.

"More than my whole exec team can chew." Chase let out a self-deprecating laugh. "I know I'm going to make mistakes, and the company's going to suffer because of them. Can you help me prevent that from happening? I know you care about the business, the employees, the customers…."

Chase had just hit on the one thing Mathias couldn't flat out refuse: preserving the integrity of the T-Group, and he hoped Chase hadn't read his expression. As much as Mathias hated Chase Richards right now, he could not stand by and let Chase ruin the T-Group if he could do something to prevent it. But working with Chase? Mathias wasn't sure he could handle being around Chase all the time. His heart was pounding at the prospect. There were still entirely too many mixed feelings that Mathias couldn't begin to try and figure out.

It could only work if they kept everything to a strictly professional relationship, Mathias decided. He needed time to think about Chase's offer, but he wouldn't let on to Chase that he'd even consider it.

Apparently Chase had interpreted Mathias's long silence as disinterest.

"Look, I can see I'm wasting your time," Chase said, almost sadly. The evil Chase would say he'd been wasting his time here with Mathias. Had Chase learned *something* after all? "I don't know what to do to make you believe anything I'm saying. When I figure that out, I'll be back. And I will be back, I promise. I'd like your help, and I'm not giving up this time." Chase got up to leave and started walking to his truck. He'd left the contracts on the bench.

"Chase." The word slipped out before Mathias could stop himself.

Chase stopped, but didn't turn around. Not right away. When he did, Mathias noticed his eyes were glistening and bright. Chase swallowed, loud enough to hear fifteen feet away.

"Chase," Mathias said again, wondering how much he would put himself through to protect the T-Group. How much he needed to be protecting himself right now. From Chase Richards. "Let me think about your idea, the partnership—business partnership. Whether or not it could work. You have a lot of resources that, if used properly, could grow both businesses, and make a really successful enterprise with a little bit of work, and some new business practices."

"I'm working on some proposals, crunching some numbers, maybe we could go over those, and you can tell me what you think, or at least tell me why they won't work," Chase added.

"Okay. I can take a look at them when you're finished." Mathias focused on not sounding too eager to see Chase's ideas. The man was a genius when it came to financial innovation, and if he could put his talents to good use…. That report would give Mathias a good idea of how serious Chase was about actually running the T-Group. He recalled how impressed he'd been with Chase's report on the oil supply companies, and wished that Chase had put his obvious business acumen to better use after B-school.

"Maybe we could discuss some of the ideas over dinner? You look like you could use a good meal." Chase's tone was concerned and inviting and maybe even hopeful, but not mocking. Mathias knew he'd missed some meals lately, been too upset or preoccupied to eat, but he hadn't realized that he'd lost enough weight that even Chase would notice and comment on it.

"I need to get to the hospital pretty soon; it's almost visiting hours. And without your numbers, I don't think there's much to discuss yet." Mathias could see the disappointment on Chase's face. "But, I might take you up on that another time," he added.

"Fair enough," Chase said, somewhat more hopefully, and got in his truck and drove off.

As Mathias watched the truck drive off, he thought that Chase had sounded so different, so honest and open, for the first time in a long, long time. He *did* sound a lot like the old Chase, and Mathias knew he wanted to find out how much of that was real. He just wasn't completely sure yet whether or not that was a good idea. It might be the right thing for the T-Group, but it might be the worst thing in the world for Mathias Tobler.

Chase drove all the way from Dallas just for a few minutes of conversation? Mathias wondered, after Chase had left. Of course Chase hadn't known it would be such a short conversation, but he didn't even attempt to overstay his welcome, such that it was. That had surprised Mathias as much as some of the things Chase had said. Though it did also remind Mathias of that night they'd met in Colorado Springs when Chase wouldn't take a hint that Mathias didn't want to spend time with him. That old memory made Mathias smile. That was the fake, cocky Chase that night, and Mathias had been relieved that Chase had decided to be himself after that.

Maybe Chase was really capable of changing for the better, going back to the man that Mathias had spent three years with, and had wanted to stay with for the rest of his life—all those years ago. Now Mathias wondered just how much of Chase's behavior was real and how much was a façade. Could it be possible that hard-nosed corporate raider Chase was really just an act all these years?

And what had Chase been saying about his father? How had Chase's father been behind any of this? That didn't jibe with what

Alan had told Mathias when he'd returned from Venice. Mathias would need to ask Chase about that the next time they spoke.

The next time.

Mathias had clearly already accepted that there *would* be a next time. Was he going to give Chase's offer a chance? All Mathias knew was that he had to at least find out more about what Chase had in mind, if only to help protect the company.

He didn't have time to think about that right now. He needed to get to the hospital and visit his father. There was no telling how much time he had left, and Mathias wouldn't let Chase keep him from spending as much of that time as possible with his dad.

MARTA was in Jerry Tobler's room when Mathias arrived at the hospital in Austin. She was sitting on the edge of the bed, holding her husband's hand. Jerry needed to wear an oxygen mask almost constantly now, so conversation wasn't really an option at this point. Simply sitting with him and having any physical contact would have to suffice.

"Hi Dad, Mom," Mathias said as cheerfully as possible as he entered the room. He bent to plant a kiss on his mother's cheek, then sat on the opposite side of the bed, facing his father. Jerry only managed a weak wave in greeting, but under the mask he was smiling.

"You look completely exhausted, honey," Marta said after taking a good look at Mathias. "You haven't been taking good care of yourself lately. You can't keep this up much longer without getting sick, you know."

Jerry squeezed Mathias's hand as if in agreement with Marta.

"I know. I just can't sleep lately, and I'm hardly ever hungry. I've had so much to deal with the past few weeks, and I haven't quite processed it all yet. I'm still trying to figure out what my next step should be…. And then today…." Mathias's voice trailed off.

"What happened today?" Marta asked, a look of concern flooding her face.

"I don't really even want talk about it," Mathias replied listlessly.

Jerry squeezed Mathias's hand again, which Marta had noticed. Jerry wanted Mathias to talk about his problems, not keep them bottled up out of some fear for his father's health, but Mathias wasn't sure that was the right thing to do.

"You wouldn't have mentioned it if you didn't want to talk, so let's have it," she said encouragingly.

"It's just...." Mathias's voice trailed off. "Chase." He stopped, as if that were all that needed to be said.

"What happened now?" Marta asked.

"He came by the ranch today, and he was... I don't know... *different*."

"He came to *our* ranch?" Marta asked with incredulity. "It's at least three or four hours from Dallas!"

"Yeah, he came by to talk to me, all the way from Dallas. I wondered about that, too," Mathias conceded.

Jerry tugged on Mathias's hand. He was impatient to hear what Chase had to say to Mathias.

"He made me an offer to work for him and run the Tobler Group—to be a 50-50 partner with him," Mathias announced. He could tell both of his parents were shocked by this turn of events.

"He's keeping it?" Jerry wheezed. He'd pulled his oxygen mask off to speak, and Marta fought to put it back on him, while he tried to shove her hands away. In the end, Marta won. She always did.

"Yeah, Dad. He says he wants to run it, and with his capital he thinks it could be much more profitable."

"And you believed *that*?" Marta asked. Clearly she didn't want Mathias to be made a fool of again when it came to Chase Richards.

"No. I mean, I'm not sure," Mathias replied. "I'm afraid to believe a word he says, but he sounded like he meant it. He sounded almost like...."

"Like what?" Marta asked.

"Like he used to... before."

No one needed any clarification what Mathias meant when he said that.

"Are you considering the offer?" Marta asked.

"If he's serious, then yes, of course. I can't take the chance that he might damage the company, fire our employees, or ruin our good name," Mathias replied. He was tired, so tired, and he didn't want to spend the little time he had with his father talking about Chase. "I still feel so responsible for everything that's happened."

Jerry grabbed at Mathias's hand again, giving him a squeeze to let him know none of it was Mathias's fault.

"Maybe none of it would have happened if I'd let him buy those companies in the first place," Mathias suggested. "You know I actually took a look at that operations proposal he'd put together, and it made sound business sense. I didn't want to believe it, but Chase really did his homework on those companies and the industry, and if he'd done what he said and tried to actually operate them as going concerns, he would have done a good job with it."

"Do you think he could be serious about keeping the T-Group intact and working to expand it?" Marta asked again.

"I need to talk more with him, sound him out to see what he's getting at. Just with him, it's impossible to know what's an act and what's genuine."

That made Mathias think about something he'd nearly forgotten. Along with the million and one things he'd tried to forget about Chase over the past nine years. That night, years ago when Chase had told him how when he was worried or nervous, or something was dreadfully important to him, that Chase put on an act—tried to be the person he thought could handle the situation. Was the Chase he saw today the actor, or had most of the past nine years been the act? Mathias had to think about that before he could even begin to fathom the truth. He certainly hadn't listened to Chase when he'd tried to explain anything, especially about himself. Maybe Mathias needed to listen to Chase, find out what Chase seemed to want to tell him.

"Well, I think you shouldn't rule it out without some careful thought."

"Yeah, Mom, I won't. Chase said he wanted to show me some of his ideas, and I think I'll give him the chance to prove that he's serious this time. I just wish there weren't so many personal feelings tied up in the situation."

"I know, honey. It's not just about the company, or even about what happened between the two of you. Involving Brooke in all of this seems to me that he's gone too far," Marta said, her tone edging back toward caution and unease.

"I don't think Brooke would have been as easy for him to manipulate if I'd been paying more attention to her," Mathias conceded. "I don't think I made as much of an effort with Brooke as I should have… and that should have told me that she wasn't really the right person for me. I know she has a lot of good qualities, but somehow, I didn't really bring them out of her, and she didn't bring out the best in me either."

"Those are good observations. I'm sorry you had to discover all of that so late," Marta said. "But you have plenty of time to find the right person to settle down with."

"I know. I just haven't met anyone—except Brooke—who even gets my attention much less any stronger interest." Mathias couldn't keep his dark mood out of his voice.

Marta and Jerry held hands with Mathias, and he fought to brighten his frame of mind. The last thing he wanted was to make things even more depressing for his family. At that point, Mathias's older brother, Leo, entered the room. He'd come back from his assignment abroad as soon as he'd heard his father had been hospitalized and had been to visit him almost every day, though not always at the same time as Mathias. Leo had been working on local fundraising activities for Doctors Without Borders during the rest of the time, and occasionally he had appointments he couldn't reschedule.

"Hey, Leo!" Mathias said, and got up so Leo could sit at their father's side. "Good to see you!"

"Hi, Dad, Mom, Mattie," Leo said.

For the next couple of hours, Mathias concentrated on his family, and swept Chase and RichardsCorp out of his thoughts.

CHAPTER TWENTY-TWO

CHASE'S drive back to Dallas seemed much longer than the ride out. He hadn't seen Mathias since the tense morning in the lawyer's office, and he hadn't spoken privately to Mathias since that confrontation in Chase's office. He'd been looking forward to the opportunity to speak open and honestly about everything they'd just gone though. He had hoped that Mathias had relaxed and might be open to Chase's offer. Had he really expected Mathias to jump at the chance? Of course that's what Chase wanted, but it hadn't been realistic. There was still too much animosity and emotion between them. It had been there—on Mathias's side, at least—before the whole takeover started, only Chase hadn't realized it. Of course Mathias had never gotten over their breakup either. Chase had broken things off in such a cowardly way and hadn't gone to see him even if only to explain *why*. He would have begged Mathias to take him back. In hindsight, that would have been the best thing. Chase knew that now, but at the time he thought he needed to keep his distance from Mathias so they could both get over it.

He thought for sure Mathias would throw him out on his ear after he'd said he was still in love with him. Then, against all expectations, Mathias called him back. Chase hadn't wanted Mathias to see the tears welling up in his eyes. He only had himself to blame for Mathias's hatred and refusal to have anything to do with him—personally or professionally. Visiting the ranch today had been a gamble, a long shot, but Chase had to take it and lay everything out on the table, honestly, and hope Mathias really was the man who Chase not only loved but admired as much as he'd said. Nothing he'd said had been a lie or an act.

From the day when Mathias had smiled after Chase had beaten him fencing at an intercollegiate tournament, Chase knew Mathias was extraordinary. He hoped like hell he hadn't destroyed that.

Then Mathias had said he'd think about Chase's offer. But at that moment, the *last* thing Chase had been thinking about was *working* with Mathias. He imagined kissing him and touching him and making love with him. When they'd been together, Chase felt confident and successful and special—all the things that over the past nine years he'd needed to hide behind a façade or pay for in order to feel.

That night in the back of the limo had been impossible for Chase to forget, and he was determined to do whatever Mathias demanded if only he could get another chance. But if he had to wait for all that, prove to Mathias he was really changing as a person, then he would. He could do that. He had to try to do things Mathias's way; that *was* what Chase wanted.

But now, Chase could only move forward, and this time he would take his time. He wouldn't push Mathias. He'd wait for Mathias to contact him, and he knew eventually that would happen. Mathias couldn't in good conscience not try to see how he could get his company back, or at least how he could make sure the business was being run in order to protect his family's reputation and the employees he seemed to care so much about. The fact was, Chase really needed Mathias's help to run the T-Group, and he just had to make that the focus of their interactions, at least until Mathias began to trust him again.

Chase knew that even if Mathias did decide to come to work with him, that didn't mean there would be anything more to it than that. Especially if Chase tried to rush Mathias. It was going to take Mathias time—possibly a long time—before he'd trust Chase about anything, ever again. Chase was resigned to that and committed to finding a way to change Mathias's mind. And he knew how much even just the chance of getting Mathias back meant to him. He'd used up a large portion of his company's resources for the takeover, and now he was offering Mathias a half stake—for free. But Chase would gladly give up everything he had to get Mathias back. Not one single thing Chase had bought with his wealth had ever made him as happy as Mathias had without even trying, just by being himself and loving Chase back enough to give Chase the confidence he hadn't found within himself.

Chase smiled, remembering how much more there was to their relationship than just that. How he and Mathias had just clicked, complemented each other with so few points of disagreement. It had been so easy to fall in love with Mathias, and to keep loving him—Chase had never really stopped. He couldn't help but think about how much he still wanted Mathias—wanted to touch him, feel him, kiss him. Chase had never felt so alive as when he'd been with Mathias. Mathias was an amazing lover—open and giving. Sometimes it was just a touch, or even a simple glance, that could make Chase's heart race. Other times, Mathias could be hard and demanding and the things Mathias did to him then just blew his mind and left him helpless and shattered and begging for more. Like the time with the saber.

Autumn 2001

Durham

"I THINK you need to close your eyes," Mathias said, and Chase complied. He was naked and lying flat on his back in the bed in his apartment with Mathias sitting on the edge of the bed next to him. Mathias brushed his fingers along the closed eyelids and Chase smiled. He loved it when Mathias got creative, and he had a feeling something out of the ordinary was going to happen.

Mathias got up off the bed.

"Where are you going?" Chase asked, opening one eye a tiny bit.

"Okay, I can see you can't listen to directions," Mathias replied playfully. "Put your hand over your eyes until I tell you that you can take it down, got that?" Mathias demanded in a tone that told Chase not to argue.

Instead, Chase smiled and did as commanded. *Oh yes, this was going to be interesting.*

"Ooh, Tee, I love it when you take control like that!" Chase said to Mathias's retreating footsteps. Chase heard his closet door open and Mathias obviously rooting around in there for something specific.

A few minutes later Mathias came back over to the bed and sat down next to Chase.

"Lift your head up and take your hand off, but keep your eyes shut," Mathias told him and tied something around Chase's head. Chase fingers instinctively reached for it, discovering it was one of his neckties.

"Got one for my wrists?" Chase joked.

"Not now, but if I need one, there's more in the closet. Now be quiet and lie still and do what I tell you," Mathias ordered.

Chase could feel Mathias stand up, and it sounded like he was walking away from the bed and opening something else, but Chase couldn't quite place the sound. The next thing he felt was cold metal against his leg, just above his right ankle. It meandered lazily up the inside of his leg, just scraping the skin with light pressure, increasing as it moved upward.

"Is that what I think it is?" Chase asked tentatively.

"Depends on what you think it is," Mathias scoffed.

The metal thing approached the inside of Chase's right knee. Definitely a blade, and he knew immediately what it was. What he didn't expect was how much he was enjoying the way Mathias was touching him with it.

"Is that my *saber*?" Chase asked incredulously, already half-hard.

"No more questions or I'll have to gag you, too," Mathias warned, jabbing Chase's inner thigh enough to get his point across but not enough to hurt much. The blade wasn't sharpened, and it wouldn't draw blood, but the tip of it could inflict some damage and pain, and right now, that jab more than got Chase's attention. Suddenly, he was completely hard. He couldn't believe how excited he'd gotten at the way Mathias had touched him with the sword. It was hot and kinky and *so* unexpected from Mathias.

Now Chase wondered, with some alarm, what Mathias had in mind as the tip of the blade moved very close to his balls—which felt surprisingly good—but it kept moving slowly, along the crease of his hipbone before Mathias directed it toward Chase's navel. But then Mathias pulled the saber up and lost contact with Chase's body.

Chase wasn't sure if he was relieved or disappointed, probably a little of both. Until he felt the tip of the saber brushing up against the base of his cock. He'd never felt anything like this before; it was incredible, and Chase could feel himself twitching at the touch of the cold metal, which elicited a satisfied laugh from Mathias, who then dragged the blade along the length of Chase's cock and on up his torso, tickling slightly. Just below Chase's left nipple the pressure increased to just this side of pain, but by now, to Chase, it felt so good, and he wanted more pressure, even some pain. He groaned softly.

"Ah, you like that?" Mathias asked.

"Yeah, God, yeah," Chase moaned. He loved it.

Mathias increased the pressure slightly as Chase pushed up against the saber. Yes, it hurt but the pain was brief and Mathias pulled back fairly quickly. Chase was suddenly and intensely aware of every part of his body, especially his cock, which was hot and hard and aching, and he moved a hand in that direction, but Mathias parried with the saber to deflect Chase's hand.

"Fuck, your reflexes haven't slowed at all," Chase grumbled.

"That's enough playing around," Mathias told him. "On your hands and knees," he added curtly.

Chase thought the game must be over now, and Mathias would get to the part where he actually fucked Chase, because right now, Chase really wanted to be fucked, and the sooner the better. But apparently Mathias had something else in mind because he didn't walk over to the bed, eager to get his hands on Chase. Chase didn't even know where Mathias was or what he was doing. He was amazed how quietly a giant like Mathias could move.

Chase heard the whir of the blade through the air before he felt it strike him across the ass, and he groaned uncontrollably at the sharp, hot pain that lingered for a moment before easing away. But it was a groan of pleasure, not pain, and he felt his cock ache and twitch.

"Hmm, I think you liked that too much," Mathias said with a hint of disappointment. "I probably shouldn't do that again," he warned.

"No! I didn't like it!" Chase protested because he really wanted Mathias to hit him again. They hadn't really done much BDSM, so they were still exploring the boundaries of what they liked and didn't like, but so far, Chase loved everything Mathias was doing to him, and he was already so fucking hard he wasn't sure how much more foreplay he could stand.

The saber whirred once more just before it smacked him again, this time slightly lower than before, and the pain lingered for much longer this time around. Chase didn't think he wanted to be hit any harder than that. He was going to let Mathias know when he felt Mathias's fingertips softly brush the still-throbbing line where he'd just been hit, as if trying to soothe it, and Chase knew he already had a welt forming on his skin. Occasionally it happened if someone got hit by a blade during practice, and this time it had been on bare skin.

"Enough of that," Mathias said almost apologetically, but he landed a decent slap on Chase's ass instead before Chase heard him step away from the bed again.

Then, Chase felt the tip of the saber on the sole of his left foot, and it moved up the side of his calf and began climbing his thigh.

Now Mathias really had Chase's attention. *He wouldn't*, Chase told himself. Mathias just wouldn't use the saber on him like *that*, would he?

"You're gonna need this," Mathias said suddenly and tossed something onto the bed near Chase's left hand.

Chase reached out; it was a tube of lube. Well, at least Mathias was going to fuck him one way or another pretty soon, but Chase wasn't quite sure whether he was going to like it.

"Get yourself ready."

Chase still had the blindfold on, but he turned his head toward Mathias in confusion and Mathias must have guessed from the expression on his face at least part of what Chase was thinking.

"Slick up a couple of fingers, and you can figure out the rest, can't you?"

Chase sat down for a moment while he put some lube on his fingers, quite a bit trickier to do blindfolded than he expected, but he managed, then got back on his knees, reaching a hand between his legs and pushing one finger slowly into himself.

"Good," Mathias said. Now his voice was low and gravelly, and Chase could tell Mathias was just as hard and worked up as he was. "Slowly... 'cause I like watching you fuck yourself."

Chase pushed a second finger in, and it felt good. Very good. But not what he wanted. He wanted Mathias's cock.

"Tee, c'mon and stop playing," Chase gasped. Even his own fingers were getting him more and more needy, and he wasn't sure how much longer he could wait. He sped up the motion with his hand, fucking himself more than really prepping for Mathias. If Mathias wasn't going to fuck him soon, he'd just do it himself. But the point of the saber jabbed at Chase's hand and he stopped.

"You're ready enough," Mathias said and pulled Chase's hand away. "All this time, and you've never been fucked by a saber, have you?" Mathias asked. His tone was a mixture of threat and playfulness and now Chase was actually worried. But he was still hard as a rock, mostly prepped and more than ready, and completely at Mathias's mercy.

The tip of the saber dug into one cheek of his ass, again not quite painful, before Mathias dragged it slowly downward, reducing the pressure until Chase could just feel the blade scraping against his balls. The light pressure combined with some genuine fear was exciting. This was either going to be the best or the worst fuck of his life, he knew that now.

"Tee?" Chase was nearly pleading now. He wasn't even sure what he was pleading for. For Mathias to stop? Or for Mathias to jam the saber into him? But he already knew he didn't want Mathias to stop. He was hot and hard and desperate. He leaned forward, head nearly to the bed, and shoved his ass at Mathias, completely spread open and waiting, groaning with need even though he tried his best not to.

"That's *my* saber," Mathias said with a laugh as Chase felt Mathias's cock jamming into him. Chase half sobbed with relief and overexcitement. He hadn't really prepped much, and it felt like Mathias's cock was ripping him apart, tearing a shout from Chase's mouth. Almost immediately, the pain turned into the most intense pleasure, and Chase had to grab and tug at his balls to stop himself from coming. Mathias didn't say or do anything; he was too busy fucking into Chase like his life depended on it.

Chase lost track of everything except the feel of Mathias's cock splitting him open, and the way Mathias grabbed at his hips, digging his long fingers into Chase's flesh. He heard shouts and groans and beautifully filthy words, but he wasn't sure if they were his or Mathias's and he didn't care. All he wanted was for Mathias to keep fucking him, wanting him, needing him. Because Chase wanted and needed Mathias just as much, and he thrust his hips back to meet Mathias's.

Mathias slowed his movements and leaned down onto Chase's back, holding onto Chase's shoulders now, hot breath burning his neck before he felt Mathias's teeth sink into his flesh, and he let out another growl of pleasure. Now Mathias's hands were traveling down Chase's shoulders, his back, until one hand slid onto his chest, stroking down the groove between his pecs. A thumb brushed against one nipple and it shot even more waves of pleasure through Chase's already overloaded body. His balls ached and he knew he couldn't last much longer. Mathias hadn't even touched his cock, and Chase had nearly lost complete control several times.

This time, Chase didn't even try to fight off orgasm. Instead he concentrated on every point of contact with Mathias, feeling Mathias's cock dragging across that magical place inside, Mathias's hands on his body—sometimes roughly grabbing at him, other times stroking more gently and sensually, and the sounds of Mathias's own pleasure as he took what he wanted from Chase—what Chase was more than happy to give.

Mathias's hand slid lower, taking firm hold of the base of Chase's cock, and Chase knew it was over as soon as he felt Mathias stroke upward. Almost immediately, Chase started coming, groaning and sobbing as his cock exploded, shooting thick, strong jets for what seemed like ages while Mathias mumbled filthy words of encouragement into Chase's ear.

That had to be the most intense orgasm he'd ever had, Chase thought hazily as his body gave out, and he nearly collapsed onto the bed, held up only by Mathias's tighter-than-tight grasp of his chest and shoulders. But Mathias wasn't finished with Chase yet, and he sped up his movements again, grunting and gasping into Chase's ear with each stroke. Even though Chase's brain was working about as well as his body right now, he knew he'd never seen or felt Mathias quite like this before, desperate and needy, fucking him like a wild animal, and it thrilled him as much as Mathias's controlling kinkiness had.

Suddenly, Mathias stopped and shuddered. Mathias's strong arms surrounded him, and deep inside he felt the hot pulsing of Mathias's orgasm. Mathias groaned out Chase's name then fell silent, and all Chase could hear was Mathias gasping for breath as he rolled onto the bed, taking Chase with him, Mathias's arms curled around Chase, still holding him close.

CHAPTER TWENTY-THREE

Present Day
Tobler Ranch

OVER the days following Chase's visit to the ranch, Mathias mulled over what Chase had said, and what he hadn't said. He had apologized for what had happened over the past two months: for turning Brooke against Mathias and for trying to destroy Mathias's life and everything he cared about. But was his sincerity enough to make Mathias consider going back to the T-Group to work with Chase? Could he ever trust Chase again? The apology was a start. He could only imagine how difficult it had to have been for Chase to come to the ranch and say those things. It gave him a tiny shred of respect for Chase's gesture.

And the things Chase had said, about wanting to change and admiring Mathias and his family, had made Mathias reconsider his opinion of Chase. Why else would he drive out to the ranch unless he really wanted Mathias to believe it and… and *what*? Take the offer of partnership? What could Chase really be after? He had everything he could get from Mathias. Or had he? The only thing Chase didn't have was a personal connection to Mathias; it had been severed long ago. Did Chase really want him back?

Mathias stopped himself. The idea was ludicrous. How on earth could even *Chase* think trying to destroy Mathias's company could ever win Mathias back? Thinking back, Chase hadn't started out targeting the Tobler Group. He'd begun with a very reasonable offer for a block of companies that really didn't fit into Mathias's business. Mathias had sold them to someone else.

That's when it all started, Mathias realized. Chase hadn't arrived that day fuming and angry, but that's how he'd left. Mathias replayed their conversation in his mind. He'd come in asking for an explanation. He'd left in a rage only after Mathias had accused him of behaving worse than his father. Being compared to Alan Richards set him off.

Chase had also mentioned Alan when he'd visited the ranch. What about Alan was so important? Now Mathias was intrigued, and he wanted to find the answer.

He still had the card Chase had given him weeks ago with his private line and cell phone numbers. He picked up his phone and called Chase's cell.

"Richards," Chase's voice came across the line, all business.

As soon as he heard Chase's voice, Mathias wondered, *Am I doing the right thing by believing him?* He doubted his ability to judge people—especially Chase—but his parents had convinced him to at least give Chase a chance to prove he'd changed.

"Hello?" Chase asked, a hint of impatience in his voice.

Mathias had paused longer than he'd thought as those doubts flashed through his mind.

"Chase… it's Mathias." He wasn't sure how to start this conversation—or whether he should even be having it in the first place.

"Mathias? I… I… didn't expect you to get back to me so fast," Chase said, his voice anything but professional, and all Mathias could think of was a tongue-tied twenty-one-year-old talking to him in the locker room, back at the Olympic Training Center all those years ago.

Mathias swallowed a lump in his throat as he fought off the memory. Why the fuck had he remembered *that* just now?

"Yeah, I discussed your ideas with my family." Mathias spoke once he was sure his voice would sound normal again. "And I want to take you up on—"

"The partnership?" Chase asked, a bit too eagerly.

"Not so fast, Chase…." Mathias bit his lip as he forced himself to keep this professional. "I meant your offer to go over some numbers and plans with me."

"Yeah, sure," Chase replied, but the disappointment was obvious.

"Let me know where and when is convenient for you. My schedule is pretty free right now."

"Right… I …," Chase paused. "How about Thursday evening?"

"Evening's no good, actually. I'll be visiting my dad, but the early afternoon would work for me," Mathias suggested.

"Your dad…. Mathias, I'm really sorry to hear he's in the hospital again. Whether you believe me or not, it's true," The clear regret in Chase's voice made Mathias feel guilty for doubting his sincerity.

Well, maybe Chase has a conscience after all. But how far did it extend? Mathias would discover the answer on Thursday.

"Thanks," Mathias said honestly.

They discussed the details of their meeting and disconnected.

WHEN Chase hung up from his short conversation with Mathias he couldn't believe it. Mathias had called and was actually considering the idea of a partnership. Mathias had only agreed to look at the ideas, but it was progress! He needed to take things slowly—and calmly—this time for sure. Mathias's tone had been completely professional, so Chase tried not to read any more into the call. There was nothing personal at all about the call. Chase must have sounded like an idiot to Mathias—tongue-tied and unsure. He had to be himself with Mathias going forward—the real Chase, shy, occasionally goofy, but honest—no matter what. Lying and acting had only gotten him heartache and a lot of things he didn't really want. But it had lost him the one thing he still wanted more than anything: Mathias.

Thursday couldn't come fast enough, but Chase fought to keep focused on work the rest of the week. He'd pretty much abandoned RichardsCorp's normal business to Mike Killian and the rest of the executive team and spent all of his time on Tobler Group business. He'd taken an office on the top floor of the T-Group's building—he wasn't about to take over Mathias's office, for so many reasons—and spent most of each day listening to Mathias's executive team's reports and making decisions about things that he quickly discovered he knew very little about. Sure, he knew how to run a company in general, but there were so many things specific to this company that put Chase out of his depth immediately. He relied on Mathias's executive team to steer him in the right direction.

Chase wouldn't be able to keep this up if Mathias didn't come back. The entire executive team had already presented him with letters of resignation effective on the date the change of ownership became official—in less than a week. Chase had offered each of them substantial pay raises to stay, even for an extra month or two, and to a man—and woman—they'd turned him down flat. He couldn't handle the job on his own and it would take time to find a suitable replacement team.

What the T-Group really needed was Mathias running the show, making the right decisions and encouraging his well-chosen executive team to stay, despite the fact that Chase now owned the company.

THURSDAY afternoon, however, Chase had decided that they should meet on completely neutral territory. He couldn't ask Mathias to meet him in his new office in the T-Group headquarters, and he certainly wouldn't expect Mathias to ever set foot into Chase's office again— not after what Chase had done to him the last time he'd been there. He cursed himself for the millionth time over how badly he'd handled *everything* with Mathias. He'd let him get on that plane to Italy alone then strung him along for over a week, and then practically forced Mathias to make it easy for Chase to break things off.

He'd been such a fucking coward. He'd folded under his father's pressure when he should have stood up and made it clear what was really most important to him. Why had he let his father fuck with his life? He should have figured out that Alan was pulling the strings from the beginning, but Chase hadn't understood until it was too late. He hadn't realized in time that Mathias was the most important thing in his life, and it was no one's fault but his own.

He had to make the first move in order to heal things and maybe someday—Chase could wait—Mathias might begin to trust him again.

Chase drove himself to the restaurant in the Spyder, with the top down. He'd reserved a table for the patio area. It wasn't a popular place for business and it was well past lunchtime, so he and Mathias would have privacy for their discussion. It was a lovely sunny day with a light breeze, and Chase enjoyed the sun on his face as he walked into the restaurant from the parking lot. He'd noticed Mathias's Lexus was already there, and parked next to it.

The hostess showed Chase out to the patio, where Mathias was waiting, sipping iced tea with thick slices of ripe peach floating in the glass. He nodded slightly as Chase took his seat but didn't say anything.

"Hi," Chase said.

"Peach tea." Mathias gave an abrupt nod and raised his glass. "Just like the place we used to love in Durham."

"Right," Chase said, remembering. He'd completely forgotten this place had peach tea. He hadn't been here in ages. He hoped Mathias didn't think he'd chosen this place because of the tea and its nostalgic connection. But then again, Mathias *had* ordered the peach tea, and brought it up, his tone sounding reminiscent and not at all accusatory. "Great place. They never threw us out, no matter how long we stayed, as long as we kept ordering pitchers of tea!"

"They made the best carrot cake in the world, if I remember correctly," Mathias added, laughing softly.

Their reminiscences were interrupted when their waitress walked up with menus and rattled off the daily specials.

"Can you please bring us a pitcher of the peach tea, and another glass? Then give us a few minutes to decide?" Chase asked when she had finished.

"Sure thing." She added a cheerful smile, then turned on her heel and headed back inside.

"I don't have all day this time, remember that. I need to get to the hospital, and I have a long drive," Mathias reminded Chase. "Now I thought you had some proposals to show me," he added, his tone showing a tiny hint of suspicion.

"I do." Chase noted with disappointment how quickly Mathias had brought the conversation around to their sole purpose for meeting.

But Chase realized he didn't have the folder with him. Did Mathias think Chase had brought him here under false pretenses—that there was no proposal? Did that trigger his abrupt change of attitude? "Damn! I left it in the car. I'll be back in a minute."

"Why don't you order first, then go get them." Mathias opened his own menu and began skimming the offerings. "What's good here?"

"I don't know. I haven't been here for a long time, and it looks like they've completely changed the menu. I just remembered I liked the patio here."

Mathias looked around appreciatively. He certainly *seemed* to be in a good mood. Chase took a moment to really look at Mathias, while Mathias's attention was elsewhere. He definitely looked a lot better than he had the other day at the ranch, much healthier. He'd shaved and put on casual business clothes, rather than the loose, torn jeans he'd had on before. He smelled like sunshine and shampoo. The way he'd always smelled. The scent brought back an almost physical pain that must be locked into his memory banks. Mathias and the scent of peach tea. The sun shone on his glossy black hair, the longish bangs temporarily tucked behind one ear. They'd slip out and into his eyes sooner or later. Chase smiled at the familiar recollection.

The last time they'd sat across a table from each other had been in the lawyer's office, and Mathias had looked exhausted, sleep deprived, and defeated. Now Mathias sipped tea, looking relaxed. Chase's heart skipped a beat at how normal things seemed between then. They hadn't been this close and this comfortable in years. Even better, Mathias hadn't jumped right to the main reason for this lunch; he'd chatted, even mentioned their favorite place in Durham.

"Yeah, this patio is wonderful, nice and quiet. Doesn't seem like the kind of place you'd choose." Mathias tone held no hint of the sarcasm Chase expected, but it still felt like a backhanded compliment.

"Why not?"

"I guess I expected you to pick some trendy place with pretty but inedible food," Mathias said. "Not a place like this with homey southern comfort food."

"They have great key lime pie, too. Or at least they used to. I remember that now." Chase tapped the dessert section of the menu. He decided not to let Mathias's comment about expecting a place that was all about appearances bother him.

"What kind of Texas boy are you if you don't have pecan pie?" Mathias joked, and Chase relaxed a bit.

The waitress came back with a pitcher of tea and a glass for Chase, which she set down on the table in front of him before pulling a pad out of her back pocket, pen poised. Once she'd written down the orders, she went back inside.

"I'll go get the folder." Chase stood, reluctant to actually get up and leave.

"I'll be here when you get back," Mathias assured him with a smile that warmed Chase's heart as he headed back into the restaurant.

He walked quickly to the parking lot to retrieve his notes, wondering again whether things were going well or not. Mathias had laughed and smiled, but he'd also insulted Chase with that remark about trendy restaurants. No matter. Mathias had put him at ease, and for a little while, it almost seemed as if the past nine years hadn't happened at all. Yes, Mathias had given him mixed signals, but at least they were here, talking, even if Mathias only cared about protecting the T-Group. Chase could live with that. One step at a time. As much as he was disappointed there hadn't been any sparks, at least Mathias didn't seem to hate him as fiercely as he had when they'd talked at the ranch. *That* was progress.

MATHIAS watched Chase head back inside the restaurant and thought about the way the sun glinted golden on his hair and what it might be like to run his fingers through it again. Then he stopped himself and wondered what the fuck was wrong with him. What was he even doing sitting here chatting with Chase and talking about a place they'd gone to years ago when they were still together? *What the fuck made me say that?* Seeing peach tea on the menu had given him a pang of emotion that threatened to knock the wind out of him.

Fucking stupid sentimental idiot to even order the tea in the first place. What must Chase think of him now? That he was still pining away? Especially since Chase had seemed somewhat surprised about the tea in the first place.

But Chase's mind couldn't just be on business, either, if he'd left the reports in the car. Did Chase want to get him back or just fuck with him some more, like some sort of toy? Had Chase chosen this place for the effect he must know it would have on Mathias? He badly needed to turn the focus back on business. He couldn't let himself get distracted by anything personal when it came to Chase Richards.

Just then Chase returned with a thick manila folder, which he set down heavily on the table then settled back in his chair. Mathias studied Chase's face as Chase flipped through pages in the folder. He didn't look as tanned as he had the last time they'd sat across a table from each other—in the lawyer's office as Mathias signed papers giving up his company. If he'd looked this pale at the ranch, Mathias hadn't noticed—or cared. Now Chase looked slightly drawn and tired, but his tawny eyes sparkled as brightly as ever, and his perfect white smile still radiated. Best not to even consider the way Chase's full lips looked as he'd read over the menu, trying to decide what to order. Or the way his eyes crinkled, making Chase look kind and innocent. The takeover appeared to have taken its toll on Chase, too, which surprised Mathias.

"Take a look at this," Chase said, handing Mathias a thick batch of stapled sheets. "I've got a copy, too. We can go over some of these ideas, and you can give me your feedback."

The waitress interrupted, carrying a tray laden with their lunch, and served them before smiling and silently heading back inside.

"You put all of these together in just over a week?" Mathias asked around a mouthful of sandwich, surprised by the effort Chase had contributed. He decided to concentrate on food for the moment, and put the report aside for the time being.

"Give or take." Chase attacked his meal, chewing hungrily. "I put together the framework after I met with the heads of some of the departments. Then I asked Lewis McDonald to check for any errors in the data and calculations. He had a lot of suggestions for me based on his more specific knowledge. You know that guy is worth his weight in gold?"

"Twice his weight." Mathias nodded and poured himself another glass of peach tea.

"Well, I'll be sorry to see him go," Chase said, then wished he'd phrased that differently when he saw how Mathias reacted.

"See him go? You're sacking him?" Mathias snapped and Chase flinched.

"No. No! I mean he's given me his resignation. He offered to stay only until the sale is finalized. The whole executive team's followed suit. Next Friday's their last day. I couldn't convince him— or anyone else—to stay," Chase explained. "Without experienced executives, who the rest of the employees trust, it's going to be next to impossible to keep the company running the way you did. You don't have any obligation, but I'd really appreciate some advice from you about who I can promote into some of the leadership roles. I'm way over my head already, and I can't get up to speed fast enough on food and retail to avoid making some bad decisions starting out. That isn't going to inspire people to stay, is it?" Chase asked in a self-deprecating tone that surprised Mathias.

But he didn't reply right away, chewing slowly while he thought about what Chase had said. So far Chase seemed 100 percent sincere about running the business, treating Mathias's team with respect, seeking *and* taking their advice. That surprised Mathias, too. Chase had even admitted that he couldn't run the company on his own. That didn't sound at all like the man that had pulled off a well-planned and -executed takeover by financial market manipulation. Mathias was beginning to think he needed to revise his opinion of Chase after all.

After they finished eating, they spent another hour and a half discussing Chase's plans, sipping another pitcher of peach tea and enjoying huge slices of key lime pie. Mathias actually found himself reluctant to leave when he realized he needed to get going for the long drive back to the ranch and then the hospital.

"I'm going to show these to my father and get his opinion. Is that all right with you?" Mathias indicated the proposals.

"Yeah, that's fine. I'm curious to hear what your dad thinks of these ideas." Chase laid a pile of money on the tray, including a very generous tip for their waitress.

"You are?"

"Sure. I wouldn't want to take the company in a direction he wouldn't approve of. It's still your family name on half the businesses, right?"

"Yeah, but that didn't seem to stop you before, did it?" Mathias asked with a bit more acerbity than he'd intended.

"I really fucked that whole takeover thing up. I don't even know how to begin to apologize so I didn't even think it was worth trying, I'd dug myself in so deeply." Chase's voice sounded sincere and remorseful.

"It's not like we can undo what's done. We need to move forward."

"I really wanted to make a change… I tried to let you know at the first meeting we had about the oil companies. And I needed for someone—for you—to believe and trust me. No one has trusted me for a long time."

"Brooke believed and trusted you…," Mathias said, and immediately wished he hadn't.

"Brooke…." Chase's voice sounded strangled.

The waitress was heading toward them but she must have noticed the look on Chase's face and silently turned around, realizing she shouldn't interrupt their conversation.

Chase let out a sigh. "Brooke was a huge mistake… for both of us. I know you don't want my opinion, but it was way too easy to win her trust and turn her against you. I'm sorry but I don't think she felt a shred of loyalty to you."

"I know. Her only loyalty was to herself. I realized entirely too late, but I would have figured it out before I'd actually married her; I know that much."

"I still can't picture you getting married—to anyone," Chase said.

"Well, you don't need to picture it. It's not going to happen. I figured that out, too…." Mathias felt unexpected heat surge to his face. He couldn't continue on this topic, not now. "I need to get on the road, Chase. I'll get back to you after I've made my decision."

Mathias stood to leave.

CHAPTER TWENTY-FOUR

TWO days later, when Mathias paid his father another visit in the hospital, he found Jerry sitting up in bed reading Chase's proposal. Marta sat in a chair next to the bed skimming absently through a magazine, and she looked up when Mathias entered.

"Son!" Jerry's excited tone surprised Mathias. "I finally made it through the whole proposal, and I'd say some of these ideas are brilliant. I'm not sure all of them will work, but they are a somewhat different approach than we've taken before. I agree about the integration aspects and the value of the crossover customers. It's a brilliant way to get people from one line of business into our other lines, and I think you should consider further study of most of the suggestions. You don't even need to study the items in the 'Protect' section. They should all be implemented."

"We could just start with 'hello'," Mathias joked. "And where's your oxygen mask? Mom, you're falling down on the job."

"Don't need it anymore." Jerry grinned and Marta nodded.

Mathias noticed that there seemed to be fewer tubes and wires attached to his father today, and Jerry's color looked better than it had for weeks.

"The doctors said his condition's improving, thanks to the experimental treatment." Marta's smile lighted up the room, and Mathias's spirits.

Mathias had heard positive progress reports before, but this was the first time he actually believed them. "Well, that's great, Dad! Just don't overdo it." As thrilled as he was to see improvements, he didn't want to get his hopes up that his father might actually recover.

"I won't. Your mom is still in charge around here. She lets the doctor and nurses come in now and then, but everyone knows who's boss." Jerry winked at Marta. "But let's talk about these ideas in Chase's proposal. Like I said, there's a lot of potential here!"

"I agree. I just wanted to get your take on it." Mathias sat down on a chair next to his father's bed and pulled his own copy of the proposal out of his jacket pocket.

"Mattie, I remember you had suggested integrating the restaurants and the grocery stores along these lines, when I was still working... why didn't we implement those ideas?"

"That was right around when you got sick, Dad, remember?" Mathias replied. "Without you, we had our hands full with day-to-day operations, and we didn't really have the resources to study or implement anything new. Later, the Board decided it was too radical a move to make without you. They weren't convinced I could keep the company running, much less accomplish anything like this."

Mathias remembered the uncertainty of that time much more clearly than Jerry did. He'd been in and out of the hospital, and Mathias hadn't let him know how little support he'd initially gotten from the Board. But after hitting all revenue and profitability targets for six months, they'd begun to relax and eventually to trust Mathias's abilities. Even after he'd been officially named CEO, he'd been reluctant to test how far that trust went, choosing to fight other battles instead.

"Idiots," Jerry grumbled. "Maybe this time it will happen, now that Chase's calling the shots, and he doesn't have to listen to them."

They spent the next half an hour discussing details and numbers in the report. Mathias scribbled notes and hoped he'd be able to read his handwriting later on.

"So, the next move would be a more rigorous study of each proposal, and then go forward with the one promising the greatest return in the shortest period of time. Once that's in place, we could consider implementing the others." Mathias paused. "I mean if I was running things, that is."

"One thing I can say, even if you don't end up implementing any of them...," Marta interjected.

"What's that, Mom?"

"I think that Chase's taken a very serious look at our—" She paused. "At the T-Group… and come up with well-considered and appropriate suggestions in just a very short time. Maybe you give him a chance to show he's really changing. I think his partnership offer is genuine. He really wants to work with you to run the T-Group."

"I agree, son," Jerry added. "I know there's a lot of history between you two, particularly because of the way he acquired the T-Group. You don't know whether or not you can trust him or work with him, but if you want to keep running these businesses, you might give that partnership a shot. You can always quit if you find you can't trust him. But I can't imagine why he'd go through all the trouble of putting together these proposals to show you if he was just playing a game or trying to cheat you."

"Good point, Dad," Mathias admitted. He'd been asking himself the same question for days. He didn't like the answers his mind supplied. Or the ones his body suggested. "But I don't think he intended to break up with me the way he did when we first met either, so just because *today* he thinks he wants to be business partners with me doesn't inspire huge amounts of confidence in him."

"Mattie, honey, if you had that attitude when you first met him—or anyone—you'd never have had the good times you did have together, right?" Marta pointed out. "Yes, things ended badly, which is unfortunate, but you just have to give people a chance at the beginning, and if they don't live up to your expectations, you can change your mind about them. Nothing will ever happen if you start out mistrusting everyone's intentions, will it?"

"But I *know* his track record—in business and in personal matters—and it would be the height of idiocy to trust him now!" Mathias didn't know if he was trying to convince his mother—or himself. All he knew was he couldn't let Chase Richards break his heart a second time. Was this enough of a foundation to try again, even as business partners?

"So, don't trust him completely, but give him a chance to show you his true colors, one way or the other," Marta replied. "People can and do change. He could have bought a lot of other companies if he just wanted to run a business. I do think there's something else here—something personal—and he wants to work with you."

"He has a fine way of showing that, doesn't he?" Mathias asked, feeling fully justified in his suspicions.

"Didn't you say Chase wanted to buy those oil supply companies?" Jerry replied. "That sounds like he did try the standard approach to start with. I'm not condoning what he did or how he did it. I'm simply saying that I think he's really trying to change his business style, and your mom's right, you should go with it until you get a good idea whether or not there's something sinister going on."

"Dad, you're making this sound so dramatic," Mathias said, though he was smiling.

"You don't really have much to lose at this point, do you?" Marta asked. "And maybe you'll be pleasantly surprised."

"I'd like to come out of this with some dignity and self-respect left. I wouldn't have either if I let Chase take advantage of me again."

"So, don't let him take advantage of you. Go in there with a clear idea of what you want out of this, and at what point you'll leave if you're not getting it," Jerry suggested.

Mathias thought about that for a minute. Why did his father always have the right answer for everything? Even the most difficult problems Mathias had faced. He wished he'd asked for his father's advice a lot sooner; maybe he could have avoided some of the problems with Chase and the takeover battle. But Mathias hadn't wanted to burden his father when Jerry had been so seriously ill.

Now that Mathias thought about it, it seemed that his father's health was actually taking a turn for the better the past week or so. Could Mathias's obvious need for advice actually be helping? Maybe all Jerry needed was to feel needed and part of something important to him: namely, having Mathias take him into his confidence and rely on his advice, experience, and love.

"I think I'm going back to the ranch to look over this report more closely." Mathias got up and kissed both his parents good-bye. "Thanks for your suggestions about how to approach Chase's offer."

"You be sure and call if you want to talk any more about any of this, before you make your decision," Marta said.

"Did you tell him when you would get back to him?" Jerry asked.

"No, and he didn't give me any deadline," Mathias replied before departing.

No deadline. He hadn't given Chase any time frame when they'd discussed Chase's offer for the oil supply companies. Had he acted too quickly, Mathias wondered as he drove back to the ranch. Could this entire takeover battle have been avoided if he'd simply listened to what Chase had to say at that first meeting? Possibly, but he had good cause for not trusting Chase—then or now. How could he have known Chase was serious?

Back at the ranch, he fed and watered the dogs and the horses, then sat out on the porch with a cold beer as he looked over Chase's proposal again. Even Mathias's father had been impressed with the ideas. Chase could have just hired some consulting firm to crunch some numbers and toss out a bunch of ideas, Mathias decided. He pulled his cell phone from his pocket and dialed Lewis McDonald.

"McDonald." Lewis's voice came over the line.

"Lewis, it's Mathias."

"Mathias, how are you doing? Enjoying some free time or a vacation with Brooke?"

Mathias was surprised how little the mention of Brooke hurt him. He hadn't completely forgiven what she'd done, but he had no feelings for her anymore.

"No, I'm out at the ranch, reading a proposal Chase Richards put together." He decided to keep this call professional and didn't correct Lewis's misapprehension that he and Brooke were still together. "What did you think of the report?"

"I was really impressed with what he came up with, to tell you the truth. He asked for some data, and I know he met with people in the different chains before he visited the factory and several of the stores. I even had a couple of calls asking me what he was authorized to see," Lewis explained. "That was all in the first week or so, I'd say. Then he set himself up in one of the offices down the hall from me, and I guess he spent a week or so working on this."

"Whose office is he using?" Mathias asked. "He's not using mine?"

"He's using one of the summer intern slots. It was empty. And no one's in your office. Pam probably wouldn't let anyone touch anything in there anyway." Lewis chuckled.

"I'd pay to see Pam and Chase go at it actually. My money's on her." Mathias couldn't picture Chase Richards using some tiny office they'd put an intern in, rather than the biggest office in the building. Compared to Chase's own enormous and luxurious office at RichardsCorp, the office must be like a closet. Mathias almost laughed at the image.

MATHIAS took the rest of the week to make a decision, then called Chase late one evening to let him know.

"Hang on just a minute, Mathias?" Chase's voice betrayed exhaustion, but the tone indicated his pleasure in hearing from Mathias.

Mathias heard Chase speaking with someone in the background, before he came back on the line.

"Sorry, I had Lewis in my office, and I—"

"You're still at work? It's after nine o'clock!" This definitely surprised Mathias. But then again, a lot of things about Chase had surprised him lately.

"Yeah, we had to put in some overtime to draw up new contracts with the suppliers. I think we need to lock in pricing for at least six months to eliminate random cost increases… and avoid the choice between cutting into our margins and passing the increases on to customers." Chase paused. "But you know that, it was one of my proposals…."

"It was a good idea. Glad it's working out." Mathias was a little surprised at Chase's use of "we" when referring to the T-Group.

"You have something to tell me?" Chase asked.

"Let's meet tomorrow and discuss it, okay?"

"Sure."

Mathias suggested a place and time to meet. He'd chosen a popular brunch spot; on a weekday it wouldn't be crowded once the breakfast rush was over.

THE following week, Mathias returned to the Tobler Group as a 50 percent partner. He convinced his entire executive team to stay, even the people who had already accepted job offers elsewhere. Then he offered everyone a raise; he hadn't needed a lure to keep anyone, but he felt they all deserved something for their loyalty to him. The raises were being funded by RichardsCorp, and Mathias couldn't refuse the deal when it wouldn't cut into their own profitability. To a person, everyone admitted Chase had treated them professionally and with respect, and they'd quit out of loyalty to the Toblers. Otherwise, they had no problems working with Chase Richards, as long as he continued the way he'd started. But Mathias's team was glad he was back.

Slowly, over the next few months, they began implementing some of Chase's suggestions, adjusted a bit for Mathias's opinions and admittedly superior knowledge of the firm and the industry. But revenue and earnings were growing, and Mathias knew that the improvement was due at least in part to Chase's ideas. Their competitors faced a less rosy outlook, due to the economic downturn. Once Chase actually tried, he showed remarkable ability to put his all into a project. Mathias realized he'd never have discovered Chase's business talents—or benefited from them—had he sold those companies to Chase in the first place.

Loath to ruin the successful détente they'd achieved, they'd avoided discussion of their personal issues. But the topic lay between them, a mountain range neither dared to cross, and at least to Mathias, the divide seemed to grow wider as their professional relationship improved.

He found it excruciating to spend long hours with Chase, in one office or the other, or hunched over spreadsheets or laptops, or endless hours in the car driving between one location and another, and realized how much Chase had changed. He wasn't a new person, but he seemed to be peeling back layers and turning back into the man Mathias had loved for years. Mathias had never stopped loving that Chase, the one who stared at him in a long-ago locker room and with one kiss turned his entire world upside down.

Chase's topaz eyes glittered and danced as he detailed ideas for the T-Group, the way they used to devour Mathias and get his blood boiling. Now, he just hoped Chase couldn't see that at times his body responded, pulse racing, nipples tingling, when Chase got close enough for Mathias to detect Chase's essence beneath the soap-and-shampoo clean smell.

But Chase remained the perfect gentleman, the more Mathias wanted him to be anything but.

CHAPTER TWENTY-FIVE

December 2012

ONE evening, they finished work late, with no time for a dinner break, and rode together in the elevator to the T-Group HQ garage. Chase had given up his chauffeur-driven cars; it wasn't who he really was anymore, and he owned half a dozen cars he'd rarely driven, until now. He'd already given up his back-of-the-limo activities—the night Mathias climbed into the back of his limo had been the last. Since then, Chase hadn't been with anyone. He didn't want anyone but Mathias, and he'd do whatever he needed to try and make that a reality. No one-night stand could replace Mathias, and a quick fuck would provide more guilt than pleasure.

"Tee, want to come over for dinner? I'll cook...." Chase's mouth went dry as he made the suggestion. He'd kept their interactions strictly professional, but tonight the offer slipped out before Chase could stop himself.

"To the pleasure dome? No thanks." Mathias shook his head and let out a soft chuckle.

Fuck! Other people called his house that? He'd thought it was just his personal opinion of the place. *Fuck!* "I'm actually thinking of selling it. It's way too big for me, which is why I wouldn't mind some company." Chase shrugged, hoping he sounded casual, but his heart raced in his chest. "It might be your last chance to see it."

"Tell you what. Why don't you come over to my place, and you can cook there?" Mathias countered, then lowered his gaze to his shoes.

Chase could tell from Mathias's face that as soon as he'd made the suggestion, he had second thoughts.

"I don't know...," Chase began, giving Mathias a way out, though he desperately wanted to take him up on the offer.

"No, I'm serious, you're welcome to come over," Mathias insisted, giving Chase a wide grin as if to prove it.

"Okay." Chase tried not to sound too excited about the idea. Going over to Mathias's condo could be awkward. Brooke had lived there until Chase intervened, but maybe Mathias didn't hold that against him anymore. Brooke hadn't deserved Mathias, but Chase didn't think *he* deserved Mathias either.

He didn't want to rush things, or get too optimistic that Mathias had forgiven him and could begin to consider getting back together. Hell, Chase didn't even know whether or not they were even *friends* at this point, much less anything more intimate. But Mathias had extended a personal invitation, and it was the first time they'd had anything even remotely approaching purely social contact for more than nine years.

He reminded himself Mathias's invitation was nothing more than dinner.

Chase followed Mathias home. They took the elevator up to the penthouse, accessible only with Mathias's key. Had Brooke given her key back or did she show up sometimes just for kicks? Mathias appeared to be completely over her, though obviously they'd never discussed the topic.

Mathias's place was furnished in a spare—elegant and clearly expensive—modern style that reminded Chase of the apartment Alan leased and had decorated for him back in Durham. Impressive, but very impersonal. It didn't seem like Mathias's style at all.

"Brooke decorated the place." Mathias must have read Chase's mind. "It's not really me, but I've been too busy to deal with it. I should sell it and get a smaller place, too."

"You could just redecorate."

"Nah. Too many bad memories. I can't redecorate those away, unfortunately."

"I guess not." Chase replied, his tone subdued. Even though Mathias had brought Brooke up, Chase didn't want to risk Mathias recalling his role in the debacle.

Mathias walked into the kitchen, Chase close behind. Peering inside the refrigerator, Chase noticed it held only a carton of orange juice, two six-packs of a local craft beer, some assorted lunch meats, and random condiments. Mathias must not have realized he didn't have anything to cook. Most nights they worked late and ordered food into the office. Mathias obviously didn't cook for himself much anymore.

"What's in the cupboard?" Chase asked somewhat more hopefully, then started opening cabinets. "Hmm, pasta—" He retrieved a box of penne to examine the contents. Enough for two. "—and here's a jar of sauce. Some spices… that'll perk it up a bit."

"Knock yourself out." Mathias pulled a couple of beers from the refrigerator. He opened them and handed one to Chase, then sat at the kitchen table watching Chase forage for dinner.

Chase managed to find enough ingredients to make the sauce palatable, and prepared a very basic but tasty-enough meal.

"Who would expect that two multimillionaires would be sitting around eating pasta with sauce from a jar on a Friday night?" Chase chuckled as he opened the third round of beers.

"Is that a dig at my hospitality? What have you got in your fridge, caviar and truffles?" Mathias shoveled pasta into his mouth. Either he was famished or he liked it.

Chase shrugged, but he felt his cheeks tingle. "No. Well, yes, but the caviar's for the cat… and the housekeeper. She eats all the best stuff before I get a chance to. So it won't spoil."

"You have a cat?" Mathias asked in disbelief.

"Yeah, why is that such a surprise?" Chase replied, slightly defensively, but knowing the comment wasn't meant as an insult. When Mathias didn't reply, Chase went on. "My housekeeper, Claudia, started feeding a stray, and the cat sort of decided to move in," he added laughing. "Now, I don't know why I never got a cat before. I love having her around. She keeps me company when Claudia's not around. Not that I'm at home much anymore."

They sat at the kitchen table talking about nothing at all as they made their way through the second six-pack. This marked the first time since Mathias had come back to the T-Group they'd sat around relaxing and not going over work. They'd somehow managed to just be Chase and Mathias again, and not CEOs or rivals, even if just for a little while. Mathias looked as comfortable with the situation as Chase did—no pressure to stay formal and distant with each other, but yet no expectation of anything more than simple company.

They'd spent hundreds of nights like this, back when they'd been together. Tonight Chase felt like he'd stepped back in time to a night at the table in Mathias's Durham kitchen. Pasta and beer after a day of studying. Difference was in those days they often rushed through dinner unable to keep their hands off each other, or forgot about dinner, only to remember when they smelled something burning. A familiar tingle went through Chase's body as he watched Mathias tuck a swath of dark wavy hair behind an ear. How he wanted to kiss those fingers, that ear, earlobe, all the way down the curve of Mathias's jaw

"If you have any more to drive you won't be able to drink home." Mathias laughed, but he opened up another bottle and set it in front of Chase.

"Yeah, I know… Huh?" Chase laughed, too, when he realized Mathias had just said something utterly nonsensical. His arm bumped the bottle which rolled off the table, splashing its contents into Mathias's lap. "Fuck! I'm sorry!"

"It's okay, there's more in the fridge," Mathias started to get up, then fell back into his chair unsteadily, laughing the whole time. Then he noticed the extent of the spill. "Aw, fuck is right."

"Aww, Tee." Chase tried to look contrite and not to laugh, failing miserably. He grabbed a handful of napkins from the table and knelt next to Mathias's chair. Chase started to mop up the mess before he realized precisely what he was doing and stopped, suddenly a lot less drunk than he'd been a minute before.

Chase just stared into Mathias's eyes, gray-tinged blue like the Mediterranean in winter. But not cold; warm and welcoming Chase to dive right in and be transported. Mathias didn't utter a word, though he communicated a million things with his eyes. Suddenly, they weren't in Mathias's enormous sterile condo in downtown Dallas.

They were back in a dorm room in Colorado Springs with their whole future ahead of them.

Mathias pulled Chase toward him, so his lips were close enough to brush against Mathias's. *Is this really happening or am I imagining things?* Chase's lips made contact, light tentative contact that screamed through his entire body. Mathias's hand burned where it gripped Chase's wrist and his lips tingled. A slow warmth spread out from his balls, and he wondered how he'd survived all this time without Mathias, all these months of looking and never touching. Wanting but being afraid to hope. Mathias parted Chase's lips with his tongue and Chase's body smoldered with need. And just from a kiss? A kiss from Mathias felt like a dream. Then Mathias's arms went around him, and Chase knew it was really happening, right now.

They kissed more deeply, hungrily, and more passionately, and Chase stopped questioning reality. As much as he wanted this—wanted Mathias—he was scared. Scared this was happening too fast and not at all the way he had expected. What if Mathias was just drunk and horny and there wasn't anything more to it?

"Couch," Mathias mumbled into Chase's mouth, and Chase decided he didn't fucking care. Because he was kinda drunk and plenty horny, too, and he wanted Mathias more than he'd ever wanted anyone. He would do this and enjoy it, and they could pick up the pieces later.

Somehow they managed to move into the living room, kissing, hands searching and seeking and exploring and remembering once-familiar curves and angles.

MATHIAS sat on the couch and pulled Chase onto his lap. He hadn't forgotten that night in Colorado Springs, that very first time Chase had crawled into his lap—and changed his world forever. Tonight would be like a first time for them. Another first time for a new Chase and Mathias. Older, wiser, maybe slightly jaded and disappointed with how life had turned out for them. Nine years ago, they'd both made mistakes, and many more since then, but now Mathias knew what he wanted—needed—from Chase, and he wasn't about to let that go ever again.

He hadn't planned for this, but he knew to his core it was right. He'd never gotten over Chase. All that stood in the way was fear of trusting Chase again. But if he didn't open up and trust, he'd never know. He'd end up lonely and unhappy. Maybe all of this was a mistake, and he'd get hurt again, but if Chase had really changed, there was nothing to fear. He and Chase had everything most people could ever want, but they didn't have what they really needed: each other. *Someone to love and be loved by.* Love made all the difference.

They tore at each other's clothing, heedless of popping buttons or the sound of ripping fabric. Nothing mattered to Mathias but the way Chase's skin felt, the heat radiating up from the core, burning through the years of mistrust and hatred. It burned away everything but their need for each other. Once they were naked, they stroked and kissed and licked and bit and sucked at each other, desperate to relearn and reclaim. When touching wasn't enough, Mathias led Chase into the bedroom. He pulled lube and condoms from his night table and climbed into bed with Chase.

Chase took Mathias's hand and slicked the fingers with lube, then lay back, opening himself up for Mathias. Mathias looked down at Chase's beautiful body and wanted to kiss and touch and explore all of it, and there would be time for that later because right now they were both too excited to wait. When Mathias noticed the way Chase gazed up at him, eyes dark with desire but so full of love, Mathias knew this couldn't be a mistake. Even though they'd been together hundreds of times, his fingers still shook as he slipped them into Chase, just like that very first time. Whether it was nervousness or eagerness, Mathias wasn't sure, but his heart felt like it was bursting all the same.

Chase slipped the condom onto Mathias, then slicked on some more lube. Mathias pressed the tip of his cock against Chase's entrance and leaned down to kiss Chase, possessing his mouth, as he slowly pushed inside. To Mathias, it was even more thrilling than it had been that very first time he'd been inside Chase—inside of a man. Now, it was even better, Mathias thought. Like coming home after being away for a long time and finding everything exactly where you'd left it, and feeling such joy and relief. And when Mathias pushed in, Chase made that beautiful sound again, so Mathias knew that Chase felt it all, too.

"Tee, I never stopped loving you or wanting you or—"

Mathias's kiss cut off Chase's words. And when the kiss ended, Chase still couldn't speak, barely managing a few groans and unintelligible noises as his body gave itself up to the pleasure Mathias offered.

Neither of them lasted long that first time. But as they lay in each other's arms, gasping for breath, trading sweet kisses and caresses, they knew there would be many, many more times to make love to each other more slowly and more perfectly. For now, this was just what they wanted and needed. It was a new start, and that was the most important thing.

CHAPTER TWENTY-SIX

WHEN they woke in each other's arms the next morning, there was no hesitation, no doubt, or regret. They pulled each other close and were already hard and needing each other's touch. They made love again, slowly, as if by taking things too fast and rough they'd shatter the beauty of the moment. Afterward, they took a lazy bath, washing each other carefully and tenderly before heading back to bed for a nap.

"Chase?" Mathias asked tentatively, wondering if Chase were still asleep. They hadn't yet opened the curtains, but the afternoon sun peeked through the gap, spraying bright beams of light across the room.

"Hmmm?" Chase replied without opening his eyes.

"Are you awake enough?"

"Awake enough for what?" Chase asked in a low gravelly tone.

"For... talking."

"Talking?" Chase's eyes popped open.

"Yeah. I wondered...."

"Wondered what?" Chase asked, his voice soft and curious. He rolled onto his side and propped his head on one hand so he could look at Mathias.

"How we ended up where we were... during the last nine years," Mathias continued, not sure how best to bring up the subject, but he had to know. "I thought I hated you... and that you wanted to destroy me. But it seems like neither of us stopped caring.... What went wrong?"

"It's my fault," Chase said regretfully. "I could have fixed it… prevented it really, but I made a terrible mistake. I trusted the wrong person."

"So, why didn't you fix it?"

"I was so ashamed of how I'd acted—*why* I'd broken up with you—I was afraid to explain. And then by the time I got my courage back, it was too late, and you wouldn't return my calls, or speak with me."

"Ashamed of what? Can you explain now?" Mathias tried to not let his curiosity or shock come through. *Chase could have cleared this all up years ago?*

"I fell into a trap. A carefully planned, long-term trap, set by a master chess player."

"What are you talking about?" Mathias asked, not following Chase's line of thought at all.

"My father… I didn't realize at the time, not until it was entirely too late—how he'd played me. Set me up and watched me take the bait…."

"Can you please drop the metaphors and just explain what you mean?" Mathias said, slightly exasperated.

"During that spring break when I came home from Durham, my dad got me involved in a deal," Chase began slowly. "It was exciting, and I felt like I was succeeding at something—making my dad proud of me—and that the other people on the team respected me for my ideas and not because of my father." As he went on, Chase's voice sped up, the emotion propelling the words out of his mouth.

"And that wasn't true?"

"No, it was. I think it was…." Chase wrinkled his brow. "But, I'd been putting on an act—that confident act you hate so much—starting during spring break, because at first I was really… really scared about working for my dad." Chase looked slightly ashamed as he said it, but Mathias gave him a supportive look, and Chase continued. "Then I got caught up in the thrill of doing the deal—of finally earning my dad's approval—and then he wanted me to help close out when I got back from Durham, and I didn't want to let him down."

"Yeah, I know about that part; he told me…," Mathias trailed off, remembering how he'd felt when Alan had explained everything. "… about how you wanted to do this deal so you could get a huge bonus, and that you'd obviously chosen the job and the money over our plans—over *me*."

"What the fuck? He talked to you? *When?*" Chase sounded completely taken aback.

"He came to visit me right after I got back from Venice and explained how sorry he was it had turned out the way it had—that you had chosen a job over… me. He said that you had even disappointed him by the way you'd acted," Mathias explained. He also remembered that feeling of unease as soon as he'd seen Alan in the living room and how that feeling had grown. Alan had been up to some sort of game; only now it seemed he'd been playing both Mathias and Chase—against each other. "Didn't you know he came to see me?"

"No. The man is even more unbelievable than I imagined, and I already thought the worst about him," Chase said heatedly. He sat up in the bed, his body tensing, anger flashing across his features. "'Evil genius' isn't even strong enough for that man!"

"But that isn't how it happened, then?" Mathias asked hopefully. "He just lied?"

"Not exactly. I did choose the job over you—wait, just let me finish—because he forced me to make a decision…. Originally, he'd led me to believe the deal would only take a few days, and he even had the gall to tell me what a wonderful trip we could have with my bonus. You have no idea how much I wanted to surprise you with a luxurious trip, so I didn't tell you *why* I had to stay in Dallas. Then he kept dragging the timeline out."

"Till I put you on the spot when I called and forced you to make a decision about whether or not you'd join me?" Mathias asked, with a touch of guilt.

"Worse. He wanted more than to fuck up our trip. All my life, he'd glorified the idea of the family business and family loyalty. Built it up to be the highest goal I could achieve, and over the years I believed him. Fell for it hook, line, and sinker. He questioned how I could possibly turn down the *honor* of being part of our family business to be with you. Claimed you held me back from the beginning, and he blamed you for me not making the Olympic team. He warned that you'd always hold me back, and if I wanted to work with him, he didn't want any distractions." Chase was nearly sobbing, his body shaking with emotion. "Said when I didn't compete in Sydney, it was the biggest disappointment in his life. He forced me to choose between him and *you*—" Chase gulped air and his eyes misted over. "—and I just couldn't bear to disappoint him again."

"Chase, calm down! Please." Mathias tried to soothe Chase, stroking his shoulder and arm gently. His own heartbeat raced and caressing Chase helped Mathias calm himself down. He took a deep breath.

The story and Chase's terrible choice left Mathias cold—he'd had no idea Chase had gone through anything as horrific as being forced by his father to make a choice like that. *What the hell kind of father does that to his son?* And Chase had kept it all inside the entire time. If only he'd told Mathias what was happening instead of trying to handle it himself, they could have worked it out *together*. No wonder that Chase had turned into the man he'd been when he took over the T-Group. But Mathias was worried about Chase now.

"No. I can't calm down, Tee. Not when I see how far he went to get what he wanted. He lied to you so subtly, twisting the truth so you would blame me. You wouldn't even *want* to work things out with me. Well, I got back at him!" Chase's voice turned cold. Anger distorted his beautiful face and turned it nearly as ugly as the emotions inside. "Once I figured out what he'd done—I started planning how to make him pay. I knew RichardsCorp was the most important thing in the world to him. More important than me or my mother—or anything. That's when I decided to take the company away from him. The way he'd taken you away from me." Chase was breathing hard and Mathias stroked his cheek, willing him to relax.

"Wow, Chase, that's a lot of hate for one person to keep inside." Mathias hated to see him like this, hated to hear that Alan really had turned Chase into a monster. It frightened him to see that vengeful man at the surface now, and he understood how he'd provoked Chase into plotting revenge against him—because Mathias had compared him to Alan. No wonder Chase had struck back so hard. "You pushed your father out of the business to get back at him for breaking us up? Why didn't you just try to explain it to *me*?" Mathias saw a look of shame and regret on Chase's face that tore his heart in two. "Of course, I was angry with you, after what he'd told me, but I would have listened if you'd told me you'd made a huge mistake...."

"I was too ashamed. I hated myself for not realizing how important you are until too late." Chase breathed more calmly. The anger was gone from his face, but his eyes were still dark, haunted. "So, I hid behind one of those characters I used to make up. Only I pretended to be my father, and it worked so well I just kept doing it... until I turned into the man I hated, with a life I never wanted. The only thing that saved me was you believing me, finally, that I wanted to change back...." He looked deep into Mathias's eyes.

Mathias leaned forward and brushed his lips against Chase's. "No, I believed the *way* you said it. I could tell you were sincere. That didn't mean I trusted you yet—that took a long time—but I knew you meant what you said. The hardest part was waiting for you to follow through and make sure you wouldn't revert to the man I thought you'd been for the past nine years. You surprised me time after time, and finally I found myself trusting you again." Mathias paused for a moment, twining his fingers in Chase's. "The truth is I never stopped loving you either—the old you, the one I first knew in Colorado. I couldn't be around the man you turned into, but I still wished that the Chase I loved would come back. And you have."

"Thank you. I'm so sorry it had to happen in such a destructive way. I'm still trying to clean up the entire mess. I hope someday you'll forgive me for what I put you through. Not just you, your family and the shareholders and employees...."

"The fact that you realize what you did, and how many people it affected—not just me—is all I need. I can forgive you, as long as you promise me to always be yourself, and no matter what, talk to me. Tell me when something is wrong so we can fix it together. Because when you're being yourself, you're totally worth spending time with."

Chase laughed, probably recalling the first time Mathias said those exact words to him. Mathias smiled and kissed Chase.

"You know I'll promise you anything if you keep kissing me like that."

Mathias had a similar thought, but he could see Chase wasn't finished. "I mean to keep my promises this time. I have too much to lose if I don't."

While they kissed, Mathias's cock responded to Chase's familiar touch and taste and feel, and he found he was suddenly hard and wanted Chase again. Chase broke the kiss, and when their bodies separated, Mathias unconsciously drew the sheet up to cover his hard-on. The motion caught Chase's attention.

"You can't possibly hide something that big, Tee, why even try?" Chase teased.

Mathias looked down and cursed to himself. *Fucking Brooke!* She'd messed him up to the point where he often felt the need to hide his arousal, and he was still half-ashamed of it, even months later. He didn't even know what to say to Chase.

There was no need to say anything, as Chase took Mathias's mouth in a hard, passionate kiss, before moving his mouth lower, lips and tongue trailing down Mathias's throat to his collarbone, caressing the contours. Mathias focused on the wonderful things Chase's mouth was doing to him, now at his nipples, spending long, agonizingly delicious minutes at each, flicking his tongue over the nub, licking, sucking, brushing his full, beautiful lips across one, then the other until Mathias arched off the bed, begging for those lips to move even lower.

Chase happily obliged as he glanced up at Mathias from under long eyelashes with a wonderfully mischievous sparkle in his eyes. After teasing Mathias mercilessly by going so slowly, finally Chase's lips reached Mathias's navel. His tongue circled it twice before it flicked inside a few times, then resumed its southerly progress along the faint trail of hair that bisected Mathias's lower abs.

When he reached the sheet concealing Mathias's erection, Chase leaned back, then with a playful smile, took hold of the sheet somewhere near Mathias's knee, and slowly pulled at it, revealing just the tiniest glimpse of the tip of Mathias's cock. Chase leaned over and licked delicately at the visible portion, causing Mathias to shudder and his cock to twitch.

Another half an inch.

Chase glanced at Mathias with that sly look again, then focused his gaze back on Mathias's cock as he slowly unveiled it, making certain to lick and kiss as each new slice of skin was revealed.

Mathias thought he was going to explode—or worse: die of such extreme arousal he might expire before he even came.

"Are you trying to kill me?" Mathias moaned.

"No," Chase replied. "Just want to enjoy something as wonderful as your cock for as long as possible. It's much, much too beautiful to cover it up, especially when it's so hard... and thick... and dark and heavy," he added, his voice low and guttural and in such a marvelously obscene tone that it sent shivers up Mathias's spine and made his cock ache even more. He couldn't help the groans that escaped his mouth.

When Chase had uncovered the full length of Mathias's erection, he paused for a moment to look at it again, clearly enjoying the sight of it. Despite Mathias's impatience for Chase to suck him, he couldn't help but love how Chase wanted Mathias to know how much he loved his body and loved touching it or using it, and that Mathias should never be ashamed or shy about showing it off.

"I love knowing I can get you so hot and hard and desperate for me," Chase whispered, mouth hovering over Mathias's cock.

Chase had got him harder-than-rock hard—just as Brooke had before. But Brooke couldn't understand Mathias's arousal was a compliment to her, not an insult. She had never taken the time to celebrate the beauty of either her own body or Mathias's, while Chase had no trouble at all with that. In fact, at the moment, Mathias could do with a lot less celebrating and a lot more sucking.

"Wouldn't you like it even more to know what a wonderful orgasm you gave me?" Mathias suggested. He could come at any second and Chase hadn't put more than his lips on Mathias's cock yet.

"Perfection can't be rushed," Chase laughed. "And this is going to be a perfect blow job."

And it was.

Chase took his time exploring every millimeter of Mathias's cock with lips and tongue, then lavished plenty of attention on his balls, licking at them, sucking them into his mouth with gentle pressure that made Mathias gasp and shudder. Finally, Chase opened his mouth wide and took nearly all of Mathias's cock inside, moaning and humming so vibrations shot straight to Mathias's balls, and he thought he was going to come immediately. But Chase knew what he was doing and eased back, letting Mathias's cock slip out completely. He bent again and wrapped his hand around the base as he took just the head into his mouth, sucking hungrily.

Mathias fought to keep his eyes open, to hold back the wave of pleasure that was building in his body. He loved watching the way Chase's lips wrapped around his cock and the way it slipped in and out of Chase's mouth. It was even better, knowing how much Chase was enjoying this. Mathias had one hand loosely on Chase's neck, for the enjoyment of the contact and not to try and direct him at all, and Chase's eyes danced, and he groaned his own pleasure. Occasionally, he reached down to stroke himself, but he was concentrating on Mathias.

Unable to stop himself, Mathias rocked his hips up slightly, pushing himself deeper into Chase's mouth. Chase stopped moving and glanced up at Mathias, his eyes messaging that it was okay for Mathias to keep thrusting, and Chase let go of the base of Mathias's cock, taking hold of his own instead.

Mathias was close to the edge now, but he acknowledged Chase's offer. He took a firmer grip on Chase's neck and started thrusting up into Chase's mouth in short, quick movements. Their gazes locked, and Chase was clearly waiting for more, *wanting* Mathias to fuck his mouth harder and deeper. Mathias only needed a few more strokes before he was coming, still holding onto Chase's head and shooting down his throat. After the long, slow buildup, Mathias's orgasm was short and very intense, and it had definitely been the best blow job he'd had in years.

Chase was still kneeling between Mathias's legs, and Mathias sat up and pulled Chase in for a long deep kiss, enjoying the taste of his come mixed with the taste that was pure Chase. Reaching down,

Mathias covered the hand that Chase still had wrapped around his own cock, and together they pulled and stroked and soon Chase was grunting and shuddering and coming, splashing thick pearly strands on them both before they lay back together on the bed to recover.

IT WAS Sunday evening, and they had just finished eating Thai food they'd ordered from a place a couple of blocks away. It was the first time all weekend they'd actually dressed completely, and in this case "better late than never" didn't apply. The restaurant's delivery guy wouldn't forget this order, thanks to the surprise he got when Chase—naked and wet from the shower—walked into the living room while Mathias was paying for the food. Chase grinned, waved and turned back into the bedroom, but the man stared after him for a few moments, mouth open. Mathias wasn't sure if he should be embarrassed or jealous, and simply tipped the guy an extra ten dollars.

As they munched on pad thai, basil chicken, and coconut rice, washed down with ice-cold Singha, they were both happy and comfortable and most of all *together*. Despite the time they'd been apart and everything that had happened in the interim, they fell back into the easy companionship much more quickly than either of them expected.

"I'm really sorry about your shirt," Mathias said, only half meaning it. He wasn't entirely sorry he'd ripped Chase's handmade shirt well beyond repair on Friday night. Chase had found another shirt to wear in Mathias's closet. "That shirt looks great on you, fits you really well," Mathias noted, eyes traveling over Chase's chest and arms.

"It should fit well; it's my shirt," Chase replied with a chuckle.

Mathias lifted his brows. "It is?"

"You're kidding me, right?" Chase asked skeptically. "Here I was thinking you'd saved it in a 'brokeback' moment, and now you tell me you didn't even *know* you still had one of my shirts?" Chase said in mock offense.

282 | EM LYNLEY

"Yeah," Mathias replied, unrepentant, and stuffed more pad thai into his mouth. He'd never admit to Chase now that he'd known about that shirt all along.

"CHASE," Mathias asked, his voice tentative but curious. "What did you end up doing with that million dollars, if you don't mind me asking?"

"Ah, yes. The bonus money." They were sitting on the couch in Mathias's living room after dinner, and he paused for a moment, looking at Mathias and wondering how much he wanted to reveal. *Everything*, he decided. It was the only way for things to work between them; he couldn't keep any secrets from Mathias. "It turned out to be nearly four million dollars by the time my father finally decided to close out the deal," Chase began. "He was definitely right about the timing, I have to give him credit."

"*Four* million dollars?" Mathias asked, eyebrows up near his hairline.

"It seemed even worse to explain when it was so much," Chase continued. "But I didn't spend it on the kind of things you'd expect… no cars or plane or anything remotely extravagant. Shortly after I got the money, I discovered how long my father had been trying to break us up, and I used the money to get back at him."

"What do you mean?"

"I overheard him talking to someone about how he'd finally fixed my problem—he was referring to you—even though it had taken three years, but I wouldn't have another distraction or anyone to make me question my priorities again. It didn't sink in until he called me into his office and asked me if I wanted to take time off to train full time at fencing—he'd arranged for me to try out for the Olympic team the following spring—for Beijing.

"'This time there's nothing to keep you from making it all the way. No distractions, *no one* to hold you back,' he told me, and I finally understood the extent of his disappointment about Sydney. He blamed you and had been planning his revenge since then."

"But he was always pretty nice to me, inviting me for visits or trips with your family, and he didn't tell you to stop seeing me, did he?" Mathias asked, clearly confused. "He didn't want you to come out, but in private he supported you. Us."

"No, he *seemed* like he was fine with our relationship most of the time, but he always preached 'know your enemies.' I think he wanted you around to get to know you, and figure out how to come between us. The fact that it took him three years, and he finally had to give me an ultimatum and make me choose...." Chase couldn't continue.

"That he couldn't find any other way to break us up, because we really were good together?" Mathias finished Chase's thought.

"Yeah, Tee, we were great, weren't we?" Chase asked wistfully.

"I thought we were, but after you broke things off, I doubted myself... doubted whether or not I had just misjudged you, us, our entire relationship," Mathias added sadly.

"Oh, God, no! It was never about me wanting to leave you," Chase admitted. "It was about me thinking that getting—and keeping—my father's approval was even more important. I was so afraid I'd disappoint my father and lose the chance to be part of the family business, the chance to do the job that I'd wanted to do since I was a kid... or thought I wanted, because he'd steered me toward it." Chase added.

"So, how did you use the money?" Mathias prompted.

"My dad's success was built on getting and using information he normally wouldn't have access to, insider information. Some of it legal; some of it not. I turned his tactics against him. If I got information he wanted, I leaked the intel to prevent him from putting together a deal—tipping off the target company, or one of our competitors. I even paid for information I never shared with my father, and did the deal with my own team. I bought off a couple of people at RichardsCorp to be loyal to me rather than him. It took a while, but after a bunch of *his* deals failed while I had some pretty clear successes, I managed to seduce enough of the executives to back me, and got control of the company and kicked him out."

"All by using his own tactics against him? I guess you learned pretty well after all." Mathias nodded, but his tone was hard to discern.

Chase couldn't tell if Mathias was impressed or disappointed how well Chase had learned Alan's lessons. Mathias had every right to judge him, but Chase wanted to come clean completely about everything he'd done and *why*. Things he should have said years ago, when he'd still had a chance to win Mathias back without all the pain and destruction Chase had caused since then.

"Yeah," Chase said. "I know it doesn't say much about me...." He looked away, unable to bear the disappointment he expected to see in Mathias's eyes. "And in the end, I turned out just the way he'd always wanted me to be. For a while I enjoyed the game. But even after I took his company away from him, I was just going through the motions for a long time. I never really understood why achieving what I'd set out to do didn't make me happy."

"So, it became an act you couldn't stop. But why did you try to change?"

"When I saw your engagement announced to Brooke, it hit me. I realized what was missing. It was you. I needed to know whether Brooke really made you happy. Even though I wanted you back, I wouldn't have tried to ruin things for you if you belonged together...." Chase couldn't meet Mathias's gaze. "I know that doesn't count for much now, especially after I tried to take over your company."

"Tried? You succeeded!" Heat crept into his voice.

"I know I fucked it up when I got mad at how you accused me of being like my father. It was about the worst insult you could make, and it was so untrue." Chase didn't want to tackle the issue again, but Mathias had every right to still be upset. "It had only been an act. *Until that day.* I was so hurt and disappointed and scared that I'd never get a chance with you again that I really *did* turn into my father—worse than my father." Chase was relieved he could finally admit everything to Mathias.

"Which is totally the way to win back an old boyfriend," Mathias said sardonically. But he laughed and leaned over to kiss Chase, and Chase relaxed.

"Worked like a charm." Chase managed a half smile, but he understood. Even though they'd managed to work things out between them, and the T-Group's finances had actually improved, Mathias could not forgive or forget easily, and Chase didn't expect him to. He would strive every hour, every day, to prove he really was a man worthy of Mathias's love.

And Chase resolved to do it.

CHAPTER TWENTY-SEVEN

IT HAD been over a week since the night Chase had come over for dinner and stayed for the rest of the weekend. Though they decided to take things slowly, it hadn't worked out that way so far, and Chase had ended up staying at Mathias's almost every night since, except for the nights Mathias spent at Chase's. It wasn't quite like it had been twelve years earlier when they'd first gotten together, when they had so much to learn about each other. This time around, it was comfortable and familiar, and they both realized how much better their lives were with them together.

One evening, while Chase waited in bed for Mathias to wash up, he tugged open the top drawer of the night table, looking for the bottle of lube. Something in the back of the drawer caught his eye, and he pulled the drawer completely open.

He couldn't quite contain his surprise when he discovered a black silk blindfold. Was this the one Mathias had worn in the limousine, months earlier? Sheppard said he had taken it but Chase could not be completely certain. What did this mean?

The lube completely forgotten, Chase pulled the blindfold out, and his fingers twisted the smooth strap, remembering the mix of excitement and fear when he'd discovered Mathias climbing into the limo, and the way Mathias's body had responded to Chase. For Chase, neither his mind nor body forgot, replaying each moment during those months before they'd reconnected, never believing he could have another chance.

Caught up in the swirling emotions and memories of that night, it barely registered when the bathroom door opened. Looking up, Chase briefly caught Mathias's eye before turning his gaze back into the drawer, dropping the blindfold and grabbing for the lube.

"Just getting the lube out," Chase managed to say. He looked up again, but the bathroom door had closed once more, with Mathias on the other side of it.

Did Mathias have any idea it had been Chase with him that night? How the hell could they even discuss this? Mathias wouldn't want to admit to Chase he'd been with a stranger, but Chase didn't think he'd be pleased to discover Chase had fucked him in the limo and not revealed his identity? Either way, any discussion of the blindfold—or that night—was a minefield. He couldn't bear to lose Mathias again over something they both had enjoyed, but couldn't talk about.

But this was one secret Chase needed to keep from Mathias.

Knowing he'd kept the blindfold secretly thrilled Chase—a sign that Mathias remembered their night in a positive light. Maybe he wouldn't be upset. Not now after they'd started to build a life together. He hated the idea of keeping any secrets. He had to tell Mathias it was him and hope their bond was strong enough.

Then a ray of light flickered through the chaos in his brain. Had Mathias meant for him to find it? It wasn't exactly hidden. Was this a test?

He weighed the options in his mind for a few more moments while he waited for Mathias to come out of the bathroom.

MATHIAS had washed up and undressed down to his boxers. He opened the door to the bedroom, happy to see Chase already waiting for him in bed. Until Mathias noticed the open drawer and the *blindfold* in Chase's hand. Suddenly, Mathias couldn't breathe as the memories of that night came flooding back. His eyes briefly caught Chase's gaze as he closed the bathroom door again, deciding just how he was going to handle what would happen when he stepped out of the bathroom.

Especially after he'd seen the look in Chase's eyes. A look of shock and something else that Mathias had yet to identify. He calmed himself and tried to analyze the situation. Had Chase been pleased at seeing the blindfold?

Mathias had pondered that night for months, replaying every pleasurable moment of it. He'd come to only one conclusion. Or at least only one he could live with. His mind hadn't been playing tricks on him after all. The man had reminded Mathias of Chase, because *he had been Chase*. He'd wanted to believe it was Chase—even that night—and he'd convinced himself it had been, in order to erase the guilt because he'd enjoyed being with that stranger so much.

But Mathias couldn't just ask Chase about it. If Mathias was wrong and it had been someone else, he couldn't risk Chase knowing he'd done something so dangerous—and enjoyed it so much. He thought it was better to keep those doubts than to ever know for sure, and he considered never bringing it up. Wasn't that the safest thing to do now?

No. After he and Chase had gotten close again, Mathias realized he had to know. He had to find out the truth. About that night and about whether Chase Richards was the man Mathias needed him to be if they had any chance for a real future together. He had put the blindfold in the drawer before bedtime and waited to see what Chase would do when he found it.

I want to believe it was Chase. It was *Chase*, he repeated over and over until his breathing and pulse returned to normal. Then, slowly, he opened the bathroom door and walked into his destiny.

Chase lay on the bed with the blindfold in his hand and a serious look on his face.

"Mathias, there's something I have to tell you. I just don't know how you're going to take it."

CHASE held his breath as Mathias walked out of the bathroom, a towel loosely wrapped around his waist. He avoided looking into his eyes, not sure he could handle what he saw there. But he had to do this. If he didn't come clean, Mathias would never trust him again.

Oh God, how did I get myself into this situation? By being an arrogant asshole. By scheming and manipulating and for not realizing what was really important in his life. He had changed so much since he'd let Mathias go, but only since that stupid takeover plan had he actually grown up and taken real responsibility. And sometimes that meant you failed.

He took a deep breath and prayed Mathias was a better man than Chase could ever hope to be.

"Tee…."

"Yeah?" Mathias sat down on the edge of the bed. He reached toward the blindfold and took one end in his fingers, absently playing with it as he turned his gaze on Chase.

Chase looked up and saw a question in the blue eyes, now dark like a summer storm. "Tee…."

"What?" His voice held a note of worry.

"The day you came to my office…." Chase stumbled over the words, and his chest felt heavy. He couldn't breathe. Was this what a heart attack felt like? He almost hoped for one, just to avoid this, but if he didn't say it now, the lie would stay there between them, blocking out the sunlight. Their relationship would wither and die, and there would be no third chance for them.

Mathias waited.

"After that… that night. There's a bar, you know it, Black Knight." Chase thought the words would choke him. "The limo." He held up the blindfold. Mathias hadn't let go and the movement pulled his hand up. "It was me." Chase looked away. "I should have told you, but I wanted you so much. I never stopped wanting or loving you and it was the only way I could ever be with you again. You—"

"I know."

"What?" Chase looked up, but tears welled in his eyes, stinging. He couldn't see anything clearly, but he thought maybe Mathias had the hint of a smile on his lips.

"I know. I didn't know for sure at the time, but later… somehow I knew." Mathias paused, eyes shining as his gaze settled on Chase. "The way you touched me, kissed me, you were rough but also so gentle."

"I should have said something."

"No." Mathias shook his head and reached for Chase's hand. "If you'd said something then, when I hated you more than anything, it would have been a disaster."

"You have no idea how I felt, with you in my arms, knowing the only way I could be with you was like that, another lie."

"I do know. Because even after what happened that day, I wanted it to be you. It felt so good, so familiar being with a man I thought was a stranger, but I couldn't stop thinking of you. The way you used to be, not the one in the office that day. And I hated myself, my body, for still wanting you."

"You kept this?" Chase tugged at the blindfold again, and Mathias moved closer.

"I wanted it to be you." This time Mathias looked away, and Chase couldn't breathe for the hard lump in his throat.

"Tee." Chase reached out and pulled him close, and they lay together, in silence, Mathias's head on Chase's chest and the blindfold still entwined in their fingers. He didn't want to make love to Mathias tonight. He just wanted to feel the warmth of his skin and the soft black hair against his lips and know that after everything they'd put each other through, there was still a love so strong between them, it shone even in the darkest night.

THE next morning, Mathias opened his eyes to see Chase staring down at him. They'd survived. Chase broke down in tears as he apologized for not telling Mathias it was him that night, and Mathias forgave him. It was such a relief to put the worry and fear behind him and to know that despite everything that had happened between them over the years that somehow their love had still survived, under all the hate and resentment and scheming. They'd found each other that night, and later they had come back to each other openly and honestly.

They could build a future on a love like that.

"Finally, you're up," Chase said with satisfaction, wrapped himself around Mathias, and leaned in for a rough kiss that said his patience had finally run out. "I was getting lonely."

"You could have woken me up, you know."

"That was the plan. You had three more minutes."

"It's Sunday, what's the rush?" Mathias attempted an innocent grin. "The sun's barely up."

"But *I* am." Chase tightened his arms around Mathias and leaned down for another kiss.

Mathias felt Chase's erection digging into his hip, and he was rock hard in an instant. He pulled Chase's head in and deepened the kiss as his hands traveled over Chase's body. Suddenly, Mathias couldn't wait another minute, and he rolled Chase onto his back, pressing him down into the mattress. He wasn't rough or overly forceful, but the intensity of his desire was obvious.

"Are you reading my mind?" Chase whispered.

"I'm not very good at that, so why don't you tell me what you're thinking?" Mathias said playfully, and Chase whispered into his ear again.

MATHIAS had done everything Chase had asked for—one of them twice—and it seemed like they weren't going to make it out of bed at all that day. Chase decided that was just fine as he watched Mathias nap. He could watch Mathias sleep all day or all night, he just liked *looking* at Mathias that much.

The last week had been like a dream come true for Chase. Mathias had finally opened up and accepted Chase back into his life, and at times it felt as if the past nine years had never happened. They had quickly fallen into easy, familiar patterns with each other, and Chase knew it would kill him if he lost Mathias again. He was savoring every single minute they spent together, even now, while Mathias was asleep. Chase hadn't realized just how unbearably lonely it had been to wake up alone every morning, until he'd woken up next to Mathias again.

Chase knew Mathias had been happy with Brooke at first and he still envied the attempt to find someone to share his life—something Chase hadn't done. He'd been too afraid that he'd never find anyone like Mathias ever again. And if he managed to find someone "good enough," Chase expected to fuck that up, too, so he'd just given up wanting a partner—convinced himself he didn't need one.

But now, back with Mathias, Chase knew he needed Mathias in his life, to make his life worthwhile. He rolled closer to Mathias, who was facing him and snoring very softly. Chase reached out a hand to stroke Mathias's hair and tangle his fingers lightly in its soft length. One finger traced its way along Mathias's cheek, lingering at the mole under his left eye, before Chase began to trace Mathias's lips, feeling the gentle rush of air as he exhaled.

Suddenly, Mathias's hand came up and caught Chase's wrist, startling him.

"Hey, how long were you awake?" Chase asked accusingly, but with a smile.

"Long before you started playing with my hair." Mathias let out a low chuckle and released Chase's wrist. "I was hoping you'd leave me alone for some rest. You're wearing me out, you know?" he added in a low, gravelly voice.

"I thought you came with a lifetime warranty."

"That only counts for normal use, and I think you're bordering on extreme wear and tear here."

"Oh, too bad."

"It just means next time you can make love to me," Mathias said, his voice still slightly sleepy and low.

"Fine," Chase said.

"Fine," Mathias agreed and pulled him into his arms.

CHAPTER TWENTY-EIGHT

Six months later

"TEE, I had an idea for your birthday," Chase said near the end of June. "It's right around the time we'll get preliminary numbers for the fiscal year-end, right?"

"Yeah," Mathias agreed. T-Group's fiscal year ended on June 30, and it took a few weeks to crunch the numbers. "What's the connection?"

"None, really. I thought we could do something special, and hopefully we'll also have good results from this past year to celebrate, since we implemented some of the new strategies." It was more than that. It wasn't much more than a year ago that all of this had started, when Chase had seen the announcement of Mathias's engagement. Chase wanted to close off that year and put it all behind them, so they could start the next phase of their life—*together*.

They'd already moved in together, three months earlier. Chase had put his house up for sale. The steep asking price meant it wouldn't sell quickly, though plenty of "prospective buyers" had called to see the property. Chase engaged an experienced real estate agent who quickly separated the real buyers from the gawkers. Mathias had sold his downtown condo easily, and together they'd purchased a nice restored house in the Oak Lawn district at the center of Dallas's gay community. Their home had a huge backyard where Oskar and Trinka could run and play to their hearts' content. Mathias finally had the room—and a partner who welcomed them—and he'd brought them to Dallas from the ranch.

In their private lives, they were out, though they'd told only their senior management team directly. There was some initial surprise, considering the circumstances of the takeover, but they managed to smooth that over fairly successfully, and for the most part it was a nonissue since Mathias and Chase worked so well together. They didn't hide their relationship, but kept their behavior professional while at work. So far, it hadn't created any problems, and if anyone saw them together outside of work they were open and honest about it. It had been a big step for Chase; Alan had convinced him that coming out would harm him professionally, and he was pleasantly surprised at how little effect any of it had on the business. For Mathias, it had been a relief to drop the act they'd started back in Durham.

"You know, Chase, I don't need another reminder I'm getting older, thank you very much!" Mathias let out a burst of mock anger. "I already told my family not to do anything special, and I'm telling you the same thing, okay?" His tone softened, but his expression remained serious.

"Oh, well I sort of already made reservations." Chase shrugged. He'd come up with a pretty elaborate plan, but he wasn't sure whether Mathias would appreciate it. He'd play it by ear until the date got closer, and maybe he'd check with Marta.

Mathias's parents lived nearby, having moved back into their Fort Worth house. Jerry had made a substantial recovery, thanks to an experimental treatment being done by a specialist who had since moved from Austin to Dallas, prompting the Toblers' relocation. Chase and Mathias visited them at least once a week, and Mathias's parents were thrilled that not only was the T-Group thriving, but that Chase and Mathias had been able to make a new start together.

"How about if we just go away for the weekend somewhere, just the two of us?" Chase suggested.

"I don't know. I don't want any kind of fuss," Mathias repeated. "Promise me you aren't going to plan some big surprise party with everyone I know or something utterly embarrassing like that?"

"I promise, no fuss," Chase said in a conciliatory tone, and Mathias looked as if he only half believed him.

"So how come back in February you made me promise not to do anything special for *your* birthday, but now you're making plans when you know I don't want you to make a big deal out of it?"

"I guess I must love you more than you love me, or something." Chase flashed a cheeky grin.

"Fuck you!"

"Can you wait till we get home, at least?" Chase replied, and Mathias just huffed in reply.

July 14
Dallas

ON THE day before Mathias's birthday, he and Chase left the office together in the early evening. They headed down to the garage and got into Chase's car, a silver Mercedes CLK. As soon as he pulled out of the garage, Mathias realized he wasn't heading in the direction of their house.

"Where are you going, Chase?"

"We're going away for the weekend, remember?" He turned to Mathias with a sly grin.

"I thought you'd given up on that idea." Mathias wasn't amused by Chase's reply—or that smile. It gave him a sinking feeling in his gut. "I didn't pack a bag or anything, so I hope you don't think we're leaving now."

"We *are* leaving now. I packed something for you after you fell asleep last night." Chase's smile got even bigger when he realized he had succeeded in completely taking Mathias by surprise.

"You did?" Mathias usually loved Chase's deviousness, but he couldn't decide whether he was more intrigued or annoyed in this instance. "Where are we going?"

"It's a secret. You won't know till we get there."

Chase drove out of Dallas, and it didn't take long for Mathias to guess at least the first destination.

"Are we going to the airport?"

"Yup. They have plenty of great restaurants and hotels. You'll love it." Chase teased as he took the airport exit.

"Airport hotel for my birthday? That's kind of insulting. Okay, I changed my mind. Make a fuss!"

Chase responded with raised eyebrows but didn't reply. He turned off the main airport road toward the private hangars located far from the commercial airline terminals. "You know I still have a plane, which comes in handy every once in a while. Today is one of those times."

Mathias's mouth went dry. "You have a plane?"

"You said 'make a fuss'." Chase winked and ran his hand along Mathias's thigh.

Butterflies danced in Mathias's belly at the touch, and the mystery Chase had created around his birthday excursion. *Chase's own plane?*

They drove into one of the enormous private hangars, and Chase parked the car. A ground crew was hurrying around the only plane inside, which bore no company name or logo, clearly preparing it for a flight. Mathias stared at it, his mouth hanging open.

"You okay?" Chase asked with a touch of concern.

"You own a fucking *Boeing* jet?" Mathias asked, still shell-shocked. It was the size of an airliner. It *was* an airliner! Who the hell owns their own 747?

"My dad bought it, if that makes you feel any better," Chase replied. "I just never sold it."

"Unbelievable!" Mathias didn't hide his disapproval. That certainly sounded like Alan, and hopefully long-gone "evil Chase," but Mathias wondered why Chase kept a plane he admittedly used only rarely.

"Good evening, Mr. Richards." One of the uniformed crew walked up to the driver's side of the car and greeted Chase politely. "We'll be ready to take off in about fifteen minutes. I'll have someone take your bags, and you can board anytime you like."

"Thank you, Trey." Chase popped the trunk open and started to get out.

Mathias hadn't moved yet. This was overkill. He wasn't impressed or thrilled that Chase had planned an elaborate weekend with a private airliner. Mathias hadn't fully decided whether he would even get in the fucking plane. Had Chase really changed after all? The secret plan and talking Mathias into this trip seemed a bit too much like the old manipulative Chase for Mathias's liking, and he was beginning to worry he'd jumped back into this relationship too soon.

He glanced over at Chase, conversing with the crew member. A lot had happened between them during the past year, but lately, Chase had been perfect, been the man Mathias had first fallen in love with. He hadn't done a single thing to make Mathias doubt that his old Chase was back for good. Their relationship would only work with complete honesty and trust. And Mathias just had to believe Chase had a good reason for everything he did.

"Sir, after we drop you off at the destination, we have a supply run scheduled before we can pick you up. Unless, of course, there is some sort of emergency," Trey told Chase.

Mathias listened to that rather mysterious conversation— especially as the "destination" hadn't been specified. He expected Chase to explain, but he didn't, clearly wanting to keep Mathias in the dark about something. Mathias wondered not only about where they were going, but about what kind of "supply run" they'd been discussing. He finally opened the door and got out of the car.

"That's fine, Trey," Chase said. "Mathias, meet Trey Wheeler, our pilot."

Mathias came around to Chase's side of the car and held his hand out to shake Trey's, and Trey shook, giving him a polite, if slightly formal, nod.

"So, Trey, where are we going?" Mathias asked, his curiosity now getting the better of him. Chase had obviously gone to great lengths for this, so maybe he should just relax and enjoy the surprise.

"Bahamas." Trey smiled, gave a little salute, then turned away from them and began to pull the luggage from the trunk.

"Nice," Mathias replied, rethinking his opinion of Wheeler, who hadn't evaded his question. "Are we going to be diving or sailing?" he asked, excitement for the trip now building.

"You'll find out when we get there," Chase said cryptically, and led Mathias toward the boarding steps.

Inside, the plane was possibly more luxurious than Mathias had feared. It was comfortably appointed, with separate sections laid out: a few scattered tables with leather-covered armchairs, a dining table with eight chairs, a bar area, and in the back, a door leading to what was most likely a bedroom. The furnishings and décor were of the highest quality—Would Alan Richards have settled for less?—and Mathias didn't even want to contemplate the cost. Chase sat in one of the armchairs, and Mathias settled across the table from him, not saying a word.

A female uniformed crew member came through a door from the front of the plane.

"Good evening, Mr. Richards," she said warmly. "I have the champagne on ice as you requested, and I'll be serving dinner in about ninety minutes, once we're at cruising altitude. Would you like me to pour champagne now before we take off?"

"No, thank you, I'll take care of that myself." Chase nodded, then introduced Mathias to the flight attendant, Janice, a petite blonde with an infectiously bubbly personality.

"It's very nice to see you again, sir," she added, almost shyly, as if not sure that she should venture to make a personal comment to the boss.

"I don't fly much myself anymore, but this time it's a special occasion," Chase added genially.

"Well, I hope you'll enjoy your trip to Martha's Vineyard. I hear it's lovely this time of year." She flashed a smile and a nod toward Mathias; then she turned and headed back through the door to the crew's area.

"Martha's Vineyard?" Mathias shook his head, incredulous. "The pilot said we're going to the Bahamas!"

"He did?" Chase gave another sly grin, then got up and headed back behind the bar. He pulled out a bottle of vintage Pol Roger and two champagne flutes from under the counter.

"I see." Mathias finally realized the joke was on him. Chase wasn't going to tell him where they were really going.

"If you ask the co-pilot, he'll tell you we're going to Bali." Chase grinned as he skillfully opened the bottle and poured two glasses full of champagne, then came back around the bar to Mathias. "Does it really matter where we go to celebrate?"

"No, I guess it doesn't matter at all, especially since we weren't supposed to celebrate in the first place. But now that you've started, it would be rude of me to stop you," Mathias agreed, with a laugh and a huge improvement in his mood. He took the glass Chase offered him and they sat back down on the comfortable chairs, this time with Chase seating himself next to Mathias.

"Happy Birthday, Tee," Chase said simply, raising his glass toward Mathias.

"It's not my birthday yet," Mathias replied, smiling.

"It's past midnight somewhere, right?" Chase touched his glass to Mathias's.

Mathias immediately thought back to that birthday celebration in the Colorado Rockies. A huge lump grew in his throat, and he didn't trust his voice, so he just smiled and sipped at his champagne in silence for a few moments. Evidently, Chase hadn't forgotten either— the night that Chase had made love to him for the first time, and Mathias had finally drummed up the courage to tell Chase that he loved him.

He could tell from the look on Chase's face that the memories had a similar effect on him. Chase gazed for a few long moments at Mathias, his eyes full of love—and regret—probably deeply ashamed of the wasted years and the pain he'd caused Mathias.

"I wish I could—" Chase began in a shaky voice, but Mathias put a finger gently to Chase's lips, silencing him.

"I know. Me, too," Mathias whispered, his own eyes stinging at the painful memories.

Chase set his glass down and took Mathias's from his hand, placing it on the table. Then he leaned toward Mathias, taking his mouth in a gentle, loving kiss—not hungry or passionate, but full of so much more emotion because of its sweetness and restraint. They kissed for long minutes, hands caressing cheeks and chins and tangling in hair, trying to say everything they felt, but without words.

A gentle throat clearing from the direction of the cockpit caught their attention and they broke the kiss, both looking slightly embarrassed at being caught in such an intimate moment—it wasn't the kiss itself, but the obvious feelings it demonstrated. Janice's expression indicated she regretted having to interrupt the obviously emotional moment between them.

"We're ready to taxi for takeoff; you'll need to put the seatbelts on, and watch out for the glasses, just in case," she said nervously, then turned and left them alone again.

Takeoff was uneventful, and approximately an hour later, Janice set the dining table for them. When she announced that dinner was ready, they sat at the table, seating themselves across from each other at one end of the ridiculously long table.

Dinner was served, and Janice left the cabin with a polite bow and a large, friendly smile. And a wink.

Mathias expected Chase had planned some sumptuous feast for their dinner, in keeping with the luxurious surroundings—caviar and truffles, and perhaps some foie gras. So, he was more than surprised and thrilled when Janice served them delicious barbecue beef brisket—from Mathias's favorite restaurant—paired with admittedly the most decadent macaroni and cheese Mathias had ever eaten, made with a blend of several cheeses, including tangy Gorgonzola and sprinkled with a crispy breadcrumb topping. Add the delicious spicy coleslaw on the side, and it was one of the most enjoyable meals Mathias could remember.

"Wow, this is amazing." Mathias's mouth watered as he inhaled the heavenly aromas and began eating. Even though Chase had arranged a fairly simple meal, everything was top quality and prepared perfectly.

"So, Trey and Janice and the co-pilot work for you, or do you just rent them when you use this thing?" Mathias asked as they enjoyed their meal, half joking, his disdain for the plane and what it represented was only thinly veiled by humor.

"They're employees of RichardsCorp if that's what you're asking." Chase seemed like he didn't want to discuss the plane, which only made Mathias more determined to ask.

"And they just sit around gathering dust, since you apparently don't use the plane much." Mathias pushed on, disgusted by the waste of money and resources.

"I don't use the plane *personally*, but it gets used on a regular basis, and they crew for all the flights."

"What, for drug runs from Central America?" Mathias kept at the topic, his tone almost sarcastic.

"Mostly it's used for transporting supplies and personnel for a couple of international organizations," Chase replied almost enthusiastically. He wasn't letting Mathias's cynical comments get to him, and now Mathias's interest was piqued.

"What?" *That* had stopped Mathias in his tracks. "What organizations?"

"Doctors Without Borders, mainly. Sometimes the World Health Organization. I'm not sure of all the details; Trey Wheeler coordinates it all. I just pay the bills."

"Doctors Without Borders?" Mathias repeated, surprised. "My *brother* Leo works with them. You're kidding, right?"

"No. I actually got the idea from Leo," Chase said, and apparently noticing Mathias's startled expression, he continued. "Not directly from him. I mean knowing what Leo did gave me the idea how an organization like that could use a plane, and like you said, it was just gathering dust."

"How long have you been doing that?" Mathias asked, not quite believing what Chase was saying. He didn't sound like the Chase who used to throw money around to impress and control people, the way he had until he'd changed—for Mathias. But it put everything in a whole new light, Mathias admitted, realizing how easily he'd jumped to a conclusion about the plane without even waiting for any details.

"I guess since I took over the company from my dad." Chase shrugged. "And I never made much of a fuss about publicizing it because quite frankly, donations to charitable organizations didn't exactly fit into the persona I was cultivating at the time," he added with a smile.

Mathias laughed, but he wondered again what else he'd misjudged about Chase and why. In retrospect, so many things made sense, and Chase clearly hadn't been evil incarnate as Mathias had once assumed.

After dinner, Janice cleared the table, dimmed the lights, and left the room.

"Is that the signal to get cozy?" Mathias joked.

"Definitely, let's go get cozy over there." Chase nodded in the direction of a couch about halfway down the cabin, and they got up and relocated.

Mathias was just leaning in to kiss Chase when the crew door opened again. Janice had returned, but this time she was carrying a small chocolate cake with three lit sparklers lighting her way toward them.

"I'll spare you the singing," she said with a barely suppressed giggle and everyone laughed. "Happy Birthday, Mr. Tobler!" She put the cake down in front of Mathias and turned to leave.

"Happy Birthday, Tee." Chase moved in for their interrupted kiss.

Mathias hesitated slightly.

"Don't worry, she's not coming back unless we buzz her," Chase assured him then leaned in again. This time they kissed long and deep and passionately, until the sparklers had long burned out.

"Don't I get any of my cake?" Mathias asked.

"Why don't we have cake in bed?" Chase suggested.

"Bed? Just how long is this trip? We must be near Australia by now," Mathias joked, but he was really curious now. How long had then been in the air? Three hours? How fast did this plane go, he wondered and tried to calculate how far they'd traveled.

"One of the nice things about having your own plane is that you can land whenever you want. Who knows, we may still be over Texas," Chase teased. "But there's plenty of time to show you the bedroom, and have a nap after, just in case the tour tires you out," he added suggestively.

Mathias stood up and stooped to pick up the cake.

"Lead the way!" he said eagerly.

Chase didn't have to be told twice, remembering to bring the tray with the rest of the champagne. He opened the door with one hand and ushered Mathias inside.

On top of one pillow lay a black silk blindfold. Mathias smiled and shut the door.

Happy Birthday. Oh, yes, it certainly would be.

WHEN he woke up, light was already streaming through the tiny windows, but he had no idea what time it was. It seemed they'd just fallen asleep, after feeding each other cake rather messily and making love—also rather messily—twice. All he could tell was they were still in the air.

Mathias's movements woke Chase, who sprawled across Mathias's chest, one leg pinning Mathias firmly to the surprisingly comfortable bed.

"Morning, birthday boy," Chase said with a sloppy kiss. "I'm pretty sure it'll be your birthday in Botswana when we land there."

"Fuck Botswana." Mathias rolled Chase off of him roughly and sat up in bed, leaning toward the nearest window, but before he could peer out, Chase had grabbed his arm and playfully pinned it behind his back, while shutting the shade with the other hand.

"Do you really want to ruin the surprise?" Chase asked. "If you can't control your curiosity, go ahead and look, but I'd really prefer you don't," he added, completely serious.

As much as Mathias wanted to know, he wouldn't look yet. Chase had gone to a lot of trouble to preserve the surprise, clearly expecting to enjoy Mathias's reaction when they landed.

"Okay, you win. I won't look," Mathias promised, and Chase released his arm. They both flopped back into bed.

Chase picked up the phone on the bedside table.

"How long till we land?" he asked. "Okay, great, that's perfect, thank you." He put the phone down and turned to Mathias. "About an hour. Just time enough for a shower, which we both certainly need."

SEVENTY minutes later, they were both dressed, sipping coffee in the main cabin, hair still damp after a long, very enjoyable shower. All the shades were closed in here, and Mathias didn't venture a peek, even when Chase's back was turned.

Finally, they landed. They'd been in the air about eight hours, and they could really be anywhere in the US, Canada, Hawaii, even South America. They could also be back in Texas, Mathias thought with a laugh. Though if Chase had really just wanted to fly around all night in a plane, he wouldn't have made such a fuss about hiding their true destination. Mathias had to admit, this certainly was a classy way to join the mile-high club.

He glanced over at Chase, who had been watching him attentively. There was something in Chase's expression Mathias couldn't quite identify. As they prepared for landing, Chase's gaze darted around the plane, never landing on Mathias, and he rolled his hands into fists. Was he afraid of something? Mathias knew he wasn't a nervous flyer, so it had to be something else, and it intrigued him. He smiled lovingly at Chase, hoping to put him at ease, but for some reason, Chase seemed to be even more anxious once they'd touched down, as if he wasn't completely confident about the birthday surprise.

Outside the plane, Mathias heard muffled voices and equipment being moved. The three crew members came into the passenger cabin and Chase thanked them all for a smooth flight and their service.

"We'll see you back here as scheduled, barring any unforeseen problems," Trey assured him, and the crew members deplaned, bringing the luggage, leaving Chase and Mathias alone in the plane.

"Are you ready?" Chase asked, his voice a bit shaky.

"Are *you* ready, Chase?" Mathias asked, concerned. "What's wrong?"

"I've never been here before, and—"

"Well, don't waste the whole day, then! Let's get out and explore Outer Mongolia! I've always wanted to go there, how did you know?" Mathias joked and got up and went out through the door of the plane before Chase could stop him.

What he saw when he looked out was not at all what he had expected. Of course it wasn't the Bahamas or Botswana. Or Outer Mongolia. But Mathias didn't expect to walk out the door to discover they were in… Venice.

The distinctive silhouette of San Mark's was visible across the vast lagoon, and Mathias had figured it out immediately. Besides, he'd been there before, hadn't he?

He turned around and Chase was right behind him at the top of the stairway leading down to the tarmac. He still looked worried, and Mathias didn't know what to say. Wasn't even sure he could speak. He didn't even know if he was happy or sad to be here, spending his birthday with Chase—in Venice—ten years after….

"You definitely surprised me." Mathias reached for Chase's hand but he didn't have a chance to say more.

"*Signori!*" a man called from the foot of the stairway in Italian. "Your taxi is waiting!" he shouted in accented English and waved furiously to them to hurry.

Mathias walked down the steps in silence, Chase behind him, and they were shuttled into a private water taxi which headed across the lagoon to the main islands of Venice.

The day was warm, but a refreshing breeze whipped Mathias's hair into his eyes. At least that's how he'd explain that fact that he could barely see anything as they approached the beauty of the Grand Canal and the ferry slowed down. Mathias wasn't ready to admit he was crying, and he couldn't stop himself. Thankfully, the boat crew was busy piloting the boat and not witnessing Mathias making a fool out of himself.

Chase wrapped one arm around Mathias's shoulders as they sat on a bench near the front of the ferry, allowing them a spectacular view as they moved along Venice's main waterway.

"You haven't said anything since we got off the plane, Tee." Chase leaned in, lips brushing Mathias's ear, voice rising and tremulous.

Mathias blinked and sniffed and tried to smile.

"Please, *please* tell me those are happy tears and not I-fucked-everything-up-worse-than-before-tears," Chase asked hopefully, almost fearfully.

"Happy tears," Mathias said in a squeaky voice he couldn't control, though he was sure he sounded anything but happy. He really was happy—ecstatic in fact—because Chase had gone this far to set things right between them.

"Thank God!" Chase said, sounding slightly relieved. But Mathias could tell he hadn't relaxed completely, now nervously playing his fingers along Mathias's arm.

Then Chase slid closer to Mathias and put his arms around him, pulling him in close for a kiss. Not long, not short, but enough for Mathias to know it meant much more.

"Mathias," Chase said, fingers on Mathias's chin, looking deeply into Mathias's eyes, his tone subdued.

"What?" he sniffed.

"If I had to choose between you and anything else ever again, there is *nothing* on earth I would choose over you. I was an idiot to think otherwise, and right now I'm the luckiest man in the world that you've given me a second chance to prove how much you mean to me."

Mathias looked into Chase's eyes and saw tears pooling in the caramel depths.

"You don't deserve me," Mathias shook his head slightly, but turned a huge smile on Chase.

"No, I don't," Chase agreed with a laugh.

"Keep saying that; I like how it sounds," Mathias laughed back, and Chase leaned down to kiss him and stop his smug laughter.

"I love you, Mathias," Chase said as they embraced again, kissing as the sound of church bells echoed along the canals.

EM LYNLEY has worked finance, the wine industry and high-tech, though she'd rather be writing hot man-on-man romance. She spent ten years as an economist and financial analyst, including a year as a White House staff economist, but only because all the intern positions were filled. Tired of boring herself and others with dry business reports and articles, her creative muse is back and naughtier than ever. She has lived and worked in London, Tokyo, and Washington, DC, but the San Francisco Bay area is home for now.

Visit her website at http://www.emlynley.com
her blog at http://emlynley.livejournal.com
her Twitter page at http://twitter.com/emlynley
and her Facebook at http://www.facebook.com/emlynley.

Precious Gems from EM LYNLEY

http://www.dreamspinnerpress.com

Also from EM LYNLEY

http://www.dreamspinnerpress.com

www.ingramcontent.com/pod-product-compliance
Lightning Source LLC
Chambersburg PA
CBHW070048030726
47506CB00002B/394